GW00367897

To Mourn
a Mischief

By the same author

Storm Islands
The Ragusa Theme

To Mourn
a Mischief

Ann Quinton

PIATKUS

All the characters in this book are
fictitious and to the best of my
knowledge bear no resemblance to any
living person.

Copyright © 1989 by Ann Quinton

First published in Great Britain in 1989 by
Judy Piatkus (Publishers) Ltd of
5 Windmill Street, London W1

British Library Cataloguing in Publication Data

Quinton, Ann
  To mourn a mischief.
  I. Title
  823'.914 [F]

  ISBN 0 – 86188 – 894 – 4

Phototypeset in 11/12 Compugraphic Times by
Action Typesetting Limited, Gloucester
Printed and bound in Great Britain by
Butler & Tanner Ltd, Frome and London

To Joan and Peter

I should like to thank the many people who helped me with my research for this book, in particular Michael Adams, Ann Colvill, Simon Grew, Len Lannigan, William Poulter, Dr. Jeremy Trowell and Jonathan Wilkinson.

To mourn a mischief that is past and gone
Is the next way to draw new mischief on.

OTHELLO, Act 1, Scene iii

Prologue

October 1942

The Junkers 188, loaded with its deadly cargo of explosives, crossed the Dutch coast and started to climb over the North Sea. German meteorological experts had informed the K.G.6 crews that fog over southern England would render them immune to British night-fighters. The forecast was incorrect. As the pilot headed towards the English coastline, still climbing steadily, a steely moon illuminated the sky, penetrating the low cloud bank and touching the gently swelling waves beneath with phosphorescence. Cursing the unfavourable weather, he nosed his plane over the Suffolk coast where broad sluggish estuaries crawled like silver ribbons across the flat muddy shores.

The RAF Mosquito from 85 Squadron at West Malling, alerted by Sandwich radar, hurtled towards him like a bolt from the blue. Desperately, the German took evasive action. Twisting violently to port and diving steeply he tried to shake off his pursuer, but the Mosquito followed, homing in on him and opening fire. Shells ripped through the fuselage, damaging the controls and setting alight the port engine. The *Flugzengführer* wrestled to keep the stricken plane under control. Behind him, his gunner screamed and slumped back, severely wounded. He attempted another dive but a second burst of shellfire inflicted further damage, and with flames licking along the stricken craft's fuselage, he gave the order to bale out.

The escape hatch had jammed and for precious minutes the remaining crew wrestled with the faulty mechanism before

1

forcing it open. The unconscious gunner was pushed out first, the ripcord of his parachute pulled as he fell through the hatch. The plummeting aircraft had dived to a height of 7,000 feet before the other three crew members managed to bale out. The hapless wireless operator was struck by one of the propellers as he jumped and his left arm severed.

There was an explosion as the plane hit the wet, marshy ground near the creek and sliced through the heavy clay soil. Overhead, the Mosquito banked sharply, levelled out and flew back to base, reporting mission accomplished.

Chapter One

The tide crept silently along the creek, nibbling at the reed beds, edging across mud and shingle flats, spilling gently into dappled shallows where waders foraged. The old sluice gates shuddered as the brown salty water nudged the blackened timbers, and over the other side of the river wall the brackish water in the ditch sucked and slurped at the tangled roots of the willows that marked the edge of the water meadows. Beyond this ditch was a thicket of low-lying hawthorn and bramble bushes, and from behind this cover three pairs of eyes watched with interest the drama that was unfolding over in the far corner of the meadow.

Ex-pilot officer Neil Hopkins and Kenneth Batson of the East Anglian Aircraft Research Group exchanged a look of quiet satisfaction as the giant digger, a Komatsu PC50LC, tracked for maximum support on the marshy ground, chugged slowly round the saucer-shaped depression, cutting a swathe through the saturated soil. This was the culmination of months of speculation and research; they believed that the crater held the remains of the first Junkers plane to be shot down over the British mainland during World War II, the site pinpointed earlier by magnetometer reading.

Permission to excavate had been given by the landowner and the Ministry of Defence, but the latter had granted a licence only on condition that a team from the Explosives and Ordnance Disposal Unit was present. Contemporary records had stated that the bomb load had exploded on impact but as a precautionary measure an EOD team from RAF Wittering was on the scene, organising the excavation.

Already many finds had been made: pieces of wing structure, a propeller and parts of a BMW engine, and some more personal belongings − a tool kit, maps, first aid equipment, and even a packet of cigarettes. Carefully and methodically, the digger worked away at the sizeable hole, uncovering numerous cannon shells and further plane debris. A shout from the driver alerted the men who were picking over the finds. A scoop of grey clay swept cleanly from the crater had revealed part of a large cylinder pointing nose skywards from an oily pool.

'Christ! What have we here?' Flight Sergeant Patterson, in charge of the operation, lowered himself cautiously down the fifteen foot crater and approached the ominous find. It was obvious to all the apprehensive onlookers that what had turned up was a bomb, not the expected 50 kg-sized bomb that was usual, but a much larger one which was soon identified as a deadly 1,000 kg Herman bomb, named after the portly Reichmarschall Herman Goering. It was intact and still contained its full complement of explosive.

Reinforcements were sent for and it was decided to lift the bomb out of the crater and try to defuse it on the spot. The continuous wet weather over the summer months had turned the marshy ground into a quagmire and Clive Patterson's men slithered around in the mire as they manually dug away the stinking mud to uncover enough of the Herman to enable them to attatch a harness. Dutch Rings, circles of aluminium, were placed round the bomb, forming a metal tube in which to work, and after a nerve-wracking struggle the lethal find was lifted out. A blast barrier was built round the bomb and Flight Sergeant Patterson arranged for the police to warn the inhabitants of nearby Croxton village to keep their windows and doors open as a precaution. He then began the serious business of washing out the explosive.

Several hours later, after a delicate trepanning and steaming operation, the Herman was pronounced comparatively harmless and the RAF team took it back with them to Wittering to carry out further tests and check the fuse mechanism.

'Whew! I feel as if I've been holding my breath for hours.' Neil Hopkins stretched and scratched the back of his neck as

4

he watched the little convoy rumble off. 'That was certainly a big surprise. To think that it had been lying there hidden for forty-five years.'

'I suppose it was harmless enough, buried under all that mud,' said Kenneth Batson, 'but I wonder what the locals would have said if they'd known they were sitting on that little lot.'

'Some of the older inhabitants must have known about the plane crash but these things get forgotten in the march of time. Well, I suppose we're finished here now for the time being. The digger can go home to bed.'

The driver was only too glad to take himself and his machine away from the treacherous Suffolk marshes. He swung his massive Komatsu round and headed for the river wall. Even as its treads bit into the soft ground, seeking purchase, a large portion of bank broke away, sliding towards the dyke, and the digger slewed sideways and tore into a pillar of mud.

'Hell, that's all we need!' exclaimed Neil Hopkins. The driver swore and slammed his engine into reverse. The machine roared and shuddered but remained firmly wedged in the landslip.

'Thank God this didn't happen when it was excavating the crater or it would have been curtains for us all.'

With each thrust from the accelerator the digger seemed to settle further into the morass.

'Cut your engine, man, you're making it worse!'

The driver switched off and jumped down from the cab, slithering as he landed on the track.

'This looks like another little stint of manual digging. Any volunteers?'

The small knot of men crowded round the machine to assess the task. It was well and truly embedded, tilting at an impossible angel, steaming in a cloud of exhaust. Above it a clearly defined semi-circle had been gouged out of the collapsing bank, revealing a shelf of gleaming mud. On this shelf, in neat array, was a collection of bones.

To Neil Hopkins's inexperienced eyes it looked like a complete skeleton.

*   *   *

Lee Garfield was returning from her morning ride when her attention was drawn to the activity down on the edge of the marshes. As she ambled slowly up the rutted track that led from the creek over the bluff of hill towards The Hermitage, she was momentarily blinded by light reflecting off something large and metallic held in the hands of one of the distant figures scrambling amongst machinery and mounds of earth. She reined in her mare and fumbled for the binoculars round her neck. Thoughtfully she studied the scene for a few minutes, then the mare fidgetted and side-stepped, and Lee dropped the glasses and bent forward to scratch her mount's neck.

'Okay, old girl, I know you think it's time we were home. Let's go.'

It was a warm humid day and the horse was blowing by the time they clattered into the stable yard. Lee unsaddled the mare and rubbed her down before fixing her feed. The ugly black gelding in the next stable leaned over and nipped her shoulder as she walked past with the bucket.

'Give over, you devil! Your turn next, but not if you try tricks like that.'

She finished the stable chores and made her way up to the house. The Hermitage was an impressive Neo-Classical building which had been built on an incline overlooking the marshes and distant river and even farther distant sea. From the terrace which ran the length of the rear elevation, one could see part of the creek and the surrounding farmland. Lee had never discovered why it was called The Hermitage. It was in fact the dower house of the now non-existent Croxton Hall and had been sympathetically modernised several years earlier. As she was about to go through the back porch she remembered the scene she had witnessed earlier, and walking to the edge of the terrace, she propped her elbows on the balustrade and swung up her binoculars.

It was here that PC Tom Drake found her when he drove up to the house a short while later. He was a square, solid young man who took his duties as recently installed village policeman very seriously. This was the first time he had had occasion to visit The Hermitage and until now he had only seen Mrs. Lee Garfield at a distance. He had not realised that she was as young as this. Early thirties, he reckoned as he took

6

in the tall, well-built dark woman who turned from her absorbed contemplation of the scene behind her to greet him.

'Good morning, Constable, what can I do for you? Is anything wrong?'

'No, ma'am, but I've come to give you warning.'

'That sounds ominous. What have I done? What felony have I committed in all innocence? You'd better come inside.' She turned to lead the way back to the house. 'By the way, do you know what is happening over there?' She gestured behind her.

'That's what I've come about. They've found a bomb, a very large one.'

'A bomb?'

'A German bomber came down there during the war. The East Anglian Aircraft Research Group are excavating the site. From the records they thought that all the bombs had exploded on impact but they've found a big 'un, a 1,000 kg job, that's still alive. They've got the bomb disposal squad from RAF Wittering here and they're going to try and defuse it. I'm warning everyone to leave their doors and windows open in case something goes wrong. I came here first as you're the nearest.'

'Good heavens! I wonder if Tony knows about the plane crash. That land used to belong to the family before Great-aunt died and the estate was sold off.'

'Is your husband at home, ma'am?'

'No, he's up in town at a conference. He wouldn't be very pleased to come home and find the ancestral pile about his ears.' In the face of the solemn young man before her, she couldn't resist facetiousness.

'We hope it won't come to that,' he replied stiffly. 'Are you alone in the house? Are there any members of staff about?'

'Actually, I'm alone. Mrs. Collins, the housekeeper, has gone into Woodford — her husband drove her in — and the local help doesn't usually come in at the weekend unless we've got guests or a shoot. Are they likely to cause much disturbance? That area is the favourite haunt of a marsh harrier — I've seen it several times in the last few weeks.'

Another member of the conservation lobby, thought Tom Drake, his heart sinking; still, it was a change to meet one

7

amongst the landowners, they were usually on the other side of the fence.

'If that goes up it's going to be more than a bird that's disturbed! In the interests of safety, I think you should leave the premises for a few hours.'

'You're evacuating me?'

'You are closest to the scene, as I said; I think it would be prudent.'

'Prudence is a rich, ugly, old maid courted by Incapacity', she quoted to the mystified policeman. 'Blake, *Proverbs of Hell*. But why should you know that? I had a very literary father.'

Stephen Bates' initial reaction when he heard the police van going round the village issuing the warning over its public address system, was one of anger. After an exchange with the driver he stomped indoors and took out his ill temper on his long-suffering wife.

'Why wasn't I told? Carstairs must have given his permission for the excavation. Apparently the water meadows are crawling with Ministry of Defence boffins and bomb disposal squads. You'd think I would have been informed, consulted, but no, I'm only the resident gamekeeper.'

'Calm yourself, man. What's it all about?'

'They've turned up a bomb – apparently a Geman plane crashed there in the war. Do you remember hearing anything about it?'

'No, but it was before my time. What's happening, then?'

'They're trying to defuse it, and as a precaution they're telling everyone to open their windows and doors. I should have been told!'

'I think you're well out of it. If they think it could damage the houses all this distance away, there wouldn't be much hope for the poor men down there if it went off.'

'Well, I just hope they made good the damage. Imagine it – they've got a digger down there. It's probably cut the ground to pieces, it's like a quagmire after all the rain we've had.'

'At least it's a nice day today,' replied his wife, breaking off

8

from her baking to go round and open the windows, 'it's not too cold to open the house to the elements.'

Ada Cattermole paused in her washing up and, with suds up to her elbows, leaned out of the kitchen window to hear better. A not upleasant frisson of fear and excitement ran through her sturdy frame. She wiped the scummy bubbles off her hands and arms with a tea-towel and went outside to find her husband, Arthur, who, when last seen, had been making off up the garden path. She ran him to ground in the old ramshackle shed that formed the natural dividing line between flower and vegetable garden. It was almost obscured by the display of large, garish-coloured dahlias that rioted in front of it and leaned over the path to scatter silken petals and earwigs. The vegetable garden was Arthur's serious work, the dahlias his pride and joy, carefully nurtured with an eye on the local horticultural show from which he usually carried off several prizes.

The shed was his den, his bolthole, the place to which he retreated to daydream and potter. To this end he had installed an old armchair near the door; its rexine covering was split in several places, and curls of snuff-coloured stuffing leaked down the sides and were snagged on the gardening tools stacked against the walls.

Ada burst in and flopped into this chair, fanning herself with a hand that was still red and wrinkled from its recent immersion in hot water.

'Did you hear that, Arthur? Gave me quite a turn it did.'

'What do you mean?' growled her husband, who had been about to sit down in the chair himself for a quiet smoke.

'Brought back the war, the bombing and all that.'

'Don't be so daft, woman! They had sirens in the war to tell you when the Jerries were about — they didn't go around with no loud-speaker vans.'

'Yes, they did,' said his wife triumphantly, 'I remember in Blackhaven right near the end of the war, must have bin 1945, a landmine dropped near the docks and didn't go off. They evacuated everyone in the area and went round the streets with a van just like that, warning people. I were working in the munitions at the time and it caused quite a scare. It went off too when they started messing about with it; shattered windows for miles around and made a lot of people homeless. Funny how it brings it all back. I'd forgotten about that there German plane. Now I remember my old dad telling me about it at the time. Did you get to hear about it?'

'Yes, it happened just before I came home on leave. I remember old Fred Roberts down at Ramsey telling me. He said there were shells going off all over the place and shrapnel flying about − his son Frank nearly got hit coming home late that night. They saw the plane go down in flames and the next morning they found this German airman propped up in the hedge nearby, dead as a doornail.'

'Horrible. I know he was our enemy but you can't help feeling sorry for the poor man. He was only doing his duty, and he probably had a wife and kiddies back home in Germany. I wonder where they buried him, if his family ever knew.'

She settled herself more comfortably in the chair and carried on with her musing.

'I don't know why they have to go around digging up the past, it's all over and done with now. Risking us being blown up by an owd bomb that's been there forty years!'

'Did you do what they told you?' asked her husband, seeing an opportunity to repossess his chair. 'Did you open all the doors and windows?'

In the Old Manse Matthew Betts, retired headmaster, widower, and currently involved in an intensive programme of wine-making, pondered the same point as he carefully fixed the airlock on one of the demi-johns ranged on the table before him. He had heard the van going round the village but he hadn't obeyed its commands. Many of the Manse's window frames were so old and warped that they hadn't been opened for years. It would be just too bad if some freak blast blew them out.

He recalled reading a recent magazine article about aircraft enthusiasts who travelled the country, excavating sites of reported wartime plane crashes. He supposed these were the people involved at present. He couldn't see much point himself in men spending all their spare time rooting around digging up the odd piece of shrapnel or engine part and putting it proudly on display in some museum. The war was over, had been for more than forty-three years, why couldn't they let sleeping dogs lie? He'd been patriotic enough in his time, had fought for his country, but he was becoming increasingly pacifist in his old age. He hadn't yet got to the stage of actually going on a peace march, he was too old for that, but the young people who supported CND had his sympathy. Far better to seek means of averting a new war rather than dwell on the old one. That hadn't done these aircraft enthusiasts much good — they seemed to have found more than they bargained for.

He wondered what was actually happening down on the marshes. With one of the first fine days of the summer — albeit early September — a Saturday and a midday tide, there were probably a lot of children in the vicinity. But no, the local children nowadays seemed to shun the simple pleasures of free swimming in the creek. They preferred to spend their time and money at the new Leisure Centre at Felstone. How different it had been when his children were young. He and Ella had spent many a happy hour picnicking on the river wall with Mary and Stephen and hordes of their friends; waiting patiently for the tide to reach the little shingle beach, hunting for crabs along the high tideline, poking and prodding amongst the reeds and grasses. There was nothing quite like the feel of the silky, opaque water on one's skin, the faintly rotting smell of mud and seaweed and salt, the sibilant rustle as a ripple of wind winnowed through the reed beds.

The youngsters nowadays didn't know what they were missing; they were . . . no, he had sworn he wouldn't do this, wouldn't harp about the good old days. God, he was getting old, and what the hell was he doing making all this wine? There was no-one to drink it.

Bradley Scott was amused when he heard the announcement. He risked life and limb on his jaunts, researching for the travel books he wrote; when he was back home in Croxton he

11

expected peace and quiet in which to recharge his physical and mental batteries. Perhaps he attracted trouble. He had often thought this. In fact it was this penchant for getting himself involved in bizarre situations — for turning up in a place just as a revolution broke out or an earthquake erupted or a power-cut paralyzed a city — that had prompted his series of books, *The Alternative Guides*.

It was surprising how lucrative they had become. The public, it seemed, enjoyed reading about the hazards one could face in foreign travel; the unbuilt hotels, polluted water supplies, buses and trains that didn't run, the grossly over-priced local dishes that were unfit for human consumption. People wrote to him with suggestions culled from their own experiences for inclusion in the next editions. It helped him to keep his star system up-to-date. Six stars against a place denoted the utter pits, one or two stars were more an indication of local vagaries and eccentricities, something the less intrepid traveller could actually enjoy.

He decided to take a stroll in the direction of the creek and see for himself what was happening, then changed his mind. The area would be swarming with officials; he had endured enough brushes with officialdom on his travels to give him a healthy dislike of tangling with any representatives of the law unless absolutely necessary.

He opened the fridge to get a can of beer and glared at the empty rack. Damn, he had meant to go into Felstone and replenish his stocks! He had a thirst on him after cutting the hedge; he would go down to the local and get a bite to eat with his pint, seeing that the fridge was as empty of food as it was of beer. He washed his hands, splashed water over his face and neck, ran a comb through his damp hair and beard, and after extracting a note from his wallet and stuffing it in his jeans pocket, set out towards the village.

As he passed the edge of Croxton Woods and caught a glimpse of Smoky Cottage through the trees, he remembered that its occupant, Julian Lester, had promised to lend him a book on nineteenth-century rail networks which he had picked up in a recent sale. He swung over the stile and made his way towards the cottage. With any luck he'd find Julian in and would be invited to share a jar with him. The old bugger seemed to exist on a mostly liquid diet.

Julian Lester, antiques' dealer and writer manqué, had not heard the police anouncement. Smoky Cottage was off the beaten track and village traffic was only a distant background hum. He was a small, dapper man in his fifties with a carefully barbered goatee beard and a rather precious manner. He was fingering his beard as he sorted through the notes on his desk, one eye on the clock interspersed with longing glances at the gin bottle on the nearby sideboard. Why had he made this stupid rule about not touching a drop before midday? Because he had got smashed out of his mind last week, lost a whole day and broken a valuable piece of porcelain into the bargain, that was why.

Drink was rotting his guts and blurring his judgement; it was time he took himself in hand. At least he still preserved the niceties; he didn't swig it out of the bottle or drink it neat. The mixer drinks, bitter lemon or tonic, were carefully measured out, he even went to the trouble of twists of lemon when there was one in the fridge, though a lot of good that did him!

He was glad of the distraction when Bradley Scott arrived on his doorstep.

'Come in, man. You've come about that book?'

'Yes, I was just passing and thought I'd give you a look.'

'Help yourself to a drink whilst I look it out. Is gin all right?'

'I'd prefer a beer if you've got one handy.'

'Horse piss, but you know your own poison. There's some in the kitchen, I think. Hang on.'

Whilst he was gone, Scott flung himself into a chair and looked round the room. For an antiques' dealer Lester did himself badly. He lived in something approaching squalor, and the dark, heavy furniture and bits and pieces lying around were certainly not valuable antiques. His place was not a good advertisement for his trade; perhaps he kept his choice things in his shop at Woodford? The desk was overflowing with folders and notebooks and the sheet of paper in the typewriter looked as if it had been there a long time. Julian Lester was writing the definitive book on Lowestoft porcelain. It had been a long while in the making.

13

'How's the magnum opus coming along?' Scott jerked his head towards the desk as his host handed him a glass of beer and poured himself a generous measure of gin and tonic.

'It's not. Every time I think I've finished a section, new information comes up. It's soul-destroying.'

'The trouble is, you're flogging a dead horse. There are so many books already on the subject.'

'You can talk — think about all the hundreds of guide-books that exist.'

'Ah, but I've latched on to a different angle, something new, something unique. Why don't you try it — *The Alternative Guide to Antiques*? You could write up all the fakes and forgeries, it would make fascinating reading.'

'It's an idea but I'm sure that it's been done before. And think of the research that would need doing. This lot's bad enough. Anyway, we can't all be successful writers,' Lester added petulantly.

'You do all right in the antiques' business though, don't you? I understand it's the thing to be in nowadays, what with the American bases on our doorstep and all the interest engendered by programmes like the "Antiques Roadshow".'

'I earn a crust but it's not what it used to be. Too many amateurs muscling in on the act. All these antiques' fairs around — there's one nearly every other week — and half the stall holders are amateurs doing it just for the fun. Bored housewives who've knocked off a cupboard of Grand-mother's pretties and are flogging them for pin money; young trendies who are doing it for weekend perks and look on it as an amusing little hobby — they're spoiling it for everyone. Anyway, let me get this book. I found it in a box of oddments I bought at a sale near Debenham. I thought you might be interested.'

He rummaged in one of the tea-chests ranged round the room. 'Published in 1922, it's got a lot of stuff about the old LNER line that used to operate in East Anglia. Here we are.' Lester dusted it off and handed it over.

'Are you loaning it to me or expecting me to buy it?'

'Have a look at it, and if you decide you want it we'll settle a price later. Now you know why I'm not a millionaire.'

14

'Thanks, Julian. I'd better be on my way. I see you didn't take any notice of the edict either.' He nodded at the closed windows.

'What are you talking about?'

'Didn't you hear? They've dug up a bomb down on the marshes. Some German plane came down there in the war — and now the police are going round telling people to leave their doors and windows open in case its cargo of bombs goes up. Why, what's the matter, man? I shouldn't think the blast is likely to reach you here.'

Julian Lester had paled and was looking at the younger man in alarm.

'Where did you say it was?'

'Somewhere near the creek, I think. Are you alright?'

'Yes.' He poured himself another drink. 'It was just a shock hearing you say that. My mother was killed in the war like that. A plane came down in the road where we were living. They thought all the bombs had been ejected over London and that it was returning empty, but she went out into the backyard and there was a bomb stuck in the toilet door. It went off as soon as she touched it and blew her to pieces.'

'How awful. Where were you?'

'I happened to be spending the day with an aunt on the other side of the town. My father was at the front.'

'You can't have been very old.'

'Eight. I was eight. She was the only wartime casualty in the family. My father and various uncles and cousins all came back safely; it was my poor mother, sitting at home waiting, who copped it. Anyway, don't just stand there, man, help me to open them.'

He flung open the front and back doors, and charged round the cottage wrestling with stiff windows. Bradley Scott shrugged and gave him a hand. He was secretly rather amused. Julian Lester liked to project an image of well-bred gentility. He took care in conversation to hint at his upper middle-class background and bemoan the fact that he had come down in the world. He must be rattled to admit so openly to his working-class roots.

An hour later Bradley Scott was still there, listening to

15

Lester's maudlin ramblings and trying to quell the effects of three cans of beer on an empty stomach.

'I suppose you'll be off on your travels again soon?' The older man eyed him through the liquid in his glass.

'In the autumn.'

'Where is it this time?'

'The Canaries. They're very popular with British tourists at that time of the year. It will be good to be on the move again, I seem to vegetate if I spend too much time here.'

'That's not what I've heard,' said Lester slyly. 'I didn't think you'd be so keen to shake the dust of Croxton off your feet this time.'

Ginny Dalton was in her garden when the van went by. At first she thought the announcement was something to do with the Anglian Water Board cutting off water supplies; it had happened before. Glad of an excuse to pause in her labours, she put down the shears, pushed back the hair tumbling over her forehead and scrambled to her feet. Dora Adams, the postmistress, was cycling past as she reached the gate.

'Ginny, my dear, did you hear that?' she asked, slipping off her bike. 'They've found an enormous bomb down near the creek and we've to open all our windows and doors in case it explodes! Whatever next? You're looking very hot and bothered — not doing too much, I hope?'

'Just trying to keep up with the garden. Everything's gone mad this summer with all the rain we've had.'

'Don't I know it! Henry's been having to cut the grass twice a week, three times some weeks. Is young Simon helping you?' Her darting black eyes probed the dense vegetation behind Ginny, who had to admit that her son was out with his friends.

'Don't spoil him, my dear. I know he misses his father but he's growing up fast — it wouldn't hurt him to give you a helping hand about the place.'

'He's having a last fling before he goes back to school. I'm glad he's making the most of the weather.'

'So should you be, Ginny. I suppose it's back to school for you too next week? It must be a strain — teaching full-time and looking after Simon and the house. Though I don't suppose it is as bad as teaching maths or one of those real subjects — all those exercises to correct and lessons to prepare.'

Ginny resisted the temptation to read her a lecture on the work involved in being the head of the art department in a large comprehensive. Dora Adams meant well, it was just that she and tact were strangers. Besides, how could she know that cramming her day with activity from morn to night was the only thing that kept Ginny sane?

Dora cycled off down the road and Ginny went into the house and opened those windows not already open. She drank a glass of orange juice, ate a pear and some plums that were visibly wrinkling in the heat and flipped through the newspaper before returning to her labours in the garden. It was late afternoon before she decided to call it a day. She collapsed on the garden seat and eased her aching limbs. The little knot of apprehension that had been gathering in the pit of her stomach ever since her exchange with Dora Adams was growing. She hadn't realised how late it was. Where was Simon? As far as she knew he had taken no food with him and he had been gone since nine that morning. She mustn't be over protective but he was only thirteen, still a boy but liable to hurtle into adolescence at any moment.

When he rode up the path a short while later she pounced on him in relief.

'Simon, *where* have you been? Do you know what the time is?'

'We've been down at the creek.'

'The creek? But I thought ...'

'They've dug up the remains of a plane and there was a bomb as well. If it had gone off it would have made an enormous crater and done ever so much damage.'

'You mean you were down there — whatever were the police thinking of?'

'They didn't know we were there. We weren't really close, we were hiding behind the hedge on the other side of the meadow. Do you know — the plane was a German bomber and when it crashed two of the airmen were killed. They found an arm lying in a field!'

'How gruesome — however do you know that?'

'Alfie said so.'

'So he was there too?'

Alfie was what would have been known in earlier times as the village idiot. It would have been a complete misnomer. He was a scruffy old man of indeterminate age and immense cunning who took great care to appear half-witted to all those with whom he had no wish to get involved. To the chosen few he was an inexhaustible supply of country lore and local gossip. Simon was numbered amongst the latter; Ginny was never sure whether she should rejoice in this or remove her son from Alfie's pernicious influence.

'Don't tell me he's acquired a bike?'

He was usually to be seen shambling through the village trailing a stick behind him like a dog on a lead.

'Mark gave him a lift on his carrier.'

Ginny tried to visualise Alfie perched on the back of a bike, rotund figure encased in its ancient raincoat belted with a piece of rope like a sack tied in the middle, stick catching in the spokes, and her mind boggled. She refused to be sidetracked.

'Do you realise that you could have been killed if that damned bomb had gone off?'

Reading his mother accurately from long practice, Simon tried diversionary tactics.

'They used a digger to get it out.'

Ginny stared at him in amazement. 'You surely don't mean that they actually used one of those great mechanical diggers for such a delicate operation?'

'Yes, it got stuck in the mud. Is there anything to eat?'

'Go and make us a pot of tea and then I'll see about a meal. I take it the scare is over − that they managed to defuse the bomb?'

'Yes, but it took ages. Do you know they drilled a hole in it to get the explosives out − trepanning, they call it.'

'If I'd known you were down there watching it, I'd have gone out of my mind. I presume the little drama is all over now that you've deigned to come home?'

'No, it isn't. They found a body − in the bank where the digger got stuck. Actually, it's a skeleton. Alfie said that all the airmen had been accounted for when the plane came

18

down; two of them were found dead and two were taken prisoner, but there was always talk of a fifth man — a spy. Isn't it exciting?'

Ginny Dalton felt no twinge of foreboding.

Chapter Two

'You'd better get the local bobby back, this will be his pigeon, a case for the police.' Neil Hopkins rocked back on his heels as he crouched over the bones they had uncovered and fumbled for his notebook.

'Here we are: *Staffelkapetan* Helmut Mueller — survived this little lot but killed in a car crash in 1949; *Oberfeldwebel* Kurt Werner and *Unteroffizier* Dietrich Wallfisch — both killed at the time; *Obergefrieter* Ernst Fischer — survived, and still alive and well and living in Wiesbaden. All crewmen accounted for, so what have we here?'

'There must have been a fifth member.' Kenneth Batson tentatively poked the bleached bones with a muddy toecap.

'Looks like it — perhaps the apocryphal spy who seems to have been sighted all over the place, though how he wound up here, dead, near the actual crash, needs some explaining.'

'I thought those rumours had been discounted.'

Neil Hopkins shrugged. 'Perhaps Ernst Fischer can shed some light on the matter when we're in touch. Anyway, that's up to the police, they can sort it out.'

He got to his feet and dispatched one of his men in search of the local constable. The late afternoon sunshine slanted through the sedge and marram grass and shimmered over the tussocky grass of the water meadows. Over on the far side a herd of black and white cows, looking like toy animals at that distance, plodded methodically out of sight answering the call to milking parlour. Hopkins, Batson, and their helpers

20

perched on the river bank and opened up their thermoses and packets of sandwiches.

Tom Drake was annoyed at having what was left of his Saturday afternoon ruined by this bunch of aircraft enthusiasts; they had already caused a deal of trouble that day. Disgruntled, he parked near the end of the track leading down to the creek and plodded along the grassy wall, noting the crater and mountains of soil marking the excavation and the gap torn in the river bank where the digger had come to grief. Old Carstairs would have something to say about this. It was surprising he was not on the scene already, shouting his mouth off.

'So you've turned up one of the crew?'

Hopkins led him to the spot and pointed out the skeletal remains.

'They were all accounted for at the time, supposedly.'

'A stowaway?'

'Constable, this was a Junkers 188 on a very dangerous mission in wartime Britain, hardly the occasion for joyriding.'

Tom Drake walked round the skeleton and scanned the surrounding ground. 'Well, we're down to bare bones after — how long — forty odd years? But I should have expected some of his gear to remain. He would have been wearing a helmet, I presume, a belt, parachute harness — all we seem to have is his boots.'

'But they're not boots, are they?' Hopkins bent down to look closer.

'Don't touch, don't disturb anything further,' said PC Drake sharply, 'this will have to be investigated properly. I'm getting in the CID and the scene of crime officers.' He hurried back to his vehicle and called up HQ.

Detective Sergeant Patrick Mansfield leaned against the listing digger and gazed thoughtfully around him as his officers went into action. To Neil Hopkins and his men, hovering on the periphery of the scene, he appeared to be half asleep, daydreaming, but very little escaped those dark eyes, deepset beneath bristling, greying eyebrows. He was a heavily

21

built man in his mid-forties with a square head and closely cropped dark hair showing generous touches of grey. A local man, currently living in the neighbouring village of Wallingford, he displayed the stolid, impassive mien of a born and bred Suffolk man; but these very characteristics, so easily mistaken by the outsider for stupidity and dullness, hid a dry wit and a strong core of common sense. Patrick Mansfield was nobody's fool but it was often in his interests to appear so.

The sun was low in the sky and a damp mist rolling in from the river by the time the scene of crime officers had carried out their task of photographing the skeleton from every conceivable angle and measuring, sifting and probing the surrounding area.

'We've finished, sir, nothing else has turned up. Do you want us to bag the bones?'

No, I don't think we will. I'm getting Doc Brasnett out here to view it in situ.'

Dr. George Brasnett, the local Home Office Pathologist, was none too pleased to be disturbed in the middle of his pre-prandial drink, richly deserved after an exhausting round of golf. He refused point blank to turn out that evening but agreed to put in an appearance at ten o'clock the following morning.

'It's not going to run away, is it?' he boomed down the line. 'And a few hours are not going to make any difference to my findings. How do I get to this place?'

Patrick Mansfield gave him instructions and arranged to meet him the next day, then he put through a call to his immediate superior, Detective Inspector James Roland, and reported the situation.

James Roland was no more pleased than Doc Brasnett at being disturbed on his Saturday off.

'You've got it all under control your end, haven't you? What's the flap?'

'No flap, I just thought you should be put in the picture.'

'It *is* one of the German crew you've found?'

'Well, there is a slight doubt ...'

There was a groan from the other end of the line. 'That's all I need, an ambiguous bone case, just when I'm up to my

22

eyes in this larceny business at the Docks. Any idea how he died?'

'From what I can see without disturbing it, the top of the skull appears to be damaged.

'Which would be consistent with a plane crash?'

'Ye-es. I've sent for Doc Brasnett. He won't come down this evening but we're meeting him there tomorrow morning.'

'Sensible man! It will be dark soon, there's no earthly point in either of us turning out tonight. Who have you got there at the moment, apart from the Force?'

'The bomb disposal men have gone. There's just this bunch of Aircraft Research enthusiasts and the digger driver.'

'Get rid of them. I presume the area is already cordoned off? I don't have to tell you what to do — rig up a tarpaulin over the bones and leave someone on duty overnight. There's nothing more to be done at the moment.'

Mansfield returned to the scene of the excavation.

'You can go now, sir,' he said to Neil Hopkins. 'We shall want a statement from you later, and you may have to attend the inquest.'

'An inquest on a skeleton?'

'He hasn't been pronounced dead yet, sir' said the DS solemnly.

Detective Inspector James Roland overslept the next morning and woke up feeling decidedly hung-over. He had taken part in a sponsored squash marathon the night before and had celebrated too well afterwards. He dragged himself out of bed, frowned as a shaft of sunlight struck his face, and limped downstairs to the kitchen where he made himself a mug of black coffee and swallowed some aspirin. The thought of food nauseated him but he pushed a slice of bread in the toaster and swore when it jammed and filled the room with smoke and the acrid smell of burning.

This was the part of the day that he hated most. Other men living on their own complained that the evenings and nights were the worst, that that was the time when loneliness took over, but James Roland didn't agree. You could go out in the evening, there was always something to do on the social scene and he'd never been short of a sleeping partner when he felt so

23

inclined; but it was now, at breakfast time, that he missed a permanent companion. Someone to bring him a cup of tea, to fuss over him, to share the papers in bed; not that he often got the chance of a lie-in in his job. And not that he intended getting permanently involved with a woman ever again and laying himself open to hurt.

It was five years since Karen had walked out and he still felt very bitter. It was his unsociable hours that had got to her; never being able to rely on his presence at any given time, the ruined meals, the disturbed nights, the illogical plaint that he was more committed to the police force than he was to her. It was something that put an intolerable strain on many of his colleagues' marriages but somehow they soldiered on whilst his had come unstuck. He had been working day and night on a case over at Woodford, and the day he had cracked it and had come home in a state of euphoria and exhaustion he had found her gone. Later he had discovered that she had been seeing this other man for a couple of years, had been having it off with him, and just about everyone in the local force had known about it before him. That had hurt.

He sighed and looked round the kitchen with a jaundiced eye. He was still living in the same house in which they had started their married life. When they had split he had bought out Karen's share, enabling her to set up in a luxury flat with the hated Don Culbert, and he had continued living here on his own. It had been a mistake. He should have sold up and moved elsewhere. He told himself this frequently but was too apathetic to do anything about it. He did the bare minimum about the place to keep it in repair and from becoming too much of a pig sty. He ate and slept here when nothing better turned up, but it wasn't a home in the accepted sense of the word.

He glanced at the clock. Hell, Patrick would be picking him up in less that half an hour, he had better get a move on. He showered and shaved, squinting at himself in the bathroom cabinet mirror. Dark smudges underlined the light grey eyes that blinked back at him and his black, unruly hair was plastered in damp wedges over his forehead. God! He looked far older than his thirty-one years this morning − and felt it too. He towelled his hair, ran a comb through it, and hurriedly donned trousers and shirt. It was going to be another hot day but it was a humid, sticky heat, not conducive to a feeling of well-being when you had a hangover.

There was a thunderous knocking on the front door as he was bending down to tie up his shoelaces; it echoed the thumping in his head.

'The back door's open,' he yelled down the stairs, and sorted out and pocketed his keys and small change from the pile of debris he had dumped on the dressing table the night before. Patrick Mansfield was waiting for him in the kitchen when he descended a few minutes later. He was seated on the edge of the sole chair, staring disaprovingly at the dirty crockery piled up in the sink.

'You really shouldn't be so free with invitations. You never know who you might have asked in.'

'Only you could knock loud enough to disturb all the neighbours − early on a Sunday morning too.'

'It's half-past nine. And how is the Big White Chief this morning?'

'Cut it out, Pat, I'm feeling decidedly delicate.'

'How did it go?'

'We reached the target. I'll be after you for your sponsor money in the near future.'

'Well, it's for a good cause but you want to watch it − you're not as young as you used to be, trying to keep up with all these youngsters.'

'Much as I hate to admit it, this morning I think you're right. I'm definitely feeling the signs of incipient middle-age.'

'A nice breath of river ozone is just what you need. I've said the same to DC Evans − he's out in the car.'

'Still hankering after the bright lights, is he?'

'He still looks as if he's crawled out from under a stone. "Come along with me," I said, "and we'll get some good country air into your lungs and get rid of that city pallor."'

'The altruistic copper. How are Jean and the children?'

'Jean's fine and so are the kids. The trouble is they're not kids any longer. Gavin starts his second year at Leeds in a few weeks' time and Jane goes into the lower sixth. Proper little madam she is, thinks she's really grown-up. No more school uniform now, and if you saw the kind of gear she gets herself into ... the teachers are in for a culture shock.'

'It's called the generation gap. Come on, let's go. We mustn't keep DC Evans waiting, or Doc Brasnett come to that.'

It was well after ten o'clock before George Brasnett joined them at Croxton Creek. He came bouncing down the incline, a short, portly figure, plump legs encased in shiny green waders.

'Christ! What is he wearing?'

To James Roland the doctor looked absurdly like Toad of Toad Hall. He only wanted a cloth cap and goggles to complete the picture. 'But perhaps he had the right idea.' He glanced down at his own shoes which were already thickly caked with mud, and at the grey smears and grass stains decorating his trouser bottoms.

'Good morning, James, Patrick, lovely day. What have you got for me?' Doc Brasnett nodded briefly to DC Evans who was gazing unhappily over the mud flats and beamed up at the tall inspector and his hefty sergeant.

'Sergeant Mansfield put you in the picture yesterday evening, I presume? You'd better have a look.'

Roland led the way along the river wall. The police constable, who had spent a sleepless night guarding the side under a make-shift shelter, saluted groggily and moved aside. The pathologist produced a pair of hornrimmed spectacles, which added to his remarkable likeness to an amphibian, and trod carefully round the exposed skeleton, blowing gently through his pursed lips.

'Well, he appears to be all here. Was this how you found him or has he been disturbed?'

'Just as you see. It was extraordinary really, a section of the bank broke away leaving this cavity behind. Are you going to be able to date him?'

'You know better than to ask me that, James. How old would you like him to be?'

'Circa the 1940s?'

'Hhmm.' The pathologist bent down, and with beautifully manicured hands began examining the skull.

James Roland watched the podgy fingers delicately probing the bleached cranium, and sighed. It was a cause of constant annoyance to him that dating a skeleton accurately was an impossible task. Carbon dating could sort out your really old bones, and a high nitrogen content inducated something more recent, but within the tenet of police criminal memory — about thirty years — it was anyone's guess unless you had something else to go on; scraps of clothing, a watch or jewellery or something other than mortal remains, which in this case could be the footwear. Forensic scientists could work miracles these days; a minute sliver of fabric, a trace of saliva, a few grains of soil, could be married up to solve a crime, convict a murderer or whatever, but your actual skeleton . . . In his opinion forensic science had advanced far more than morbid pathology.

Dr. Brasnett interrupted his musing. 'I don't want to worry you but there are gunshot pellets lodged in the cranium.'

Roland groaned. 'Modern ones?'

'That's your problem. If he copped it in this little lot,' he flapped a hand at the crater, 'one could expect perhaps a piece of shrapnel embedded somewhere, not gunshot pellets. And he didn't come down with the plane either — there appear to be no broken bones.'

'So you're saying he definitely wasn't connected with the shot down plane?'

'I'm not committing myself at this stage, but you're right about the sex, he was male. Get him up to the lab and I'll do a detailed examination later.'

'How long will it take? Can you give me a report later today?'

'It's Sunday. If you're lucky I may have something for you by tomorrow afternoon. If not, Tuesday morning.'

With this, James Roland had to be content. He arranged for the removal of the bones and the footwear was carefully taken off and sent to Forensics. He had a horrible idea that when cleaned up they would look not unlike an old pair of shoes that he still had knocking about in the back of his wardrobe. Definitely not German Airforce issue boots of 1942.

* * *

27

Later that morning drinking coffee in his office at Felstone Police HQ, he and Mansfield mulled over the problem.

'Supposing he was one of the airmen ...' The sergeant produced his pipe and tobacco pouch and began the complicated ritual of lighting up. 'Say he parachuted down safely and one of the locals took a pot-shot at him with his shotgun?'

'Then why hide the body? He would have thought himself perfectly within his rights, at a time like that, to defend hearth and home against the enemy. Besides, surely the surviving members of the crew — two of them were taken prisoner — would have alerted the authorities to the fact that there should have been a fifth body or survivor to be accounted for.'

'What about this spy business? Neil Hopkins, the chappie from the East Anglian Aircraft Research Group, says there were many rumours circulating locally at the time, of a spy who was seen in the district in civilian dress carrying a briefcase.'

'Pie in the sky, I should think. We'll have to check with the German authorities — didn't you say one of the crew was still alive? Perhaps he can throw some light on it. Any more theories?'

'You're shooting them down as fast as I put them up.'

'We're clutching at straws, aren't we? You don't think it's a German airman, do you?'

'No. I had a pricking in my thumbs as soon as I saw him, if you'll forgive the expression; it was all too neat. And I think Tom Drake had the same feeling — he was quick to get on to us and set things in motion.'

'So, what have we? We have the skeletal remains of someone who was killed — we can rule out natural causes with gunshot pellets in his skull — but who he was, why, and when it happened is anyone's guess.'

'There'll be no way either of finding out after all this time whether he was killed on the spot or taken there afterwards, will there?'

'Too true. Let's hope the Forensic boys come up with something. We must pin our hopes on the shoes. The very fact that there was nothing else left behind suggests someone was trying to prevent identification.'

* * *

'And how is our upwardly mobile Lothario today?' Jean Mansfield threw over her shoulder as she stirred the sizzling pan on the hob with one hand and dexterously shook the contents of a second one with her other hand. She was a small, neat woman with cropped curly hair and warm brown eyes. She had been a social worker when she had first met her husband but had relinquished the job early on in their marriage because of their clash of interests. She had always insisted that she had stopped work to concentrate on producing a family but Patrick had been aware of the sacrifice she had made, and the reason for it, and he now encouraged her in all the voluntary work she undertook. She was an active member of the W.I., ran the village Brownies Pack and was on the committee of the local Nature Conservation Trust as well as helping out at Felstone's Citizens Advice Bureau.

Her husband eyed her affectionately but said gruffly: 'I do wish you wouldn't refer to our James so disrespectfully.' He dropped a kiss on the top of her head and perched precariously on a kitchen stool. 'The Super wouldn't like it.'

'I know he's the Super's blue-eyed boy, but I don't think it's fair. Oh, I know you don't like me whingeing, Pat, but you're a damn good policeman with years of experience. It doesn't seem right that you're stuck at sergeant whilst he goes through the ranks like a dose of salts. Just because he's got a university degree.'

'You know that's not true. We've been into all this before, Jean. I know my limitations. We can't all be high-flyers like James Roland, but we make a good team. He needs me as much as I need him, and he never pulls rank.'

'I should hope not, with you so much older!'

'What's got into you today? It's not like you to act the nagging, ambitious wife.'

'I'm sorry. I don't really mean it. It's not the fact that he's your boss that gets to me ... I suppose it's his attitude to women.'

'How come?'

'You know perfectly well what I mean. He treats us as sex objects.'

'That's coming it a bit strong.'

29

'But it's true – everyone says so.'

'Everyone?'

'Jane and her friends were ...'

'Jane?'

For one horrible moment he thought his friend and colleague had flipped and was tangling with under-age teenagers.

'You know that a lot of her friends' parents belong to the Felstone Sports and Social Club,' continued his wife, unaware of the momentary shock she had just delivered, 'It's common knowledge that anything in skirts is fair game to him, strictly on a love 'em and leave 'em basis.'

'Presumably these mythical women participate of their own free will. And he certainly doesn't dirty his own patch, there's never been a breath of scandal at the Station.'

'Well, there wouldn't be, would there? He's no fool. But he uses women. I'm not surprised that his wife left him.'

'It all stems from that. He adored her and he's never really recovered from it. It destroyed his faith in women and now he takes good care not to let anyone get close to him again. Personally, I can't see what women see in him.'

'There speaks your typical male. Those, dark, brooding looks are a real turn-on, especially coupled with that little boy air he has about him at times.'

'You're getting me worried.'

'Don't be ridiculous, I can give him a dozen years – but it's easy to see why women fall for him. That black hair and those light eyes – he's got a touch of the Paddy about him. It's funny, he looks Irish and you've got an Irish name, but there's not a drop of Celtic blood in either of you, is there? Are you ready to eat yet?'

'What is it?' He sniffed suspiciously.'

'Don't be like that. It's stir-fry pork. The children are always going on at me about being more adventurous in my culinary efforts so I thought I'd experiment while they're both out.'

'Using me as a guinea pig? Where are they, by the way?'

'Gavin's working this evening,' he had a holiday job as a part-time barman in Felstone, 'and Jane has gone to a party in Felstone. She asked if you could pick her up about eleven-thirty.'

'I'm just a damned taxi service, and that's far too late for someone her age.'

'She's not back at school yet. This is their last rave-up to mark the end of the holidays. At least we keep tabs on her this way. You wouldn't like her wandering home on her own at that time of night, would you?'

'Heaven forbid! I'm sure Gavin was much less trouble at that age.'

'Only because you didn't worry so much about him. It's the old double standard again; however much you intend to treat them alike you can't help being more anxious and solicitous over a daughter, especially in this day and age.'

'That's true. I feel quite sick with worry sometimes when I think of the dreadful things that can befall a young girl. That's part of the penalty of being a policeman.'

'She's a sensible girl, and you've never tried to hide the hard facts of life from her. We have to give her some freedom and show her that we trust her, though it's not easy to know where to draw the line.'

Jean Mansfield bent down and took two plates out of the oven. 'I think this is the moment of truth. It smells good, doesn't it?'

'We-ll, different ...'

'Don't be such an old stick-in-the-mud.' She deftly ladled out the contents of the frying-pan. 'Talking of mud, what's this I hear about your dredging up bodies down at Croxton Creek?'

'I don't believe it — where did you hear this?'

'It's all over the village. Is it true?'

'One skeleton has been found.'

'And ...?'

'And nothing. You know I can't discuss my work, but between you and me I think we've turned up a murder victim, though whether we'll ever get to identify him or pin it on anyone is another matter.'

'Has the Press got on to it yet?'

'Have you seen this?' It was the next morning and James Roland flung himself back in his office chair and waved the

31

morning edition of the *Felstone Courier* at his sergeant. The headline jumped out at him:
LETHAL BOMB CARGO DISCOVERED 44 YEARS AFTER GERMAN PLANE CRASHES.
'I suppose we can be thankful that there are no photos. I don't think they've managed to pinpoint the actual site.'

'It's private land surely, they wouldn't be allowed near?'

'There's a public footpath running along the top of the river wall — it only needs an enterprising reporter with a zoom lens and all would be revealed. However, I've been on the phone to old man Carstairs who owns the land and he's pulling in his gamekeeper and farm hands to patrol that area and make sure no-one strays off the straight and narrow.'

'At least they don't know about the skeleton.'

'I was saving that till later.' Roland flipped over the newspaper and pointed a long, elegant finger at the 'Stop Press'.
SKELETON FOUND AT PLANE CRASH SITE. HAS THE MYSTERY OF THE GERMAN SPY BEEN SOLVED AT LAST? read Mansfield to himself, and sighed. 'I don't know how they do it — talk about the village grape-vine. I don't suppose you've heard from Doc Brasnett yet?'

'Give him time, Pat, give him time. He knows there's no frantic hurry over this one. He's not going to put himself out over some bones that are God knows how old. Hopefully, we'll get more help from Forensics over the shoes.'

The rest of the morning was taken up with routine work, and Roland became so immersed in a report on co-ordination between H.M. Customs and the Dock Police that had landed on his desk that when the pathologist rang him late afternoon, he had almost forgotten about the mystery skeleton.

'Brasnett here.' The voice boomed down the line, immediately conjuring up for Roland the bouncy, forceful character at the other end. 'I suppose you are all agog to hear my report?'

'Er ... yes. Good of you to get back to me so soon. Anything interesting?'

'Male, five foot nine, slender build, early twenties.'

'And he died from ...?'

'There are five gunshot pellets lodged in his cranium.'

'So they would have killed him?'

'You don't usually walk around with your skull full of shot. But, of course, he could have been killed in some other way first and shot afterwards, bizarre though that would seem. There's no telling, after all this time.'

'Suicide?' asked the inspector without much hope.

'No way. He'd have blasted half his head off.'

'Teeth?'

'I was wondering when you'd get around to that. The jaw is broken but I can get you a good dental impression.'

'Ah, good, at least it will be something to go on, though I'm not hopeful. Thanks, George.'

'There's nothing else you need to know immediately, I'll send in my written report later with full details. I wish you joy.'

'Just one thing — how close was his assailant?'

'Close enough to be seen. In other words, he wasn't hiding behind bushes a long way off. He was shot at quite close range — it will be in my report — approximate distance, trajectory angles, points of entry. Much good it will do you at this distance in time.'

'What it is to receive a colleague's encouragement.'

The official report when it came through added nothing significant to the information already garnered. The Coroner had been informed and the inquest was set for the following week. Neil Hopkins, the digger driver, and PC Drake were amongst those called to attend and, as expected, an open verdict was recorded. The Coroner ordered the bones to be stored until identification was carried out or until all further avenues of enquiry had been exhausted.

The information that Forensics supplied them with the following week was startling in that it widened the field of enquiry considerably. The call came through as Roland and Mansfield were getting down to the onerous task of tackling the backlog of paper work that had accumulated over the past weeks.

'Paul Robertson here, I've got the gen on those shoes your lot sent us. I don't know whether this is going to please you or not but your bone case wasn't wearing English footwear.'

'You mean they *were* German?'

'No, no, I think you've got a Colonial laddie.'

Roland raised his eyebrows at Mansfield who came close and perched on the edge of the desk, craning forward to catch the conversation.

'Stop talking in riddles, what are you trying to tell me?'

'They're Hush Puppies — a style called "Kirby" — and they were manufactured and sold only in Australia.'

'Australia! Any idea of their age?'

'First produced in 1975, and available subsequent to that.'

'Are you quite sure about this — is it official?'

'Yes, we've been in touch with the head office of Clarks Shoes in Street. They're very good and have often helped us in the past, and the Public Relations Manager informs us that Clarks do not make Hush Puppies in this country, and only have the franchise in Australia. This particular style was only on sale in Australia.'

'This is most unexpected. We've got a date to work from but I can't say this information has eased our task. Thanks, anyway. At least we've now got some definite facts.'

'Always happy to oblige. Good hunting!'

'Did you get all that?' Roland put the phone on its cradle and leant back, clasping his hands behind his neck. A look of mock despair flickered across his usually enigmatic face.

'An Aussie turing up on our patch and getting himself done in — where does this leave us? I can't see that Missing Persons are going to be much help.'

'He doesn't have to be Australian,' pointed out Mansfield, scratching his head. 'He could be a local man who'd been on a visit or working over there.'

'True. We'll have to check with them and put out some feelers locally. Surely if somebody's got a relative over there they're going to know if he's gone missing? I mean, it's all of ten years, possibly more. We'll have to see if we can get a lead from the Australian authorities.'

'You're hoping the murderer is local?'

'If he's not we haven't a hope in hell, not after all this time. I tell you one thing, though — whoever he is, he isn't *au fait* with local history. Either he was too young to know about the plane crash or else he moved into the district after the war.'

'Unless he was trying to be too clever — thinking that if

34

ever the body was discovered it would be neatly identified as a German airman.'

'In which case he over-reached himself. We may have a very worried man living on our patch − or woman.'

It was a week later when the first real break-through came. Roland was in his office when the duty sergeant phoned from the front desk.

'I've got a Mr. Neil Hopkins here, sir. He's asking to see you, says it's important.'

'Neil Hopkins?'

'He says it's to do with the recent bomb excavation at Croxton Creek.'

'Ah, yes, send him up, will you.'

Whilst he waited, Roland recalled that Neil Hopkins was the leader of the team of Aircraft Research enthusiasts who had discovered the skeleton. Now what can he want? he mused. Shouldn't think he's got any more information that could be of help to us ... more likely he's fishing for information himself to complete his records. Well, he's going to be unlucky.

'Mr Hopkins? I believe we met at the inquest.' Roland got to his feet and shook hands with the man who was shown in. He saw a man of medium height, in his mid-sixties with greying ginger hair and a handlebar moustache. 'Do sit down. I believe you have something to tell me?'

'I understand you are in charge of the investigation into the skeleton that was found at the German plane crash site? Has it been identified?'

Roland indicated that it had not. 'Why? Can you tell me something about it − you have some information?'

'Not information exactly − I have something to give you.'

Hopkins looked uncomfortable as he reached into his pocket and produced a small package. 'I'm afraid it stems from some very unprofessional behaviour on the part of one of our members who was with me on the excavation,' he continued whilst he started to unwrap the package. 'He found this by the skeleton. It's a medallion, a St. Christopher medallion.'

He peeled the wrapping back and tipped the jewellery on to

35

the desk under the startled eyes of the inspector who tried to hide his excitement as he picked it up.

It was the size of a ten piece coin, of some blackened metal. An attempt had been made to clean it up.

'He thought it belonged to the German airman and took it as a souvenir. Later, when he learnt that the skeleton probably wasn't one of the original crew, he realised that it could be an important piece of evidence. I'm only sorry his conscience took so long to prompt him. He handed it over to me yesterday.'

'You're saying it was round the skeleton's neck? Was there a chain?'

'Apparently it was lying near the sternum. The chain must have rotted − not silver like this.'

The medallion was indeed silver. On one side, moulded in base relief, was the hunched figure of St. Christopher and his child burden; on the other side, just discernible to the naked eye, was the hallmark, and above it what looked like an engraved pattern of entwined initials.

'Will it help your identification?'

'It is quite possible. It will certainly help with dating. The hallmark will show in what year it was manufactured.'

'And presumably one set of those initials belongs to the dead man?'

'That is also quite possible.' He had already arrived at this conclusion but was surprised to hear his thoughts echoed by the man opposite him. Hopkins was a shrewd man. 'We shall certainly look into it. Thank you for bringing it in, Mr. Hopkins.'

'You won't take any action . . .?' He hesitated. 'I mean, you won't bring any charges against my colleague?'

'How can I charge someone who has no name or address?' replied Roland blandly. 'Though it would have been a help if we had had this earlier. Just don't let him loose next time round, that's all. Or . . .'

Neil Hopkins cocked an enquiring eyebrow.

'. . . make sure you run a metal detector over him afterwards,' Roland finished dryly.

After Hopkins had departed he allowed some of his elation to show. He tossed the medallion in the air and caught it then went in search of his assistant, whom he ran to earth in the station car park, locking up his vehicle before reporting for duty.

'Patrick, me boyo, we've had our break.' He opened his fist and showed his mystified sergeant the medallion. 'Our bone case had a taste for jewellery — he was wearing this little gew-gaw round his neck when he copped it.'

'How . . .? I mean. Where did it turn up?' In a few succinct sentences Roland put him in the picture, and the older man examined the medallion eagerly.

'This is going to give us a lead, isn't it?'

'I hope so. I think we stand a good chance now of tracing him, though it's surprising his killer didn't remove it. It must have been tucked inside his shirt or whatever. There's not much point in sending it to Forensics, it's been mauled about too much to tell them anything. Take it to Gilpin's in the High Street. They're the most prestigious jewellers in the area. They can translate the hallmark for us, identify the makers. It would be too much to hope that they actually sold it and kept a record of the transaction, or did the engraving, but you never know your luck.'

'It may come from Australia.'

'Yes.' Roland studied the obverse side again. 'St. Christopher is the patron saint of travellers. Suppose our chappie was given this as a talisman before he started his travels Down Under?'

'You mean he could still be a local man?'

'Who came back and met a sticky end. We'll have to check with all the local jewellers. If they can't give us a lead we'll have to make a door-to-door in Croxton and neighbourhood — someone may recognise it.'

Mr. John Gilpin of Gilpin and Sons, Silversmiths and Horologists since 1874, was quite happy to help the police with their enquiries. He tutted over the state of the medallion when Sergeant Mansfield showed it to him but the careful application of an impregnated cloth did something to restore it to its former condition and revealed more details. He screwed in his eyeglass and applied himself to reading the hallmark.

'Ah, yes, it was tested at the London Assay Office — the

37

lion's head tells us this, and the letter A gives us the date of 1975.'

'There's no doubt about this?' queried Mansfield. 'There is no way it could be before 1975?'

'Oh, no, Sergeant.' The elderly Mr. Gilpin was quite shocked. 'This is quite indisputable. All silver is dated and this is included as part of the hallmark. In fact, from 1975 onwards all four British Assay Offices have used the same date letter. Before then you had to identify the Assay Office before you could find the date.'

'So this was produced on sale in 1975. Can you identify the manufacturer.'

'Very popular these were about that time. They were produced in great quantity − all part of the young man's macho image. You know, Sergeant, the silver or gold coin glinting on a suntanned chest.' He gave a little titter. 'We sold many of them.'

'Have you any records of sale?'

'Not for something of little value like this. As I say, they were mass-produced, not the sort of thing we would normally have retailed but we have to bow to contemporary fashion. I should think that every high street jeweller in the country stocked this or something similar.'

'What about the engraving?' Mansfield hid his disappointment. 'Would it be possible to trace the purchaser through this?'

'If you can find out who did the engraving then you probably have the purchaser. This is an amateur attempt,' he said disparagingly.

'You mean, it wasn't done professionally?'

'No. It is a very clumsy job. No professional engraver would own up to this. Having said that I must admit that whoever did it had an eye for design and must have had access to a graver. Probably some young woman bought it for her sweetheart and had a go at engraving their initials on it herself.'

'I think you are probably right. Well, thank you for your help, Mr. Gilpin.'

Back in the inspector's office Mansfield brought his boss up-to-date with developments.

'I checked with all the other jewellers in Felstone and they all told me the same thing; it was a very popular line and they had all stocked it at the time.'

'It's a pity about the engraving. At first sight I thought it was a gift. Well, the date fits in with the forensic evidence from the shoes. Our chappie was alive and well in 1975. From the state of the remains he must have been dead at least seven years so that gives us a time scale of about five years. I'm afraid it means a door-to-door but I can't spare you for the moment. We'll have to shelve it for the time being; the Great Man himself has ordered that we pull out all the stops on this illegal immigration caper. He wants a check run on all the container-lorry drivers using Felstone Dock. That article in the national press alleging that Felstone was the main back door for people sneaking into the country has really caught him on the raw.'

In the event nearly a week elapsed before a start was made on the house check. The weather had deteriorated badly and any hopes that the fine spell in early September had heralded an Indian summer were soon dashed. There were heavy falls of rain and those farmers who had not managed to cut their corn earlier despaired of ever harvesting their crop. Autumn had settled in early. The trees and hedgerows dripped with moisture and the sodden leaves hung in a dull green, grey and brown profusion with none of their usual pyrotechnic display.

Patrick Mansfield took William Evans with him on his enquiry and the young detective constable, born in Cardiff and late of the Metropolitan Force, viewed the mist-wreathed fields, overflowing ditches and puddled lanes with something approaching horror.

They had had no luck so far. Several people had recognised the type of medallion, they were even shown an identical one at one household, but nobody had recognised the engraving or could lay claim to any knowledge concerning it. They had quartered the village of Croxton and were now left with one remaining road, Duck Lane, to cover. Mansfield had left this until last as his friend and old headmaster, Mathew Betts, lived here and he was hoping some refreshment would be forthcoming.

Duck Lane ran behind the Post Office and village store and

dissected the fields belonging to Church Farm. At one end was a thatched cottage, the oldest building in the village, belonging to a nonagenarian who had lived there all her life; at the other end was the Old Manse. The chapel that had once stood next door had been pulled down several years earlier and replaced by a pair of cheap, nasty semi-detached houses that looked ill-at-ease amongst their older neightbours. Newcomers to the village lived in these houses and as Mansfield had expected, it had been a waste of time calling on them. Old Mrs. Tandy had likewise been a dead loss and the occupants of two of the cottages farther up the lane had been out, probably doing their Saturday morning shopping.

The next cottage along, a rather attractive red brick structure with dormer windows jutting out of the mossy, Suffolk-tiled roof belonged to Mrs. Ginny Dalton. Mansfield knew her by sight, she taught his daughter at Felstone High School. She had been widowed tragically when her husband, considerably older than herself and also a teacher at the same school, had suffered a coronary just over a year ago. He did not expect to get any joy from her but called as a formality.

She answered the door dressed in an old pair of paint-stained jeans and a skimpy tee-shirt that emphasised her slenderness and made her look absurdly young. Far too young to hold a responsible teaching post and to be the mother of a teenage son, though he seemed to recall that this son was actually a stepson. She had a mass of red-gold hair of the shade known as strawberry blonde, tied back from a face that had a streak of blue paint across one prominent cheekbone.

Patrick Mansfield introduced himself and DC Evans and explained that they were trying to trace the ownership of an article that had come into police possession.

'You'd better come in, Sergeant, though I really don't know why you've come to me.'

'It's routine, Ma'am, we're visiting everyone in the vicinity. It won't take long.'

She led them through the small hallway into the living room. It was a large room and he guessed that the dividing wall between two smaller rooms had been knocked down at some time to make this spacious, light sitting-cum-dining room. It was furnished in a mixture of old and new, which blended surprisingly well. Most of the furniture looked old but the cushions and curtains were fashioned from batik-printed material, possible executed by her, and there were many modern paintings on the walls and bright, gay ceramics dotted around.

'What is it you want me to look at, Sergeant? Are you trying to identify stolen property?' She gazed at him disarmingly and he noted that she had odd coloured eyes. One was blue-grey, the other hazel. 'Never trust a person with odd-coloured eyes.' Where had he heard that? Still, it was disconcerting, rather like trying to look in the eye a person with a squint.

'Rather more serious than that. We are trying to identify a person. Have you ever seen this before?' He held out the medallion to her.

She went very still and a frown crossed her face but she made no attempt to take it from him. Instead she stared at it as if mesmerised.

'It is engraved on the other side.' At that she did react. She had the pale, clear skin that often goes with red hair and the colour drained from her face, leaving it white and papery.

She held out her hand, and when he gave it to her she seemed to hesitate before tentatively turning it over. A single word escaped her.

'Tim . . .'

Chapter Three

'You recognise it?'

She stared at the medallion as if it were a living entity that would up and bite her.

'I . . . Where did you get it from?'

'Are you all right Mrs. Dalton?'

'I . . . Yes . . . It was just a shock seeing it again. I don't understand . . . How did it come into you hands?'

'Suppose you just sit down, Mrs. Dalton, and tell us all you know about it.'

'I gave it to Tim many years ago.'

'Tim?'

'Tim Spencer. We were childhood sweethearts. I gave it to him before he went to Australia.'

William Evans caught his breath audibly and was frowned into silence by his superior.

'Who is this Tim Spencer? Did he live locally?'

'He's a distant cousin of Tony Garfield of The Hermitage — they were brought up together. Sergeant, what *is* this all about? How did you get hold of this medallion?'

He ignored her question. 'Are you quite sure that this is the medallion you gave him? The engraving . . .?'

'I did it myself. Look — T.S. and G.M. My maiden name was Merrivale.

When was this — how long ago?'

'1975. Early 1975.'

'And did you keep in touch?'

'Yes . . . no . . . for a couple of years he . . . communicated, then I heard no more. I guessed he had found pastures new ... we were very young.'

'Extremely young in your case, Mrs. Dalton, I should think.'

'I was seventeen. Old enough to be passionately in love, or think I was. But why all these questions? Has Tim turned up after all these years? I still don't understand where you got hold of this?'

She fingered the medallion and looked at them expectantly.

Mansfield groaned inwardly. This was the part he always disliked. After years of experience he still found this one of the most distressing parts of his job: the breaking of bad news to the next-of-kin or close friends. She must have sensed his unease. It triggered instant comprehension on her part.

'Something's happened to him, hasn't it? He's dead.'

'I'm sorry to be the bearer of bad news but I'm afraid it looks as if he's been dead a long time.'

'You'd better tell me.' She seemed to compose herself, and with those odd eyes fixed compellingly on his he knew that he had no option but to put the facts before her.

'You know the recent bomb excavation at Croxton Creek? A skeleton was found ...'

'It was Tim? You're saying that was Tim?'

'This medallion was found round the skeleton's neck, so unless your Tim passed it on to someone else ...'

'It can't be him. He's in Australia!' She was denying it to herself rather than to him but her head had already accepted what her heart rejected.

'I'm afraid he came back.'

'Is there any way of making sure?'

'Do you happen to know what dentist he went to?'

'Dentist? Oh – dental records.' She gulped. 'I don't know but I'm sure he went to a local one in Felstone; Tony would probably know. Sergeant ...' she hesitated '... how did he die?'

'He was shot through the head.'

'You mean murdered!' She was horrified.

'Well, he certainly didn't die a natural death. I suppose it could have been an accident but nobody ever owned up.'

'I can't believe it, it's horrible! What will happen now?'

'We are treating the death as suspicious. You will be required to make an official statement later. Is there anything else you can tell me in the meantime?'

'No, I don't think so. He went to Australia in 1975 and I never saw him again.'

'Had he no parents or close relations?'

'No. He was a great nephew of the late Mrs. Fellingham of Croxton Hall, the grandson of her brother. He had no brothers or sisters and his parents were killed in a plane crash in 1964. After that he went to live with Tony Garfield's family who were also relatives of Mrs. Fellingham.'

'And nobody kept in touch or heard from him after he went to Australia? Isn't that rather extraordinary?'

'Yes, they did . . . I mean . . . well, it was rather difficult.'

Mansfied raised his craggy eyebrows eloquently and she sighed.

'I'd better explain. Tim was . . . er . . . rather high-spirited. We . . . he upset Great-aunt Gertrude and she packed him off to Australia to "make good", as she called it. There were family connections with Australia,' Ginny said vaguely. 'Anyway, three years later she arranged a big party to celebrate her eightieth birthday. All her relatives were invited − she had no children of her own and had been a widow for years − and Tim was summoned home for the occasion. But he never came back.'

'It rather looks as if he did, Mrs. Dalton.'

'But if he came back, somebody must have seen him.' Patrick Mansfield put his beer glass on the low table in front of him, tipped back his chair and got out his pipe. He and Roland were mulling over the latest developments in the Duck and Spoon, the local pub to which they sometimes repaired when in the Croxton district.

'The murderer did.'

'But he wasn't just beamed down. He must have used public transport, been seen on the journey by people.'

'And you're hoping someone will remember after all this time? Wishful thinking, I'm afraid. Ten years is a long time. But let's hope we can get a positive identification through dental records and confirm the dates. I think a visit to Mr.

Tony Garfield of The Hermitage is called for. Have you done your homework?'

'He's another great-nephew of the old girl who used to lord it up at Croxton Hall. She died several years ago after the hall was burned down. The estate was sold off and a Mr. Harry Carstairs bought up most of the land and built himself a palatial modern house on the old site. Garfield bought The Hermitage. I understand he inherited some money from the old lady and settled there with his wife − I believe she came from South America or the States. Only a small portion of land went with The Hermitage and he doesn't farm it himself − rents it out to Carstairs, which makes sense − but he retains shooting rights and owns frontage on to the river and creek.'

'You have done well. How old would he be?'

'Late thirties, I think. He's a businessman, a property speculator, and spends a lot of time in the City.'

'I wonder how close he was to Timothy Spencer? It sounds as if they were brought up virtually as brothers.'

'You'd have thought they would have kept in touch. There's something odd about this, I'm getting a distinct whiff of fish.'

'We must get this identity confirmed. If it is Tim Spencer, perhaps our Aussie friends Down Under can turn up something. How did Mrs. Dalton strike you?'

Mansfield considered this whilst he had a second go at lighting his pipe. He re-packed the tobacco, tamped it down, and by the third match it was sizzling nicely and added considerably to the smoke pollution in the room.

'I think our William was quite taken by her, she'd gobble him up for breakfast.'

Roland waited, knowing that he could rely on his assistant for an accurate summing-up and thumbnail sketch of anyone with whom he had been engaged in conversation for longer than a few seconds. He wasn't disappointed.

'Gives the impression of being very young and ingenuous, looks it too − slim, boyish figure, but a nice pair of tits. Dresses like my daughter on one of her androgynous days − but I think there's more to her than meets the eye. To coin a phrase, I think still waters run deep.'

45

'She's not as naïve as she appears?'

'Can't be, can she? Head of the Art Department at the High School, and with a teenage son. Of course, she was only a school kid herself when this great romance blossomed. It can't have had too lasting an effect — she's been married and widowed since then.'

James Roland coughed and made to get up.

'If you're quite sure you've finished giving me my third passive smoking session of the day, I think we'll go and find out what light Garfield can throw on the investigation.'

'Is it official yet?'

'The Big Man's kicking, but once we can convince him that his anonymous skeleton was a relative of the late Grand Dame of Croxton, he'll have to give the go-ahead.'

'It's got you hooked, hasn't it?'

'I'm intrigued, yes.' Roland drummed his fingers on the stained table top and frowned unseeingly into his empty glass. 'I don't like to think that a young chap can be cut down in his prime like that and buried in the ancestral acres without any sort of hue and cry. I think it's time he was avenged.'

There was a cool breeze blowing from the direction of the river when they stepped out of the car in front of The Hermitage. It dispelled the mists of earlier in the day and brought with it a hint of smoke and burning leaves. Someone was struggling with a bonfire in the far corner of the kitchen garden where it sloped down towards the green-houses. There was a mass of thick, damp smoke wreathing the runner-bean cones and partially obscuring the figure wielding a pitchfork.

'Our Mr. Garfield does well for himself.' Mansfield's shrewd eyes assessed the signs of good husbandry; the well-kept fences and neatly gravelled drive, the pristine paintwork and gleaming windows.

'He certainly doesn't seem short of a penny.' A distant whiney from the direction of the stable block made him mentally add a nought or two to Garfield's net worth. 'I wonder how he actually earns his shekels? "Property speculator" covers a multitude of sins.'

Their feet scrunched on the gravel as they walked towards the door. The viginia creeper that clad the porch rustled in the wind and shook scarlet strands over the brickwork. The bell was answered by a man of medium height, with brown thinning hair and caramel brown eyes. His well-upholstered figure was impeccably dressed in a well-cut dark suit and club tie. It could only be Garfield himself. Roland stepped forward and showed his I.D.

'Mr. Garfield? I am Detective Inspector Roland and this is Detective Sergeant Mansfield. We've come ...'

'I think I know why you've come,' he cut in, a look of distress crossing his face. 'In fact, I was about to get in touch with you. Ginny Dalton rang my wife — they are old friends. This is a shocking business, Inspector. You had better come in.'

He led the way into a beautifully proportioned sitting room with a high ceiling and long windows overlooking a verandah. It was furnished with large, comfortable sofas and chairs upholstered in chintz, and there were bowls of chrysan-themums and autumn leaves on the occasional tables scattered around. It looked like a photo from *Country Life* and this impression was heightened by the inevitable labrador stretched out in front of the log fire. An old dog with a greying muzzle,his tail thumped as they entered the room but he made no attempt to get up.

Mansfield effaced himself by moving over to one of the windows. There was a panoramic view of the creek and surrounding countryside. In the distance he could see the sluice gates dissecting the river wall and beyond them the water meadows, flat and grey and uninviting. Although he craned his neck he could see no signs of the recent excavation; the bend in the river bank and the screen of scrubby willows hid it from sight.

'Inspector, are you sure this skeleton is Tim's? I just can't believe it!'

'That's one of the reasons we've come to you, Mr. Garfield. We're hoping you can help us to get a positive identification.'

'You want me to identify the ... the skeleton?' He was alarmed.

'Oh no, sir, we're hoping dental records will give us positive identification. Do you happen to know which dentist he went to?'

'Dentist? Well, yes, we went to old Gregory Fentin in Felstone when we were young. He died recently and I believe his practice has been taken over by a husband and wife team.'

Roland's heart sank. He had been counting on the dentist, whoever he was, keeping his records for longer than the required five years; but with a new broom it was quite likely that the earlier records had been swept away and consigned to the shredder.

'Do you really think it is my cousin Tim?' continued Garfield, 'I just can't believe it — he's supposed to be in Australia. And Ginny tells me you think he was murdered?'

'I'm afraid this is so. If you can tell us something about his background and the circumstances leading up to his decision to emigrate to Australia, it will give us a clearer picture of the situation.'

'Yes, of course. Do sit down, Inspector, Sergeant . . .' He waved his hand vaguely in the direction of the easy chairs positioned in a semi-circle round the fireplace. 'I will give you all the help I can of course, but where do I start?'

Roland sat down in one of the chairs indicated. He bent forward and scratched the recumbent dog behind its ears. Mansfield stayed where he was, ostensibly miles away in contemplation of the view but with his ears pricked.

'Nice dog.' The said dog rolled over onto its back and rolled its eyes at the inspector in ecstasy.

'He's an old softie, very ancient and full of rheumatism now, I'm afraid. He spends most of his day asleep in front of the fire but he's earned his honourable retirement. Now, what do you want to know?'

'Anything you can tell us, sir, that will help with our investigation. Suppose you start with his boyhood — I understand he lived with your family after his own parents were killed?'

'Yes, they died when Tim was about seven or eight, and he came to live with us as he had no other close relations.'

'And you got on well together?'

'Of course, why shouldn't we?' Garfield asked in surprise.

48

'It can be rather traumatic, accepting a substitute sibling at short notice.'

'I was an only child and I was pleased at the prospect of company. Of course, Tim was a lot younger than me. I was fifteen when he came to live with us and I left home myself a few years later so we were never really close; but yes, Inspector, we got on well enough.'

'So he would have been how old when he went to Australia? What led to that?'

'Nineteen. He left school as soon as he was old enough, wouldn't stay on for higher education, and drifted from one job to another. He left home, wanting to be independent, and one way and another was a bit of a tearaway, rather wild. I think it was just high spirits. There was no real harm in him, he would have settled down in time, but then he got himself into a spot of trouble and my Great-aunt – Mrs. Gertrude Fellingham – arranged for him to go to Australia. Uncle Bart, her late husband, had had a business there. He had been a merchant and had done quite well for himself there and in the Far East.'

'And where does Mrs. Dalton fit into this?'

'What did Ginny tell you?' he countered.

Roland raised his eyebrows in feigned surprise. 'I understood she and Tim Spencer were childhood sweethearts, and because of some misdemeanour connected to that he was banished to Australia.'

'Yes, well, that is the long and short of it.'

'So what happened?' prompted Roland.

'I suppose you will have to know, thought I don't see what this has got to do with his death.'

'That is for us to decide, sir.'

Tony Garfield grimaced. 'They were both very headstrong and imagined themselves madly in love. They wanted to get married. Of course, it just wasn't on. Ginny was still at school and her father was very strict, and Tim hadn't two pennies to rub together. They planned to elope – mind you, this is hearsay. I wasn't around at the time and I only pieced together what happened afterwards.'

'I take it the elopement went wrong?'

'You could say that! Look, Inspector, this is putting me in

a very embarrassing situation, but I suppose you will have to know the facts. I hope Ginny will forgive me ..' He hesitated and looked very unhappy. 'Tim helped himself to some of Great-aunt's jewellery and a sum of money that was in the house at the time. He also took her second car — a Vauxhall estate — in which they went off, only there was an accident.'

'And ...?'

'There was an accident and a child was killed.'

'You mean he was joyriding and caused the death of a child? Did he get a prison sentence?'

'No, I think he was charged with causing death by reckless driving but he got off with a hefty fine which Great-aunt paid. You see, there were mitigating circumstances, some doubt whether the accident was his fault; the toddler was wandering in the road where he had no right to be, unaccompanied, and Tim came round a bend too fast and couldn't stop. Of course, he was speeding at the time ...'

Roland was aware that his sergeant had ceased his perusal of the landscape and was watching the speaker with interest, a gleam of remembrance stirring in his deep-set eyes. Good old Patrick! Of course, he had been around at that time and it looked as if he had some recollection of the case.

'And what about the little matter of the stolen car — to say nothing of the jewellery and money? Was he charged with theft?'

'Oh no, Inspector.' Garfield was shocked. 'Great-aunt certainly didn't press charges — it was agreed that she would stay her hand as long as Tim went along with her plans for him to go out to Australia and settle there. She fixed up a job for him on a sheep farm in Queensland — some connection of Great-uncle Bart's — so he was packed off there and forbidden to communicate with Ginny.'

'Was she cited as accessory?'

'No, she was only seventeen at the time and she hadn't realised he was committing theft against his own family. He had told her that he was allowed the use of the car when he wanted and had spun her some yarn about the money and jewellery really belonging to his parents and being kept in trust for him. She was completely shattered by the death of the child.'

'Was it a local child?'

'Yes, the accident happened on the outskirts of the village. It was the four-year-old son of Stephen Bates, the head gamekeeper. He now works for Mr. Carstairs.'

'And what was his reaction — apart from very natural grief — at what must have seemed to him to be the murderer of his son getting off almost scot-free?'

'He was very bitter,' admitted Garfield, 'he thought it had all been hushed up because of Great-aunt's money and influence. I'm surprised he went on working for her.'

'Perhaps he knew on which side his bread was buttered. I presume he was living in a tied cottage and had other family to provide for. Is he the sort of man to bear a grudge?'

'He's a very surly character. I think the whole thing embittered him and he's never really recovered from losing his son.' Garfield looked at Roland with dawning enlightment. 'Inspector, you're not saying that he took a pot-shot at Tim when he came back, are you? In revenge?'

Roland ignored the question.

'What is this about Tim Spencer being summoned home a few years later?'

'Great-aunt's eightieth birthday party, I presume you mean? She . . .'

He broke off as the door opened and a woman dressed in trousers and a polo-neck sweater under a sleeveless Barbour jacket came into the room. The proprietorial air with which she sauntered in immediately marked her out as Mrs. Garfield, and Roland recognised her as the person seen earlier tending the bonfire. She was as tall as her husband and well-built, giving the impression of robust good health. She wore her dark bushy hair in a long bob with a ragged fringe and her eyes were so dark as to be almost opaque. There was something faintly foreign and exotic about her; she didn't quite blend in with the *Country Life* setting.

'Darling, this is Inspector Roland and Sergeant . . . they've come about Tim.'

'Cousin Tim — this is all quite unbelievable, Inspector.'

'You knew him, Mrs. Garfield?'

'No, it all happened before my time, but of course I've heard about it. He was the black sheep of the family but he

51

didn't deserve to come to such a nasty end.'

'The Inspector is trying to establish a picture of Tim's background and family to help him in his investigation.'

'Well, I wish him luck and I hope Tim's killer is brought to justice. Can I get you some tea? I presume that doesn't count as drinking on duty.'

'That would be most kind, ma'am.' Roland's tone was deferential but his eyes glinted as he held open the door for her. He returned to his seat.

'You were telling me about your Great-aunt's birthday party?'

'Ah, yes. Great-aunt Gertrude had no family of her own and she'd been a widow for years but she decided to celebrate her eightieth birthday in style — throw a big party. The few relatives she had were invited, and her many friends and acquaintances, from her employees through to the county set in which she moved.'

'Those relatives would be you and Timothy Spencer — am I right?'

'There was another cousin in America, but Leslie didn't turn up either though I believe Great-aunt was in touch by correspondence.'

'But Tim was definitely invited and expected? When would this have been?'

'July 1978, mid-July, I can't remember the exact date, and Tim was certainly expected. She'd always had a soft spot for him and I think she may have engineered the whole exercise so as to have an excuse to summon him back home and put on the big forgiveness scene. She was very upset when he didn't show up.'

'Yet she didn't make any attempt to contact him afterwards? He's been missing ten years.'

'She died the next year, and somehow . . . this may sound strange to you, but I hadn't realised how much time had passed. I've never thought of Tim as being missing. There's always been this picture in the back of my mind of him thoroughly enjoying life in Australia and doing well for himself, and I've always half-expected to see him turn up on the doorstep one day, larger than life, sunburnt, loaded, and talking Strine. I just can't believe it.'

52

'What can't you believe, Tony?' Lee Garfield re-entered the room, carrying a large tray which she deposited on a low table before busying herself with teapot and milk jug.

'That Tim's dead. And not just dead but murdered too! If he came back, why didn't we know? And who could have wished him harm?'

'That's what we're here to find out.'

'Is it possible, after all this time?' Lee Garfield paused, the teapot held in mid-air. 'Milk and sugar, Inspector?'

'Just milk, thank you.' He accepted the cup from her. 'The trail is cold but we never give up.'

'I'm sure you don't.' She looked at him appraisingly. 'What about the funeral – can we have one?'

'Once he has been formally identified, I'm sure the Coroner will release the bones for burial and you can go ahead with funeral arangements.'

Lee Garfield took a cup of tea across to Mansfield.

'Do sit down, Sergeant, you make me feel quite nervous looming over me like that.'

'I'm enjoying the view, ma'am.'

'It is lovely, isn't it? I never get tired of it, there's always something new to see, but I never realised that I was looking out over a grave.' She shivered and changed the subject. 'Haven't I seen you before, Sergeant? Your face looks familiar.'

'It is quite possible, Mrs. Garfield. I live in Wallingford and I'm often out and about in the district in the course of my duties.'

'What is your name?'

'Detective Sergeant Mansfield.'

'Mansfield? Of course – you're Jean Mansfield's husband, aren't you?'

He admitted uneasily that he was and wondered just what connection his wife could have with the volatile woman before him.

'We're both on the committee of the local Nature Conservation Trust. I've seen you with her at functions. She does a good job of work – very keen.'

He admitted that once his wife got her teeth into anything, she applied herself conscientiously.

'I wish I could get my husband more interested in conservation. Birds to him mean gamebirds conserved for the gun, and schemes to destroy the habitat of our Suffolk wildlife.'

'Don't exaggerate, darling. I'm trying to open up the countryside to people who normally see little of it – you're just being a dog-in-the-manger about it.

Mansfield caught Roland's eye. Whatever was meant by this little exchange it was evidently a bone of contention between them. Garfield intercepted the look and gave a little deprecating laugh.

'Don't mind us, Inspector, this is an old dispute. Now, is there anything else we can help you with?' It was a dismissal.

'You've been most helpful, sir. Just one thing – have you got a photograph of Tim Spencer?'

'A photograph?' The request surprised him. 'I don't think I have. There may be some snaps of him as a boy somewhere around, but I'm pretty certain nothing as an adult. Why do you want one?'

'Mr. Garfield, he came back to Croxton. Somebody may have seen him, somebody *must* have seen him. Although it is a long time ago, I'm hoping we can jog somebody's memory.'

'I hadn't thought of that. Perhaps Ginny Dalton can help you. The only way I can describe him is ... he looked rather piratical – black hair and a lot of restless energy. The girls fell for him, he conformed to their picture of a romantic hero.'

'What have I missed?' murmured Lee Garfield, and then looked contrite. 'Sorry, that was in very poor taste, I take it back.'

'Well, I wish you success in your investigation,' said her husband, ignoring her remark and ushering his guests to the door. 'And I hope you'll keep us informed.'

'We shall certainly be in touch, sir. Thank you for the tea, Mrs. Garfield.'

It was raining when they stepped outside, and the smoke from the bonfire had dwindled to a faint wisp curling above the beech hedge. The rain drummed on the car roof increasingly loudly as they drove back towards the village. In a couple of places puddles stretched right across the private concrete track that linked The Hermitage with the road

54

leading into the village. When they reached a convenient lay-by, Roland pulled into it and cut the engine.

'Well, Pat, what do you think of Garfield?'

'He seemed genuinely upset and bewildered.'

'Yes, though it's a pity he was forewarned. I wanted to break the news to him myself and watch his reaction.'

'You're putting him on our list of suspects?'

'We've got to start somewhere, though what motive could he have?'

'Money? The old lady was well-heeled, and the three great-nephews were her only relatives so presumably they were in line to inherit. With one out of the way a bigger share would go to the other two.'

'Yes, though she may have willed most of it to a cats' home or a refuge for fallen women. As you mentioned before, it is rumoured that he certainly inherited from her but it may not have been very much. Anyway, he seems to be doing quite well on his own account. It will be interesting to find out in just what financial pies he has his fingers and what exactly happened to Mrs. Fellingham's estate. What did you think of his good lady? She certainly wasn't the county type I was expecting.'

'You mean because she mixes with the likes of my Jean?' said Mansfield stiffly.

'I mean nothing of the sort as you know full well! She was pleasant enough but she didn't seem quite to fit in with her background. They seemed to me an ill-sorted couple.'

'PC Drake, the local chap, said she quoted poetry to him the first time he met her.'

'Am I right in thinking I could hear an American inflexion in her voice?'

'She certainly sounded as if she had spent some time in the States. I wonder why they have no children?'

'Thinking about it, that's one of the things that has struck me as odd, the family as a whole seem singularly unprolific. Old lady Fellingham had no children, Garfield and Tim Spencer were only children and their parents must have been too. Was it planned or do you think there was a low fertility factor passed on in their genes?'

'Speaking of children, what about this business of the

toddler being killed by Tim Spencer? How about that for a motive? The father is a gamekeeper which means that he carries guns around with him as other men carry plastic money. He sees Spencer back in the district and he's overcome with rage and the desire for revenge and fires a blast.'

'Very good, but you'd have a hell of a time proving it after all this time. Still, Mr. Bates will certainly feature high on my list of suspects. Do you remember the case?'

'It rang a bell, but I can't really remember any details. I'll check back. He was lucky if he got off with a fine. It could have been five years.'

'Your Mrs. Dalton didn't exactly come clean either, did she? Her account was conspicuous for what it left out rather than what it contained. She certainly needs interviewing again, but first we must check those dental records. I want someone down at that dentist's surgery first thing on Monday morning, and let's hope the new man hasn't ditched all the old records.'

'I've got a job for you, Taffy — very important.' Mansfield collared DC Evans as he reported in on the Monday morning. 'Get yourself into town and check this dental record. The surgery is at 21 Gladstone Road — used to be run by a Gregory Fenton but the old boy kicked the bucket recently and a husband and wife team have taken over. We need this confirmation so lean on them if they jibe at searching through his old records. And, William — watch the accent. We don't want them thinking the Suffolk Constabulary talks funny.'

'I don't talk funny!' Evans was very indignant. 'And talking of accents, some of the people around here I could mention sound proper daft. I reckon they ought to be sitting on a stile, dressed in smocks and chewing straws.'

'Cut it out, laddie, dew yew'll make me wholly riled, dew yew doan't want that, dew yew?' Mansfield rolled his eyes and struck an attitude. 'Run along and take Pomroy with you.'

Darren Pomroy had recently been seconded to the CID on temporary training attachment and needed constant reminding that detective work was 90 per cent hard slog and routine business rather than the cops and robbers dramas that had enlivened his childhood television viewing.

'Can we have a car?'

'What's wrong with your own feet? It's only a ten minute walk from here, get on with you. And Evans ...' The young constable waited with an expression of weary patience. '... what's that on your face?'

'My face?' He fingered his well-rounded cheeks and snub nose warily. His carrotty hair stuck up round his head like a fiery halo.

'You're not presenting your usual clean-cut profile to the world, the contours are a little mussed, a little ragged at the edges. I repeat, what's that on your face?'

'My beard,' said Evans stiffly.

'You could have fooled me. Do us a favour, lad, cultivate it in your own time — when you're on a long leave. Spare us the growing pains.'

Evans took himself off in umbrage and nearly collided with Roland in the doorway.

'What was all that about?' Roland looked after the retreating figure.

'DC Evans is having trouble with his image.'

'Not fitting in very well?'

'I'm afraid he thinks most of us are country bumpkins. I often wonder what he's doing here in little old rural Felstone.'

'I can tell you. He's followed his auntie.'

'His auntie?'

'He's an orphan, was brought up by an unmarried aunt in Cardiff. He joined the force down there, and after his probationary period decided to try his luck in London. In the meanwhile, in advanced middle-age, this aunt ups and married a docker who is almost immediately transferred to Felstone. Young William decided to follow them; I think he has some idea about keeping an eye on the old girl, for altruistic reasons I hope.'

'I should have known all this, he's one of my lads, but he's a very prickly customer, inclined to put up the backs of his colleagues.'

'He's probably scared stiff.' As his sergeant looked at him, mystified, Roland continued: 'All these open spaces and the raw countryside around him when he's used to being hemmed

57

in by bricks and mortar, high-rise flats. Don't be too hard on him, he has potential.'

'I'm sure you're right. Did you happen to notice what young Pomroy was wearing?'

'A very trendy leather jacket. That must have cost him an arm and a leg.'

'It's his idea of casual wear in which to merge with the background; his effort at copper-in-disguise.'

'What it is to be young.'

When Evans returned he was in an excitable mood and as a result his Welsh accent was even more pronounced, the sentences tripping skywards or dipping dramatically.

'Sarge, you'll never believe this, we were only just in time! Another day and it would all have been to no avail.'

'What are you on about? Did you get the confirmation?'

'Yes indeed, they fitted sweet as a bird, Timothy Spencer is our man. But I'm telling you − old Mr. Fenton had kept records of his patients right back to the time he started the practice in Felstone in the 1930s. Cupboards full of them, drawers overflowing, and Mr. and Mrs. Gardiner − that's the new couple − have been going through them and chucking out all the stuff over five years old. They'd just reached the 'R's', would you believe! Just a few more hours and it would have been too late − fancy that!'

'Spare us the superlatives, Evans. Get it down in writing.'

'Well, there you are, James. It's all yours.' Superintendent Bob Lacey eyed his subordinate with a suggestion of malice in his protruberant pale blue eyes. 'It's come from the top. Go ahead with your investigation, but be discreet.'

'What exactly is that supposed to mean?'

'It means he wants it cleared up and out of the way without any sordid details coming before the public eye. In other words, the Chief Constable is a shooting friend of Mr. Tony Garfield.'

'Then I should have thought he would be pressing for the culprit to be found and brought to justice. After all, Garfield is the next-of-kin.'

'Do you think he did it?'

58

'At first reckoning he's the obvious suspect. But a bit too obvious, and I really can't see what motive he could have had.'

'It's a cold, cold trail. Could have been a shooting accident, manslaughter at the worst; difficult to prove anything after such a long time.'

'Is that the official line? Because it just won't do, sir. I'm not going to be hamstrung by the CC breathing down my neck because I'm embarrassing his friends. If I open up a can of worms, then it stays open. I'm not conniving at any sort of cover-up.'

'Good God, man, whatever gave you that idea. You're reading more into my remarks than I meant — I just thought I would drop a hint, for your own good, that he's touchy on this one. Of course, he could jump the other way. If you turn up something really startling, he could be hollering for the Yard to be called in. I thought you ought to know the score.'

'Thanks, sir. I presume I can have Sergeant Mansfield? And DC Evans and young Pomroy have already done some preliminary work on the case.'

'Go ahead, and good hunting. Do you have any line to go on so far?'

'Let's say that the more I'm learning about this case, the more intrigued I become. I don't think it is as straightforward as it first seemed. I don't think it was an accident. I think he was deliberately killed in cold blood, and once we can get a line on possible motive we're half-way there. Someone must have thought they were very safe after all this time; they're conceivably panicking now and may make a careless move.'

'Well, keep me in the picture and go easy on the telex calls to Australia — we *are* working to a budget, you know.'

After Roland had gone, Chief Inspector Lacey chuckled to himself and eased his bulk out of his office chair which had been fashioned for a less well-upholstered rear. Roland had really got the bit between his teeth on this one! He had taken James' measure a long while ago and learnt how to motivate him. He worked better when he came up against a little opposition. He was a good policeman but a high-flyer, and Lacey had the uncomfortable feeling that Roland was only too ready to step into his own shoes. It didn't hurt to slap him

59

down now and again and remind him that he had a long way still to go.

He strolled to the window and glowered at the louring rainclouds seemingly stitched to the towers and steeples of Felstone. God! Was it ever going to stop raining? If it kept up much longer they'd all be growing fins.

Stephen Bates lived in a brick and tile cottage on the opposite side of the wood from Julian Lester. It was set in a clearing amongst the boundary trees and had a good-sized garden, mostly given over to vegetables and fruit trees. Amongst the latter were several very large and ancient Bramleys, their trunks and branches knotted with age and blackened by the rain. Their crop of apples lay rotting in the long grass and a blackbird, disturbed at his feast, flew shrieking and scolding across the garden as Roland and Mansfield trod the path to the front door.

'At least we've been spared the wasps this year,' commented Roland as he side-stepped to avoid a large slug blazing its trail in lustrous slime, 'but other beasties seem to have taken their place.'

The door was opened by a woman who was possibly younger than she looked. She was probably in her forties but there was a worn, resigned look about her as if, long ago, she had given up any pretence at disguising the ravages of time. Her greying hair was styled in a frizzy perm from another age, and her sallow complexion was devoid of make-up. Was this what losing a child could do to you? Damn! thought Roland. I didn't check whether there were any other children.

They explained who they were and asked for her husband.

'He's out the back, I'll tell him you're here.' She made no attempt to ask them in but paused in the act of pulling the door to.

'I was afraid you'd come. Don't upset him, will you?'

'Hardly an encouraging welcome, she seems more in awe of her husband than us,' said Mansfield, grimacing.

'Tell me, are there any other kids?'

'There's at least one, a daughter at school with mine.'

They waited on the doorstep and a collared dove mocked them from the nearby wood, its 'coo-cuk' full of derision;

from the bottom of the garden a pheasant squawked harshly.

'Taking his time, isn't he?' Roland turned from his contemplation of the garden which was run on strictly utilitarian lines. Mrs. Bates had apparently neither the time nor the inclination to soften the effect with flower beds or floral displays, although there was a small patch of lawn and a few over-grown chrysanthemums under the front windows. This was not a garden in which anyone had ever relaxed and enjoyed the sunshine; a deck chair would have been as out of place as a piece of garden statuary. Still, with all these trees massed the other side of the fence, it was probably in shade for the best part of the day.

Stephen Bates caught them momentarily unawares by appearing round the side of the house. There was something dark and puritanical about him, like a latter-day preacher, but where there should have been serenity his face was twisted with anger.

'What do you want?' he demanded, and the lurcher at his side snarled and leered at them with baleful eyes.

'Mr. Bates? There are some questions I should like to ask you in connection with the skeleton found at Croxton Creek. It has been identified as Timothy Spencer's. I believe . . .'

'So I heard. So he got his just deserts. If I'd met up with him, I'd have done for him myself!'

'Are you sure you didn't?'

Bates gave a bitter little laugh, totally devoid of humour.

'Supposing I had . . . you'd never prove it, not after all this time!'

61

Chapter Four

'Mr. Bates, do you think we could come in? I'm sure you don't want us discussing this on the doorstep.'

He led the way indoors with ill grace. The hall was narrow, tiled with vinolay in a hideous mock porphyry pattern the colour of offal, and the walls were papered in a heavy flock wallpaper featuring bamboo canes, identical to that seen by Roland in the vestibule of the local Chinese restaurant. Bates made as if to take them through to the back of the house, presumably to the kitchen, the hub of the household, but he hesitated and instead pushed open a door to the right.

'You'd better come in here, I suppose.'

The old front parlour syndrome still existed, even in people of this generation, thought Roland, looking around. The room kept solely for important social functions or unwanted guests; coming out of wraps only at Christmas, or a funeral, or on an occasion such as this. But no, that was not quite true. The covering on the bulbous-legged table had been pushed to one side and a pile of books stacked on the shiny surface. On the seat of one of the high-backed wing chairs, a Sony Walkman had been abandoned.

'My daughter does her homework in here.'

It was a dark, uncomfortable room, sparsely furnished in a style chosen to meet the Bates' idea of conformity rather than comfort, and the gloomy atmosphere could not all be attributed to the arboreal excess encroaching on the cottage. This room was a stranger to laughter and happiness and light-heartedness, but there was one incongruous note: a large, unframed painting pinned to the wall above the sideboard. It was an abstract; vivid swirls of paint chased each other in a convoluted pattern like a Catherine Wheel out of control.

'Did she do that?' Roland indicated the picture.

'Yes. Her mother insisted on putting it up − it's out of the way in here.'

'She has an eye for colour. Perhaps she is going to take up art?'

'Not if I have my way,' Bates growled. 'She can get a proper job like her sister when she leaves school.'

'And what age are your daughters, Mr. Bates?'

'Sharon, my eldest, is nineteen. She's a hairdresser in Felstone. Tracey is fifteen and still at school. Two daughters I have, Inspector, my only son is dead − killed by that homicidal maniac thirteen years ago.'

'A tragic accident.'

'Accident? It was murder! He should have been sent down for years. Instead he got off scot-free!'

'Not quite true, Mr. Bates. There was a heavy fine, and his life in this country was finished.'

'The old lady − Mrs. Fellingham − paid it, every penny, and being sent to Australia was no punishment. How many youngsters today wouldn't give their eye teeth for a chance like that − a future with prospects in an up-and-coming country?'

'Yet you went on working for Mrs. Fellingham.' Mansfield guided him back to the matter in hand.

'Well, she was a good mistress and I had my remaining family to think of. Mind you, she didn't live long after that, only a few years; I reckon all the scandal finished her off, that and the fact that Spencer never came back to her eightieth birthday party.'

'I understand that this party took place in July 1978. Spencer was summoned back from Australia but he didn't take part in the celebrations. But he came back, Mr. Bates. He came back and someone murdered him. Are you sure you didn't see him?'

'What are you getting at?'

'The very nature of your job means that you're out and about in the countryside. Are you sure you didn't see him or hear of him being in the area?'

'I tell you, I never set eyes on him after the court case. He was hustled away, kept out of my reach. If anyone saw him it would be Ginny Dalton – why don't you ask her?'

'Ah yes, Mrs. Dalton, Ginny Merrivale that was. How did you feel about her part in the accident?'

'She was only a kid with her head stuffed full of romantic nonsense – what could you expect with a father like hers? I didn't blame her and I reckon she's been punished now. She hasn't prospered – been widowed since and with no kids of her own. No, it's him I blame, and all I can say is that I'm glad he met a sticky end! He deserved it, and you won't get me crying crocodile tears. And just you try to pin it on me!' he challenged.

'I can assure you, justice will be done. What sort of gun do you own?'

'Gun, eh? A twelve-bore shotgun. I stick to the old side-by-side model, I don't like the up-and-over. And that information won't get you far. I reckon half the adult population of Croxton owns a shotgun, and that's just the ones that are licensed. There's a lot of shooting around here, Inspector, and I'm not talking about organised game; there's pigeons and rooks and rabbits, pests all of them, to say nothing of the poaching that goes on.'

'Well, thank you, Mr. Bates, there will be someone round to check your gun. I take it you have no objection?'

'Wouldn't make any difference if I had, would it? You'd better make sure that I'm not out on the job.'

'What an embittered old sod,' said Roland as they made their way back to the car.

'You can't help feeling sorry for him, though. I mean, he has got a reason.'

'I feel more sorry for his family. I'm surprised his elder daughter still lives at home. You'd think she'd have upped sticks and cleared out as soon as she was old enough.'

'Perhaps she stays to support the mother. I wonder if he blames his wife for having let the kid run out on the road in the first place?'

They opened the gate and stepped out into the lane. A muscular-looking man with a shock of tow-coloured hair and a full curly beard, dressed in cords and a green anorak, was walking past their car. He paused and eyed them cagily, then gave a curt nod and strode on.

'His face seems familiar,' remarked Roland, unlocking the door and getting into the car.

'You've probably seen it staring out at you from a book jacket. That was Bradley Scott, the travel writer. He lives in Croxton when he's not away on his travels.'

'The *Alternative Travel Guides*? I didn't know he lived locally. Well, let's away to Duck Lane and see what Mrs. Dalton has to say for herself.'

'Ma, there's someone to see you.' Simon Dalton climbed to the bend in the stairs and shouted up the stairwell.

'Don't call me Ma! Who is it?'

'Policemen.' Simon's voice held a nice mixture of curiosity and disdain. When his mother made no reply he continued up the stairs and burst into her bedroom where she was pinning up her hair at the dressing-table. 'I said, it's policemen.'

'All right, I heard you the first time. Where are they?'

'At the front door. I say Ma − Mum − are you all right?' She was staring at her reflection in the mirror with an odd expression on her face.

'You'd better ask them in. And, Simon . . . run down to the Barkers for me and pick up that bag of wool. I promised her I'd call today and take it off her hands.'

'What − now? Can't it wait?'

'Please, Simon, it won't take long.'

He was not so easily distracted. 'Mum − what do they want?'

'The policemen?' she shrugged. 'It's probably just a formality. That skeleton that was found on the marshes − I used to know him.'

He was thunderstruck. 'You mean − you actually *knew* him!'

'What's so strange about that? We were both local people. I imagine they are interviewing everyone in the village.'

'Do you think they've got a search warrant?'

'Don't be ridiculous, what would they want a search

65

warrant for? Now go and ask them in whilst I finish doing my hair, and then go and do what I told you.'

After he had gone she sat with her hands idle in her lap, half her hair coiled on top of her head, the remainder tumbling round her neck and shoulders while her thoughts ran riot. Tim ... Ever since the day the sergeant had called and shown her the medallion, she had been unable to get him out of her thoughts. Tim — the handsome, impulsive, dare-devil Tim who had loved her and promised her the moon, but who had not kept faith. What did those policemen want? They were like the turnstones that flocked to the shore in winter, turning over the pebbles, poking and prying amongst the seaweed and shingle. Who knew what hideous truths they were going to uncover?

She gave herself a mental shake and twisted up the rest of her hair. Why was she so apprehensive? That part of her life was over and done with, should have been banished to the shadows years ago.

She ran down the stairs and paused in the hall. Through the half-open door she could see two tall figures with their backs to her; one was burly and middle-aged, the other slimmer and younger with black, unruly hair ... Tim! It was Tim, come back to haunt her. She gripped the newel post. God, she must be going mad ...

The figure moved over to the hearth. She saw his face reflected in the mirror above the mantelpiece and the illusion was shattered. She must pull herself together, this was crazy, imagining she saw Tim in every slim, dark man. Her eyes met his in the mirror and another shock flooded through her. Oh no, it couldn't be ... James! James who had told her he was a policeman. What cruel irony ...

James Roland sensed the eyes boring into his back and looked up into the mirror. Christ! It couldn't be ... Virginia. Ginny — why hadn't he made the connection? And she had told him that she was a widow and a teacher, had told him many things that had beguiled and misled him that night a couple of months ago.

It had been at a Charity Ball organised by the Rotary Club that they had met. He hadn't wanted to go, disliked functions like that, but had been persuaded by the wife of one of his ex-colleagues to buy a ticket and join their party. Emma was a very forceful character and wouldn't take no for an answer. Paul was doing very well for himself since leaving the Force and joining a finance company, and membership of the local Rotary Club was part of the scene in which he now moved.

'You look handsome in that dinner jacket, James. You'll slay the ladies.' Emma had pounced on him as soon as he had entered the hotel where the ball was taking place. 'Come and meet the rest of our friends.' He had known several of them by sight but he had been drawn to the solitary woman, the only one in the party who seemed not to be partnered, who had sat still and aloof from the rest of the frenetic crowd. She had not appeared lonely or a wallflower, just self-contained and serene. Her red-gold hair was piled high on her head in a style reminiscent of a figure on a Greek coin, and she was wearing a white, draped dress that complemented the effect.

Emma had followed his glance. 'Let me introduce you.' With her usual insouciant style she had announced: 'James — Virginia. James is a policeman, one of the clever mob Paul left behind. James, Virginia is a teacher and widowed last year, be kind to her.' And she had flounced off to greet another guest.

'Typical Emma! How tragic to be widowed so young, how are you coping?'

'I . . . I'm coping, let's leave it at that. I'm sorry, I didn't catch your name?'

She had been staring at him, almost as if she were seeing a ghost. Her eyes, odd coloured he noted, drank in his appearance. It was almost as if she recognised him. He couldn't remember what they had talked about but she had literally thrown herself at his head, or so he had thought at the time. She had hung on to his words, ignoring the rest of the guests in preference to him, and when they danced the messages that had sparked back and forth between their bodies had been unmistakable. The poor woman is sex-starved, he had thought, and had felt his own libido rising in excitement.

Somehow he had got through the evening, aware of her eyes following his every move, devouring, promising, inviting, sending out signals. Signals he had totally mis-read, he recalled with disgust and anger. She had lured him on, a prick-tease, and now when he thought of it he felt anger and the urge to punish her stirring through his innards, coiling in his guts. He had offered to see her home, and he remembered how they sat in his car and he had said to her: 'Your place or mine?'

She had stared at him out of those strange eyes and it was as if his words had smashed through some barrier she had erected around herself; as if she were coming out of a trance. She had shrunk away from him and spoken in agitation.

'No, no. There's been a mistake . . . I'm sorry. I'm afraid I've given you the wrong impression . . . I don't sleep around.'

'Don't you?' Disappointment had fed the anger flaring through him, and he had grabbed her arm and snarled at her: 'You want me as much as I want you, don't pretend differently!'

'No, you don't understand. I'm sorry, it's all my fault. I must be going mad.' She had shook her head violently, as if trying to rid herself of an annoying insect buzzing around her. 'Please forgive me, you're right to be angry, I've behaved badly. Please let me get out — I'll get a taxi.'

He had wrenched open the door and she had practically tumbled out on to the tarmac.

'You know something VIRGINia?' he had called after her, stressing the first two syllables of her name. 'It's women like you who get themselves murdered!'

And here he was, meeting up with her again, this time on a murder enquiry. He didn't know who was the more taken aback. Christ, he mustn't let a thing like this throw him! He pulled himself together and turned to greet her.

'Detective Inspector Roland, CID, Mrs. Dalton, and I think you've already met Detective Sergeant Mansfield? I believe you can help us with our enquiries into Timothy Spencer's death.'

So that was the way he was going to play it, she thought. He was going to ignore the fact that they had met previously. Well, that was all right by her. Her cheeks still burned when she thought of what had happened that evening, of how she had behaved . . .

'I have already told the sergeant everything I know, I can't think why you want to see me again.'

My God! thought Mansfield, eyeing the two protagonists facing each other. One of James' inamoratas! There was no mistaking the recognition, the tension sizzling between them. It was bound to happen at some time. Well, well, how was his superior going to ride this one, and what difference would it make to their enquiries? He settled back to enjoy the exchange.

'I don't think you have, Mrs. Dalton. I think you left out some very significant facts. Mr. Mansfield, did Mrs. Dalton tell you about the circumstances leading up to Timothy Spencer's banishment to Australia?'

'No, sir,' replied Mansfield stolidly, 'but then, the true facts don't make very pretty hearing.'

'I didn't think they had any relevance to what has happened.'

'No relevance? A man has been murdered, a man whom you claim to have loved, and you say the events leading up to his leaving home have no relevance to what happened? I think you are kidding yourself, Mrs. Dalton. There is a string of criminal offences — stealing, cheating, joyriding, the death of an infant — to be taken into account, apart from the little matter of an elopement.'

'I suppose Tony Garfield told you? Well, it's true, but I still don't see what those facts have to do with Tim's death.'

'Nor do we — yet. But we'll get there. Why weren't you charged?' he snapped at her suddenly, and she started.

'Because in the eyes of the law it was decided that I had nothing to answer for,' she replied defensively, 'but don't think I haven't suffered for it, Inspector. The death of that child will always be on my conscience, will haunt me for the rest of my life.'

She stared unseeingly out of the window and Roland was moved to pity. 'Do you think we could sit down, Mrs. Dalton? There is a lot to discuss and we might as well be comfortable.'

He took her silence for acquiescence. After he and Mansfield had seated themselves at the table, she went and sat on the leather pouffe near the fire and stared into the flames.

'So, Timothy Spencer was sent to Australia and you were left behind — did you keep in touch?'

'Not exactly ...' She said nothing further and the silence stretched.

'Would you care to explain that?' asked Roland politely when nothing further was forthcoming.

'You had difficulty in recalling that part when we spoke before, I seem to remember,' prompted Mansfield.

'The truth of the matter was, we were forbidden to correspond. My father made me promise we would not communicate until I was twenty-one, or Tim ... Tim was made welcome here again by his family.'

'But ...?'

'We arranged that he would send a message through the personal column of *The Times* each year on my birthday.'

'And did this happen?'

'For two years, then during the third year I heard that his great-aunt had invited him back to celebrate her eightieth birthday so I expected him home. He didn't come, and shortly after that my birthday passed without a message so I reckoned that he wanted to cut himself off from me and his family, had found a new life and new interests in Australia.'

'So you upped and married someone else, taking on a widower and a stepson?'

'I married my late husband in 1979. What are you implying?'

'I'm implying nothing, just trying to establish that you were not exactly heartbroken at Spenser's defection. That it was a part of your life that was over, an adolescent romance that was behind you and forgotten?'

'Yes, that is so.'

'Then why,' broke in Mansfield, 'were you so shattered when I showed you the medallion?'

'Surely it was natural? I had given Tim that medallion and it was a shock suddenly seeing it again, especially when I understood the circumstances.'

'So you had no communication with him after his second year away. Didn't he send you a message to say he was coming home?'

'No. Tony told me that the old lady had sent for him and

I just expected him to turn up one day, larger than life.'

That was the second person who had used that expression about Tim Spencer, thought Roland. He must have been an impressive character, the type who could charm the birds out of the trees.

'Mrs. Fellingham must have been in touch with him if she summoned him home?' he persisted.

'Well, yes, but I think it was probably done through the business connections the family had in Australia.'

'Did you go to the party?'

'Me? Oh no. Perhaps if Tim had returned . . . The family must have been quite thin on the ground. I suppose Tony would have been the only one, unless . . . there was supposed to be another cousin in the States. To tell you the truth, I don't even know for sure that the party actually took place.'

Well, that could easily be checked thought Roland, but whether it would have any bearing on their enquiries was another matter. This third great-nephew of the old girl must be checked out too. He changed tactics.

'Can you think of anyone who had reason to want him dead? Anyone he had harmed?'

She hesitated and looked distressed. 'I suppose the obvious answer is Stephen Bates whose child we killed. He naturally held Tim responsible, and at the time made no secret of the fact that he would kill him if he got his hands on him. But I don't think it could have been him. I mean, Bates was quite capable of shooting him but he wouldn't have tried to cover it up afterwards. He would have claimed it was an eye for an eye and a tooth for a tooth; he's very fond of quoting the Old Testament.'

'Is he a religious man?'

'He has never been a churchgoer but I believe he holds some odd religious beliefs.'

'And you can think of no-one else who could have had a grudge against him?'

'No — it all seems crazy, Tim was such a happy-go-lucky, likeable sort of person. He never did anyone any harm.' She saw the expression on his face and added hurriedly: 'Not knowingly, that was just an unfortunate accident — things went horribly wrong. I've thought and thought and I can't see how anyone could have hated him enough to have killed him.'

'Someone did, Mrs. Dalton. Well, thank you for your help. If you think of anything else, no matter how insignificant it may seem to you, please let us know.'

She nodded her head but did not speak and showed them to the door in silence. As they stepped outside Roland paused as if he were going to say something further, but he bit back the remark and bade her a curt good-day as he strode out to the car.

Mansfield had noticed his hesitation and managed to contain himself until they were in the car and on their way.

'Come on, Inspector, don't try to pull the wool over my eyes. You know Mrs. Dalton.'

'What gives you that idea?'

'You didn't have to be psychic to sense the currents flowing between the two of you. What happened?'

'Nothing happened. I have met her socially but you can take that expression off your face. I haven't laid her.'

'The one that got away?'

'Damn you, Patrick, don't presume.'

'Sir!'

They drove in silence for a short distance before Mansfield spoke again.

'Do you think she could have done it?'

'It's possible, and how about this for motive? The Tim affair was a youthful peccadillo she thought she had put behind her. She is being courted by an older, serious admirer — she was still quite young herself — and is all set for marriage and a life of respectability when Tim turns up and expects to carry on where he had left off. She repulses him, he threatens to reveal all to her new admirer, so she kills him to stop him carrying out this threat.'

'And how would we ever prove it if it were the truth?'

'That's the rub. At least there *are* things we can check. I want you to find out who the family solicitor is and make an appointment for me to see him. Also, check back with Garfield and see if you can jog his memory to come up with the date on which this party was actually held. We must ferret around the Australian angle too. He may have only come back for a visit and expected to return there — surely someone

72

would have noticed he had gone missing? He must have made some friends over there, and what about his employers and workmates? By all account he was a genial, friendly sort of chap.'

'A lot of good it did him.'

'If we don't get a lead soon, this case is going to be shelved, and *that*, Patrick my friend, is going to grieve me very much.'

Over at Smoky Cottage Julian Lester was pottering in his garden and vacillating between various courses of action. Ever since he had returned from his September holiday, spent touring the museums and art galleries of Brussels and Bruges, and had learnt that the skeleton found on the marshes was that of Tim Spencer, he had been dithering over what to do, what move to make.

The light was fading fast as he swept up the last of the fallen leaves from the lawn and trundled them off in the wheel-barrow to the compost heap. From the surrounding woods came the mournful call of an owl which was picked up by another one nearby and echoed as a wavering hiccup some-where over to his right. That was a real sign of autumn, he mused, when the owls became vocal, socialising in moans and murmurs like a group of old women comparing their ail-ments. It was well into October and autumn was established. He had long ago given up waiting for the summer that never was. The inside of his cottage beckoned; a hot bath and tea and toast. But first, whilst he was running the water, a good strong nip of mother's ruin.

But still he lingered outside, dead-heading the chrysan-themums whose golden flowers glowed eerily in the gathering dusk. Should he put certain facts before the police? Should he sit back and do absolutely nothing? Or should he get in touch with a certain person? He reviewed his finances. He should never have spent all that money on a holiday, not when the roof needed re-felting and his premises in Woodford needed decorating. He made a decision, and leav-ng his boots in the back porch, shrugged off his coat and padded through to the living room, snapping on lights as he went. The gin bottle and glasses stood on the table but he ignored them and made for the phone. He picked up the receiver and dialled a number.

The funeral of the late Timothy Spencer took place on an October morning that was for once bright and sunny. The verger had switched on the lights in the church of St. Michael but they were not needed. Sunlight slanted in through the tall, perpendicular south windows, setting the dust motes dancing above the pews and firing the brass handles of the coffin that rested at the foot of the chancel.

Roland and Mansfield sat at the black of the church and watched the congregation. It was pitifully small. Apart from a handful of elderly women, whom Roland was sure were there out of curiosity rather than genuine respect, and two men, one of whom he recognised as Larkin Senior from Larkin & Webb, Solicitors, of Felstone, the only other mourners were Garfield and his wife and Ginny Dalton, accompanied by her stepson Simon. He was surprised to see the boy there. Boys of that age didn't usually participate in funerals unless they happened to be close relatives of the deceased. She must have kept him away from school and got time off herself.

She was dressed in a long, full black skirt and black boots but the traditional mourning image was contradicted by the vivid red jacket that topped the ensemble. It should have clashed horribly with her hair, which was flowing down her back Pre-Raphaelite fashion, but she looked stunning. He plucked his eyes from her and studied the stepson. There was something vaguely familiar about the boy, something that niggled at the back of his memory. He had dark, untidy hair and was at that stage of adolescence when all his features seemed too big for his face; the generous full mouth, the snub nose, the large grey-blue eyes, all jostled for position in the freckled countenance. He was not as yet very tall but was all arms and legs. There was a rip in the back of his anorak, Roland noted.

He turned his attention to Garfield. He was wearing a dark overcoat and a black tie, and seemed to be the only member of the congregation who was genuinely sorrowing. His wife beside him, dressed in an elegant grey coat with a blue shawl

74

draped across her shoulders, looked bored and fidgeted with her prayer book.

In the churchyard Roland drew Mansfield to one side and indicated the elder of the two men following the cortège.

'Who is that?'

'Matthew Betts. He's the ex-headmaster of Felstone High School, retired several years ago. He lives here in Croxton and probably knew Tim as a child. He's an old friend of mine, taught me years ago, and I think it would be a good idea to talk with him. He knows everybody and everything that goes on locally, might be able to give us some useful pointers.'

'Good idea. I'll leave that to you if you know him.'

Roland had just remembered that he had forgotten to ask Ginny Dalton if she had a photograph of the dead man. He had been so rattled, remembering his first encounter with her, that it had been overlooked. Hell! He must be slipping if he let personal concerns interefere with his professional competence.

The committal was over and the group of mourners at the graveside started to disperse. The Garfields were talking to Ginny Dalton. They seemed to be pressing her to some action but she shook her head and walked up the path to the main gates, with Simon dawdling behind. When she saw the detectives standing there she veered sharply to the left and hurried off along the path that wound through the yews to a side exit leading on to the Woodford road. Not by so much as a flicker of an eyelid did she acknowledge their presence, but the boy looked at them curiously before following his stepmother.

Tony and Lee Garfield greeted them and exchanged pleasantries, and Roland excused himself and hurried after the solicitor. He intercepted Larkin as he was about to get into his car.

'Mr. Larkin? I am Detective Inspector Roland. I think you may be able to give me information that may help me with my enquiries into the death of Timothy Spencer.'

'I believe you have an appointment to see me, Inspector?'

'Yes, later in the week.'

'Then save your questions for then. I don't charge for my time at a graveside.'

He drove off before the astonished policeman could recover himself.

Roland rejoined his sergeant. They were the only people left in the graveyard. The sun dodged in and out between peach-edged clouds, throwing long shadows across the uneven ground and lichen-covered headstones; the tall stand of chestnut trees that flanked the north wall rustled and soughed in the strengthening breeze. There were four wreaths on the new mound: a large affair in the shape of a cross, in vivid autumnal colours, from the Garfields; a smaller one in similar shades of orange and gold that they noted in surprise was from the East Anglian Aircraft Research Group; a sedate ring of carnations and evergreens bearing the respects of Larkin & Webb, Solicitors; and a simple spray of white rosebuds that bore a card containing a single word — "Ginny".

'Well, no mysterious strangers hanging around to gloat or check out the scene,' said Mansfield, straightening up from his examination of the floral tributes.

'That would have been too much to hope for.' Roland gazed down at the grave. 'Twenty-two years of vibrant living reduced to this. May he rest in peace.'

'Now that you're mixing with the élite, can you give me a few tips on how the other half lives?'

'What are you talking about?' Jean Mansfield looked up at her husband in astonishment. She was seated at the dining table surrounded by sheets of paper, cardboard boxes, paints and all the paraphernalia of a craft session.

'The Garfields. She's on one of your committees, isn't she? How does she strike you? Or more to the point, what do you know about her husband?'

'Do you mind if I carry on with this whilst I talk? I've got a meeting this evening.'

'Which hat is it this time?'

'Brownies. What do you think of this?' She held up a string of cardboard shapes interspersed with twisted ribbons.

'Very nice — what is it?'

'Christmas decoration, or it will be when I've finished.'

'Christmas decoration! In October? That really is going too far. It's bad enough when you get it pushed down your throat on the box from September onwards – I don't think you ought to encourage it with the Brownies.'

'There's a big competition coming up soon and our pack has entered. It's amazing what you can do with a few egg boxes and paint and fir cones.'

'What a lot "Blue Peter" has to answer for! To get back to the Garfields . . .'

'I like her.' Jean Mansfield screwed up her face and considered the question. 'There's no side to her, she's just like one of us. Joins in everything and does her stint of hard work. Having said that, though, she's not quite the same, there is a difference . . .'

'Explain.'

'I suppose it's because she never has any money problems. I don't mean she flaunts her money around or anything like that. It's just that the concept of having to stick to a budget or mind the pence and pounds is alien to her. She's never grasped that ordinary mortals such as us have financial hiccoughs, cash flow problems and the like, from time to time. She's never been short of a penny and never will; it must colour her attitude to life. As for Tony Garfield – he's a property dealer of some kind, but he seems a homely sort of man, not the type you usually conjure up when you think of financial whizz-kids. He spends a lot of time away from home – pulling strings in the City, I suppose – but I get the feeling that theirs is not a very happy or fulfilled marriage.'

'Why? You must have your reasons for thinking that.'

'They seem to go their own ways. He makes all that money but they have no children on whom to spend it, and I don't think they share many interests.'

'I wonder why they have no family?'

'She hinted once that it was her fault. Some accident when she was in her teens.'

'An abortion that went wrong?'

'Could be. What a nasty mind you've got.'

'That's what comes of being a policeman. So the money they have he has earned – it wasn't inherited?'

'I really don't know, but I believe she has money of her own. It must be an empty life with no kids. Can you imagine this household without Gavin and Jane?'

'I have pipe-dreams sometimes.'

'Patrick Mansfield, you should be ashamed of yourself! Still, she has her horses and garden and she's very keen on conservation work, but I have heard ... ' She hesitated and looked shrewdly at her husband. 'Is all this important? Do you really need to know all the gossip?'

'We're groping about in the dark at the moment. Any piece of scandal, no matter how irrelevant it may seem, we need to know, so don't hold out on me. What have you heard?'

'That she has an admirer.'

'What an old-fashioned expression. Do you mean she's two-timing her husband?'

'I don't know. There's just a whisper going around that there's another man in the offing. I don't know if there's any truth in it. Honestly, Pat, don't read too much into it. It may be just idle gossip, malicious tongue-wagging.'

'Well, you know what they say about no smoke. Do the rumours give a name?'

'Not that I've heard. There's probably nothing in it; someone has blown up an isolated incident out of all proportion, and you know how things grow in the telling.'

'You never know when these little snippets of information may come in handy, so keep your eyes and ears open.'

'I suppose this is all to do with your investigation into that young man's death. Poor chap, he was scarcely more than a boy.'

With a sense of shock Mansfield realised that she was right. Tim Spencer had been less that two years older than their Gavin when he had met his death. Suddenly, it seemed all the more imperative to track down his murderer and bring him to justice.

'Have you finished your cross examination?' said his wife, carefully cutting up drinking straws and pasting them across bands of gold foil.

'Just one more question: does Tony Garfield know or suspect that is wife is carrying on with someone else?'

'I shouldn't think so. He'd probably be the last to know.'

'The husband usually is.'

* * *

Matthew Betts greeted his old friend and ex-pupil warmly when Mansfield called to see him that afternoon.

'Come in, come in, this is a pleasure, or is it an official visit?'

'A little of both. I've been intending to call round for ages — I need to pick your brains.'

'It's to do with Tim Spencer's death, I suppose? A nasty business, quite unbelievable. Take a seat.'

Through the open door of the living room that opened into the kitchen, Mansfield could hear movement and the clatter of pans.

'Have I come at an inconvenient moment? You've got company?'

'It's only Mrs. Cattermole. She does for me, comes in several times a week. She's baking and I haven't the heart to tell her that I can't manage to eat half of what she produces. She's a good soul but a terrible gossip.'

'Perhaps I should have a word with her.'

'You will, when she knows you're here. I'll get her to make us a pot of tea in a minute.'

'How well did you know Timothy Spencer?'

'He didn't go to my school, of course. He went to Rapley Hall in Norfolk, but he was around in the holidays and I got to know him fairly well. He was rather wild but a little discipline in his formative years would have worked wonders.'

'There speaks the dedicated teacher.'

'I can't leave it behind, can I? But I don't think there was any real badness in him. He just went off on these ill-considered ventures and one of them went horribly wrong.'

'You mean the elopement and the fatal accident?'

'The whole village was aghast at the time. There were those who thought he should have been put away for life and others who considered that what happened was just bad luck, an unfortunate twist of fate, and that he was punished enough by the ghastly results.'

Ada Cattermole appeared in the doorway. Her stout body was encased in an old-fashioned wrap-around apron, liberally streaked with flour and scorch marks, and her cheeks were flushed.

79

'I thought I heard voices. Would you be wanting a nice cup of tea?'

'That's a good idea. Thank you, Mrs. Cattermole.'

She stayed where she was and looked at Mansfield with shrewd little eyes. 'You're a policeman, aren't you? I've seen you about.'

'Detective Sergeant Mansfield is an old friend of mine. Now, how about that tea.'

She ignored him and addressed Mansfield. 'Do they know who done it yet?' Then, as he busied himself with lighting his pipe and eyed her with raised brows, 'I mean, who killed Tim Spencer? Poetic justice, I call it.' She savoured the phrase and tried it out again. 'Poetic justice, I said to my Arthur: he kills that poor little Bates lad and gets done in himself.'

'The tea, Mrs. Cattermole.'

She disappeared into the kitchen with bad grace and Mathew Betts shrugged helplessly at Mansfield. 'Sorry about that, what was I saying?'

'What about Mrs. Dalton? I presume you know her?'

'Ginny? Oh yes, I've known her all her life. I got her her first teaching post at the school, and of course Alec, her late husband, was one of my senior staff. Fine chap, it was a great tragedy when he died so suddenly like that – heart, you know. She's had several misfortunes in her short life but Ginny is a fighter.'

'The time we're really interested in is three years after the accident when Tim Spencer came back here. Mrs. Dalton insists that she did not correspond with him during his time away, that she was obeying a directive laid down by her father not to communicate with him until she was over twenty-one. I find it quite extraordinary that in this day and age a father could extract a promise like that, behaving like a Victorian patriach and expecting to be obeyed.'

'She were the Rector's daughter, weren't she?' Mrs. Cattermole stuck her head inside the door and nodded to Mansfield. 'Had some funny ideas, he had, but if he made her promise not to do a thing, she wouldn't have done it.'

'The Rector's daughter?' Mansfield looked enquiringly at Betts.

'Yes, sorry, I didn't realise you wouldn't have known that.

80

The Reverend John Merrivale, did you ever meet him? You must have heard of him, a real eccentric if ever there was one.'

'Yes, it rings a bell, but I didn't realise his daughter was Mrs. Dalton. He's not alive now, is he?'

'No, he died about five years ago. There's a young chap holds the living now, very proper and law-abiding after old Merrivale. He was a character, quite notorious in his way. He married divorced couples in his church but often refused to marry more eligible candidates if he thought they were mismatched. He made up his own rules about many church matters.'

'That must have gone down well with his bishop! Wasn't he disciplined?'

'I think they gave up on him years ago. He was a law unto himself, an avid socialist, and the right person to have on your side if you were an oppressed minority.'

'Ginny's mother died when she was a baby.' Mrs. Cattermole was determined not to be left out of the conversation. 'He brought her up on his own, poor little mite. I useta feel real sorry for her. He were in his fifties before she was born, and what with no mother and a father like that, it's no wonder she got into trouble.'

'Mrs. Cattermole, *please* . . .' protested Betts, trying to shoo her back into the kitchen, but Mansfield shook his head.

'Mrs. Cattermole, you seem to know a good deal about what goes on locally, what can you tell me about Mrs. Gertrude Fellingham?'

'The old lady? Well, now, I was never lucky enough to be taken on at the Hall.' She spoke as if it were their loss not hers. 'Mind you, I could tell you a tale or two what I've heard, but if you want to know about the set-up there you want to talk to Ethel Parker. She were the housekeeper – companion to Mrs. Fellingham, knew everything that went on.'

'Does she live locally?'

'Not now, she's in a home at Dunham Market. She must be in her eighties.'

'Eighties?' Mansfield's heart sank.

'She's bright as a button, don't you worry. Crippled up with arthritis but she's still got all her marbles. Arthur takes me over to see her two or three times a year and she don't half go on about the old days. There's nothing wrong with her memory, I can tell you.'

'What about other staff at The Hall? She must have employed several.'

'Well now, let me think.' Ada Cattermole propped herself against the doorpost and twitched at her apron. 'There were Nelly and Tom Herring — she were the cook and he were in charge outside, but they're both dead now. Nobody else lived in. He had a lad to help him in the garden and there were a couple of young gals usta go in and do the skivying and rough stuff. They've both married and left the area since. I reckon Ethel Parker's the one you want to speak to.'

'You've been most helpful, Mrs. Cattermole. Someone with local knowledge is a boon in this business. I suppose you don't remember hearing anyone mention Tim Spencer being back in the area ten years ago?'

'There now, I weren't around at the time, more's the pity. I were over at Colchester where my youngest were having her first baby.'

She managed to convey that had she been in Croxton at the relative time she would certainly have known if the murdered man had been seen locally. And she probably would have, too! thought Mansfield. She was one of the older generation of yeoman stock who considered it her business to know everyone's affairs; not as a busybody but as a participant in her friends' and neighbours' lives.

'You could have a word with Alfie Coutts,' she continued, glancing at her employer to see if he agreed with her suggestion. 'Mind you, dew you get any sense outa him, you'd be lucky. Proper bats in the belfry he is, though I say it myself and he do be a cousin of my Arthur.'

'He's the local village simpleton,' said Betts. 'They say it was caused by shellshock in the war. He's certainly missing something in the top storey but he's cunning with it. I don't think he misses much of what goes on.'

'He knew Tim Spencer, usta to take him poaching.'

'I thought most of the land around her belonged to Mrs. Fellingham in those days. Are you saying Tim poached his own great-aunt's game?'

'Of course he did, Mr. Betts, that were half the fun! Proper

82

young limb he were, wholly mischievous. Well, I can't stand here gossiping all afternoon, I've got work to do.' She exited with dignity and the two men managed to keep straight faces.

Mansfield eventually got his cup of tea, and after extracting from Mrs. Cattermole the name and address of the home where Ethel Parker was resident, he went back to the car and waited for his superior who was furthering his enquiries at the Dalton reisdence at the other end of Duck Lane.

Chapter Five

Roland rang the doorbell for the third time. It was a futile exercise. Damn! He had expected her to be home from school by now. There was no sign of the boy either. He stepped back from the porch and looked up at the dormer windows which glimmered blankly back at him.

A path led from the front door round the side of the house and he followed it, ducking to avoid the overgrown shrubs that massed blackly against the darkening sky. There was a lawn running almost up to the back door and in the far corner was a pond. He could make out the ramrod spikes of bulrushes and untidy clumps of reeds clustered round the expanse of water gleaming eerily in the gathering twilight. It was in no way an ornamental pool; there were no lily pads or fancy paved margins or fountains. It was a natural pond, and the idea of a wildlife garden was carried over into the vegetation. Massive buddlias arched over the grass, their rusty brown bracts no longer alive with butterflies, and there was a luxuriant bed of nettles over near the garden shed.

A pale shape detached itself from these nettles and insinuated itself between his legs. It was a large fluffy cat with creamy grey fur, and darker blue-grey points. It looked to Roland like some kind of long-haired Siamese and he bent down to stroke it. The cat trilled and wound itself in and out of his legs, flicking its bushy tail and arching its back.

'You're a beautiful fellow but I'm not the person you want. Ah, maybe we're both in luck.' He could hear a car approaching the cottage. It slowed down momentarily and then there was a roar as it swung into the drive and its headlights cut a swathe through the gloom of the bushes. 'Let's go and find your mistress.'

He walked back round the house. Ginny Dalton was standing beneath the porch, fumbling in her handbag for her key. She started and gave a little inarticulate cry of fear as he loomed up beside her, then turned on him.

'What do you mean by creeping up on me like that? What are you doing, prying round my property?'

'Your cat gave me a friendlier welcome.'

'What do you want?'

She had got her key in the lock by now but she made no attempt to open the door.

'Just a couple of points I want to clear up.'

'Shouldn't there be two of you?' She glared suspiciously.

'You've been reading the Police Manual. I am not taking down official evidence or charging you — yet. May I come in?'

She shrugged and pushed open the door, and went through the house snapping on lights and drawing the curtains. He and the cat followed on her heels, the latter giving voice vociferously, determined not to be overlooked.

'I must feed Faience first, there'll be no peace till I do.'

'What an unusual name for a cat.'

'"Decorative creamware, often overlaid by a blue-grey glaze." Don't you think that describes her well?'

'Admirably.'

He watched as she took off her coat and scarf and hung them over the back of a chair. She got a tin of cat food out of the fridge and forked its contents into a bowl which she put down beside the cat basket, tucked under one end of the pine worktop. The floor was laid with quarry tiles which were in turn partly covered by mats which consisted of hundreds of pieces of multi-coloured material. Mansfield could have told him that they were traditional rag rugs and were either museum pieces or the result of someone local remembering an almost forgotten art. Pots of dried seed-heads stood on the worktop and on the table was a half-finished *papiermâché* structure that looked as if it were shaping up to be the bust of a young boy.

'Where is Simon?'

'Doing his paper-round.' She washed the fork under the running tap, re-filled the cat's drinking bowl and put it down on the floor, dried her hands and then led the way back into the sitting room.

'I really can't think why you want to see me again.'

He felt desire stirring in him once more and bit back the obvious reply. She was dressed in a severely-cut dark green dress with which she wore thick red tights and clogs. Her hair was wound into an elaborate knot in the nape of her neck. There was about her the same aura of touch-me-not and allure, all the more potent for being uncalculated, that had turned him on before. With difficulty, he dragged himself back to the business in hand.

'Have you got a photograph of Tim Spencer?'

It was not the question she was expecting and her eyes widened as she considered the implication.

'No, I destroyed any I had years ago.'

'A pity, but it can't be helped.'

'But if you want to know what he looked like ...' she paused and fanned out her hands '... just take a look in that mirror.' She gestured towards the mantelpiece.

'You mean ...?' Enlightenment dawned on him.

'You're the spitting image of him. No, that's not true. You're taller and much older, but at first sight there is a startling resemblance.'

'So that's why ...'

'Why I couldn't take my eyes off you? Yes.'

'I was going to say − couldn't take your hands off me.'

She jumped back as if she had been slapped and her colour rose, flooding upwards from her neck, bathing her pale skin in a fiery flush. He watched, fascinated. That a woman of her age and experience could still blush like a young, bashful girl was extraordinary ... then he realised it wasn't from embarrassment. She was angry, furious, and the red tide was rage. He thought in that second that she'd be quite capable of murder; of snatching up a gun and blasting the object of her hatred in the heat of the moment. And who was to say that Tim Spencer's killing had been premeditated anyway?

'I think you had better go, Inspector.'

'When I've finished Mrs. Dalton, when I've finished.'

86

At that moment there was a sound from the kitchen and a few seconds later Simon Dalton burst into the room.

'Can I have a piece of cake — I'm starving!' Then he saw Roland and pulled up abruptly, looking warily from the inspector to his stepmother.

'Yes. Have you finished?'

'I've just got Bankers Lane and Smith's farm to do.'

From the hall the telephone started ringing. 'Answer that, will you, Simon? Whoever it is, I'm busy. Say I'll ring them back later.'

She had recovered her aplomb and sat down in an easy chair, eyeing Roland challengingly. He had no intention of losing the initiative. He sat himself down opposite her and unzipped his jacket as if he had all the time in the world. Simon came back into the room.

'It's Julian Lester — he says it's urgent.' She got up quickly and they went out together. Roland strained to hear the telephone conversation through the door which she hadn't quite closed. Most of the conversation seemed to be on the caller's part. There was a long pause, and then he heard her say: 'All right, I'll come over as soon as possible. Goodbye.'

The receiver was replaced with a little click and he straightened up and pretended interest in the bookcase beside him as she came back into the room. She was eager to explain the phone-call.

'That was our local antiques' dealer; he's lending me a chaise-longue for the school play — "The Importance of Being Ernest".'

'I thought you taught art, not drama.'

'I'm in charge of props and painting the scenery. Now, Inspector, if you have nothing further to say — I'm rather busy. I have a meal to produce and a Parents' Evening later.'

'Can you handle a shotgun?'

She stared at him in astonishment, then laughed ill-humouredly.

'Are you asking me if *I* shot Tim Spencer? I should imagine anyone with the full complement of physical attributes was capable of hitting someone in the head at close range with a shotgun.'

'How did you know he was shot at close range in the head?' he rapped.

She wasn't rattled. 'You underestimate the village grapevine, Inspector. And I would hazard a guess that I knew about the skeleton before you.' She suddenly seemed to equate the word "skeleton" with her lost love, and her face crumpled in distress.

'You haven't answered my question.'

'No. I don't number shooting amongst my accomplishments.'

'Did your family own a shotgun? I presume you were living at home then before your marriage to Mr. Dalton?'

'I was home from college in the holidays, and yes, my father did own a gun, despite his calling.'

'His calling?'

She smiled triumphantly. 'You haven't done your homework very well, Inspector. My father was a man of the cloth.'

'A parson?'

'The eccentric John Merrivale, late incumbent of this parish.'

'And he went in for shooting?'

'You could say, in a most unconventional way.'

'You mean he had no licence?'

'Oh, he had a licence all right, but he didn't follow the sportsman's calendar. He refused to recognize the closed season.'

Roland raised his eyebrows and she continued: 'You must understand that my father was a very keen gardener, and the rectory grounds abutted on open countryside as well as on the churchyard and the southern tip of Croxton Woods. We were overrun by pheasants as well as pigeons, rabbits and squirrels. If he saw something attacking his precious vegetables, he'd open the window and — BANG! No matter if it was a pheasant out of season.'

'But you didn't share in this slaughter?'

'We didn't see eye to eye at all on that subject. Let's put it like this — if this were hunting country, I'd be the one with the fox in my arms, defying the huntsmen and hounds.'

'A charming picture,' he mocked. 'So what happened to the gun?'

'I don't know.'

'Don't know?'

'My father died in 1983,' she enunciated carefully, as if speaking to a child. 'I was married and living here then and Alec, my husband, saw to the winding up of his estate. There was no property involved, the rectory naturally going with the living; only furniture and his personal effects, books and things. I have no idea what happened to the gun.'

'How careless, Mrs. Dalton, to mislay a firearm. Well, that's all for the time being. Thank you for your help.' He got to his feet and she jumped up with alacrity and moved towards the door.

'I hope you're not going to pester me again.'

'Pester you? You're helping the police in the course of their enquiries. As a public-minded citizen, and I trust you are that, it is your duty.'

She wrenched open the front door and stood back so that there was no chance of accidental contact as he stepped outside.

'Just one more thing,' he turned back to her, 'I'm here on official business, but I'd like to say — that evening at the Rotary Ball — I'm sorry for any misunderstanding, please don't let it worry you.'

'I haven't given it another thought, Inspector,' she said freezingly, and slammed the door in his face.

Roland and Mansfield exchanged notes in the car going back to Felstone. Both agreed that although they had learned several interesting facts they were no closer to discovering who had murdered Tim Spencer.

'This Reverend Merrivale sounds as if he was quite a character.'

'Oh, he was. It all came back to me as soon as Betts mentioned him. He did a lot of good in the parish but he also got across many of his parishioners. Apparently he had a good line in sermons but was not above denouncing or even threatening from the pulpit.'

'I suppose he could have done it. He owned a gun and used it indiscriminately, according to his daughter. He may have heard that young Spencer was expected back, lay in wait and shot him, to stop him corrupting Virginia again. All supposition, of course, but we must add him to our list of suspects. It's a pity we have no photograph of Spencer.'

'Couldn't Mrs. Dalton give you a description?'

'Dark with light eyes, and incredibly handsome,' said Roland with a grin. 'I think we must check out his old school. They may have a group photo and be able to put us in touch with some of his friends. It sounds as if he was quite a popular character; he may have kept up with some of his old schoolmates. Get Evans and Pomroy on to it. And perhaps Garfield can tell us where he worked and how he occupied himself between leaving school and going to Australia. I want to see him again anyway but we'll wait till after I've seen the solicitor about the inheritance. You and I have a mountain of paperwork to catch up with but I think our next priority, after my appointment with Mr. Larkin, is a visit to that old people's home at Denham Market, though I don't hold out much hope of getting any factual evidence from an octogenarian.'

The offices of Larkin & Webb, Solicitors, were situated in Marlow Square, just off Felstone High Street, in a tall Georgian-fronted building still boasting its original windows. The firm consisted of three other partners besides Larkin and Webb, and several junior members, including a Paul Larkin whom Roland took to be Larkin Senior's son. In addition to Larkin *père* and *fils*, he soon understood that there had been a Larkin *grandpère*, one of the two original founders, who had dealt with all the legal business pertaining to Gertrude Fellingham, deceased.

The receptionist, a smartly dressed woman in her forties with buck teeth and a Roedean accent, informed him that Mr. Cyril Larkin would see him when he had finished with his present client, if he would care to take a seat. Roland took a seat and looked about him. The furnishings of the room were discreet and expensive. The chairs were upholstered in leather, the long, low table was of solid carved oak, and the magazines displayed on it were current copies of *Country Life* and others of that ilk.

There were two paintings in heavy gilt frames displayed on the wall that looked, but surely couldn't be, genuine Smythes. He noted that the receptionist's blouse, a soft muted blue was exactly the same shade as the wall-to-wall carpeting – accident or design? He pondered over whether it was by accident or design that he was kept waiting long past the appointed time. The minutes ticked by without any indication of Larkin Senior's presence in the building, plus or minus a client, but just as his patience was about to give way the buzzer on the receptionist's desk sounded and she flashed him a toothy smile and said: 'Mr. Larkin will see you now.'

The solicitor was taller and thinner than Roland had remembered from their encounter at the funeral, but then he had been wearing a bulky overcoat. He must be close to retiring age, thought Roland, and he's not at all happy about seeing me. I wonder why?

'What can I do for you, Inspector?' asked Cyril Larkin after he had indicated the visitor's seat and himself sat down behind the vast, leather-topped desk that occupied a good fifth of the book-lined room. Roland explained his business and the other man steepled his fingers and looked over them with a pained expression.

'This is all most unfortunate, Inspector, but I really can't divulge a client's business. It would be most unethical.'

'Mr. Larkin, I am investigating a murder. All I'm asking for is information about the beneficiaries of a testator who is long dead. You and I know that I can get a copy of that will from Somerset House; I prefer to save time and come to the person who drew it up and implemented it.'

'Well, I suppose in the circumstances ... But I was not involved, Inspector. Mrs. Gertrude Fellingham was a client of my late father. He drew up the terms of the will and implemented them.'

'But presumably you are *au fait* with the business?'

Larkin sighed and indicated that he was. 'Apart from a few small bequests to former friends and servants, and an annuity to her housekeeper, the estate was divided between her two great-nephews, Tony Garfield – who now lives at The Hermitage in Croxton – and Leslie Drew, the grandson of her late sister Ivy, residing in the United States.'

'And Timothy Spencer, the other great-nephew, received no mention?'

'Timothy Spencer had blotted his copybook. I was given to understand that he was her favourite, and according to Mrs.

91

Fellingham's whim could have inherited the whole estate, but when he failed to answer her summons home for her eightieth birthday celebration she cut him out of her will.'

'So Tony Garfield and the American cousin benefited considerably from Timothy Spencer's disappearance?'

'I suppose you could say so,' it was wrung from him grudgingly, 'but I don't think I care for your imputation.'

'Mr. Larkin, we in the Force have a dictum: find the motive and nine times out of ten you've found your murderer.'

'You're surely not suggesting that Mr. Garfield . . . ?'

'All I'm saying is that a legacy involving a large sum of money is a very powerful motive.'

'Mr. Garfield is a successful businessman who was very comfortably off before his inheritance. In point of fact, the inheritance was not as large as expected. Mrs. Fellingham had made some very unwise investments in her last years.'

'Are you saying she played the Stock Market?'

'Let us say that she refused to listen to advice and did some very imprudent buying. My father tried to restrain her, but I'm afraid in her latter years she became very independent and . . . er . . . difficult.'

'You mean she became gaga?'

'Oh no, Inspector.' He was shocked. 'Mrs. Fellingham was a very shrewd old lady right up to her death. No, what I meant was . . . she became wilful . . . kicked over the traces somewhat, I suppose you could say. Her late husband, Bartholomew Fellingham, had started out with hardly two pennies to rub together. He amassed the family fortune through hard work and astuteness. He never made an ill-considered move, everything he did was planned and researched – none of those gambles or flashes of genius one sometimes reads about in connection with self-made men. He got where he did through sheer hard work and perseverance, and I suppose that coloured his attitude to life. He wasn't a mean man, Inspector, but he was careful. After he died, Mrs. Fellingham followed the same pattern, but then, in ripe old age, she seemed suddenly to realize that she possessed a deal of money and no children or close relations to whom to leave it, and it went to her head.

She had all the material possessions she needed, she was not a do-gooder, so she used the money to buy and sell on the Stock Exchange.' He paused and carefully polished his gold-rimmed glasses on his handkerchief. 'You do understand that this is in confidence? I don't want you to think that Mrs. Fellingham was a gambler, I was just trying to convey why the bequests were not as large as expected.'

'What was the sum involved?'

'Less than a quarter of a million, divided between the two. A hundred and twenty thousand plus is a nice little windfall but not *that* large a sum nowadays, what with escalating house prices etc.'

'But worth considerably more nine years ago?'

Cyril Larkin conceded that this was so.

'This nephew in America — did he come over here to claim his inheritance?'

'No, we had an address for him in Los Angeles — he was in real estate — and it was all done through his lawyers over there.'

'There is one point I am not clear about: did Croxton Hall burn down before or after Mrs. Fellingham's death?'

'Before — just. It happened in the autumn of 1979 and Mrs. Fellingham died shortly afterwards. A direct result of the fire, my father always thought.'

'You mean she was injured in the fire? How did it happen?'

'She wasn't injured, but the shock to her system . . . I had better explain.'

He removed his glasses and swung them gently to and fro.

'Mrs. Fellingham was a heavy smoker. I always knew when she had been here because of the distinctive smell of the Balkan Sobranie cigarettes she favoured. Anyway, she took to smoking in the bedroom, a dangerous habit for anyone, but especially in one as old and frail as she. She fell asleep one day after she had lit up and you can guess the rest. Fortunately the housekeeper smelt smoke and raised the alarm and they were both rescued safely, although the fire had got such a hold by the time the fire brigade arrived that there was little they could do to save the bulk of the building. That night Mrs. Fellingham suffered a stroke. It was only a mild one and she was taken to a private clinic where she was expected to make a full recovery, but unfortunately a second stroke a few weeks later carried her off.'

'And the fire was quite definitely caused by her smoking habits?' asked Roland sharply.

'Yes, Inspector,' replied the solicitor dryly, 'it was thoroughly investigated by the insurance company. You can rest assured that it was an accident and not arson.'

'Well, thank you for your help, Mr. Larkin. Just one more question – do you act for Mr. Tony Garfield?'

'Mr. Garfield's business is centred in the City,' the lawyer replied stiffly. 'He has no need of a local solicitor.'

'So there you have it.' Roland was bringing his sergeant up-to-date before they set out on their visit to Downham Market.

'Tony Garfield would have inherited considerably less, possibly nothing at all, if Timothy Spencer had kept on good terms with the old lady. How's that for a motive?'

'A very good one, I should have said, but you don't seem to like it.'

'It seems too obvious, and besides, Larkin is convinced that he was doing very nicely, thank you, without Auntie's money and I am inclined to believe him. I still favour a crime of passion.'

Mansfield opened his mouth to reply but thought better of it and bit back the remark. Perhaps Ethel Parker would be able to throw some light on the subject.

The two men snatched a hurried lunch in the police station and set off shortly afterwards.

Denham Market was a small market town lying about fifteen miles inland from Croxton. The old peoples' home, "Restacres" was situated on the outskirts in a former Victorian rectory standing in an acre of grounds. Roland had spoken to the matron, a Mrs. Golding, over the phone and elicited that a visit might be well worth the making. Ethel Parker was one of their star guests; a sprightly old lady with a remarkable memory.

Torrential rain had been falling for several hours as they set out, and the further they journeyed into the heart of Suffolk the greater the scene of desolation. The River Bent had

94

overflowed its banks in several places and whole fields were flooded; lakes of water lay on either side of the road, out of which sprouted sodden hedges and trees. Many minor roads were impassable and they drove through sheets of water on the main road, throwing up spray like a speedboat.

'This had better be worth our while.' Roland swore as a lorry overtook them, hurling such a volume of water on to their windscreen that vision was obliterated for a few seconds. He overshot the turning to the approach road to "Restacres" and had to back into a field gateway to turn round where the car nearly got bogged down in the gleaming black ruts.

"Restacres" was Victorian Gothic at its worst; an ugly, grey building bristling with towers and crenellated turrets, set against a backdrop of sombre pines.

'God! What a place in which to end your days,' muttered Mansfield as they approached the main door.

'Don't forget we're seeing it at its worst. The sun must shine sometimes and one hopes the interior has been modernised.'

They parked beside a minibus that stood in front of the east wing and made an undignified dash through the rain to the front door, a massive structure in solid oak with wrought iron knocker and handle. A modern bellpush was let into the wall beside the door. Mansfield pressed it. They could hear the bell echoing inside the house but nobody answered for a long while.

'Perhaps they get taken for outings?' Mansfield indicated the minibus which had peeling stickers in the back windows.

'The fees here are quite substanital. It's a private home, not funded by the council. Ethel Parker must have money.'

'Didn't you say she was left an annuity in her ex-employer's will?'

They could hear someone approaching the door. There was the sound of bolts being drawn and chains unlocked.

'This is like getting into Fort Knox. Are they trying to keep the inmates in or us out?'

The door eventually opened to reveal a young woman in check overall and cap, but before they had a chance to explain their presence, another woman came through a doorway over on the other side of the hall and hurried towards them.

'Inspector Roland? I am Mrs. Golding, the matron. Sorry

95

about the security but we have one resident who likes to go walkabout if he gets the chance, and for his own good we try to keep all the doors securely locked. Please come into my office.'

She was a trim, middle-aged woman with carefully coiffured hair and had the bright, forced voice that some people adopt when talking to old people or children. Wearing a well-cut navy suit with a white frilled blouse and a beautiful cameo brooch at the neck, she exuded an air of discretion and authority and Roland was sure that she ran her little empire efficiently and autocratically; he had met women like her before.

The room into which she ushered them was more a sitting room than an office, although it did contain a desk and typist's chair besides a sofa and easy chairs and a handsome rosewood side table and cabinet.

'Now, Inspector, Sergeant, I'm sure you would like some coffee before I take you to Miss Parker. I'm surprised you managed to get here; if this rain continues, we'll soon be marooned.'

'I believe wind is forecast, perhaps it will help to dry things out. Does Miss Parker know we are coming?'

'I told her two gentlemen were visiting her who are interested in hearing about the time she spent at Croxton Hall. She is quite excited. Of course, I didn't tell her you were police officers, I thought it might upset her, and I knew you wouldn't be in uniform.'

'How long has she lived here?'

'She came in 1979 after she left Croxton Hall. She was working there, as you know, as housekeeper-companion to a Mrs. Fellingham. When her employer died, Miss Parker found herself without employment or accommodation and was too old to seek another post, even had she been capable of doing so. Between you and me, Inspector, I've gathered that they were two frail old ladies propping each other up. Who helped who the most was a moot point.'

'I understood Miss Parker to be entirely compos mentis.' Roland began to think the journey had been a waste of time.

'Oh, she is, Inspector. I was talking about her physical health. She's very arthritic and her sight is failing, but there's nothing wrong with her brain.'

96

'And is she likely to remember events that took place ten years ago?'

'Like many old people, the past is more real to her than the present. She's more likely to remember something that happened several years ago than what she had for dinner yesterday.'

Coffee was brought in by another young woman dressed in identical overall and cap to the one who had opened the door to them. Staffing problems seemed to have been overcome here, thought Roland; they were obviously not at the inadequate level of many retirement homes. Perhaps they were better paid. The coffee was served in delicate china cups and there was a choice of cream or milk, and brown or white sugar.

'How many residents have you?'

'Fifteen, and a waiting list. We don't have to advertise. They are very comfortable here and word gets round.'

'I'm sure it does. And the fees?'

Mrs. Golding raised her eyebrows delicately as if he had committed a faux pas. Obviously any discussion of finances was not encouraged in this establishment. She'll be telling me next that trade is vulgar, he thought.

'Miss Parker was left an annuity in her late employer's will. That covers her expenses. Is that what you wanted to know, Inspector?'

He admitted that it was.

'Do they ever go out?' This was Mansfield. Used to mug-sized helpings of coffee he was suffering withdrawal symptoms after swallowing the contents of the small cup he had been given.

'Go out?'

'Apart from in a box.'

She was affronted. 'We arrange outings and visits for them as much as possible, if that's what you mean, Sergeant. It is very rare for one of our guests to move to other accommodation. They are happy and content to end their days here, as long as ...'

'... the money doesn't run out?'

'We have never turned anyone out, and I resent your choice of phrase.'

97

'Mrs. Golding, I can see that you run a very superior establishment here.' Roland threw a warning glance at his sergeant. 'One has only to look at your china.'

'Really, Inspector?'

'Yes. I always say look at the crockery if you want to get a true picture of a place. None of your inch-thick pottery beakers or tinny spoons here. That tray is laid fit for a queen, and I'm sure your residents get the same treatment. It's class, Mrs. Golding and it talks.'

She was mollified. 'We try to make it a home from home, and, of course, most of our guests are from the more ... er ... privileged sections of the community.'

'And do they get many visitors?'

'Some do, some don't.' She shrugged. 'It is quite distressing how some families think they have done their duty once they get their elderly relative into a place like this; they opt out of any further commitment. If they only realised how much it means to these old people to know that they're not forgotten. Just the odd visit, a birthday card, the Christmas reunion — it's not much to ask, is it?'

'But Miss Parker has no relatives?'

'No, so your visit will be doubly welcome. If you have finished your coffee, I'll take you up to her.'

She led the way across the large, square hall with its parquet flooring and sombre panelling, and up the broad, shallow staircase.

'We have a lift but we try to reserve use of it for those who really need it, the wheelchair bound, etc.'

The corridor was illuminated by a long stained glass window set in the far wall. It was coloured predominantly in shades of green which gave Roland the feeling that he was swimming underwater. She tapped on a door near the far end of the corridor and pushed it open.

'Here we are, Miss Parker,' she said brightly, 'I've brought the two gentlemen to see you, the ones I told you about.'

She was sitting in a high wingchair near the window, a gaunt, brittle figure with a rug clutched across her knees by hands with the swollen knuckles of the arthritic. At first sight she did not look as old as Roland had expected. He decided that this was due to her hair; it still showed a generous amount

98

of it original colour, a light brown, amongst the silver and white strands. There were men half her age in the Force who were much greyer. She was wearing glasses and she peered through the thick, pebble lenses and spoke in a surprisingly strong voice that still held traces of a Scottish accent. Miss Parker had originated from across the border and was ending her days far from her native roots.

'Come over here and sit in the light so that I can see you better. My sight is not what it was.'

They complied and she studied them carefully and then looked over her shoulder.

'Has she gone?'

'I'm here, Miss Parker, do you want me?'

'Certainly not, I don't need an audience.' Mrs Golding prepared to depart but she got in a last word.

'We mustn't tire ourselves, must we? Don't forget the concert party is visiting this afternoon.'

'Silly woman,' said Miss Parker after the door had closed behind the matron. 'She treats us all as if we've lost our wits. I've forgotten more than she ever knew.'

'Not too much I hope, Miss Parker,' said Roland, 'we want to pick your brains.'

'You're policemen, aren't you?' she shot at them. 'You can't fool me.'

'I'm sure we can't and you're quite right. I'm Detective Inspector Roland and this is Detective Sergeant Mansfield of the CID. We're hoping you can tell us about the time when you lived at Croxton Hall.'

'I was there over thirty years, that will take a lot of telling. How much time have you got, Mr. Inspector?' She cackled at him.

'I'm really interested in the last few years but I bet you could tell me everything that happened during those years, couldn't you?'

'That I could. I haven't forgotten anything that happened in those days, it's just the last few years I get muddled about. And why shouldn't I? Nothing happens here ever, it's the same day after day. *She* thinks I'm going senile because I can't remember whether the doctor came last week or the week before, but why should I bother? I've got better things to remember.'

99

'A wise philosophy, Miss Parker.'

'What do you want to know? My Mrs. Fellingham never got into trouble with the law.'

'I'm sure she didn't. We're interested in another member of the family. Do you remember Tim Spencer?'

'Tim? He was a young dare-devil — what's he done now?'

'When did you last see him?' asked Roland gently.

'A long time ago, just before he was packed off to Australia. Do you know about all that?'

'Yes, but I understand he was invited back for Mrs. Fellingham's eightieth birthday party.'

'That's what I could never understand.' She shook her head and plucked at the rug with agitated fingers. 'Why didn't he come and see me? I was his Parky — he always used to call me that — he would never have come back to Croxton without seeing *me*. We were great friends, he could twist me round his little finger. Many's the time I would hide him in my room when he had played a trick on one of the maids, and he always knew where to come when he was hungry — he loved my cake. Parky's Parkin he used to call it. And my, but he was one for the ladies. "You'll leave a trail of broken hearts behind you, but one day you'll be caught," I used to tell him.'

'And was Ginny Merrivale the one?'

'Huh, she was a match for him all right. It was like fire meeting fire. But she soon forgot him, and a lot of good it did her.'

'So you and Mrs. Fellingham were expecting him back and you were disappointed when he didn't come?'

'But he did, didn't he? That's what I meant — why should he come all the way back to Suffolk and then not come and see us?'

'You seem certain he came back, Miss Parker, what makes you so sure?'

'Because he saw him, didn't he?'

'*Who* saw him?'

'Mr. Lester, the antiques' man. He met him on the train.'

'Let me get this clear, Miss Parker.' Roland leaned towards her, his eyes narrowing in concentration. 'Are you quite sure that Mr. Lester saw him? How do you know?'

'Because he told me, that's why. I was in Gypswyck that

day, and I bumped into him near the station and he came up to me and said: "Kill the fatted calf, Miss Parker, the Prodigal Son has returned." Those were his exact words, and then he told me that he had travelled up from London on the same train as Tim. I was so excited.'

'And when was this?'

'About a week before the party. It would have been early July, 1978.'

'Are you quite sure about this?'

'Of course I am — it was the day I had my accident, that's how I know. Mr. Lester said he'd have given me a lift back to Croxton but he had to go over to Woodford, more's the pity. If I'd gone with him it would never have happened.'

'Accident?'

'At the bus station. I was getting on the bus when it jolted forward suddenly and I slipped and broke my hip. I was in hospital for months, missed the party, and just when Mrs. Fellingham needed all the help I could have given her.'

'So you were away from Croxton Hall for a while and didn't realise that Tim hadn't turned up?'

'I was upset when he didn't come to visit me. I thought as soon as he heard about my accident he would come and see me in hospital, but he never did. Then later I realised that he hadn't turned up at all.'

'But didn't that strike you as strange? You had been told that he was back in Suffolk but nobody else saw him, neither his great-aunt, nor his cousin Tony Garfield, nor Mrs. Dalton — Ginny Merrivale that was?'

'Well, I always supposed she had. Stands to reason, doesn't it? He would have gone to see her first, and I reckon she told him she was in love with someone else and didn't want to see him again. And he was so upset that he just took off and went back to where he'd come from.'

'And you never mentioned to Mrs. Fellingham or anyone that he'd been seen locally?'

'Well, no, I didn't. I've often wondered since if I should have said something at the time, but you see it was a long while before I knew that he hadn't put in an appearance, and then I thought it would hurt her more if she knew that he'd come back and hadn't got in touch than if she thought he just

101

hadn't answered her invitation in the first place, so I held my tongue. Mr. Lester couldn't have said anything either.'

'Well, you have been most helpful, Miss Parker. I wish everyone had so good a recall of events as you.'

Roland and Mansfield got to their feet, but if they thought the interview was over Miss Parker had other ideas.

'But you haven't told me why you want to know all this. What has Tim done? Has he got into trouble with the police again?'

'He hasn't done anything, Miss Parker. I'm afraid he's dead.'

'Tim, dead?' Her voice quavered and she suddenly looked her age. 'He can't be! Not my boy dead!'

'I'm sorry to be the bearer of bad news but I'm afraid it's true.' He put a hand on her shoulder and she whimpered and seemed to shrivel up.

'It's not fair. Why should he be snatched away when I'm left? An old woman like me who's got nothing to live for − it's not fair!'

Her voice followed them as they walked back along the corridor.

'At least someone genuinely mourns him,' remarked Mansfield, as they went in search of the matron. 'But why didn't he show up at Croxton Hall.'

'Because his murderer got to him first. But why was he murdered? I think a vist to Mr. Julian Lester is our number one priority now.'

The rain ceased later that day but the wind got up. It rippled the puddles and soughed through the dripping trees, causing misery to anyone unfortunate enough to be working outside. The weather men forecast strong winds that night. They went no further but the animals and birds knew better.

Afterwards it was reported that the deer had left the forestry commission woods north of Croxton and had been seen bunched together in the open fields in the days leading up to that fateful night of the 15th−16th October. The squirrels, interrupted in their busiest foraging season, likewise deserted the forest giants and the birds relinquished their usual roosts and huddled low in the hedgerows. As the wind strengthened, those ships close enough inshore ran for the shelter of Felstone harbour; those further out to sea, hove to and prepared to ride out the storm.

Not many people ventured out that evening. From the safety of their homes they predicted that there would be a few trees down by the morning. Nobody comprehended the magnitude of the hurricane about to unleash its force on the unsuspecting Suffolk countryside.

Chapter Six

The persistent clamour of the telephone penetrated Julian Lester's subconscious as he lay slumped over his desk. Somehow he dragged himself back through layers of torpor and forced open his eyes. The empty bottle stood within reach of his elbow. God! They had sunk a whole bottle of Jenever. His visitor had gone – whatever time was it? He groaned and held his head in both hands. He must have passed out, he felt terrible and his head was spinning. All he wanted to do was to sink back into sleep, but there was something he had to do first.

He was dimly aware of the telephone shrilling and with a mammoth effort he dragged himself to his feet. There was a terrible noise outside – or was it just the cacophony in his head? He swayed upright, clinging to the back of the chair, and at that moment the door burst open and a gust of wind howled round the room. Somehow he staggered to the doorway and tottered out through the porch. The night was full of sound and above him the trees threshed and milled their jagged limbs against a backcloth of turbulent sky.

The whole wood was alive, it was closing in on him – he must get back into the house. In sudden terror he lurched forward, trying to find the door, but in his befuddled state he moved in the wrong direction. He tripped over a tree root and crashed heavily to the ground, rolling over on to his back. He struggled to right himself but was as helpless as an upturned beetle.

He gave up the attempt. It was too much effort and all he wanted to do was sleep. The grass was cool and silky, he would rest awhile and bestir himself later ... later ...

At five a.m. the electricity supply to Croxton was cut off as tree after tree crashed to the ground, taking with them the overhead power cables and felling the poles like snapped matchsticks. Fifteen minutes later Felstone was plunged into darkness and many of the roads leading out of the town were blocked by fallen trees.

A tanker carrying a consignment of dangerous chemicals broke loose from her moorings in Felstone Docks and precipitated a major alert. As she plunged helplessly about in the heaving water, a mass evacuation of the area was planned in the event that she ran aground or smashed into another vessel or the harbour pilings and leaked her lethal cargo.

Whole plantations of trees were toppled, roofs and chimneys were ripped off, fences flattened, and greenhouses and sheds smashed like eggshells. A large percentage of the households in the area found their telephones dead and the only communication with the outside world was the news and reports broadcast over the local radio. The police headquarters at Felstone switched to its emergency generators and all the available workforce was drafted in to cope with the crisis.

By eight a.m. the worst of the hurricane had blown itself out but conditions were still horrendous and people ventured out at their peril. All schools in the county were closed and people were warned to stay at home unless their journey was absolutely necessary. James Roland had found his driveway blocked by a fallen tree and had struggled in on foot, dodging flying tiles and branches. Detective Superintendent Lacey had managed the journey by car and was sitting in judgement on any unfortunate subordinate who had allowed commonsense to over-ride his sense of duty. He lingered in the control room, annoying his uniformed colleagues, and pontificated on the situation.

'We must thank our lucky stars it happened when everyone was tucked up in beddy-byes. A few hours later and we'd be littered with corpses. It's quite remarkable − not a single fatal casualty.'

'Excuse me, sir,' the young constable on the switchboard

interupted, 'a report has just come in that a man has been killed in Croxton.'

'What's that about Croxton?' Roland caught the name as he was passing by and stuck his head through the doorway.

The constable repeated himself and added: 'He was found under a tree in his garden.'

'There you are, James, another corpse turned up on your patch.' Lacey heaved himself to his feet and made for the door. 'I don't suppose the poor bugger was connected with your murder hunt.'

Roland stared after his superior and then turned back to the constable. 'Who was he – do we know yet?'

The constable checked. 'the owner of Smoky Cottage in Croxton Wood. An antiques' dealer by the name of Julian Lester.'

'I don't believe it! Where did the information come from?'

'PC Drake, the local man, reported in.'

'Call him up for me, this is important.'

When Drake was eventually raised, the static over the air waves was so bad that they could have been on different continents.

'Who found him?'

'The local gamekeeper.'

'Have you moved him?'

'He's under a tree, sir, but I'm arranging for a tractor and lifting gear ...'

'Hold everything,' cut in Roland. 'Don't touch or move anything till I get there. I suppose there's no doubt that he's dead?'

'None, sir, but I've sent for the doctor.'

'Probably the wrong one. I'll be with you shortly – is the road passable?'

'Just about. There's a tree down on the corner of Piper's Lane but you can just about squeeze past.'

Roland signed off and went in search of his sergeant. Together they made the journey to Croxton, appalled at the scenes of devastation they encountered on the short journey. Gale-force winds were still blowing and those trees not already stricken were whipping about like members of an

106

orchestra, obeying the commands of some primeval conductor. As they turned off the main road the sun came out momentarily, highlighting a frieze of silver birch trees that danced in golden frenzy against the indigo clouds piled up behind them in the western sky.

'I can't believe it's coincidence,' grumbled Roland as he swung the car on an erratic course to avoid tiles and fencing panels scattered across the road. 'We've got a lead at last — someone who actually *saw* our victim — and he turns up dead before we can interview him.'

'You're saying it's not an accident? How could a tree falling on him be anything but an accident?'

'I know, I know,' Roland snapped, 'it's just our bad luck. We should have questioned him on our way back from Denham Market yesterday.'

They left the car at the end of the lane leading to Smoky Cottage and picked their way along the debris-strewn track.

'It's unbelievable that this sort of thing could happen in East Anglia.' Mansfield pointed to a giant oak tree that lay on its side, exposing a great cavity and an enormous fractured root system where it had been torn out of the ground. 'It's the sort of thing one reads about happening in the Caribbean — tornadoes and hurricanes and such-like. That tree is probably two or three hundred years old and it has been plucked out of the ground as if it were a blade of grass.'

'It's the same with most of them. The trunks haven't been severed, they've been uprooted. I suppose the water-table is very high with all the rain we've had and that's why they've been uprooted so easily. After one of our normal dry summers they would be embedded in the ground like concrete.'

'It's a wonder the cottage wasn't demolished — luckily the trees have all fallen the other way. It's fortunate it wasn't an east wind.'

Smoky Cottage stood exposed amongst the devastated trees, looking strangely vulnerable. From the side from which they were approaching the only damage visible was to the gable end which had lost all its ridge tiles. The water butt was also lying on its side and a piece of guttering swung aimlessly to and fro above it like a bent pendulum. They waded through a

107

sea of leaves and rounded the corner of the house. A solitary pear tree was still upright in a corner of the garden; the other fruit trees were laid low as if a giant had been playing skittles. A Scots pine that had stood sentinel by the gate had crashed across the path, taking with it the electricity cable and smaller saplings. Under this tree was the body of Julian Lester.

'Have you touched him at all?' Roland asked Tom Drake who was beside himself with curiosity as to why an innocent storm victim should command the interest of the CID.

'Only to make sure he was dead. I think he must have been hit by a branch whilst the tree was actually falling and that must have killed him. He's underneath it now but it doesn't seem to have crushed him or even be pinning him down.'

Roland crouched down beside the corpse and immediately saw what the constable meant. Julian Lester was lying on his back in a slight hollow in the ground beside the path. The tree had crashed over him but the full weight of it was caught and held by a bank supporting a rockery that curved round that part of the front lawn. One limb of the tree was resting aslant the chest and left shoulder of the dead man, and a delicate tracery of branches and twigs from this bough arched over his face and upper torso. There was no sign of blood.

'Right, I want the scene of crime team out here, and Doc Brasnett. When they've finished we'll get that tree off him and the doctor can do a proper examination. Get the electricity people out here too. I don't care how busy they are, this is top priority. I reckon that cable is live,' he pointed to the electricity cable hanging slackly in loops, 'and I don't want another accident.'

'Could he have been electrocuted?' asked Mansfield, bending over the corpse.

'It's possible, but he doesn't look like an electrocution case, does he?'

'No way.'

'Excuse me, sir, but has he got anything to do with the skeleton found down on the marshes?' PC Drake was rapidly putting two and two together and not liking the answer.

'He was the only person, to our knowledge, to have seen

108

the murdered man when he returned to Croxton prior to his
fatal accident.'

'You think he was the murderer?'

'I think he may have known too much.'

'You were right, James, he was dead before the tree fell on
him.' George Brasnett cleared his throat ostentatiously,
crammed his deerstalker more securely on his head and turned
back to the corpse.

The late Julian Lester had been photographed, finger-
printed, and thoroughly processed, and after an exacting
operation the tree had been lifted from his body and the
pathologist had been able to examine him more easily.

'How long?'

'I can't possibly tell you at this stage.'

'Have a try.'

'We-ll, that branch certainly crushed the top of his shoulder
but the lack of bleeding immediately made me suspicious.
Rigor mortis has started in the jaw and arms ... I reckon he's
been dead over six hours, say between midnight and three
a.m., but don't quote me on that.'

'Any idea what caused death?'

'Look at his face.' Roland stared down at the body. 'There
are traces of dried vomit round his mouth and nose. Could
have been drinking, vomited and inhaled it.'

'He was known to have been a heavy drinker, sir,' said Tom
Drake who was assisting the CID team by keeping away any
curious locals.

'There you are. He wanders outside in a drunken stupor,
falls over and ends up on his back and − hey presto! But why
should I tell you your job?'

'So it was probably an accidental death?'

'Were you expecting it to be murder? Help me turn him
over.'

Together they rolled the body over and Brasnett carefully
peeled back the dead man's shirt and trousers. 'There you are,
look − dorsal lividity.' The skin over the back of the body
was suffused red and purple. 'Postmortem hypostasis − yes,
he's certainly been dead several hours.'

Mansfield had been peering through a window of the

cottage and he called out to them: 'The electric clock on the mantelpiece stopped at 5.05 a.m. so that must have been the time this little lot came down.'

'Good man, that's pinpointed it nicely. He was certainly dead before then.' He turned to Brasnett. 'Any more you can tell us at this stage?'

'No, get him to the lab and I'll open him up.'

Roland sent DC Evans in search of Bates, and whilst the body was being removed he and Mansfield went into the cottage. The door opened on to chaos. Leaves and twigs littered the floor, mixed with blank sheets of A4 paper which were scattered about the room like overblown white blossoms. The curtains were twisted up round the top of the dresser, and a stool and chair had been overturned.

'Christ! There's nearly as much debris in here as there is outside. He must have tottered out and left the door open.'

'He was hardly likely to worry about a little thing like that if he was inebriated. It probably stayed open until a particularly violent gust slammed it to later.'

They examined the room. A chair was drawn up in front of the desk on which stood a typewriter, and beside this an empty bottle and a glass. Roland took out his handkerchief and wrapped it carefully round the neck of the bottle. He picked it up. "Oude Jenever." He read the label and sniffed at the top. 'Potent stuff. I wonder what made him go outside?'

'Probably heard the wind sending things crashing and went to see what was happening.' Roland pulled open the drawer of the desk. It contained a box of typing paper and an A4 folder containing a manuscript. He flicked through a few pages and noted that the contents dealt with porcelain. He put it back and shut the drawer.

'Typical bachelor pad — you did say he wasn't married?'

'I believe he was divorced, but it all happened many years ago. There's been never a mention of a wife or any close relation since he's lived here, which must be all of twenty years or so.'

'That will be a task for someone — tracing his family.'

There was a bureau in the corner but it was locked and Roland left it for later. The kitchen was small and conspicuously lacking in mod cons. There were a couple of dirty plates and a mug on the draining board, and a saucepan, half filled with water, stood in the sink. The other downstairs room was filled with tea-chests, and crates of bric-à-brac and piles of books stood around on the chests of drawers and tables lining the walls.

Upstairs yielded little of interest. Julian Lester's bedroom contained a single bed, which didn't look as if it had been properly made for days, and a wardrobe, dressing table and bedside cabinet. There was a large assortment of medicines and pills and potions in the latter. Lester had obviously been something of a hypochondriac. The second bedroom had been used as a further storeroom for his antiques' business, and the bathroom was small and squalid with a chipped washbasin and a pile of dirty linen in one corner. Roland and Mansfield shut the door on it and returned downstairs.

Stephen Bates was not happy to be recalled to Smoky Cottage.

'What do you want now? I did my duty and reported him, didn't I, what more do you want?'

'What time did you find him, Mr. Bates?'

'I've told Drake all this. It was about seven-thirty.'

'That was early to be about on a morning like this.'

'It's my job, isn't it? I had to see what was happening. I've never seen anything like it ...' He broke off and shook his head and Roland saw through the surliness to the man beneath who was clearly badly affected by the damage he had witnessed. Roland was sure that he was more upset by the harm suffered by the wildlife than he was by the death of a solitary man. 'We'll never recover from this — it will take years to repair the damage.'

'Just tell us how you came to find him.'

'I wasn't too keen on going anywhere near the woods, not the way it was blowing, but I thought I ought to give him a look and see if he was okay — I was afraid a tree might have crashed through the roof. So I came round by the road and it looked as if nothing was standing in the garden. I could see that great Scots pine was down and had taken the electricity lines with it, and then when I got close I saw him underneath.'

111

'So what did you do?'

'I had some stupid idea that maybe I could roll the tree aside and get at him but I soon realised that was impossible. Anyway, I could see that he was dead so I went and got Drake.'

'Was the cottage door open?'

Bates stared at them suspiciously as he thought back. 'Yes, it was. I remember thinking how odd that he should have gone outside and left it open in weather like that.'

'And did you close it?'

'Yes, I did. No harm in that was there?' He asked belligerently. 'What are you getting at? You're not trying to pin this one on me as well, are you? I suppose I should have put him to bed and locked him in last night?'

Roland and Mansfield exchanged glances.

'Are you saying that you saw him last night – you were drinking with him?'

'Too late, wasn't I? He'd already had a skinful and was out cold.'

'What do you mean?'

'What I say. I was passing by last night and I saw the light on in his downstairs window and thought I'd give him a look. It was no night to be abroad and I reckoned he was good for a noggin. He drank a lot but he was generous with it – preferred sharing it with someone than drinking it on his own.'

'And . . .?'

'When I got close, I could see he'd already had too much. He was slumped over his typewriter out cold, and there was an empty bottle nearby and an aspirin bottle beside him.'

'Are you sure about this, it could be important.'

'Of course I am – look, the bottle's still there.' Bates jerked his head at the desk in the window embrasure.

'There's no aspirin bottle, are you sure you saw one?'

'Well, I don't know if it was aspirin, I couldn't read the label, but it was a little pill bottle. I remember thinking to myself, "You'll need more than a couple of aspirins to cure the head you'll have in the morning."'

'And is everything else as you saw it?'

Bates considered. 'Well, the letter's gone out of the typewriter.'

'Letter?'

'Well, the paper he was typing on. He was writing a book and I suppose he was typing out a bit of that.'

'Are you quite sure?'

'Yes, because his head was resting on the paper. I distinctly remember that.'

'What time would that have been?'

'Just after nine, I reckon. Between nine and nine-thirty anyway.'

'So what did you do?'

'I carried on home, didn't I? And glad I was to get inside.'

'Did you see anyone else in the vicinity?'

A look of cunning flickered across the gamekeeper's face. 'I reckon I did.'

Roland sighed impatiently. 'Come on, man, this is worse than extracting a tooth. We're investigating a death, and I'm trying to establish whether anyone saw him after you.'

Bates fingered his cap. 'I heard somebody in the woods, going away from here.'

'Are you sure? The night was pretty wild, even as early as nine o'clock. Are you sure it wasn't the wind?'

'I can tell the difference, can't I?' He was contempuous. 'Natural noises are different from man-made ones, as any countryman will tell you. I heard movement and I thought at first it was Alfie Coutts. Damn poacher he is — the bane of my life — but I'd seen him earlier, over the other side of the wood going in the opposite direction, so I couldn't understand how he'd got here so quickly. Anyway, I followed and then I could see a light flickering up ahead and I knew it wasn't Alfie. Poachers don't advertise their presence by carrying a light, so I reckoned it was the other one, taking a short cut through the woods, though I thought I heard a car starting up soon afterwards and he usually does it on foot.'

'The other one? You mean another poacher?'

'No, of course not. I mean the writer chap, up to his tricks again.'

'I don't follow you, Mr. Bates.'

'When the cat is away the mice will play. I can tell you something — I'd bet my life on it — your high and mighty Mr. Tony Garfield was away from The Hermitage last night.'

'And what is that supposed to mean?'

'It means that Bradley Scott was out visiting where he had no right to be. You want to investigate people like him and that stuck up Mrs Garfield, who's no better than she ought to be, instead of harassing innocent people like me.'

'Are you saying that Bradley Scott and Mrs. Garfield are conducting an affair?'

'That would be telling, but you'd be surprised what I see and hear patrolling my territory. There's a lot of loose living about nowadays, Inspector, and it should be punished!' Bates' narrow face darkened and there was a fanatical gleam in his eyes. 'There are no moral standards any longer, and the telly and the newspapers encourage it; fornication and depravity — it's all you see and hear, day in, day out. If I thought my daughters were behaving like that, I'd kill them! I'd rather they were in the grave than carrying on like harlots.'

The man was possessed, thought Roland, carrying on like an Old Testament prophet. His sympathy went out to the Bates' girls and their unfortunate mother.

'So you think the person you heard in the woods last night was Bradley Scott?'

'Could have been. I don't know, do I? Couldn't catch up with him.'

'Could it have been a woman?'

'You mean *she* was visitin' *him?* Well, I suppose so.' The idea seemed to amuse him. 'She must have been keen, to venture out on a night like last night.'

'How well did you know Julian Lester?'

'He was only an acquaintance.' Bates was alarmed. 'He kept open house but I don't think anyone was really close to him.'

'Well, thank you, Mr. Bates, that will be all for now, but I shall want an official statement later and you will be called to the inquest.'

After Bates had left, Mansfield made a face. 'I reckon he's a dirty old man underneath all that proselytising. It's just a cover-up for his lecherous mind.'

'Interesting, though. I wonder if he really *did* hear and see someone around yesterday evening, or whether he was just

114

throwing out titbits he's gathered on other occasions to stir up trouble. It will bear looking into.'

'Especially as Jean has heard rumours that Mrs. Garfield has a boyfriend, identity unknown. What now?'

'We get down on our hands and knees and search. Somewhere amongst all these papers should be the sheet that was in the typewriter, though I'm surprised the wind was strong enough to snatch it out of the carriage. The pill bottle should be on the floor as well, it's probably rolled under something.

They searched for it unsuccessfully, and between them gathered up all the loose sheets of paper scattered around the room. Each one was blank.

'That's odd, where can it be? It looks as if Lester must have roused himself after Bates saw him and taken it out of the typewriter himself.'

'Well, we know he must have roused himself, else how did he get outside?' Roland was thinking furiously. 'I expect what happened was this: he's sitting there in a drunken stupor when an extra strong gust of wind blows the door open. All hell would have been let loose and I reckon he comes to and wonders what's happening. He sees the page in the typewriter, probably creased up or spoiled where he's been leaning against it, and takes it out. Then he notices the door is open and ventures outside to see what is wrong. He trips over and collapses outside, too drunk to get up, and the sheet of paper is snatched out of his hand.'

'And is probably miles away by now, if it hasn't been torn to shreds.'

'On the other hand, maybe he shoved it in the top of the boiler.'

There was an old-fashioned solid fuel boiler in the corner of the room; a large, cumbersome affair with a wide stove pipe leading into the chimney. Mansfield put his hand on the black, chipped surface; it was still vaguely warm. He lifted up the fuel lid and peered inside.

'That's funny, it looks as it it's been stoked up recently.'

'It's not still alight, is it?'

'No, the pump and fan would be electrically operated so it would go out in a power cut, though not straight away.'

115

Roland joined him by the boiler and looked in the coke hod which stood nearby. It was nearly empty.

'Very odd. Very odd indeed. The power was cut off just after five so until then the boiler would have been functioning normally. Lester would last have stoked it sometime during the evening, before Bates saw him at nine o'clock. These things are gravity fed and between then and the boiler going out, due to the power cut, it should have consumed most of the fuel. But, as you say, it's nearly full. It can't have been replenished by Lester this morning − he'd already been dead for several hours.'

'So who, and why?'

'To get rid of something? Come on, let's have it all out.'

Mansfield found a newspaper under a cushion and they spread it out on the floor near the stove and painstakingly removed the anthracite nuts, shovel by shovel. The sheet of paper was near the bottom, crumpled, blackened and singed in one corner. Roland carefully smoothed it out and carried it over to the window. As he made out the typed message his eyebrows shot up and he whistled through his teeth.

'A suicide note? Now why . . .? Don't get your dabs on it as well,' he snapped as Mansfield put out a hand. He laid it on the table and the two men bent over it. The first part of the opening sentence was scorched and indecipherable but the rest was just legible. Mansfield read out slowly:

'. . . to end it all. There is nothing to look forward to except a lonely old age and increasing dependence on the bottle. What is the point? I choose to go whilst I still have some self-respect and a few friends.'

'But it doesn't make sense!' Mansfield frowned and spoke slowly. 'Unless he decided to do himself in last night, takes a lethal dose of something mixed with alcohol − whatever was in that pill bottle − slumps out cold over the typewriter where Bates sees him through the window; then he somehow comes to, changes his mind and tries to destroy the note, staggers outside to get help, collapses and lies there in a coma until he's carried off. And then, just by accident, a bloody great tree falls on him. How's that?'

'What happened to the pill bottle?'

'In his pocket?'

'It's not. I want the scene of crime boys in here and everything given the full treatment − if the bottle is anywhere around they'll find it. The letter goes straight to Forensics and I'm getting Doc Brasnett to run a check for barbiturates in the body.'

'You think he really did commit suicide along the lines I've suggested?'

'Think, man − the note. If he had put that note in the stove last night it would have been thoroughly incinerated by now as we've already noted, and the stove would have burnt out. That note was not put in there until *after* Lester was dead and the stove had gone out − by someone who hadn't realised it had, or the significance of the power cut. He put it in expecting it to be consumed immediately, and for good measure topped up the stove with the fuel in the hod.'

'You think Bates was lying? That he found the body as he said and had a poke around in here, discovered the note and decided to destroy it so that it would be thought an accidental death instead of suicide? Why should he do that?'

'Forget Bates. Suppose, just suppose, that our murderer realises that Lester has some information about Tim Spencer's murder that points the finger at him. He fears we're on the track and decides to silence him. He comes round armed with a bottle − it must be someone Lester knew − gets him boozed up and then slips a Mickey Finn into his glass. When Lester passes out he types the suicide note, removes *his* glass, makes sure that his fingerprints are not on the other glass and bottle and quietly departs. It could have been him whom Bates thought he heard going away from the cottage. He took a risk − only just escaped being seen by Bates though he probably didn't expect anyone else to be abroad on a night like last night.

'Something rouses Lester out of his drugged sleep and he goes outside and collapses as we've already conjectured. Now supposing our murderer decides this morning to check whether Lester really *is dead*. He may not be certain that he has given him a lethal dose, or he may be concerned that in his hurry last night he may have left some damning evidence laying around. Anyway, he comes back this morning − a brave man considering the hurricane hadn't blown itself out

117

– and discovers his victim lying in the garden pinned under a damn great tree. It must have seemed an absolute gift. All he has to do is remove the suicide note and the pill bottle and everyone will think that Lester was killed by the falling tree. He made two mistakes, though; firstly, putting the note in the stove instead of taking it with him, and secondly, not checking whether Lester's injuries were serious enough to have caused death.'

'So you think he was murdered – and by the same person who knocked off Spencer?'

'There's just one snag to my theory: why did the murderer wait all this time before deciding to shut Lester's mouth? It's weeks since we discovered the identity of the skeleton – why didn't he act straight away instead of waiting until now? He couldn't have known that it was only yesterday that we learned that Lester had actually *seen* Tim Spencer when he returned home.'

'Perhaps Lester was putting the squeeze on him, and rather than spend the rest of his natural in the hands of a blackmailer he decided to eliminate him when he got the chance – and the opportunity arose yesterday evening?'

'It's a possibility. This is all conjecture so far but we could be right. Our murderer shows an ingenious and cunning mind, though he's not above making careless mistakes – unless he's so arrogant he thinks he can get away with anything.'

'You think it is a man?'

Roland looked at his sergeant with narrowed eyes.

'There's no reason why the murderer should not be a woman. There was no physical strength involved in this death, and as for Tim Spencer's murder ... a woman would have been just as capable as a man of blasting him down with a shotgun. And once dead, any reasonably strong, healthy woman could have buried him, given the right opportunity. He wasn't a giant of a man – five feet nine inches and slightly built. No, there's no way we can rule out the gentler sex.'

'In particular Ginny Dalton?'

'We can make out a good case against her already; getting proof is another matter. Will she be able to come up with an alibi for last night and this morning, that's what I ask myself, Patrick? That's the next task ahead, checking the alibis of any one who had any connection with the original murder, no matter how tenuous. I also want a list of everyone who was on drinking terms with Lester.'

'From what I've heard, I'd hazard that was half the adult population of Croxton.'

'They must be checked out, and we must try and discover the identity of the person Bates heard near here last night, always supposing it is not a figment of his imagination. There's also the local poacher − what's his name? − Alfie Coutts. Come on, Patrick, we've work to do, though whether the big police machine will grind to a halt as a result of the hurricane remains to be seen.'

By mid-morning the gale had more or less blown itself out but horrendous reports were still coming in of the damage left in its wake. Miraculously, no-one else had died but the hospitals in the area dealt with a spate of minor injuries, and with so many places still cut-off and communications fragmentary it was some time before the authorities were able to grasp a true picture of the enormity of the natural disaster that had struck the area. The electricity board scrambled its entire workforce to cope with the crisis but it soon became clear that, even working round the clock, it was going to be days rather than hours before many homes were once more connected to the national grid, and in some isolated places this lapse could stretch to weeks. Teams were drafted in from all over the country and in the meantime people made do with candles, oil lamps, camping stoves and open fires, and those with gas ovens found themselves cooking for their less fortunate neighbours.

James Roland was caught up in the general emergency and it was some hours before he could concentrate on the tragedy at Smoky Cottage. The first piece of information confirming his theory about Julian Lester's death came from Forensics. When he heard their preliminary report he went in search of his sergeant and shared the news.

'Julian Lester's fingerprints were the only ones on the gin bottle and glass. The suicide note was more difficult − it was very smeared but they've found traces of his dabs on that and also mine.'

119

'So if he was murdered, his killer must have pressed his fingers on the paper after he was unconscious. Any others?'

'Nothing distinguishable.'

'So as our murderer was probably wearing gloves, there's no way of proving that it was handled by anyone else. I can't see why you're looking so pleased.'

'Because the note wasn't typed on Lester's typewriter.'

Mansfield looked suitably impressed. 'That's quite definite?'

'Yes. In the note, the upper case "W" is out of alignment and the lower case "a" is filled in; faults which don't exist on Lester's machine. They're sending the note to Birmingham in the hope that the Home Office Forensic Scientists can pinpoint the make or type of machine that was used. And something else − there were no fingerprints on Lester's typewriter apart from two clear prints of his on the carriage return lever − nothing on the shift bar or on the keys themselves which means our murderer must have wiped it over. If Lester was using it regularly, there should have been a mass of prints all over it. The paper used, by the way, was Watermark Bond which you can buy in any stationer's.'

'So it looks as if you're right. Any news yet from Doc Brasnett?'

'No, he's taking his time and he can't claim he's overworked today.'

The man himself breezed into Roland's office a short while later, oozing confidence and affability.

'Ah, James, I didn't know whether I'd find you here or not. Thought you might have been drafted into a tree-clearing operation.' His chuckle bounced round the room.

'Don't be too confident *you're* safe. The way things are going, we may all end up in a chain gang. What have you got for me?'

'Some interesting finds. Our friend had certainly been drinking, his blood alcohol level was 140mg per 100 ml, there was dried vomit round the mouth and nose, suggesting that whilst lying comatose on his back he vomited and inhaled; the irritant effects of the gastric juices would have rapidly produced an outpouring of fluid into the lungs, resulting in pneumonia.' He consulted his notes. 'There is turbid fluid in the air passage and the lungs are heavy, 800-1000g. each, exuding copious amounts of haemorrhagic fluid.' He looked up and grinned nastily. 'That means to a lay man like you that when you press your fingertip on the cut surface, it tears into the lung tissues quite easily.'

'Spare us the details. What else?'

'The stomach contains alcoholic-smelling fluid and a little partly digested food; the gastric mucose is congested. His liver's fatty, suggesting that he was an habitual drinker, but the other organs are healthy, showing congestion only.'

'So ... the cause of death?'

'Pneumonia aided by hypothermia and alcohol poisoning. Do you still want barbiturate screening?'

'I think he was helped to his end.'

'Right, if you insist.'

'And time of death?'

'He was certainly dead by three a.m. Possibly a little earlier, say between one-thirty and two-thirty a.m. Death would have taken place between three and four hours after inhaling the vomit, aided by the fact that he was lying outside on a cold, wet night.'

'And the damage inflicted by the tree?'

'Superficial injuries that definitely occurred after death.'

'How nice to hear you definite about something for once.'

'I'm not laying myself open to misquotation just to please you, James. This is all off the cuff. I thought you'd be panting to hear my preliminary findings. You'll get my official report later.'

'Plus the results of the barbiturate screening?'

'I presume all this ties in with your bone case? Any leads yet, or shouldn't I ask?'

'You've got the prime one on your slab.'

'Like that, is it? Ah, well ...' He went out humming the Policemen's Chorus from "The Pirates of Penzance", and Roland and Mansfield exchanged rueful grimaces behind his back.

Later Roland marshalled his team and gave out his instructions.

'The evidence so far points to Lester's having been murdered. This would appear to tie in with our investigation into Tim Spencer's death, but we mustn't overlook the fact that he could have been bumped off by somebody else for reasons quite unconnected with our case, so we'll have to check out everyone who knew him locally and also his business acquaintances. He had a shop at Woodford and I suppose he could have been indulging in some hanky-panky on the antiques' front, it's a cut-throat business. He could, for instance, have been running a nice line in fakes. That's your job, Evans. Get over to Woodford and see if you can sniff out anything along those lines. Get a list of regular customers and find out if he had any dealings with local people.'

'I want you, Pomroy, to check the people living in the vicinity of Smoky Cottage. I know it's pretty isolated but someone that end of the village may have seen or heard something last night or early this morning, even if it was only someone going about his legitimate business. They must be cleared and their alibis checked.'

Roland paused and tapped his pen against his teeth.

'You, Mansfield, had better interview this Alfie Coutts and see if you can get any sense out of him. Being local yourself, you can probably deal with him better than anyone else. I think you had better pay another visit to your friend the ex-headmaster and see if he can give us any pointers as to who was on dropping-in terms at Smoky Cottage. Whilst you're in Duck Lane you may as well see what Mrs. Dalton has to say for herself. We know she was on friendly terms with Lester.'

'Do we, sir?'

'Friendly enough to borrow furniture from him for the school play. He phoned her whilst I was there. I wonder whether she can produce an alibi for yesterday evening and this morning.'

'Are you sure you don't want to check out this one, sir?' said Mansfield woodenly.

'I am going to see the Garfields and Bradley Scott. Any questions?'

'What exactly are we looking for, sir?'

'Christ, Pomroy! I thought I'd made that clear! You're looking for anyone in the neighbourhood who was where they shouldn't have been and can't account for it; also anyone who

122

was known to have a grudge against the dead man. You can also compile a list of typewriters owned locally – make, model numbers, age and so forth – but don't exceed your powers. You haven't a search warrant.'

'Yes, sir – I mean, no, sir.'

When Evans and Pomroy had left, Roland sighed and said resignedly: 'I can't make out whether he's a complete moron masquerading as a star trainee, or whether he's really rather bright and hiding it from everyone.'

'I think he's quite bright but he's not sure what role he should be embracing.'

'Don't we all feel like that at times? Let's hope he carries conviction when he's interviewing.' Roland leaned back and clasped his hands behind his head. 'Well, Patrick, I think we're getting somewhere at last. Our murderer is alive and well and still in our midst. I was afraid we'd never bring anyone to book for a ten-year-old killing, that it would join the list of unsolved crimes, though I didn't want another murder to bring the case up-to-date.'

'You really think that Lester was killed because of a connection with the original murder?'

'It has to be so, it would be too much of a coincidence otherwise. We're going to nail the killer for both of them, so let's get moving.'

'When did you say the inquest was set for?'

'Next Thursday. We'll get an adjournment.'

Chapter Seven

Alfie Coutts lived with his widowed sister in the same row of council houses as Ada Cattermole. When Mansfield called he found him huddled in an armchair in the dining room still dressed in his outdoor clothes, including the disreputable cloth cap without which he had never been seen in living memory. The youth of the village had been known to place bets on whether he ever actually removed it or whether he wore it to bed. The question had never been answered to anyone's satisfaction.

Edith Smith, the sister, answered the door. When Mansfield had identified himself, she led him through to where Alfie was sitting and said in a loud voice: 'It's the police to see you.'

Alfie was alarmed. He seemed to burrow deeper into the chair and squinted up at the burly sergeant with frightened pale blue eyes and twitching eyebrows. He reminded Mansfield of a hamster his children had once owned.

'I int done northen.'

'No-one's saying you have, Alfie. I'm hoping you can help me with some enquiries I'm making.'

'I int done northen,' he repeated, shrinking still further into the tatty upholstery.

'I believe you were in Croxton Wood yesterday evening. Did you go near Smoky Cottage?'

If Alfie had been alarmed before, by now he was downright frightened.

'I int done northen,' he reiterated, throwing his sister an entreating glance. 'You tell 'im, Edie.'

'He don't know nothing about Smoky Cottage,' she complied, fixing Mansfield with a furious scowl.

'About what?'

'About that furniture bloke getting himself killed. T'weren't nothing to do with Alfie.'

'I'm sure it wasn't, but did you see or hear anyone else in the woods?' Roland turned back to the brother.

'There weren't northen there,' Alfie rolled his eyes, 'no bird nor beast − it weren't right.'

'I'm talking about people, Alfie, not wildlife.'

Alfie ignored him and went on muttering: 'T'wern't right, no bird nor beast − they must'a knowed. It weren't natural.'

'Does he understand what I'm asking?' Mansfield appealed to the sister. 'I just want to know if he saw anyone else about in the woods yesterday evening.'

'Alfie don't go looking for people,' said Edith Smith sullenly, and Mansfield tried to curb his exasperation. He reckoned there was very little to choose between the intellectual powers of the couple. If Alfie was the village idiot, his sister ran him a close second.

'I'm sure he doesn't, but he may have noticed something when he was − er − taking his walk. It could be important.'

'I int seed northen.' Alfie rocked to and fro shaking his head. 'Edie − where's my tea?'

In common with the rest of the village, the house was without power, but an ancient tin kettle had been placed on the fire which burned in the open fireplace and this was now beginning to hum and dribble sizzling drops on the tiled hearth.

'Do the policeman go, I'll make yew a nice cup of tea.'

Edith eyed Mansfield craftily and he acknowledged defeat. It was useless, like trying to trap water in a sieve. He took his leave, feeling decidedly disgruntled. He would have felt even more thwarted if he could have seen Alfie as soon as the door closed behind him. The scruffy reprobate was chuckling to himself and beaming round the room with a knowing eye.

Mathew Betts was in his garden, trying to pull upright the fencing panels that were leaning crazily over the footpath.

'Here, let me give you a hand.' Mansfield added his weight

125

and the two men hauled them back into place and secured them. 'Have you suffered much damage?'

'Some slates off the other side of the roof, and my greenhouse is a write-off. My chrysanthemums are now non-existent. Still, I've been lucky compared to a lot of people. Come inside and tell me what brings you to this neck of the woods on a day like this. I take it it isn't a social call?'

'Too true. You've heard about Julian Lester's death?'

Betts eyed his ex-pupil with surprise. 'Yes, killed by a falling tree. Don't tell me you're investigating that?'

'We're treating his death as suspicious. Between you and me, he was dead before it fell on him, but I can't say more than that.'

'Re-a-lly? Well ... how can I help?'

'You see and hear most of what goes on in this village. I want to know who were his friends, who was in the habit of visiting him at Smoky Cottage, drinking with him.'

'I think you'll find that covers a wide range of people. Are you sure you shouldn't be interviewing my Mrs. Cattermole if you want to know everybody's business?'

'God forbid! It may come to that yet, but if you can give me any pointers?'

'I don't think he had any close friends. He was basically a lonely man but he encouraged people to drop in on a casual basis. If you're suspecting everyone on those terms with him, you'd better add me to the list.'

'How well did you know him?'

'As well as anyone, I suppose, and I know that's not very helpful. He drank too much, you know. He wasn't an alcoholic but he was going that way, yet he had his standards. He didn't like hitting the bottle on his own; boozing with a companion seemed to square his conscience on the subject of over-indulgence.'

'So what was he really like?'

Betts pondered this as Mansfield lit up his pipe.

'Well, as I said, he was a loner. He seemed reasonably content with his lot but I always had the feeling that life hadn't come up to his expectations. He'd been married once, way back in the past, but he lived a typical bachelor existence.'

126

'And his antiques' business?'

'He made a living, I presume. I know he lives — lived — in some squalor, but it was by choice rather than circumstance. I can't think that he had any enemies or that anyone disliked him enough to kill him. You do mean that he was murdered, I suppose?'

A short while later Mansfield left the Old Manse armed with a list of names. On this list were three about which he had specifically enquired.

Ginny Dalton was also in her garden, gazing up at the stricken roof of her cottage. One of the chimneys had crashed down on to the left-hand dormer window, shattering it and leaving a gaping hole in the roof. Bricks and tiles were scattered over a wide area of the garden, together with a tangle of tree limbs and uprooted plants. The cat crouched by her side, tail lashing furiously as the wind ruffled her fur.

Ginny Dalton was looking very shaken, as well she might, thought Mansfield.

'Has it caused much damage inside?'

'Enough.' She registered his presence with a little frown. 'Mr. Bilham, the local builder, has promised to send someone round to rig up a tarpaulin as a temporary measure to keep out the wet, until it can be repaired. Did you want something?'

'A few words with you, ma'am, if you please.'

'Whatever is it now? I should have thought you'd have had other things on your mind today.'

'A murder enquiry takes priority. Shall we go inside?'

Reluctantly, she led the way indoors. 'I really have told you all I know about Tim Spencer, Sergeant, you're wasting your time.'

'I am making enquiries in connection with the death of a Mr. Julian Lester.'

'Julian Lester? But he has been killed by a tree — during the hurricane last night.'

'We have reason to believe that he died yesterday evening before the hurricane started.'

She sat down abruptly on a chair and stared at him.

'Was it suicide?'

'We're treating his death as suspicious.'

'But why come to me? What has it to do with me?' Two red blotches burned on her cheeks in a face which had drained of colour at his news.

'This is a routine enquiry. We have to check with all the people who knew him. He was a friend of yours, I understand?'

'He was a casual acquaintance, I wouldn't have called him a friend.'

'Then I'm sure you won't mind telling me your whereabouts yesterday evening between eight o'clock and ten, and again this morning between five o'clock and seven.'

'I was here. I'd had a hectic day at school, and after catching up with some correspondence I listened to a concert on the radio and decided to have an early night. I must have been in bed by ten o'clock.'

'And this morning?'

'Are you joking! I was huddled down here, listening to the gale and wondering if I was going to have any roof left over my head!'

'And can you prove this? I presume your son was here also?'

'No, as it happens he was not. He went to a scout meeting in Wallingford with a friend and he stayed there overnight to save my having to turn out to pick him up.'

'So he can't give you an alibi?'

'No, he can't, and I'm very glad – and shall I tell you why? Come with me, Sergeant.'

She jumped up and headed for the stairs.

'Mrs. Dalton ...'

'Come with me,' she ordered, and he shrugged and followed her up the stairs. She paused on the landing and then dramatically threw open one of the doors leading off it. 'There ... see for yourself!'

Mansfield stepped into the room and immediately saw what she meant. The room was the boy's bedroom, with all the belongings of a teenage boy in evidence. It was also the room through which the chimney stack had crashed. Rubble and brickdust strewed the floor and there were bricks scattered across the bed. A large chunk of masonry lay across the pillow.

'If Simon had been here last night, he would have been killed!'

Mansfield was shaken. 'He certainly had a lucky escape. Has he returned home since?'

'No, the friend's parents are keeping him there for the time being.'

'How are you making out?'

'I have an open fire, as you see — it was the other chimney stack that went — and I have a camping Gaz stove and plenty of candles.'

They were downstairs again by this time and Mansfield glanced over towards the table laden with books and portfolios which stood by the window.

'Do you own a typewriter, Mrs. Dalton?'

'A typewriter? No.' She appeared mystifed by the question.

'Thank you for your help. That will be all for now.' He turned towards the door but she stopped him.

'Sergeant, what happened to Julian Lester? How did he die?'

'That's classified information at the moment, ma'am.'

He left her staring after him with a baffled expression in her odd eyes.

The concrete track leading from the road to The Hermitage was blocked by a fallen tree, but from the scene of activity that met Roland's eyes as he drove up, it would not remain obstructed for long. The high-pitched whine of a power saw pierced the air, and through a blue cloud of exhaust he saw the pulsating petrol-driven generator that was powering the tool and the team of men at work on the operation. This was what having money and influence meant, thought Roland. Whilst the rest of the village struggled on with no power and no prospects of it being restored in the near future, Tony Garfield had managed to organise his own personal work-force and equipment to deal with a single toppled tree.

He left his car by the side of the track and approached on foot. Garfield, dressed in a sheepskin jacket and green wellingtons was standing by the cavernous hole left by the uprooted tree. When he saw Roland he walked to meet him and the detective saw that he looked grey and exhausted. He wondered what other damage his property might have sustained as a result of the hurricane.

'Inspector Roland — what brings you here?'

'Trouble?' Roland indicated the blocked track.

'No more, I suppose, than many people in the area have suffered. We should get this cleared soon.'

'Are your power lines down?'

'Yes, but I've got an emergency generator up at the house so that's not too much of a problem. What can I do for you, Inspector? It must be important to bring you out here today.'

'A matter of life and death, sir — or rather, death. I should like to ask you some questions in connection with the death of Mr. Julian Lester of Smoky cottage.'

'Lester? The poor chap was killed by a tree, I understand — what has that to do with me? I'm surprised someone of your rank has been delegated to deal with an accidental death.'

'I'm afraid it is not quite as straightforward as that, sir, there are complications. . .' He watched the other man closely as he spoke but Garfield only looked bewildered.

'Complications? What do you mean?'

The saw which had been temporarily silent roared into life again, rasping the air. By unspoken consensus the two men moved further away down the track.

'We are treating his death as suspicious.'

'You mean he wasn't killed by a tree? Was it suicide?'

'Have you reason to think he might have committed suicide?'

'No, why should I? Look, Inspector, what is this all about? How did he die?'

'I am not at liberty to divulge that at the moment, Mr. Garfield, but we're checking with all the people who knew him.'

'Are you saying he was murdered?'

As Roland still said nothing, he ruffled up indignantly.

'Are you suggesting that *I* had anything to do with his death?' It could have been righteous indignation or he could be trying to bluster to cover guilt. Either way, Garfield was now looking annoyed and offended. His features sharpened in stark contrast to his usual amiable mien, and he seemed to grow in stature.

130

'This is just routine, sir,' said Roland blandly, 'so that we can eliminate you from our enquiries. I'm sure you won't mind telling me where you were yesterday evening?'

'I was in town,' he replied shortly.

'You mean London?'

'Yes, of course. My offices are in the City and I often stay overnight through pressure of work.'

'You stay overnight at your office?'

'No, Inspector, I have a flat, a pied-à-terre, in Elbury Street. I had arranged to meet an ex-colleague for dinner, but unfortunately he cried off at the last moment and as it was a foul evening I decided to stay in town and catch up with some work.'

'May I have the address of your flat?'

'No. 6, Elbury Court.'

'And you were there from . . . ?'

'About six o'clock. I rang my wife around nine to tell her I wouldn't be home. She is used to my staying in town when I'm busy so she wasn't surprised.'

'Can you substantiate this?'

Garfield looked pained. 'I exchanged pleasantries with the janitor when I arrived. I'm sure he'll remember seeing me.'

'And did you go out later to dine?'

'No, I cooked myself a snack in the flat.'

'So no-one saw you yesterday evening after approximately six o'clock?'

'Oh no, Inspector, rest assured I have a cast-iron alibi for later.' He chuckled and looked almost playful: 'A bomb scare.'

'A bomb scare?'

"Yes. Someone telephoned the local police station and said that a bomb had been planted in the basement of the block of flats, and was due to go off in fifteen minutes. We were all winkled out of our beds and accounted for. It was rather like being back at school again, answering roll-call. We were turned out into the cold night air whilst the police carried out a search. It turned out to be a hoax, and after they were satisfied that it was a false alarm we were allowed back inside.'

'What time would this have been?'

131

'A little after eleven o'clock.'

'Well, that seems straightforward, sir, thank you for your co-operation.'

'Inspector, what is this all about?'

'We have reason to believe that Julian Lester's death is connected with the murder of your cousin, Timothy Spencer.'

Again Roland watched the other man closely to see what his reaction would be to this information. Garfield looked astonished.

'With Tim? This is beyond me – are you saying that Lester was responsible for Tim's death?'

'No, but I believe he may have known who was. Tell me, Mr. Garfield, where were you in the summer of 1978 when Spencer returned to this country?'

'I can hardly believe this – are you accusing me of killing Tim?'

'You inherited half your great-aunt's, Mrs. Fellingham's, estate. If Spencer had lived, you would only have received a third; or even, if local rumour is to be believed, nothing at all. He could have scooped the lot. Men have been killed for much less than that. But I am not accusing you, Mr. Garfield, this is all hypothesis. I am merely exploring the possibilities. I do not know yet who killed Spencer but I intend finding out and therefore I am investigating anyone who had any connections with him, no matter how remote. I'm sure you appreciate that you must figure on that list. If you are innocent, you can surely have nothing to hide.'

'Very nicely put, Inspector,' said Garfield wryly, plunging his hands deep into his pockets and hunching his shoulders. 'I can assure you that I want Tim's murderer brought to justice, so ask away.'

'You haven't answered the question I just put to you.'

'Summer 1978? That was the summer I was in partnership with an estate agent in Woodford. I was living in a flat there and spending the odd weekend with Great-aunt at the Hall.'

'And can you think of anyone around at that time who could have had it in for Spencer when he returned to Croxton?'

'Inspector, I've been wrestling with that question ever since I've known of Tim's death, and apart from Bates the game-

132

keeper, I can't come up with an answer. It's just crazy — and yet, on the other hand, I've sometimes thought that someone had it in for all the members of the family — an attempt was made on my life at about the same time.'

'What do you mean?'

'I was the victim of a hit and run accident just outside this village. I was lucky, I got away with superficial injuries, but there's no doubt that the driver of the car that struck me deliberately tried to run me down.'

'Did you report it?'

'Yes, but the police never caught him. It happened late one evening. I had run out of petrol and was walking back to the village with a petrol can when I heard a car coming along. I put out a hand to flag him down, and he slowed and then suddenly accelerated straight towards me. I tried to jump out of the way but he caught me on the hip and I was thrown against a tree trunk. I still bear the scars on my leg,' he gestured towards his booted ankle, 'and I was knocked unconscious. When I came to, the car had gone and eventually I managed to limp to the nearest house and summon help. The police never traced him — I'm afraid I was not much help — it was dark and I was unable to identify the make or model of car. I only knew that it was a dark saloon, and of course I hadn't seen the driver.'

Roland's mind was now spinning away on a new tack. A whole new angle to the case was opening up, but he was careful to disguise his suspicions from the man beside him. 'A nasty episode but hardly relevant to Timothy Spencer's death. Tell me, sir, what about the third cousin — the one in America who inherited with you? Did he ever come over here, have you met him?'

'Leslie? No, Inspector. He was the grandchild of Aunt Gertrude's sister, Ivy. Ivy's daughter married a geologist who travelled the world, and Leslie was born abroad and settled in the States.'

'You have never been in touch?'

'No. Leslie Drew is just a name as far as I'm concerned. A remote cousin with whom I really have no connection. You surely can't think that he had anything to do with Tim's death?'

Roland ignored the question and changed the subject.

'To get back to the present, what time did you get back from town today?'

'Around mid-morning.'

'By train?'

Garfield regarded the detective with suspicion. 'The line from Liverpool Street to Norwich is closed, surely you know that?'

'Yes, of course, my mistake. So you drove up — quite a hair-raising journey, I should imagine?'

'Not for the faint-hearted.'

'Is that your car?' Roland indicated the red estate car that stood by the side of the track near to where the men were working.

'No, mine is in the car park of the Duck and Spoon. That vehicle belongs to the vet. My wife's mare injured herself in the storm and he is up at the stables now, checking her over.'

'I should like a few words with Mrs. Garfield. I'll make my own way up, sir,' as Garfield made as if to go with him, 'there's no need for you to accompany me, I know you're busy here.'

Out-manoeuvred, Garfield could only watch impotently as Roland stepped off the track and picked his way carefully round the prostrate crown of the tree whose damaged, skeletal branches spread over a wide area of the stubble field.

As far as Roland could see, The Hermitage had not suffered any significant damage in the hurricane, but the garden was a shambles. Innumerable ornamental trees had been laid low, shrubs flattened, and leaves and twigs were thick on the ground. The virginia creeper had been torn from the west wing and hung down in forlorn scarlet and maroon loops from the exposed brickwork. Roland ducked beneath it and made his way round to the stables.

Lee Garfield and the vet were standing in the yard, talking animatedly. They broke off as he approached, and he was aware that they were both regarding him curiously.

'Inspector Roland, this is a surprise. Surely you're not sleuthing on a day like this — or is it a social call?'

'If you could spare me a few minutes, Mrs. Garfield, it

134

would be appreciated. I'm afraid I've called at an inopportune moment.'

'Mr. Winterton is going now. My mare got frightened in the storm, and whilst lashing out cut a fetlock.'

'Not serious, I hope?'

'She'll do fine,' the vet answered. He was a compact, weather-beaten man dressed in ancient tweeds with an equally ancient tweed trilby pulled low over his forehead. 'Try and keep her quiet and I'll look in in a couple of days.' He touched his hat to the woman and nodded to Roland. 'Is the track clear yet?'

'No, but they're making progress, it shouldn't be long.'

'Shocking business, never known anything like it in all the time I've been living in Suffolk.' He picked up his case and strode away round the corner of the building.

Lee Garfield was dressed in a purple anorak and cords. The wind had whipped a healthy colour into her cheeks and her hair was a black cloud. She was a very physical person, thought Roland. Compared with her, her husband seemed pale and insignificant.

'Well, how can I help you, Inspector? I presume you saw Tony down there?' She gestured in the direction of the driveway.

'Yes, ma'am, he told me you were here. I'm checking up on the movements of everyone in the vicinity yesterday evening and this morning.'

'Whatever for? Have you turned up another skeleton?'

'This one is clothed in flesh, so to speak.'

That stopped her in her tracks. 'You've found a body? Whose?'

'A Mr. Julian Lester of Smoky Cottage.'

'Julian? But we heard that he'd been killed in the hurricane ... I don't understand.'

'We have reason to believe his death was not accidental. We are treating it as suspicious.'

'You don't say?' She assimilated this with curiosity but no alarm. 'Perhaps we had better go inside.'

'This shouldn't take long.' He felt a strange reluctance to be closeted alone with this woman in an empty house. She exuded sexuality in a way that disturbed him. Christ! Patrick

135

would be wetting himself if he knew how his chief was reacting. What was he afraid of − her or himself? To allow any hint of intimacy to develop would be strictly out of order; better to avoid contact altogether.

'I believe you and your husband knew Julian Lester?'

'Well, I suppose you could say so. I collect miniatures and Julian kept an eye open for any coming on the market. Between us we made several interesting finds.'

'You visited Smoky Cottage?'

'Yes, Inspector, I have been to Smoky Cottage on occasion, though I didn't make a habit of it.' Damn it, the woman was laughing at him, amusement smouldering in her dark eyes.

'What about your husband?'

'Tony occasionally put business in his way. As a property dealer, he's often involved in slum clearance and that sort of thing, and he would tip Julian the wink − I think that is the expression? − if there was anything due for demolition that might interest him. It's surprising how collectable old Victorian fireplaces and such like are becoming.'

'Do you own a typewriter, Mrs. Garfield?'

'A typewriter? No.'

'What about your husband?'

'It depends on what you mean by typewriter. This is the age of the micro chip. Tony's into word processors and all that. But he probably has the odd one or two lying around in his office − you'll have to ask him.'

'I understand that Mr. Garfield spent yesterday evening and last night at his flat in London, and that you were here?'

'Yes, he had hoped to get home but he rang me about nine o'clock to say he wasn't going to make it.'

'Were you alone?'

'Why, whatever do you mean, Inspector?' She was amused rather than annoyed.

'I mean,' said Roland heavily, 'was there anyone else in the house − sleep-in staff, servants?'

'Mr. and Mrs. Collins, the housekeeper and handyman, have a self-contained flat over the kitchen quarters. I assume they were there. I saw neither of them after about eight o'clock so I can't vouch for their presence and neither can they for mine. I'm afraid you'll have to take my word Inspector, that I was here ... and alone.'

She was being deliberately provocative, and Roland wondered if she were like this with every male who crossed her path. As he met her cool, amused stare he was suddenly convinced that she had indeed had company the previous evening and was challenging him to prove otherwise. Had it been Bradley Scott? Was it he whom Stephen Bates had heard near Smoky Cottage, and had he been on his way to The Hermitage, taking a short cut through the woods? Tony Garfield had rung her at nine o'clock to tell her he wouldn't be home. If Scott was her lover she could well have phoned him to tell him the coast was clear, and if he had answered her summons straight away he could well have been near Smoky Cottage at the relevant time. It would be interesting to hear what Bradley Scott had to say for himself.

'I see no reason to doubt your word at present, Mrs. Garfield. By the way, does anyone live here?' He indicated the hay loft which had obviously been converted into a flat. Curtains hung at the windows and a permanent wrought-iron staircase led down to ground level.

'Not at present. It was the live-in quarters for the stable boy but my husband decided we no longer needed one.'

'I thought the fashion nowadays was for stable girls; one hears of all these horse-mad young women working for a pittance in order to get a ride.'

'I don't encourage young girls, Inspector, only young men.'

He managed to outstare her and get in the last word.

'If it ever becomes imperative for you to produce an alibi, I hope you will be able to come up with something more ... concrete?'

With this parting shot he left her, aware that he had come out of the interview somewhat more ruffled than she.

Bradley Scott was clearly very upset by Julian Lester's death. After Roland had identified himself and been asked into his house, the writer paced the floor, shaking his head and tugging at his beard.

'Poor old sod! To think a fluke accident like that could carry him off.'

He seemed to find nothing untoward in the fact that a CID officer had arrived on his doorstep to ask questions about a presumably accidental death.

'Julian Lester was dead several hours before the hurricane struck. The tree falling on his body is quite irrelevant.'

'Do you say?' Scott whistled in surprise. 'I suppose he had drunk himself silly and suffered a heart attack? Or do you mean it was suicide?'

'Have you reason to think that he might have committed suicide?' This time he got a purposeful answer.

'No reason that I know of, but I suppose if anyone could be said to be a candidate for suicide he fits the bill.'

'Would you mind explaining that?'

'It's difficult to explain what I mean. I always sensed that deep down he was a dilillusioned and unhappy man. Unfulfilled, I suppose you could say. He dabbled in the antiques' business but was never fully committed; he was trying to write a book but it never got off the ground. He couldn't seem to get his act together, if you see what I mean, and of course he drank too much.'

'How well did you know him?'

'Well enough. I first met him at the local. We got friendly and I got into the habit of dropping in on him when I was near Smoky Cottage – you could always be sure of receiving hospitality,' he grinned wryly, 'and sometimes he came here. He had a good brain on him and was an interesting talker, but I felt he had wasted his life and I think he knew it too.'

'How long have you lived here, Mr. Scott?'

'Eight or nine years. I was lucky, Inspector, I received a legacy that enabled me to throw up my job and do what I had always wanted to do – travel and write.'

'What job was that?'

'I was an engineer working on oil rig constructions. I travelled a great deal in the course of that work but after coming into my inheritance I was able to see the world from another perspective. I bought this house so as to have a permanent base to which to return.'

'And what made you choose Croxton?'

138

'I had always loved the Suffolk coast, and my ancestors came from these parts.'

'You have never married, Mr. Scott?'

'No. My lifestyle, both in the old days and now, doesn't leave room for permanent relationships. I value my freedom – a confirmed bachelor, I'm afraid.'

'But you look out for your comforts, I see. This is not a typical bachelor pad.'

Roland looked about him appreciatively, unable to prevent himself from comparing Scott's domicile with his own. The place was neat and agreeably furnished but somewhat spartan in appearance. One would have expected a travel writer to have accumulated a quantity of souvenirs and keepsakes from his travels round the world. Scott's walls and surfaces were singularly free from such ornamentation.

'May I see your typewriter?'

'Whatever turns you on, Inspector.'

He led the way into his study. Books and maps lined the walls and a sturdy desk occupied a prime position in the room. On this desk was a golfball-type machine. Too modern, thought Roland, but it must be checked out.

'Would you please type me out a few sentences?'

Scott gave him an odd look, then shrugged and sat down at the desk. He was a self-taught typist but had progressed beyond two finger status. Roland reckoned him a four-finger protagonist, and those fingers fairly flew over the keys. In the space of a few seconds he had finished, and with a flourish snatched the sheet out of the carriage and handed it to the detective.

On it was typed: "The Inspector has come a-visiting. I do not know the reason for the visit ????"

'Thank you, sir,' said Roland, pocketing it. 'To return to Lester's death – would you mind telling me what you were doing yesterday evening?'

'I was here.'

'All the while? You didn't go out at all?'

Scott looked surprised at the question. 'I'm getting together the itinerary for my next expedition. I'm off on my travels in a few weeks' time.'

'So you were working here all the evening – what time did you go to bed?'

139

'About eleven-thirty, and slept like a log. Didn't see anything of the gale until my garden shed was blown away and crashed against the kitchen window. What has all this to do with Lester's death?'

'We have reason to believe he was murdered.'

'Murdered! But I thought you said it was suicide?'

'It was *you* who suggested suicide, sir, if you remember,' said Roland gently but firmly. 'I'm trying to establish if you have an alibi for yesterday evening and this morning.'

'An alibi? Well, no, I was here all alone all the time but I can't prove it.'

'You're quite sure you didn't go out yesterday evening?'

'No, I've told you, Inspector,' he was getting annoyed, 'I was here all the while.'

Roland decided to try a long shot.

'Suppose I tell you that someone saw you in Croxton Woods yesterday evening, near Smoky Cottage.'

'They couldn't have done!' He was agitated and started to bluster. 'It must have been a mistake, it wasn't me! I sometimes take a walk through the woods to get some exercise, but not yesterday evening.'

'Are you sure?'

'We-ll, I may have popped out for a breather...I can't remember.'

'Can't remember? It was less than twenty hours ago, sir!'

'Yes, well, I believe I *did* go out for a short while, but I certainly didn't go anywhere near Smoky Cottage.'

'Are you sure? Your memory doesn't seem very reliable, sir. Of course, if you could prove you were nowhere near Smoky Cottage, it might be very much to your advantage.'

Roland took his leave, content that he had badly rattled the travel writer and convinced that wherever he had been last night, it hadn't been *chez soi*.

The unforeseen October hurricane totally changed the face of the Suffolk countryside. Landscapes that had remained immutable for centuries were irrevocably altered in a few hours, transformed out of all recognition; landmarks were razed and familiar outlines lost forever.

Some districts escaped relatively lightly; others would be

counting the costs for years to come. The village of Croxton came somewhere in the middle of the scale. Many properties had sustained considerable structural damage and countless trees and hedgerows had been laid low, but the main problem in the immediate aftermath was the lack of power. Those houses on the eastern side of the village nearest to the main road were re-connected within forty-eight hours, the rest of the inhabitants had to wait for up to five days. Freezers leaked pools of water from their de-frosting contents; ornamental candles, hurriedly appropriated from Christmas decoration boxes, were put to use as domestic supplies ran out, and ingenious methods of cooking on improvised stoves were thought up.

A large proportion of Croxton Woods, including Smoky Cottage, was declared unsafe and put out of bounds to the general public. Alfie Coutts, denied access to many of his usual haunts, took to spending more time in the Duck and Spoon where he regaled anyone who would listen with tales of the strange happenings in the woods on the night of the hurricane. It was not immediately understood that these phenomena did not pertain solely to the animal kingdom.

Tony Garfield wondered if his plans for developing Croxton Creek would be held up as a result of the disaster. As a partner in a well-known business consortium he had drawn up an ambitious scheme to build a marina and holiday village on his land abutting the shore. Local opposition would be aroused when the news got round; he was already having enough trouble on that score with his own wife. It would mean laying everything on the line and he needed Lee's co-operation. The knowledge that he seemed to be under a cloud of suspicion in connection with the police murder enquiry, ridiculous though it was and not to be taken seriously, was something he could well do without at present.

Bradley Scott went ahead with his plans for his forthcoming travels, but his heart was not in them. Who would have thought that after all this time events would catch up with him? Very soon he was going to have to make a decision, and whichever way he decided nothing would be the same again.

141

How had he become embroiled in the first place? Perhaps it was time to shake the dust of Croxton off his feet in a more permanent way. Once the police got on your back there was no telling where it would lead. And why was he, a professional writer, thinking in worn-out clichés?

Ginny Dalton alternated between bouts of panic and dazed abstraction. The thought of how close Simon had come to death paralysed her with horror. She had already lost the two loves of her life, Simon was all that remained to her. If anything should happen to him... Simon himself was unaware of his lucky escape. His bedroom had been cleared of debris before his return, and he exasperated his mother by complaining that he had missed all the fun.

Marian Bates, the long-suffering gamekeeper's wife, supposed she was lucky. Living as they did on the edge of the woods, their house could have been annihilated. As it was, the wind had been blowing in the other direction and everything had gone the other way. In fact, the gaps in the tree cover let in more light and lessened the gloomy atmosphere that usually hung over the property. It also meant that Stephen was kept extremely busy coping with the effects of the disaster on the gamebirds. He was out all hours of the day and although she knew it was wicked, she could only rejoice in anything that kept him out of the way of her and the girls.

She lived in daily dread of her daughters leaving home and deserting her, but how much longer could she expect them to put up with the strictures laid on them by their father? He had declared the disaster to be the act of an angry God punishing his wicked children, and she knew that she was still included in this category for having allowed little Kevin to stray on to the road all those years ago. Timothy Spencer had paid for his offence and was now at peace; she was going to go on paying whilst she still drew breath. And why was Stephen so shaken by Julian Lester's death?

Ada Cattermole, caught up in the drama of the situation, was proving very tiresome to her employer, Mathew Betts. She insisted on giving him a blow-by-blow account of every

142

mishap suffered by the entire population of the village. How she got to know all the intimate details in the first place was beyond him, but know she did and was determined to pass on the information.

Arthur's shed had been flattened and she declared that he was like a snail without a shell. Betts sympathised with him. He could understand the need for Ada's nearest and dearest to seek a refuge away from her wagging tongue; he only wished that he could stop the flow. Whilst he was prepared to admit that the hurricane, together with the Dutch elm disease of recent years, had done more to change the face of the countryside than the effects of the Industrial Revolution and World War Two combined,he didn't want to dwell on it. There were other forces at work in the village, malevolent forces that threw a pall of suspicion over the community.

As the villagers cleared up and life gradually got back to normal, a thread of speculation ran through the district. It engendered excitement, curiosity, mistrust and fear, and it centred around the death of Julian Lester. Those who knew the facts kept silent, but whispers and rumours circulated freely.

Was it an accidental death, suicide — or murder?

Chapter Eight

'Murder — we were right!' James Roland tapped the report in front of him. 'It's all here — a barbiturate level of 0.6mg per 100 ml has been confirmed.'

'So he died by barbiturate poisoning?' Mansfield knocked out his pipe in the ashtray on Roland's desk.

'I've had words with Brasnett, you know how he hates to commit himself. Apparently that amount corresponds to the victim absorbing about three capsules of Tuinal or something similar; enough to prove fatal to someone of frail build and unaccustomed to alcohol. This, of course, was not the case with Lester, but combined with inhalation of vomit, exposure and hypothermia, it was enough to carry him off.'

'Strange our murderer didn't make sure by giving him a larger dose.'

'It would be very bitter tasting, he was probably afraid that Lester would detect it — it must have been dissolved in the gin. He probably worried afterwards whether it had done the trick which is why he went back to check.'

'Any hope of tracing him through possession of the drug?'

'Barbiturates are very rarely prescribed nowadays, as you know, but it's not impossible for someone to have got hold of some Tuinal or Seconal capsules. They could have had them put by for some time.'

'So you think Julian Lester's death is definitely connected with Tim Spencer's murder?'

'It must be, I can't believe otherwise, and of course the information Pomroy turned up ties in with this.'

As expected, the inquest on Julian Lester was opened and

adjourned and the two detectives were now threshing over the latest developments and collating the evidence.

'We've heard from Birmingham about the suicide note. It was probably typed on an Adler typewriter; an older office manual model, possibly at least fifteen years old. It's not much to go on – you can't tell at a glance what age a machine is – but at least we know it's not one of your modern office wonders.'

'Evans has had no luck with the antiques shop angle, I take it?'

'He still has a few names to check out but everything seems to be above board and normal. The impression he got from the regular customers he contacted was that Lester ran a genuine business and knew his stuff, but was curiously reluctant to encourage trade. He didn't actually turn custom away but he certainly didn't go out of his way to attract it. The shop could have been far more of a money spinner than it was.'

'That could tie in with the fact that he was making his money through blackmail, and the income from the business was of secondary importance.'

'Hmm, it's worth bearing in mind. Pomroy has had no luck with the locals. Nobody admits to being out that evening except those with watertight alibis, but the general feeling seems to be that if anybody saw anything it would be your Alfie Coutts.'

'Well, it would take a better man than me, Gunga Din, to get any sense out of him.'

'Still, I think we'll have to have another go at him. Perhaps Evans can woo him with his Welsh rhetoric. Pomroy got a list of typewriters and their owners. He got samples of type from all but two, and I think they were just being bloody-minded. Needless to say, none of them match up with the suicide note.'

'So where does this leave us?'

'With the same list of suspects for Julian Lester's murder as we have for Tim Spencer's. Our enquiries so far into Lester's death haven't thrown up any new names, so let's go through them again.'

Roland consulted his notes. 'First, Stephen Bates. He could

have done it, but if so why did he tell us about having seen Lester slumped unconscious over the typewriter the night before, and draw our attention to the missing pill bottle and sheet of paper in the machine? It doesn't make sense. Mind you, he has such a warped view of life and seems so unbalanced on some subjects that it's impossible to put a rational interpretation on all his statements. I don't think he's our man but we can't cross him off.'

'On the face of it, Tony Garfield seems the one with the most motive. He stood to gain by Tim Spencer's death, but it seems impossible for him to have had anything to do with Lester's. We know that he was in London early that evening. We know from medical evidence that Lester was given the fatal dose not long before Bates saw him, which was just after nine o'clock − and that was about the time that Garfield rang his wife from his flat, and we also know that he was still there at eleven-thirty. There's no way of tracing that call from London − he won't have gone through the operator − so if his wife says he rang her at nine o'clock. . . '

'She could be in it, too.'

'Unless he rang her from somewhere else − Smoky Cottage − and pretended he was ringing from London?'

'You mean, he makes sure he's seen entering his flat around six o'clock, leaves secretly and drives to Smoky Cottage where he carries out the dastardly deed, rings his wife to establish an alibi and then drives back to London and is back in his flat in time to establish his presence during the bomb scare. But how could he count on there being a bomb scare?'

'Because he arranged it himself? He said the police were alerted by an anonymous phone-call − suppose it was he who made it?'

'Could he have done it, time-wise?'

'That's what we must find out. There would be heavy traffic coming out of London at that time of the day − all the commuters streaming home. It wouldn't have been an easy journey and he must have spent some time with Lester. He didn't just rush in, say "Drink this", and depart. He would have had to have been there by around eight o'clock. I suppose it's just possible, and the journey back the other way after nine o'clock would be quicker. The trouble is, it falls

146

apart when you consider that the murderer must have re-visited Smoky Cottage between five and seven o'clock the next morning. I can't believe Garfield drove himself back again in the middle of the hurricane — it's just not on.'

'Pity, you were making out quite a good case against him.'

'And we've also got to remember that a murder attempt was made on him too at the time of Spencer's murder. It was in the record book — he was deliberately run down and left for dead at the scene. Was the same person responsible?'

'It can't have been coincidence. I don't like coincidences at the best of times, and I don't believe that the murder of one of Mrs. Fellingham's relatives and the attempted murder of another *can* be unrelated incidents, so ...' Roland ran his fingers through his hair and squinted at Mansfield through narrowed eyes '... are you going in the same direction as me?'

'The third cousin?'

'The third cousin, one Leslie Drew resident in the United States. But is he now amongst us? I ask myself.'

'Is it possible?'

'Let's talk it through. We know that he was summoned to the birthday party. Just because Garfield never saw him doesn't mean that he didn't come back. In fact, if he intended getting rid of his rivals, he would have taken great care that Garfield or anyone else *didn't* see him. He could have shot Spencer, run down Garfield, and hurriedly left the district thinking that he *had* killed him — Garfield was left lying unconscious remember?'

'Fair enough, but how do you explain the recent events?'

'Suppose he came back? He could have come back to the area years ago under a different name. Remember, nobody knew him so he wouldn't have been recognised. He could have been living locally under an assumed name for years.'

'So why didn't he make another attempt on Garfield's life later?'

'There would have been no point; Garfield married shortly after coming into his part of the inheritance. If he had died, his money would have gone to his widow, not to his unknown cousin in America, even assuming he had no other relatives.'

147

'That's true, but if Lester was killed because he knew too much, it means that *he* must have known who Leslie Drew was – is.'

'That's the dicey part. But suppose, say, the two cousins, Spencer and Drew, met up with each other in London and travelled down on the train together? Lester saw them. He recognised Spencer but he wouldn't have known Drew so there was no reason why he should have connected Drew with the third cousin.'

'A year or so later, Drew comes to live in the district and he and Lester become acquainted. Lester remembers seeing him with Spencer and mentions it casually in passing. Drew would be alarmed but not unduly worried. He spins him a yarn about meeting Spencer for the first time that day, and says that Spencer told him he was paying a fleeting visit to his great-aunt on his way back to Australia. Lester wouldn't have known that Spencer in fact hadn't shown up at The Hall. He would have thought nothing of it, and it wouldn't have been until he came back from holiday and learned that the skeleton found was Spencer's that he would start wondering and become suspicious of Drew. What do you think of it so far?'

'One of your more far-fetched flights of fancy, sir.'

'Blast you, Pat, I'm just thinking out loud but I think we must follow this up. Get on to Larkin and find out Leslie Drew's last known address in the States. Then we must get on to Interpol and see if they can trace him. In the meantime, we must try and work out who living in the area could possibly be Drew under an alias.'

'So Garfield and Drew are our two main suspects?'

'Oh no, what we've recently learned from the Australian angle makes everything else pale into insignificance. Mrs. Virginia Dalton has a much stronger case to answer. Timothy Spencer having a wife and son who are still living in Australia – what a turn-up for the books!'

'I thought the Australian police reported that they were divorced?'

'They weren't when Spencer came back to England. That original telex to Australia certainly paid off. When I got the initial information I followed it up and our colleagues Down

148

Under were most co-operative. Timothy Spencer married within eighteen months of arriving in Australia – he didn't take long to forget Ginny, did he? Apparently it was a shotgun wedding. He got this girl pregnant and her family insisted on marriage. Our Aussie friends contacted the ex-wife and she was very forthcoming. The marriage was a disaster right from the start and they'd already separated by the time he came back to England. She, of course, never saw him again and assumed he'd done a bunk, but as she was already seeing this other chap it didn't worry her unduly. She eventually divorced him under the Australian Family Law Act and re-married.'

'So you've stood your original theory about the relationship between Spencer and Ginny Dalton on its head?'

'Yes, because it makes far more sense this way. She wasn't worried about his coming back and queering her patch with Alec Dalton – by the way, we don't even know if she knew him then – no, she was waiting for Spencer to come back and claim *her*, and then he turns up and tells her he's already married and has a son. Can't you just see her beside herself with passion, killing him in the heat of the moment?'

'You obviously can. How do you explain away Lester's part in this?'

'Think, man. She was on friendly terms with him. If he had mentioned to her later that he had seen Spencer, I'm sure she could have thought up an explanation along the lines of having had a rendezvous with Spencer and having told him that she was involved with someone else and didn't want to see him again, whereupon he upped and quit and didn't stay around to visit his great-aunt.'

'You've thought of everything. What about Lester's murder?'

'We can't prove that she did it, but equally we can't prove that she couldn't have done it.'

'Don't forget that at the time the murderer went back and removed the suicide note, she was at home coping with a smashed chimney stack and the knowledge that young Simon could have been killed. She was really shattered when I interviewed her the following morning.'

'Killing someone and going back to clear up the evidence

149

under those appalling weather conditions would be equally shattering. If she had already arranged for the boy to spend the night in Felstone, she would have had no fears on his behalf. And the business of the boiler makes more sense. A woman would be far more unlikely to realise the significance of the solenoid valve and drip-feed system than a man.'

'There speaks your male chauvinist! It's a good job Jean can't hear you.'

'But true?'

Mansfield had to admit it was. 'So what are you going to do?'

'Confront her with our knowledge of Spencer's marriage and fatherhood and see how she reacts. There is also this matter of the typewriter. She may not own one personally but she teaches at a school that must own a reasonable complement of typewriters to which she would have access. They probably run a business studies course with typing on the agenda. Damn it, they've probably got a classroom stuffed full of old typewriters!'

'How could she have got hold of the barbiturates?'

'She lost her husband last year, was pretty cut-up over it if her friends and neighbours are to be believed. It's quite within reason to think that her doctor may have prescribed something along those lines to calm her down.'

'Not nowadays, he wouldn't.'

'You can't know that for sure. She's as likely to be in possession of barbiturates as any of our other suspects.'

'As a matter of interest, James, what have you got against her personally?'

'If that had come from anyone else but you . . .' snarled Roland, glaring across the desk.

'I know, I know . . . I'd be hung, drawn and quartered. I'm speaking as a friend, not as a subordinate. I'm presuming on our acquaintance over the years, but if we're to work together successfully on this case I've got to know the score.'

'The score is this: we're going to find this killer and bring him or her to justice − got it?'

Mansfield had.

As it was a Saturday morning Roland expected to find Ginny

150

Dalton at home. He was disappointed. Simon answered the door.

'Is your mother in?'

'No,' said the boy, regarding the detective warily, and after a long pause, 'She's at school.'

'On a Saturday?'

'She's painting scenery for the school play.'

'Ah, yes. Is she likely to be there long?'

'I don't know.' He pushed back the hair tumbling over his forehead and added ungraciously, 'She didn't say.'

'Then I shall probably catch her there.' The boy said nothing more but watched guardedly as Roland walked back to his car. Part of the roof of the cottage was still covered by a tarpaulin. Ginny Dalton, along with many hundreds of others, had joined the long list of housholders awaiting repairs to their property. Roland turned his car round and drove to Felstone High School, thinking as he drove that he could probably use the pretext of questioning her also to investigate the typewriter situation.

Felstone High School had come into being in the 1960s, one of the first schools in the county to go comprehensive. At the time of its inception the old Secondary Modern school buildings were requisitioned for the development, the existing Grammar School buildings having been considered too small for the purpose. These were later turned into a sixth form college. A magnificent assembly hall, sports complex, and art and music studios had been built on to the back of the original buildings, overlooking the playing fields and the distant docks construction. It was towards this area that Roland now went, being vaguely familiar with the groundplan of the school. He parked the car and approached the back of the hall.

He heard them before he saw them; that peculiar level of noise that denotes women at work and play, their tongues sharing the task with which they are occupied. They were in a large room leading off the rear of the hall, the equivalent of the Green Room in a theatre, and as he slipped unobtrusively inside the sharp smell of size and paint assailed his nostrils.

There were half a dozen girls wielding paintbrushes on the

151

flats propped up against the walls, and they looked as if they themselves had wandered off a stage-set. Roland thought it had been a long time since he had seen such a bizarre collection of clothes and make-up. One girl was wearing what appeared to be parrots, the size of budgerigars, hanging from her ears. They must have been lighter than they looked, he thought, or her ear-lobes would have resembled those of the tribal women of the Masai.

Ginny Dalton was in their midst and looked considerably the youngest of the bunch. She wore jeans and an old paint-spattered sailing smock, and her hair was tied back in a ponytail. The girls nearest the door had noticed him by now and were giggling and nudging each other. One young madam of about fourteen flaunted her mini-clad hips and nascent bosom at him in a way that suggested that if all else failed she would be well able to earn her living at the oldest profession. He noticed with resignation that Patrick Mansfield's Jane was amongst them; his identity would soon be common knowledge.

Ginny Dalton looked up from her crouched position on the floor and sat back on her heels in exasperation.

'What do you want?'

'A few words if I can possibly disturb you at your ... labours.' She swung to her feet in a graceful, fluid movement and spoke crisply to her pupils.

'Alright, girls, carry on and finish the stonework, and then we'll have a go at the climbing roses.'

She led the way into another smaller room which opened off the scenery storeroom. It was piled high with redundant furniture and boxes of oddments. A basket of broken tennis rackets bloomed in one corner like an exotic tropical flower with a net of footballs for seeds. She left the door ajar and turned on him.

'Why have you come here pestering me?'

'I was hoping my visit would be incognito but I'm afraid my sergeant's daughter is amongst your coterie.'

'Don't worry, Inspector, I would rather they know you as a member of the Fuzz than think my boyfriend has come visiting. What do you want?'

'Is scenery painting solely a female preserve?'

152

'The boys, most of them, are involved in a rugger match; the corresponding girls' hockey match was postponed because of the weather so I took the opportunity of organising a working party.'

'Discrimination again?'

'I fear so, and for once I'm all for it. The girls are far better at this sort of thing than the boys.'

She leaned against a cupboard, arms akimbo, a slim, apricot and ivory figure, and regarded him disdainfully. He perched on an upturned desk and matched her nonchalance.

'The time has come, Mrs. Dalton, to talk of many things: of shoes — and ships — and sealing wax — and typewriters.'

'What is all this fuss about typewriters? Your sergeant has already ascertained that I don't own one. What am I suppose to have typed?'

'A school of this size has many typewriters, and I'm not just referring to the ones in the office. Is that not so?'

'I have no idea how many there are, it is hardly my province. Why can't you ask the caretaker or the school secretary?'

'I can indeed. I thought to save time by getting you to show them to me and perhaps type out a few lines.'

'I've told you, it's nothing to do with me. You would have to get the headmaster's permission, and ... and you haven't got a search warrant, have you?' she added triumphantly.

'People who insist on a search warrant are usually either guilty or bloody-minded. Which are you?'

'Inspector, this conversation is getting us nowhere and I have to return to my girls. I'm sure you didn't come here just to talk about typewriters. What do you really want?'

'Why didn't you tell me that Tim Spencer had a wife and son in Australia?'

The colour came and went in her face and the denial slipped out involuntarily.

'That's not true!'

'Isn't it?'

'It can't be, you're making it up!'

She was either a very good liar or she was appalled at his revelation. She looked stricken, and Roland had the crazy desire to take her in his arms and comfort her and tell her that

Spencer hadn't been worth her concern. Instead he said sternly: 'I can assure you it is fact. Timothy Spencer married in 1976 and a son was born the following year. He didn't keep faith with you for long, did he? It must have been quite a shock. There you were, waiting for him to come home and claim you, and instead he tells you he already has a wife and child. I suppose one can understand your blasting with a shotgun in the heat of the moment − a woman scorned and all that. A pity this isn't France, they look more favourably on a crime of passion over there.'

'I've told you, I did *not* see Tim when he came back. And, James Roland, I think it is you who are acting like someone scorned!'

A frisson went through him at her use of his first name, and her astuteness shook him. She went on, unaware of how she had scored: 'Destroying people, exposing their secrets, undermining their relationships − is that how you get your kicks?'

'The murderer is the ultimate destroyer. He destroys life − there can be no justification for that. He has put himself beyond the pale and it is my duty − my responsibility, if you like − to hunt him down and bring him to justice.'

'Noble sentiments, but I repeat − doesn't it matter to you how many innocent people you destroy in the process? Don't you owe a responsibility to them too?'

'My superintendent would tell you that there is no such thing as an innocent person.'

'My father would have agreed with him. To him all men were conceived and born in sin. The omission of that passage from the modern baptismal service was a source of great disquiet to him.'

'Your father obviously had a great influence on you.'

'No-one who knew my father could remain indifferent to him; he was not the kind of person you could ignore, was very outspoken, which earned him some enemies.'

'And how did he react to your debacle with Tim Spencer?'

'He was very . . . supportive.'

There was a burst of noise from the outer room and a girl put her head round the door. She was dark and intense-looking, and she eyed Roland speculatively.

'Please, miss, we've finished the wall — can we start on the rose pergola?'

'Yes, but go easy on the colour, it needs to be several shades lighter than the wall. And, Tracey, cut down the noise level. You sound like a bunch of first-formers.'

The girl disappeared and Ginny Dalton turned back to Roland.

'That was Tracey Bates, the gamekeeper's daughter.'

'Whose brother you killed?' He was being deliberately brutal but whilst she was still in a state of shock over his recent disclosure he was hoping to prompt her into ... what? A confession? An unguarded revelation which would help his enquiries? Or did he just want to inflict hurt?

'Whose brother's death I was partly responsible for, yes.'

'Does she know?'

'I'm not sure. Knowing her father, I think she must. She has never said anything but I see her watching me sometimes ... Who was it who said that Hell was meeting up with the people you had wronged?'

'So you teach her?'

'Yes, and she is good which makes it all the more difficult. She has a natural gift which must be encouraged. I want her to go on to Art College and train professionally — and I have the job of trying to persuade her father along these lines.'

'An unenviable task.'

'Quite. He looks on any form of further education for girls as a waste of time, and the art world as a sink of depravity. It's a shame. The eldest girl, Sharon, is in a dead-end job at a hairdresser's in town, and I'm determined that Tracey won't go the same way. She has talent and I can't bear to think of it all being wasted.'

'The dedicated teacher,' he said mockingly.

She glared at him defiantly and pushed back the hair which was escaping over her forehead. At that moment she looked absurdly like her son. He had made the same gesture a short while ago and had regarded Roland with the same mutinous, wary look.

'Well, Inspector, can I go back to work or are you going to arrest me?'

155

'Not yet, Mrs. Dalton, not yet, but it is a pity you haven't got an alibi for the evening that Julian Lester died.'

'I don't even know how he died.'

'Don't you? It was an overdose.'

'So he *did* commit suicide?'

'Oh no, Mrs. Dalton, he was murdered.'

'But why?'

'Do you really not know? Julian Lester saw Spencer when he came back to England. He saw him with you, didn't he? And when he learned a short while ago that he had been murdered, he knew who was responsible and had to be silenced.'

She whitened and her freckles stood out like the red-brown speckles on a robin's egg.

'You've really got it in for me, haven't you? I had nothing to do with Tim's or Julian Lester's deaths, and you can't prove otherwise.'

She was recovering and on the attack again. 'I am fed up with your insinuations and accusations and, in fact, I could probably sue you for harassment. I think it is time I saw my solicitor!'

'Go ahead, Mrs. Dalton it should prove interesting,' he said laconically, and jerked his head towards the door through which a rising tide of laughter and chatter was penetrating. 'You'd better go back to them — they sound as if they are going to run amok any minute now.'

He stayed in the storeroom as she swept back to her scenic artists and he heard her voice crisply commanding: 'Girls, come on, this will never do. We want to get this finished this morning to surprise the boys, don't we? Jane, mix up that red paint — and, Clare, don't lean against the flats. If you want to ruin your clothes it's not my problem, but I don't want my wall smudged!'

Miss Brodie would have been proud of her.

Back in his car Roland reflected on the guilt or otherwise of Ginny Dalton. She could have done it, but had she? Was he being vindictive by pursuing her without a shred of real evidence? Did he want to see her convicted and shut away for a long time? At least then, said a nasty little voice inside him, she would be unable to lure any more suckers with her enticing touch-me-not air. God! He mustn't get personal, and what would happen to young Simon if she were convicted? Although he had different colouring he was so like his mother with that watchful, vulnerable bearing like a cornered deer . . .

He suddenly realised what he was thinking and slammed on the brakes so hard that a motor-cyclist behind him had to swerve violently to avoid going up the back of his car. Simon wasn't her son! He was her stepson, the son of her late husband by his first wife. He pulled into the side of the road, cut the engine and let the thoughts chase themselves round inside his head.

Alec Dalton had been a widower with a young son when he married Ginny Dalton so the boy couldn't be hers – or could he? Simon would be about thirteen years old which would mean that he had been born in 1975. 1975! The year in which Ginny and Tim Spencer had made their disastrous elopement bid. Suppose they had already been lovers and she had been pregnant at the time? Was Tim Spencer Simon's real father? Was is possible? She would have been studying for her 'A' levels prior to going to college. Could the boy possibly be hers and Tim's, and had he been adopted by Alec Dalton and his first wife? Or was he imagining the likeness?

No, it had been niggling away in the back of his mind ever since he had first seen the two together. The boy was dark with light eyes, the same colouring that Tim Spencer was supposed to have had. If he himself had a son of that age, thought Roland with a jolt, he would probably look very much like Simon Dalton; after all hadn't she admitted that he and Spencer were uncannily alike?

He started up the car again and drove speedily over to Wallingford to Mansfield's home. Jean Mansfield opened the door and looked annoyed when she saw who it was.

'He's just about to sit down to his lunch. I suppose you're going to drag him off somewhere?'

'It's alright, Jean, this won't take long. Can I see him?'

She went ahead of him, calling out: 'Pat, Inspector Roland is here to see you.'

Mansfield was sitting in his shirt sleeves reading the

newspaper, a half empty beer mug on the table beside him. He looked up with alacrity. 'Has something come up?'

'You could say so. Can you get on to your friend Betts and find out if he knows whether Simon Dalton was an adopted child?'

'Adopted, eh? I'll ring him straight away. What has brought this up?'

Roland hesitated, not wanting to unburden himself in front of Jean Mansfield. She correctly interpreted his reluctance and said dryly: 'It's alright, I'm going, I don't want to hear State secrets. But I'll tell you one thing: Alec Dalton was incapable of fathering a child.'

Her husband and visitor stared at her in astonishment, and eventually Patrick found his voice.

'Are you sure? How do you know?'

'Ginny Dalton told me once, ages ago.'

'Ginny Dalton — you know her?' Roland eyed the woman in front of him in surprise and disbelief.

'We're not intimate friends but we're acquainted. We're both on the local Nature Conservation Trust committee and the School PTA. Someone once had the temerity to ask her why she and Alec had no children, and I remember her saying that he had had mumps badly as an adult which had put paid to his becoming a father. I thought she meant this had happened after he fathered Simon but maybe she meant it had happened earlier, before he married his first wife.'

'Thanks, Jean, that could be very useful. Pat — the call?'

Mansfield went into the hall and they heard him dialling. Jean Mansfield looked pointedly at the clock and Roland tried appeasement.

'I'm sorry to interrupt your meal but this is important.'

She relented. 'Will you share it with us? It's only a casserole but there's plenty to go round.'

'Thanks, Jean, I'm very tempted, but not today. Make the offer again and I'll take you up on it. Your meals are occasions to be savoured.'

'You don't look after yourself properly,' she scolded, eyeing him critically, 'I'm sure you've lost weight since I last saw you.'

'I'm the lean and hungry-looking type, but I'd love to come

for a meal soon – get Patrick to fix it up. By the way, I saw Jane at school today. Getting quite grown-up, isn't she?'

'It would make her day to hear you say that. She's been helping to paint the scenery for the school play – is that where you saw her?'

'Yes. Does Ginny Dalton teach her?'

'She did up to the end of the fifth year. Jane is not taking Art in the sixth form but she's involved with the Drama group through her English 'A' level.'

'Ginny Dalton keeps herself busy, working at weekends as well as doing a full school week and being on numerous committees.'

'I think it's her way with dealing with her grief. She works far too hard, but it helps her to cope with Alec's death.'

'She took it hard?'

'Well, naturally.' Jean was getting ruffled. 'Look, I don't know what you and Pat are up to, poking around in Ginny Dalton's past, but don't involve me. I refuse to spy on friends, even to keep the big police machine turning.'

'As if I would.' Roland gave her what he hoped was a disarming smile. 'I just wondered if the marriage had been a happy one.'

'They were devoted, I believe, and she was very cut-up when he died. After all, they hadn't been married all that long and it was so sudden that the shock must have been terrible; one doesn't expect a healthy man in his forties to drop dead of a heart attack.'

Mansfield came back into the room at that moment.

'Your hunch, whatever prompted it, was correct. Mathew says that Alec Dalton and Ruth, his first wife, were unable to have kids and they adopted Simon when they were living up in Norfolk. He seemed to think that Ruth was the one at fault.'

'That is most interesting. Your Mathew Betts is a fountain of knowledge; at this rate we'll be putting him on our payroll.'

'He doesn't like it, James. It's alright to fill in your old friend on local background information; it's another thing altogether to point the finger at your friends.'

'He hasn't told us anything we couldn't have found out for ourselves, given time,' said Roland, avoiding looking at Jean

159

Mansfield. 'Well, I'll be off and leave you to eat your lunch in peace.'

'If you won't join us, at least have a beer before you go?'

'Not now, thanks. Goodbye, Jean.'

Mansfield accompanied him to the front door. 'You're not thinking of holding out on me, I hope. What is this all about?'

'It's been staring us in the face all the while and we didn't see it. Have you looked closely at Simon Dalton?'

'A perfectly ordinary adolescent boy.'

'Who, apart from his colouring, is the spitting image of his real mother — Ginny Dalton.'

Mansfield looked flabbergasted.

'Well, isn't he?'

The elder man considered this. 'Now you've brought it to my attention, I suppose the answer is yes. Give them the same colour hair and eyes and I reckon they would look like brother and sister. So you think that Ginny had an affair with Alec Dalton before they were married — whilst he was still married to his first wife — and Simon was the result?'

'You haven't got there yet. I think Simon is the son of Ginny and Tim Spencer. The boy has his colouring by all accounts.'

'My God!' Mansfield was doing some rapid calculations. 'He must have been born after Spencer was packed off to Australia — do you think he knew?'

'I don't think he did, I don't think anyone knew. She must have gone away to have him and it was hushed up, though how Alec Dalton and his first wife come into the picture at that stage I don't know. But just think: she bears Spencer's child and is probably still carrying a torch for him three years later. She is expecting him to come back and claim her, and instead she learns that he has married another girl in Australia and has another son by her.'

'Yes, I can see what you mean, the case looks black against her; but although I can see her shooting him in the heat of the moment, I can't see her all these years later killing a witness in cold blood to shut his mouth. The two murders are not compatible.'

'People running scared are apt to do things out of character, as we know only too well.'

160

'It's going to be difficult getting proof about young Simon if he was officially adopted.'

'Yes, adoption societies are worse than the confessional.'

Roland zipped up his jacket and pulled on his gloves. 'Go and have your meal or I shall be even further in Jean's bad books.' It had started to rain again as he walked down the path and he turned up his collar and made a dash for the car.

Bradley Scott let himself in through the back door. Although it was only early afternoon the light was already fading. A grey, overcast morning had given way to thickening cloud, and twilight was not far away. It was the sort of day that invited one to draw the curtains, switch on the lights and shut out the world, but Scott did neither. He shrugged off his coat and went through to the sitting room where the coffee table was spread with maps of the Canary Islands. As far as the weather was concerned he couldn't wait to shake the dust, or rather the mud, of England off his feet and wallow in sunshine and balmy temperatures. It was time he did something about booking his flight and checking accommodation.

He picked up the phone and flicked through his telephone pad seeking the number of the travel agent he usually used. Something, a slight noise, a sensation of being observed, made him freeze, his back to the door. He was not alone; someone else was in the house.

He stood still, rooted to the spot, and listening, all his senses straining to hear the elusive sound that had alerted him. Was he imagining things? No, there it was again, the sibilant whisper of material, the merest suggestion of someone quietly breathing the same air as himself. Why did he suddenly have to think of Julian Lester? The poor old bloke had let someone into his house in all innocence and been bumped off for his pains. Without moving, his eyes flickered round the room in front of him, seeking a weapon. He, who had been in innumerable tight spots all over the world without benefit of gun, now wished he had one at hand to defend himself in the safety of his house.

About two yards away from him on top of the bureau stood a bottle of Viniak, a reminder of a journey into the interior of

161

Yugoslavia. The fiery brandy had defied all his efforts either to down it himself or pass it off on unsuspecting guests. It was three-quarters full. If he darted across the room and snatched it up without any warning, he might be able to take the intruder unawares.

He lunged forward, grabbed the bottle by the neck and swung round to face the door.

Chapter Nine

'Are you offering it to me or going to beat me about the head?'

'Lee!'

'Don't sound so surprised — it's not very flattering.'

'What are you doing here?'

She was leaning against the door jamb, regarding him with amusement, dressed in his towelling bathrobe and nothing else. It was loosely knotted at her waist and the top gaped open, revealing a considerable cleavage. Her long, shapely legs gleamed palely in the fading light.

'Not very welcoming, darling. I thought you'd be pleased to see me.' She advanced into the room, snapping on the light switch as she did so.

'For God's sake, Lee, everyone will see you. At least draw the curtains first.' He thrust the bottle on to the mantelpiece and, moving to the window, yanked the curtains closed.

She chuckled. 'You sounded just like Tony then — good old pompous, stick-in-the-mud Tony.'

'You've been drinking!'

'No, I haven't, but I'm beginning to feel that I could do with a stiff dram.'

'You're mad to come here in the daytime. Tony's in Croxton today, I saw him earlier.'

'He's over with Carstairs, fixing up a shoot, nowhere near here. Who were you going to ring?'

'The travel agent — I've got to book my flight.'

'Make it two.'

'Are you sure?'

She flung herself down on the sofa and leaned her head against the cushions, causing the bathrobe to gape open still further. Her large, creamy breasts nestled like gigantic pearls against the crimson folds.

'He's gone too far this time.'

'You're not saying he's got another woman?'

'Who — Tony? Don't be ridiculous, he's pure as the driven snow. He hasn't looked at another woman since we married; I suppose I should be flattered but he's so ... so *boring* it isn't true! No, this is something far more serious. I'm surprised you haven't heard any rumours.'

'About what?'

'His scheme to develop Croxton Creek. He's in cahoots with a group of speculators and they've drawn up these ambitious plans to build a marina and holiday village and God knows what else on our land that adjoins the shore.'

'Christ! That will put the cat amongst the pigeons!'

'Can you imagine my position? Here am I, one of the chief supporters of the Nature Conservation Trust, fighting tooth and nail to preserve the natural habitats of our local flora and fauna, and my own husband is planning to desecrate a large portion of it!'

'He'll never get it past Planning.'

'I'm determined it won't come to that. If he goes ahead with this scheme, it's going to clean him out. According to him we shall have to invest our all initially and reap handsome rewards later, and by 'all' he means my money as well. He's not going to have it. He either gives up the scheme or I'm leaving him.'

'I see. You won't give him up for me, but you'll leave him because of your precious birds!'

'You know that's not true, but I see that I shall have to convince you.'

She stretched out a foot and caressed him gently and he felt himself harden. She knew all the tricks and they were at his disposal. She was like a bitch on heat and he couldn't have enough of her — but did he want her permanently? Wasn't much of the passion engendered by the risks they ran, the snatched meetings, the excitement of a clandestine affair?

164

'Come here, Brad.'

Her eyes were black, opaque, swallowing him up, and he felt himself being sucked into their velvet depths; he was drowning and he didn't want to struggle. He thought fleetingly of the more comfortable bed upstairs but knew that any mention of it would alienate her forever.

He threw himself at her and they rolled on to the floor.

Leslie Drew where are you?

Roland frowned as he read through his notes and doodled on the pad in front of him. He drew a pin man and invested him with a stetson and cowboy boots. Above the stetson he penned a large question mark. Interpol had drawn a blank in tracing Leslie Drew. His last known address in Los Angeles had been bulldozed several years previously in a redevelopment scheme. He had left the firm of Mitchell and Sarony, Real Estate Purveyors, in 1979 and apparently vanished into thin air. Was he now living in England, or to be more precise in the Croxton district, desperately trying to cover up a crime committed over ten years ago?

Roland drew another pin man and found himself adding curly hair and beard. He stared down at the sheet of paper and made the connection between his involuntary doodling and the question niggling away in the back of his mind. Bradley Scott — was it possible? He was within the correct age range, and he had admitted to Roland that he had inherited enough money at about the relevant time to enable him to throw up his job, buy a cottage and embark on his writing career. He had even let drop that his family had originated from this area. Surely he wouldn't have been so free with this information if he were Leslie Drew, living incognito, with at least one murder on his conscience?

Yet he had been in the vicinity of Smoky cottage at the time of Lester's death, Roland was convinced of this. On the face of it he would seem to have been on his way to a clandestine meeting with Lee Garfield. Would she, he mused, give Scott an alibi if pressed?

He read through his case notes again. Julian Lester's ex-wife had pre-deceased him by several years but there was a married niece living in Newcastle who was apparently his sole relative. On her would fall the onus of making the funeral arrangements once the body was released for burial, and she would presumably apply for probate. No will had been found. So far they had had no luck in tracing the typewriter on which the suicide note had been typed. Every typewriter at Felstone High School had been checked officially, without reference to Ginny Dalton. If she was guilty she certainly hadn't typed the note on a school machine.

By some judicious probing he had found out that Alec Dalton had lived with his first wife in Norwich and taught there prior to coming to Felstone; Simon had been adopted as a baby in Norwich through the County Court. He had also discovered that Ginny Dalton had left school in June 1975, a few months after the disastrous elopement bid, and had left the district on a supposedly long working holiday, followed by her college training and a good degree. She had taken up a teaching post at Felstone High School in 1979, at the same time as Alec Dalton had moved down to Suffolk, and they had been married a few months later. It all slotted neatly into place, thought Roland. She had Simon in the September of 1975 just before taking up her college place, and he had been adopted by Alec and Ruth Dalton.

How to prove it was another matter. An adoption proceeding was confidential, sacrosanct, not to be revealed to anyone except, since the Children's Act of 1975, The adopted child, him or herself after the age of eighteen. He could go to court and apply for an order requesting the Registrar General to divulge the details registered on the Adopted Children Register; as it was a piece of information vital to a murder investigation Roland should have no trouble in getting this but it would mean showing his hand, something he was not yet ready or in any position to do. He and Mansfield had mulled this over and decided to confront Ginny Dalton with the facts as they saw them in the hope that she would admit her guilt; failing this, they would then resort to obtaining a court order.

He got to his feet and walked over to the window where he stared unseeingly down at the courtyard below. Ginny Dalton — the damned woman haunted him! No matter from which angle he looked at this case, his thoughts always went full circle and ended back with her. There was a personal involvement that he knew was dangerous and unethical. The more he saw her, the more she ... bewitched him. It was a word he hesitated to use, a word that a sane, level-headed police officer, especially one noted for his dispassionate, cool-headed approach, hesitated to bandy about even to himself but it was a fact. He was bewitched and, perversely, the more he struggled against this feeling, the greater was his desire to prove that she was a murderess and get a conviction.

It was as well that Superintendent Bob Lacey was unaware of his inspector's involvement with one of the chief suspects in the case. Patrick guessed, of course, but he had enough faith in his superior's moral principles to hold his tongue.

Roland glanced at his watch. Mansfield should now be in London checking out Garfield's alibi. In a couple of hours' time he would be starting the drive from Elbury Court to Smoky Cottage, and then back again at nine o'clock. It would be interesting to see how the experiment turned out. Mansfield was a good driver; his experience in police driving over the years would make up for the absence of Garfield's impetus. If the drive could be done within the narrow time limits, Mansfield would do it.

Roland decided to call it a day for the time being. He was meeting Mansfield in Croxton later to learn about the drive up from the City; until then he would snatch a snack and get some exercise. With this idea in mind he looked out of the window again. It was for once a dry day and the hazy autumn sun reflected pinkly off the rooftops of Felstone spread out before him. The clocks altered in a few days' time; by this hour next week it would already be dark. He decided to make the most of the clement weather and stretch his legs.

A short while later he found himself driving through Croxton and taking the track that led down to the creek. He parked and set off on foot along the path that ran along the river wall. At the head of the creek he paused; to the left the bank curved round the water meadows and the site of the plane excavation where Tim Spencer's skeleton had been found; to the right the wall dissected the marshes and divided the

167

creek and reed beds from Hermitage land, leading eventually to where creek and river met. He took the right hand path.

It was wet and muddy underfoot and he soon regretted that he was not wearing his boots. The coarse marram grass squeaked beneath his feet, and dried rushes and thistle heads rustled and caught at his legs as he walked carefully along the rutted, overgrown footpath. The tide was ebbing and the water slipped away, uncovering gleaming stretches of mud that reflected the mauve and pink sky, and popped and sucked gently at the shoreline. It was quiet and beautiful in a way that East Anglian artists had faithfully recorded over the centuries. A vast sky arched over the flat terrain, and the pinks and blues and mauves, wisped with cloud, merged almost imperceptibly with the opalescent waters of creek and river and smudged fingers of reed fringe. The only sound was the metallic piping of a flock of oyster-catchers that wheeled across the skyline ahead of him in a flash of orange, white and black.

He rounded a bend and in the distance saw three figures plodding across the marshes on the landward side of the river wall. One of them was gesticulating towards the creek and Roland recognised Tony Garfield. Were they out wild-fowling? But no, none of them carried guns. He didn't think Garfield had noticed him and, not wanting to be seen, he dropped down from the wall and made his way back along the hightide line, picking his way across the boggy ground with its tussocky grass and patches of dead sea lavender and thrift.

Down near the water's edge the bleached ribs of a long-abandoned boat curved upwards like a cadaver sprung open for an autopsy. It would not survive to see another summer. Long before that the last rotting planks would have slipped beneath the oozing mud and brackish water. So had Tim Spencer's body laid, wreathed in mud, and at times of flood the water had washed through his bones, flushing away bodily sediments.

God! He was getting fanciful in his old age. The scene was turning desolate; the light was fading fast and a mist was rolling in from the river, washing the colour from land and sky alike. If he didn't hurry he'd soon be blundering about in the dark. It was with a sense of relief that he let himself into his car and drove back to Felstone.

Mansfield had scarcely got going before he was snarled up in a traffic jam at Ludgate Hill. He crawled along Cannon Street and Fenchurch Street into Whitechapel, and tried to resist the temptation to glance at his watch every few minutes. At this rate it was going to take him all of three hours to reach Croxton. Mile End Road seemed unending with its boarded-up shops, cheap take-aways, and pavements and gutters clogged with market detritus. It wasn't until he reached Eastern Avenue that he managed to get up any speed at all. After this, conditions improved and as he sped along the A12 round the Chelmsford by-pass and headed towards Suffolk, he began to enjoy the drive and the challenge.

He reached Smoky Cottage at eight-fifteen, radioed through to Felstone HQ to let Roland know he had arrived and arranged to meet him in the Duck and Spoon a little later. As he doubled back to the rendezvous he tried to work out where Garfield could have left his car, presuming he was the culprit. He must have hidden it out of sight somewhere as no-one had reported seeing it and they had checked this angle very carefully. Mansfield supposed he could have driven it a little way into the woods themselves though this would have been risky.

He parked in the pub car park and went in search of his superior. Roland had ordered him a meal and he gratefully attacked the pie and chips whilst he brought the Inspector up-to-date with his findings in town.

'Good man, you did it. Two hours and ten minutes.' Roland was quietly satisfied.

'I didn't think I was going to, but once I got clear of the East End I managed to make up for lost time. I went along the route we worked out but it is possible that he took short cuts with which we are unfamiliar, so it could be done in less time than that.'

'How did you get on at Elbury Court?'

'Firstly, there are on-street parking facilities nearby so there is no problem there. He could have parked and come and gone without being noticed; no car park attendants to record his movements. I checked with the porter and he remembers speaking to Garfield as he was getting into the lift. He is quite sure it was that particular evening because he remembers that later on that same evening they had a bomb scare. An anonymous phone-call was made to the local police station at exactly eleven o'clock − I checked with them − and they immediately alerted the residents of Elbury Court. The building was vacated, and after the place had been searched and nothing found the occupants were allowed back.'

'What is the place like?'

'Very nice. A modern block of little boxes but definitely up-market. They don't come cheap and a resident porter and tastefully designed entrance hall add class. I managed to persuade the porter to show me over the apartment which adjoins Garfield's. It is empty at the moment − a new tenant is moving in tomorrow − and it is identical to his. It is basically a bedsitting room with a minute kitchenette, toilet and shower. Ideal for his purposes, I should think and what do you know? Just outside his door is the access to the fire escape so he could easily have got in and out without being seen.'

'What about the next morning? Did the porter see him when he supposedly left?'

'No, he can't remember seeing him but says that things were a little chaotic that morning owing to the hurricane − a nice understatement.'

'The murderer returned to Smoky Cottage before seven-thirty. I don't see how Garfield could possibly have driven back during the storm.'

'I agree. Even if he had been crazy enough to start out, he would never have completed the journey so I don't see how he could possibly have done it.'

Later that evening Mansfield did the journey in the opposite direction. He managed to knock twenty minutes off the time, meaning that if Garfield had been in the vicinity of Smoky Cottage at nine o'clock he could have been back at Elbury Court around eleven. What a pity that they had practically to cross him off the list of suspects because of the events of the following morning.

He eventually crawled into bed at two in the morning, having traversed the A12 four times in almost as few hours.

'They think I murdered Tim and Julian Lester.' Ginny Dalton set her cup down abruptly in its saucer and stared across the table at her companion.

'Ginny, you can't be serious?' Lee Garfield regarded her in amazement.

'Oh, I am, most definitely so. I expect to be arrested at any moment.'

The two women had met at Ginny's urgent request and were seated in the Tudor Restaurant in Woodford over afternoon tea. It was a pleasant place with the emphasis on everything Olde Worlde. Much of it was genuine Tudor — the oak beams, inglenook fireplace and pargetting on the white plaster walls — but it was so hung about with warming pans, horse brasses and pots and pans that the effect was overdone and, as a result, much that was actually sixteenth-century was presumed to be twentieth-century tat. A wood fire burned in the open grate and the flickering flames were repeated a hundred times over in the gleaming copper and brass that surrounded the fireplace; on a nearby coffee table a large bowl of gold chrysanthemums glowed in the reflected light. A serving wench in long skirts and mob cap would not have looked out of place; the spikey-haired waitress with her plum-painted nails and lips struck an incongruous note.

In normal circumstances Ginny would have appreciated the warmth and muted lights and the chance of relaxation, but now she sat rigidly at the table and crumbled her scone with tense, nervous fingers.

'But this is ridiculous. How *can* they suspect you, for God's sake?'

'They do.'

'But they can't have a shred of evidence for such a mad idea! What are you supposed to have done?'

'Killed Tim in a fit of pique because I discovered that he had a wife and child in Australia.'

'Had he? I didn't know that.'

'Nor did anyone else, but according to the police that gives me a nice motive.'

171

'And Julian Lester?'

'Apparently he saw Tim when he came back, and I'm supposed to have murdered him to stop him incriminating me.'

'And where's their proof?'

'I haven't got an alibi for the time of Julian Lester's death. They can't prove I did it, and I can't prove that I didn't.'

'They haven't got a leg to stand on. Have you got a lawyer?'

'There's the solicitor who dealt with things when Alec died, but I don't know whether he's active in the criminal field.'

'I'll get Tony on to it, he'll find the right person to act for you. You shouldn't be harassed like this − how is Simon taking it?'

'He doesn't realise that his mother is about to be arrested for murder but he's obviously worried about the police presence − they've been to the house several times.'

'I presume it's the same team who interviewed Tony and me − Jean Mansfield's husband and that dishy Inspector Roland. He makes me think of Heathcliff.'

'He's a cold, ruthless bastard,' said Ginny in clear, ringing tones, and lowered her voice as women at nearby tables looked towards them with interest, 'and I'm at the receiving end of a persecution campaign.'

She spooned two spoonfuls of sugar into her cup and stirred it vigorously. Lee eyed her with concern.

'You don't take sugar,' she said.

'No, I don't do I?' Ginny pushed the cup and saucer away. 'I don't smoke either, but if I had a packet of cigarettes on me I'd smoke the lot.'

'Look, Tony knows the Chief Constable. I'll get him to have a word. You shouldn't be pestered like this. This country's getting more and more like a police state.'

'I don't want to involve Tony. What happened between Tim and me happened a long while ago, and there is no reason why any other member of his family should feel responsible.'

'Nonsense, Tony's always had a soft spot for you; he'll be

172

glad to help you in any way he can, and I happen to know that the police are getting up his nose too.'

'You don't know how horrible it is, Lee, living under this cloud of suspicion. I know I didn't do it, and I spend half my time looking around me and wondering who the real murderer is. It must be someone local, someone we all know; perhaps a friend or colleague. I think and think, and sometimes I think I'm going mad!'

'Ginny, you mustn't let it get you down. You need a holiday. It's half term next week, isn't it? Why don't you go away for a break?'

'I shall probably be in a prison cell by then.'

'This is not like you. You coped so marvellously when Alec died.'

'That's just it. I've gradually come to terms with it and I'm trying to build up my life again, but it's Simon. Don't you understand? He took his father's death hard but he's starting to get over it. What effect do you think it would have on him if I were arrested? If he thought his stepmother was a murderess?'

'They've absolutely no grounds for arresting you so don't think about it. And I'm sure young Simon and his friends are consumed with excitement at having a murder enquiry on their doorstep.'

'They are little ghouls at this age,' admitted Ginny. 'Perhaps I am getting things out of proportion, but I just had to talk to someone.'

'I'm glad you did. I take it this is your afternoon off school?'

'Yes, they let us out sometimes. I hope I haven't dragged you away from anything important?'

'No, and I wanted to see you anyway; I've got something I want to talk through too.' Lee Garfield toyed with the cake on her plate and looked, for her, strangely indecisive. 'I'm thinking of leaving Tony.'

Shocked out of her preoccupation with her own affairs, Ginny stared at the dark-haired woman across the table.

'You don't really mean it? Why?' And then, as she got no reply, 'Is it because of Bradley Scott?'

'You know about him?'

173

'You haven't exactly been reticent, I think you enjoy living dangerously. Does Tony know?'

'About Brad? No, I don't think so, but he's getting suspicious. But that's not the reason I'm thinking of leaving him. Tony and I haven't had a lot going for us for some time. We are temperamentally unsuited but we've rubbed along together, each going our own way, but now ... I've got to stop him, Ginny.'

'Stop him from doing what?'

'Haven't you heard any rumours?'

'About what? What are you on about Lee? Is he having an affair with someone?'

'Far worse. He wants to develop Croxton Creek.'

'What do you mean?'

'Build a marina and holiday village, turn it into a sort of East Anglian Port Grimaud.'

'But that's appalling! He surely can't do it? What about local opinion and planning permission and all that?'

'It hasn't got as far as that yet. He's still hatching out the scheme with his cronies.'

'And you're thinking of leaving him to show your disapproval?'

'It's more practical than that. He needs my money to put into the project. I'm determined that he's not going to have it.'

'What will you do?'

'Become a travelling companion?'

'Has Bradley Scott asked you to go away with him?'

'We're two of a kind. At the moment things are good for us. I don't know how long it will last, but as neither of us wants to be tied down permanently we may give it a whirl and see how it works out. I've shocked you, haven't I?'

'I guess I'm rather old-fashioned. Are you sure you're doing the right thing — I mean, what about Tony?'

'You mean, he won't take kindly to me spiking his guns over this development scheme?'

'I mean I'm sure he cares deeply for you in his way. Are you sure you really want to leave him? What about your horses, your garden?'

'You think I'll regret my present life style? I haven't always

174

had it so good, you know. I haven't always had such a generous share of life's goodies. Anyway, I've got my own money and Brad is not exactly a pauper. But please don't breathe a word of this to anyone, especially about Tony's little project.'

'I remember now, Simon told me had had seen some men down at the creek doing a survey. I thought at the time that it was probably something to do with the ... murder enquiry.'

'You see? I don't know how he has managed to keep it quiet so long. Can you imagine what the members of the Nature Conservation Trust would think if it got out?'

'Is the committee meeting still on for the end of the month?'

'Yes, it's ironic, isn't it? I attend a conservation meeting and my husband sits in his study at home planning to decimate the wildlife of the area.' Lee gave a mock shrug and picked up the teapot. 'Do you want another cup?'

'No thanks, I must be getting back. There is a play rehearsal after school.'

'How is it going?'

'We have a superb Algernon; the only trouble is he shows up everyone else.'

'Do you know, I envy you, Ginny.'

'Me? You must be joking!'

'No, seriously. I think you've got your sense of values right. I often wish I could go back and start again, do things differently.'

'You wouldn't survive two weeks of my life style; you'd be bored to tears — that is, in the normal course of events. You enjoy excitement, stimulation ...'

'That's what I mean,' said Lee sadly.

Detective Constable William Evans was annoyed. He did not like being made a fool of and Alfie Coutts, country bumpkin par excellence, had certainly achieved that. He had, in truth, led him a pretty dance when interviewed earlier. At first the old sod had pretended deafness, but when Evans had raised his voice Alfie had reseponded with a flow of rhetoric in such a broad Suffolk accent that he was incomprehensible, and had then clammed up and spent the rest of the interview mumbling to himself and appealing to his sluttish sister who had aided and abetted him. Evans wished he had enough grounds to run them both in for obstructing the police. The trouble was, he had come to the same conclusion as Sergeant Mansfield: the old so-and-so *did* know something but was not prepared to sing to the Bill.

He had eventually given up in disgust, and considering himself now officially off-duty, had retired to the local pub and treated himself to a pint and a steak pie and chips. And now, to add insult to injury, the cause of his recent discomfiture was sitting only a few yards from him, holding court amongst a bunch of cronies who looked as moronic as he.

The Duck and Spoon had been a hostelry back in the seventeenth century and had altered little through the ensuing centuries. A single doorway led into a small entrance lobby off which, to the right, was the door leading to the public bar, to the left the door leading to the saloon bar. The two rooms were adjacent with just a frail partition dividing them, and the bar counter ran through from one side to the other without a break. The public bar, in which Evans now sat, was a dark, pokey room which had a floor of worn stone flags and ancient, black-timbered, high-backed settles at the tables nearest the walls. These settles had the advantage of allowing their occupants some privacy from the public eye. Evans, thankful that he had chosen one of these seats, leant back within the shelter of the worn, curved wing, confident that Alfie had not and could not see him, and prepared to eavesdrop.

It soon became evident that the edict banning the public from entering Croxton Woods was being ignored by Alfie. He was a free agent who roamed where the urge took him, the urge being closely connected with the task of filling his poacher's pocket. He rambled on about 'Owd Sally' and it was some time before Evans realised that he was referring to a hare and not a local crone.

'I seed 'im,' said Alfie, thumping the table in front of him, 'crafty Owd Sally, sneaking through the furze, thought I didn' know he wor there.'

'Tell us about the night of the storm, Alfie,' piped up one of his hangers-on, 'tell us what yew saw then.'

Alfie picked his teeth with a matchstick and spat.

'I reckin I seed things I worn't meant to.'

'Go on Alfie, what was it?'

He looked crafty. 'That would be tellin'.'

'You're making it up, you didn't see northen. Even you're not daft enough to hev bin abroad on a night loike that.' This remark came from one of his companions who was annoyed at Alfie hogging all the limelight.

'I know what I saw and I int tellin' the loikes of yew.'

'Who are you tellin' then – the police?'

'The POLICE!' The disgust and venom in his voice was chilling. 'Do they come round agin bothering me, I'll set the dorg on them!'

'You int got a dorg, Alfie.'

The conversation was interrupted at this point by the door opening and the arrival of a middle-aged couple who were definitely not public bar material. The woman wore a fur jacket over leather trousers and slipped a silk scarf off carefully-preserved blonde curls. Mutton dressed as lamb, thought Evans as they sat down at a table near the fire, what were they doing here? As soon as her companion spoke, Evans knew. They were Americans, set on soaking up the atmosphere of an old country pub and slumming for the kicks.

'What will you have, honey?' The husband was a heavily-built man in ill-bred tweeds.

'I guess a little wine darling, Muscadet preferably.'

This caused a hiatus at the bar but eventually the landlord found a bottle of Liebfraumilch, dusted it off, uncorked it and produced a glass of lukewarm liquid. The woman grimaced as she sipped it. The man drank gin and tonic.

'What a quaint little place.' Her glance included Alfie and his friends, and he played up to her. He tugged at his cap, rolled his eyes and leered, and sang a little ditty in a hoarse Suffolk dialect. His companions egged him on and he ventured a second verse to the accompaniment of much arm waving of his empty tankard. He set this down very pointedly in front of the visitors when he had finished, and

177

when the hint wasn't taken he gave up in disgust and turned his back.

'Do look at the floor, Jack,' drawled the woman. She had the breathless, baby voice of the southerner. 'There are no floor coverings. It looks like a church floor.'

'It's probably the same age as the church. Modern life passes these places by, that's why they're so quaint.'

'And the drapes, Jack, they look as if they ought to be in a museum.'

Evans squinted at the curtains. To him they looked perfectly acceptable, the sort of curtains one expected to see in a pub.

'I guess the inmates should be, too. Some of these little communities are very primitive, you know, they don't move far from their roots and a lot of in-breeding goes on.' He said this in a stage whisper and had the grace to look ashamed when he caught Evans' eye. To the detective's annoyance, the man tried to engage him in conversation.

'Do you live locally?'

Evans speared a last chip and mumbled something to the effect that he too was a visitor. Christ! They'd go back to the States thinking everyone in Suffolk was a straw-chewing imbecile; but the damage was done. Alfie had seen him, and the look he bestowed on the young detective constable was surprisingly shrewd and knowing.

There was no point in hanging around any longer. Evans gulped down the last of his beer, called his goodnights and went out, slamming the door behind him. The night was cold and still with a hint of frost in the air; by morning the ground would be white. He turned up his collar and made for his car which he had parked in the pub yard that ran alongside the building. As he unlocked the door and got inside he cursed the inopportune arrival of the two Americans, but perhaps it had been timely after all. It had stopped Alfie Coutts from blurting out – what? – in front of all and sundry. As it was, no-one was yet the wiser but Evans now knew for certain that the old bugger was holding out on the police.

Well, he wouldn't get away with it much longer; Evans would wait here until Alfie left the pub, or was turned out at closing time, and would tackle him and get the truth. What the

178

old rogue wanted was a good scare, and Evans was looking forward to delivering it. He reckoned that Roland had gone soft living out here in the sticks, and as for Mansfield — well, he was one of them, wasn't he? He himself was more in touch with things that the Suffolk Constabulary, having come from the Met and before that industrial Wales. You had to show them who was the boss. When you had them running scared you received some respect. That was how life was lived in the concrete jungle, and he for one couldn't see why the same concepts couldn't apply here. He switched on the car radio and settled back for a long wait.

Alfie stumbled out of the Duck and Spoon just after eleven o'clock. If not pissed as a newt he was clearly far from sober, thought Evans, watching him from the car. Would this mean he was too befuddled to make sense, not that making sense was Alfie's strong point, or would the drink have loosened his tongue? Unfortunately he was surrounded by his mates which put the kibosh on Evans' original idea of hauling him into the car. He would have to follow him on foot and tackle him when he parted from the others. He lived on the edge of the council estate at the other end of the village, a good mile away; perhaps by the time he reached his gate the cold night air would have sobered him up.

Evans got out of the car and plodded after the merry band, careful to keep his distance. Fortunately it was a moonlit night. A nearly full moon lit the scene, making a good substitute for the street lights that Evans sorely missed. The men ahead ambled down the middle of the road, arguing amicably amongst themselves, and at the corner of Duck Lane three of them parted company, leaving Alfie and one other man to continue along the lower road past Church Farm.

Evans stuck his hands in his pockets and slunk along the hedgerow behind them. He was uneasy at being out in the dark in what was, to him, an alien environment. People who went on about the peace and quiet of the countryside didn't know what they were talking about. If it had been silent he would have been quite happy, but the night was alive with incomprehensible noises; rustles and creakings, murmurings and squeakings. Something was pattering through the undergrowth beside him. He froze. Was it a rat? Did they have rats in the countryside or was it something bigger − a fox? Something swooped past him out of the trees, yelping and shrieking and nearly scared him out of his wits. He stumbled and tripped over. Bloody hell, what a bloodcurdling noise! And that was just a *bird*.

By the time Evans had pulled himself together, he realised that Alfie and companion had disappeared. Cursing, he hurried forward to the spot where he had last seen them. There was a fork in the road ahead and he could make out a man walking down the right-hand path. It wasn't Alfie; he must have taken the left-hand fork that curved out of sight behind a thicket of trees and shrubs. Evans quickened his pace but when he rounded the bend saw that the road ahead was empty. Frustrated, he stopped and looked around him. Over to the left was a break in the hedgerow, a black, gaping hole, and Evans approached this cautiously. A narrow footpath left the road at this point and wound through a tunnel of trees that led from this gap. Alfie must be taking a short cut.

It struck Evans at that moment that it would have been far more sensible to have driven to Alfie's home and waited for him there. But it was too late now, so he left the road and struck out along the footpath in pursuit. At that moment the moon went behind a cloud and the scene was plunged into darkness. He could not see Alfie but he could hear noises up ahead which he hoped meant that he was still on the right track and not being misled by some other nocturnal creature.

He literally fell over Alfie. After blundering through wet, slippery undergrowth Evans' feet suddenly encountered something large and solid in their path and he toppled over. His outstretched hands encountered a bulky, groaning form and he struggled on to his hands and knees and peered into the gloom. At that moment the moon came out again and he saw the old man huddled on the ground in front of him, blood streaming from a cut above one ear. As Evans bent over to assist him, Alfie opened his eyes and fixed him with a livid glare. His cap was missing and his nearly bald head gleamed like a billiard ball in the diffused light.

180

That was the last thing Evans saw. He sensed a movement behind him, then something crashed against his head and he collapsed over the recumbent body before him.

Chapter Ten

'Well, lad, how are you feeling?'

Evans stared groggily around him; at the cream and white walls criss-crossed by pipes and electrical equipment, at the shiny tiled floor, at the green basket-weave counterpane tucked neatly round his inert form. He blinked. At the foot of the bed Roland and Mansfield were regarding him with, if not exactly anxiety, a nice show of concern.

'Someone clobbered me.' He put a cautious hand to his head and winced as his fingers encountered the bandaged wound.

'Someone did indeed! Did you see who it was?'

'No, I was trying to help Alfie.'

'Alfie Coutts. What exactly were you doing?' And then, as he frowned and struggled to remember, 'Take your time, just tell us what you were up to and how it happened.'

'I was following Alfie Coutts. I'd heard him in the pub earlier boasting about what he'd seen in Croxton Woods on the night of the hurricane, and I went after him. Somehow I lost him in the dark and then I fell over him. He must have tripped and caught his head against a branch or something. There was blood pouring down the side of his face. He was glaring at me as if it were my fault. . . I don't remember any more.'

He saw Roland and Mansfield exchanging looks.

'I suppose the old half-wit told you I'd hit him? Well, it's not true. I didn't lay a finger on him.'

'Alfie Coutts is dead.'

'Dead! But when did it happen? How long have I been in here?'

'Since one o'clock this morning. You were found beside Alfie's body on the footpath that goes from Lower Road through Combe Bottoms to the council estate. Edith Smith, Coutts' sister, raised the alarm when he didn't return home at his usual time. She managed to persuade her neighbour, one Samuel Doggett, to turn out and look for him, and he stumbled across the two of you a short while later and rang the police and ambulance. You were unconscious and Coutts very dead. You were brought into the Cottage Hospital; you were lucky — you've got a thick skull. There's no serious damage, no fracture, just a nasty gash that's been sewn up, and concussion.'

'But what happened?'

'We're hoping that's what you'll be able to tell us.'

'I thought he'd had a natural accident. He was the worse for drink and I thought he had blundered into something.'

'Your typical blunt instrument?'

'You mean someone attacked him and then went for me?'

'Let's get this straight. You found Coutts and he was still alive?'

'Yes, and furious. When I bent over him he obviously thought I was his assailant.'

'When Doggett found you, Alfie was lying there with half his head bashed in. You're saying he was alive with only superficial injuries when you caught up with him?'

Evans struggled to sit up in bed, a dazed look on his face.

'Someone must have been attacking him when I disturbed him. He laid me out and then finished off what he'd started.'

'It looks very much like it. Did you see or hear anyone besides Alfie?'

'No. I'd lost him in the dark, and then I heard noises up ahead and saw him clearly — he certainly wasn't badly injured — and then I think I heard a noise behind me but before I could turn round...'

'So either someone was lying in wait for Alfie, which suggests it was someone local who knew his habits and route home, or else someone followed him out of the pub and got to him before you. Are you sure you didn't see or hear anyone

183

from the time you left the pub till you came upon him?'

'I don't *think* so, sir.' And then, as Roland looked pained, 'I heard a lot of noises but I thought they were made by wild animals and the like. I nearly got decapitated by an owl.'

'What happened earlier? You interviewed Coutts, didn't you?'

'Yes, and got nowhere; but I was convinced he did know something and then I heard him shooting his mouth off in the pub — boasting amongst his drinking pals that he'd heard and seen all manner of things on the night of the hurricane but wasn't telling — so I decided to follow him home and tackle him again.'

'Our murderer must have heard him too and decided he was a danger and had to be silenced. I hope, Evans, that you're going to be able to give us a list of everyone who was in the pub yesterday evening.'

'I wasn't there all the evening; after Alfie recognised me I waited outside in the car. There were only him and his friends and a gang of youths apart from myself in the public bar, and an American couple who came in for a short while.'

'American?' Roland pricked up his ears.

'Tourists. There were probably far more people in the saloon bar. I couldn't see them but I could hear them.'

'Which means they could probably hear what was going on in the public bar. Well, the landlord and barmaid should be able to help us out. Alfie was killed to shut him up and you happened to get in the way. There was no attempt to cover up the attack and make it look like robbery. Alfie had nothing of value on him and you still had your wallet in your pocket and were wearing your watch.'

Evans glanced down at his bare wrist.

'They're all in your locker,' Mansfield nodded in its direction, 'and they've fitted you up in a hospital gown till your auntie can bring in your own things.'

'I'm not staying here. I'm perfectly all right now.' Evans tried to swing his legs out of bed and sank back dizzily.

'You're staying here for at least another day. Concussion's a funny thing — we don't want you passing out on the job.'

'Have you found the weapon?'

'Half the police force is scouring the area at this moment.

According to Dr. Brasnett it's metallic and has a sharp edge, probably a tool of some sort. I don't suppose it will tell us much if we do turn it up. Our maniac's hardly likely to have left his dabs on it.'

The staff nurse came in at that moment. She was a brisk, middle-aged woman who expected to be obeyed – and was.

'You must go now, sir, our patient must rest.'

'Do you hear that, Evans? Have a good rest, and we'll see you back on duty when you're fit again.'

As they left, Roland poked his head back inside the door.

'By the way, as you're not capable of going to the morgue, I'll send someone round with the photos Benton took at the scene so that you can confirm that the lethal blows were not delivered until after you were knocked out. They're not pretty viewing.'

Evans grimaced and sank back against the pillow. He had the uncomfortable feeling that the murderer was laughing at him. He was also feeling guilty. Somehow he should have been able to prevent the fatal attack on Alfie Coutts. He had been on the scene, a police officer in the course of his investigations, and had allowed himself to be taken unawares and laid out cold whilst Coutts, the poor old sod, had been beaten to death. He closed his eyes and tried to make his mind blank, but horrible images kept passing through his imagination and it was a long while before he drifted off to sleep.

A feeling of responsibility for Alfie Coutts' death was also exercising Roland. As he said to Mansfield later: 'We should have given him some protection, put him under surveillance; if we'd done that we could have prevented his death and probably trapped the killer at the same time. We know that he knew something about what happened that night.'

'Strange that our murderer did nothing until last night, when Evans happened to be on the scene.'

'Not if you accept the premise that Evans was recognised as a police officer, and one who was interested in Alfie Coutts. Our man had to act fast – and he did.'

'Someone who was in the Duck and Spoon yesterday evening?'

185

'Yes. I'm trying to trace the American couple; they're probably just harmless tourists but there's just the possibility it could be our mysterious Leslie Drew. The other people in the public bar are all accounted for: three of Alfie's cronies were together after they parted from him until they reached their front doors, the fourth was seen rolling down his garden path at about the time of the attack on Evans by none other than PC Drake. The gang of youths weren't local. They came from Felstone on motorbikes, and at turning out time they all roared off back to the bright lights.'

'So – the saloon bar?'

'And what a turn-up for the books! Bradley Scott and Stephen Bates were both in there for a good part of the evening, and who else should put in an appearance but Mrs. Dalton and Mrs. Garfield.'

'They weren't drinking in there?'

'Ginny Dalton apparently called in to see if Burroughs, the landlord, would arrange for a bar at the school PTA disco later in the term. He can't remember what time it was or how long she was actually there.'

'But long enough to have heard Alfie shouting his mouth off.'

'And to have seen him too, and anyone else who was in the public bar. The counter runs through from one room to the other and there's a mirror running the length of the wall behind it. Anyone approaching the bar counter could see in the mirror what was going on in adjoining room.'

'And Lee Garfield called in sometime during the evening to buy a bottle of whisky because her husband had run out. Vera the barmaid was collecting glasses at the time from the tables near the door. She noticed her getting into the car. She thinks Garfield could have been in the car too because she thinks Missus got in the passenger seat.'

'We come up with the same names all the time. Take the night of the hurricane: we know Alfie Coutts was in the woods – so were Stephen Bates and Bradley Scott and God knows who else. The place was alive with people if evidence is to be believed, with the murderer stalking on and off the scene like the ghost of Hamlet's father.'

'You now think that we're definitely looking for a man?'

186

'No, Patrick, the fair sex cannot be ruled out. I know women don't usually go in for physical violence like this but it's not unknown, especially when desperation lends impetus to the action. It wouldn't have taken much physical effort to do for Alfie Coutts; he was a frail old man, inebriated into the bargain. It only needs a few blows struck in a frenzy with a weapon that was to hand.'

'The shovel? Our murderer may have killed in frenzy but he or she had enough wits about them to put the weapon back where they found it.'

The murder weapon had been found; a long-handled shovel stuck in the midden by the yard gate of Lower Farm, overlooked at first because of its obviousness.

'Yes, he or she snatched it up on the way past and returned it to the same spot. The boys are still working on it. Most of the evidence was rubbed off in the muck but they've found traces of blood and hair which match the victim's, and it was the right shape to fit the wounds.'

'Was it also used to deliver the *coup de grâce* to Evans?'

'The wooden handle end was used. He certainly didn't intend killing our William.'

The death of Alfie Coutts shocked the inhabitants of Croxton. Hated by some, held in affection by others, and looked on as a figure of fun by many, he had been one of the local characters whom everyone knew. With his passing the village would never be quite the same again, and the violent manner in which he had met his death outraged the populace. The murder of Tim Spencer was shrouded in the mists of time, and unreal to many people; Julian Lester was an outsider and the true cause of his death a mystery to most, but Alfie Coutts had been struck down viciously in their midst, an innocent old man who had never done any real harm, and local opinion was in no doubt that it was time the police got stuck in and apprehended the murderer.

Stephen Bates expressed what was in many peoples' minds when Mansfield questioned him about his activities on the evening of the murder.

'I can't believe I'll never see him again. The old bugger made my job difficult and many's the time I've cursed him, but I can't believe I'll never see him again, sneaking through the woods, his pockets stuffed with my game. Alfie Coutts was one of the crosses I had to bear but I didn't expect him to come to a nasty end like this.'

He himself had left the pub at nine-thirty to pick up his wife from a W.I. meeting. They had arrived home a little after ten and had turned in not long after that. Plenty of time for him to have gone back and attacked Alfie, thought Mansfield, and his wife would back him up in anything he said, but he decided to leave it there for the time being. Although never removed from their list of suspects, Stephen Bates now figured somewhere near the bottom. If new evidence came to light that refocussed suspicion back on to him, then his movements for that evening would be rechecked.

Bradley Scott had left the pub at closing time. It was a black mark to DC Evans that he hadn't noticed him when checking Alfie's movements. He said that he had gone straight home, which was in the opposite direction to the route taken by Alfie and his cronies, but he could probably have doubled back and taken a short cut through the village that brought him out at Combe Bottoms ahead of Alfie. He admitted that he had seen no-one on his way home and so far nobody interviewed had mentioned seeing him, so he had no alibi for the relevant time.

The other people who had been drinking in the Duck and Spoon that evening had been checked out; a hen party consisting of a group of women returning from a Keep Fit Rally who had spent about an hour in the saloon bar; three local couples who had met up and parted at closing time, each pair driving home in different directions and with no reasons for chasing after and accosting Alfie Coutts; three members of the local branch of the British Legion whose combined ages added up to more than three times Alfie's and were so physically decrepit that they could not in anyway be considered as potential murderers; and two couples who were passing through the village, had called in for a drink, were many miles away at the time of the murder and could prove it.

This left just the two women who had called in at the pub for other reasons during the evening: Lee Garfield and Ginny Dalton. Roland and Mansfield went together to question them.

188

It was a bright, crisp day and the white-powdered fields still showed signs of overnight frost as they drove to The Hermitage. The track leading up to the house had almost dried out and they met Lee Garfield on horseback halfway down it. She reined in her mare and waited as Roland and Mansfield got out of the car. Her hair was ruffled and her cheeks flushed from the exercise and cold air.

'Good morning, Inspector Roland, Segeant Mansfield. Were you looking for me?'

'Yes, ma'am,' said Mansfield. 'Just a few questions we'd like you to answer.'

'I take it this is not a social call. Do you want me to come up to the house? Is it going to take long?'

'That depends on what you have to tell us.'

'Has your mare recovered from her injuries?' enquired Roland.

'Yes, it was only a superficial cut but she's very highly-strung so needs watching.'

She certainly did, thought Roland as the mare skittered sideways and curled her lip. He edged back a little, trying not to make it look like a retreat. Why couldn't the damn woman dismount? He felt at a distinct disadvatage with her towering above him.

'Shouldn't you be wearing a hat?'

'I'm not on the public highway,' she retorted, 'and I like to feel the wind in my hair.' She made it sound very abandoned and he hastily resumed his official line of questioning.

'I understand you were in the Duck and Spoon on the night that Mr. Alfie Coutts met his death?'

'In the pub?' There was derision in her voice. 'I think you've got your wires crossed, Inspector.'

'You were seen in the saloon bar between eight-thirty and nine o'clock,' said Mansfield, consulting his notes, 'buying a bottle of whisky. There are several witnesses to that, including the barmaid.'

'Oh, that.' She gave a little chuckle. 'I thought you meant that I'd been seen in there drinking.'

'Would you care to explain what you were doing?'

'I thought you had just told me, Sergeant, I was buying whisky.'

The two men regarded her impassively and she gave a little mock sigh.

'All right, I'll come clean. We don't normally buy our supplies from the pub but we'd run low and my husband wanted some for medicinal purposes. I'd been to the station to pick him up from the London train. He felt he was sickening for 'flu or a bad cold and needed a hot whisky and lemon, so I called in at the pub on my way home to pick up a bottle.'

'I understood your husband was driving.'

'You *have* been checking up, Inspector. My husband dislikes being driven, by myself or anyone else, he is not a good passenger. When I said I picked him up, I meant that I met him at the station and he took over the driving. He waited outside in the car whilst I went inside and bought the whisky. I don't suppose I was in there longer than five minutes. Does that answer your question?'

'Did you see or hear Alfie Coutts when you were in there?'

'I'm sure you already know that I went into the saloon bar. I exchanged a few words with the landlord at the counter, and when he had produced the bottle and I had paid for it I hurried back to the car. I have no idea who was or was not drinking in the pub that night. Is that all?' She made as if to ride off.

'Not quite, Mrs. Garfield. I should like to know your movements after you left the Duck and Spoon.'

'We drove straight home, of course. Tony was feeling lousy, and I tucked him up in bed with a couple of aspirins and a nightcap.'

'What time would this have been?'

'About half-past nine. I'm not really sure, Inspector, I hadn't realised I should have been clock-watching!'

'And did you turn in then?'

'Good heavens, no! I don't retire for the night that early. I stayed up for a further hour or so.'

'And weren't you afraid of disturbing your husband when you did retire?'

'There was no question of that, we have separate rooms.' She said it shortly, and when he made no reply but just quirked an eye-brow, was stung to continue: 'It is a perfectly

190

sensible arrangement. My husband often has meetings to attend, in connection with his business, which continue late into the evening; he also often brings work home with him, so in order not to disturb me he has his own bedroom and dressing-room and I have mine — not that that is any business of yours, Inspector!'

So they don't sleep together, thought Roland. Was this because she was having an affair with Scott, or was she sleeping with him because her husband was denying her her conjugal rights?

Mansfield was envious of a house large enough to allow every member of the family their own personal suite. Jean would probably appreciate not being woken up at some of the God-forsken hours at which he arrived home... or would she?

'So after approximately nine-thirty, neither of you saw the other again — or anyone else?'

'That is correct. Why, what am I supposed to have done? Gone back and attacked that poor old man with an axe?'

'Someone did, Mrs. Garfield.'

'Yes, it's a horrible thought. I realise you are only doing your duty but...' she looked suddenly worried and subdued, the mask of bravado momentarily slipping. '...is there any reason why I have been singled out?'

'Whatever gave you that idea, ma'am? We are naturally questioning everyone who was in the vicinity that fatal evening. It's really a case of elimination; because you were seen in the pub we have to check you out in order to cross you off our list. Once we get rid of all the extraneous witnesses, we can concentrate on the real suspects. By the way, Mrs. Garfield, I hope your husband has recovered from his chill or whatever?'

'It was a false alarm, never came to anything, but you know how you men like to be mollycoddled at the first sign of illness.'

'He's lucky to have such a devoted wife,' said Roland, poker-faced.

She changed the subject. 'I hope you find the maniac who did this, for both our peace of minds. I don't appear to have an alibi for the relevant time. Good day, Inspector, Sergeant.'

And she swung the mare round and cantered off down the slope without a backward glance.

'She hasn't either, has she?' Mansfield looked after the retreating figure.

'What's more to the point, neither has her husband. We've only her word that he retired to bed at nine o'clock nursing a cold. She may well believe she is telling the truth, but he could have got up again and gone out without her knowing.'

'He'd have run the risk of being seen by someone.'

'I'm sure he could have got himself from The Hermitage down to Combe Bottoms without anyone seeing him, if he had wanted to. Evans never noticed the murderer and he was actually on the scene and looking for anything untoward. Come on, let's go and see what Mrs. Dalton has to say for herself. I think it's time we faced her with our knowledge of Simon's true parentage.'

'Our presumed knowledge.'

'Want to take a bet on it?'

Mansfield didn't.

They picked her up as she left the school grounds in the lunch hour. Roland had had a hunch that she probably slipped out to do shopping at that time and was proved correct. She walked through the main gates at half-past twelve and set off in the direction of the high street. Roland followed her discreetly until she was well clear of the school, then drew up alongside her and hooted softly. She faltered and glanced at the car without seeming to recognise its two occupants, then resumed her hurried walk. Roland followed and repeated the performance, and this time she glared at the vehicle before suddenly darting through an opening in the hedge that led into the municipal gardens. As he watched her crossing the grass diagonally towards the exit on the next street, he realised that the sun had been shining full on to the windscreen; she wouldn't have been able to see who was in the car.

'Did you ever see that film "Indiscreet", sir, with Cary Grant and Ingrid Bergman?' asked Mansfield innocently.

Roland swore and cruised round the corner. 'Open your window so I can speak to her, damn you!'

As they drew alongside her for the third time, he leaned across and spoke.

'Mrs. Dalton — it's the police. We're not trying to pick you up — or not in the way you think. I'd like a few words.'

'That was an imbecilic way to behave!' Her eyes flashed at them, one blue, the other yellow-green in the wintery sunlight, like an angry cat's.

'Would you care to get into the car?'

'No, I would not. I have to get back to school.'

'You are going in the opposite direction,' he pointed out. 'We have some questions to ask you. We can either stand here in the high street and bawl at each other in front of whoever happens to be passing, or you can get in the car and we'll drive to the Station and conduct the interview discreetly in my office — the choice is yours.'

She gave in with bad grace. When Mansfield opened the door she slipped inside and perched on the back seat as far away from him as possible, her lips compressed into a line, staring frostily ahead as if Roland, in the driving seat, were invisible.

'Mrs. Dalton, you are not under arrest, please understand that. I am not cautioning you or trotting out the old chestnut about helping the police in their enquiries. I am taking you to my office solely so that we can have a little talk away from the prying eyes and ears of your pupils and neighbours — and, of course, young Simon.'

'That is very thoughtful of you, Inspector,' Her tone was icy.

She refused all further attempts at conversation. When they reached the Station and Roland ushered her into his office, she silently sat in the chair he offered and folded her hands in her lap. Roland regarded her thoughtfully. He was used to witnesses either blustering vociferously in an attempt to cover up or protest their innocence, or insisting on their solicitor being present and refusing to speak a word in the meantime. Her silence was different. She sat, tightly buttoned up in her red jacket in the over-heated room, head bowed, eyes lowered, like a penitent nun. Except that she was no nun. God! Could she really be unaware of the effect of her innocent, yet disturbing, sexuality?

193

He signalled to Mansfield and moved over to the window. Patrick Mansfield pulled his chair closer and cleared his throat.

'Can I get you a cup of coffee, Mrs. Dalton, and a sandwich or something to eat? We have interrupted your lunch-hour.'

'No, thank you, my appetite seems to have fled.'

'You mustn't neglect your health. It is a cold day and you certainly don't need to watch your weight.'

'Don't be so patronising, Sergeant,' she snapped, 'How about getting on with the third degree.'

'Mrs. Dalton, this isn't an interview room, this conversation is not being recorded, it is entirely off the cuff; you've been brought here for a friendly chat.'

'You could have fooled me.'

Mansfield leaned forward. 'Could you tell us please, what you were doing in the Duck and Spoon on the night Alfie Coutts was murdered?'

'I was ...' She stopped abruptly and glanced over at Roland who was lounging against the window frame. 'I think I must insist on my solicitor being present.'

He answered her. 'Mrs. Dalton, as we have stressed, this meeting is not official, you are not being charged with anything. We are questioning everyone who is known to have been in the vicinity of the Duck and Spoon on the night that Alfie Coutts was killed. It is as much a matter of elimination as anything. No-one else has screamed for their lawyer; I find this rather significant, don't you, Mansfield?'

'Certain things could be read into it, sir,' agreed Mansfield.

She snorted. 'Ask your questions. I have nothing to hide, and I'm used by now to having everything I say distorted and twisted to fit your theories.'

Mansfield looked pained.

'Do you want me to repeat the original question?'

'No, Sergeant, I have perfect recall! I was not in the Duck and Spoon in the sense that you mean. I had just popped in for a few minutes to ask Fred Burroughs, the landlord, if he would run the bar at the PTA Disco next month. It means applying for a licence at the local ... but then, you know all about that, don't you?'

'What time was this?'

194

She considered. 'A little after ten. I had intended going round earlier but I forgot. I had just sat down to watch the ten o'clock news when I remembered.'

This coincided with Evans' evidence.

'Did you see Alfie Coutts?'

'I don't know.'

'Don't know? Surely you either saw him or not.'

'Look, Sergeant, I happen to know, in common with most of the inhabitants of Croxton, that Alfie Coutts spent nearly every evening in the pub. There were a group of his friends in the public bar, I saw them through the mirror at the back of the counter. I don't know if Alfie was actually amongst them; if I had thought about it at all, I should have presumed so.'

'Could you hear their conversation?'

'No, I told you, I hardly noticed them.'

'But could you have heard them if you had been listening?'

'Ye-es, I suppose it was possible. What am I supposed to have overheard?'

'Alfie Coutts boasting that he was in possession of certain facts incriminating the murderer of Julian Lester.'

'So that's why the poor old man was killed!'

The right touch of indignation, thought Roland, watching her carefully, but was it just too calculated?

'And was it true?' she continued. 'Did he really know something?'

'We shall never know now, shall we? To re-cap: you visited the Duck and Spoon sometime after ten o'clock — about ten-ten, ten-fifteen?' She nodded.

'You were only there a short time, so by ten-twenty, give or take a minute or two, you would have left?' She agreed.

'What did you do after that?'

'Why, I returned home, of course.'

'Did you see anyone on the way?'

'No, it is only a short distance and I don't remember seeing anyone.'

'A pity, but this agrees with our evidence. Nobody has come forward to say they saw you walking from the pub to your house at the appropriate time. Perhaps you were not?'

'What do you mean?' Then, as neither man spoke, 'Are you insinuating that I had something to do with Alfie's death?

195

That I hung around and went after him and beat him to death? It's preposterous!'

'Someone did, Mrs. Dalton, but perhaps your son can confirm that you had returned home by ten-thirty?'

'Simon was in bed. Anyway, can a son give his mother an alibi? Is it allowed?' She was getting increasingly annoyed and agitated.

'Young Simon looks very much like you, Mrs. Dalton.' Roland left the window and resumed control of the questioning. She gave him a startled glance.

'I beg your pardon?'

'I said, how much your son resembles you; different colouring of course, but all the same little mannerisms, the give-away traits.'

'You're being absurd, Inspector. Simon is my stepson.'

'Is he? Are you sure you're not related?'

'What do you mean?'

'I repeat, are you related?'

She made as if to deny it, then changed her mind and said slowly: 'Actually he is related to me distantly. Ruth, his mother, Alec's first wife, was my cousin.'

Wow, thought Mansfield, did this mean Roland had been mistaken? He looked by no means put out.

'Interesting, Mrs. Dalton. I suppose that could account for the likeness, only you and I know that Ruth and Alec Dalton were unable to have children!'

She blenched and Mansfield thought she was going to faint. He moved towards her.

'What are you getting at?' she whispered, staring at Roland in dismay.

'The truth. Simon was adopted as a baby. Is that not so?'

She swept back her hair with a nervous gesture and countered: 'Is that a crime?'

'Not in itself. I am sure it was all done legally. But it leads me on to an interesting paradox. If Simon was adopted, why does he look so much like you, his stepmother? From there it was only a short step to assuming that you are his real mother. I suggest that Simon is the son of you and Timothy Spencer.'

'No!' It was a protest rather than a denial. She could not get any paler but she swayed and clutched the sides of the chair as if to anchor herself to reality. Roland leaned towards her.

'Are you denying it, Mrs. Dalton?'

'You can't prove it!'

'I rather think I can. The fact is that Simon's adoption order went through the Norwich County Court in 1976. Now you and I know that information pertaining to adoption is never revealed unless under exceptional circumstances. But such circumstances certainly apply here. The police has no power in itself to enforce an adoption society to reveal the identity of an adoptee's parents, but I am investigating a murder, a series of particularly nasty murders, and in view of this I should have no trouble in getting a court order to gain access to this information. Do I have to go to these lengths, Mrs. Dalton? Because, believe me, I will if I have to.'

Their eyes met. She got to her feet and went across to the window. She stared out for a few seconds and then swung round and faced him defiantly.

'Alright, I don't know how you found out but you are right. Simon *is* my son, and Tim was his father.'

'Did Spencer know?'

'No. We were separated before I could tell him.'

'Did anyone else know the truth?'

'Only myself, Ruth and Alec. And, of course, the adoption society.'

'Does Simon know?'

'No.' She looked distressed. 'We had always intended telling him when he got older, but then Alec died and I postponed it. I thought he had enough to cope with without the added trauma of that knowledge. Does he have to know? Does anyone have to know?'

'That depends. I am investigating Timothy Spencer's murder. This gives you an even more powerful motive.'

'Why?'

'Why? Spencer was the father of your child. It would not be unreasonable to assume that you were expecting him to come back and marry you. It must have been a shock to discover that he already had a wife and son in Australia. A shock great enough perhaps to push you over the edge, and cause you to mow him down with a shotgun.'

'No! I didn't kill him! I never saw him when he came back

197

from Australia, and I never knew he had married until *you* told me! By that time, Simon had been oficially adopted by Ruth and Alec and I had got over my infatuation with Tim. Anyway, if we had met I wouldn't have told him about Simon, there would have been no point.'

Roland turned the conversation.

'How opportune, your meeting up with Alec Dalton again after his wife died and claiming the . . . er . . . affections of him and your son. You are a great manipulator, Mrs. Dalton.'

'It wasn't like that at all! Naturally I kept in touch with Alec and Ruth, she being my cousin, and after she died . . .'

'Yes, how *did* she die?'

'This is unbelievable! You're not suggesting that I killed her, are you? What a malicious, distorted mind you have, Inspector! Ruth died of leukaemia, only a few months after it was diagnosed. I helped Alec to cope with his bereavement, and with Simon who was only a toddler at the time. Gradually we grew to love each other. Naturally, I can't expect you to understand this, but we fell in love and in due course married. Simon became my stepson as well as being my real son.'

'Very touching. Sergeant, send for some coffee, or would you prefer tea, Mrs. Dalton?'

'Coffee, thank you,' she said weakly.

Mansfield opened the door, collared a young constable walking down the corridor and sent him for some coffee and biscuits. Whilst he was occupied, Roland shot at her: 'Who do you think killed Timothy Spencer?'

'You mean you believe me — that I didn't do it?'

'Supposing you just answer my question.'

'I don't know. I can't think of anyone who could have hated him enough to want to kill him, as I told you before.'

'Someone did, and that someone is making a habit of it. Julian Lester and Alfie Coutts died as a direct result of Timothy Spencer's skeleton coming to light. We have a murderer in our midst and no-one is safe until he is apprehended.'

The coffee arrived and when she had finished drinking, Roland pushed his cup to one side and stood up.

198

'If there is nothing further you can tell us, Mrs. Dalton, Mr. Mansfield will run you back to school.'

She too stood up with alacrity.

'There's no need, I was coming into town on an errand anyway.'

'Thank you for your co-operation.' He opened the door for her.

'You won't tell Simon?'

'Mrs. Dalton, I don't go around wreaking havoc in people's lives for the sheer hell of it. If the fact of his parentage turns out to have no bearing on my case, he will not be told by me. But I think he should know the true facts concerning his birth. Don't forget he can apply himself for access to the orginal record when he is eighteen, under the Children Act of 1975.'

'That is a long while ahead. May I go now?'

'Certainly.' Roland stood aside. 'Good day, Mrs. Dalton.'

She started to walk down the corridor, then hesitated and turned back.

'There is one thing I think you should know — Simon was a friend of Alfie's.'

'Simon was?'

'He and a school friend, Mark Taplin, used to hang around with Alfie; in the holidays and at weekends and on summer evenings.'

'I shouldn't have thought a half-witted old man was much company for a couple of teenage boys.'

'Alfie was only wanting in certain areas. He knew more about wildlife and the countryside than most qualified naturalists, and he chose to impart this knowledge to Simon and Mark.'

'Alfie was known chiefly for his prowess as a poacher.'

'Yes, I know. I often worried about whether I should discourage the association, but I thought it was quite harmless and that it would naturally tail off as Simon got older.'

'Is Alfie likely to have confided in Simon and his friend?'

'About what he knew in connection with Julian Lester's murder? I don't think so. They hadn't seen much of each other recently because of the dark evenings, and Simon has said nothing. I try not to pry too much. It's difficult being a single parent of a teenage boy. He resents being mollycoddled, and

199

I've always thought he was safer traipsing round the countryside with Alfie than raving it up in Felstone with some of his school contemporaries.'

'Quite so.'

'But he has been acting a little oddly just lately.' She paused. 'It's probably because he's upset over Alfie's death. He won't talk about it.'

'I shouldn't worry, Mrs. Dalton,' said Mansfield, 'young people are far more resilient than we give them credit for. I'm sure he will come to terms with it in his own way.'

'Could he be in danger?' she persisted.

'I hardly think so. You say yourself that he saw very little of Alfie recently, and he's certainly not mentioned being in possession of any information the old chap might have passed on, has he? Don't worry, just treat him as usual.'

Mansfield escorted her out of the building and returned to his superior who was tapping his pen against his desk top and scowling unseeingly at the wall charts.

'I don't like it, Pat, that boy could be in danger.'

'Not if Ginny Dalton is the murderer, or have we written her off?'

'You've never been in favour of the idea, have you? And I think I'm coming round to your way of thinking. She could have committed all three killings — on the facts we have she can't be ruled out — but I don't think she is our man, or rather woman. And if she isn't, and Alfie blabbed to Simon and our murderer realises this . . .'

'Protection?'

'I don't want to alarm the boy or draw him to the murderer's attention but I think we must do something. I wonder if we can get him to talk to us. The trouble is, he may not be willing to confide in us in front of his mother but I think we must have a go. I think you'd be the best person to tackle him; you've got teenagers of your own, you can probably get on his wavelength better than I. Stress that any knowledge he has will help to avenge Alfie. Oh — and, Pat, find out the address of the other lad, his friend. This could involve him as well. There must be no more killings.

'Je-e-an, I'm home!'

200

Mansfield let himself in through the front door and hung up his coat. The house was in darkness apart from a light showing under the door of the little room beside the stairwell which they euphemistically called the study. From behind the door came the sound of tapping. Mansfield turned the handle and poked his head inside.

'Anyone at home?'

Jean Mansfield gave a little squeal and dropped her hands from the typewriter keys. 'Patrick! You gave me a scare — I didn't hear you come in. Goodness, is that the time? I wasn't expecting you home yet.'

'I'm not, officially. I was in the area and I dropped in for a cuppa and a bit of comfort. You sounded very busy.'

'Yes, I'm just typing some notes for the next NCT meeting. Let me just do this bit and I'll put the kettle on.'

'I'll do it, you finish your typing.' He dropped a kiss on her head. 'I didn't know we owned a typewriter?'

'We don't, it belongs to the Trust and I borrowed it because I thought it would be easier to work at home.'

'You didn't carry that thing yourself?'

It was a heavy office model in two shades of grey.

'Don't worry, I had a Galahad. Andrew Simmonds, that nice young librarian, gave me a lift home and carried it in for me.'

'You want to watch these quiet young library assistants, I've heard they get up to all sorts of things behind the book stacks!'

'What rubbish you do talk, Pat. Have you had a hectic day?'

'I'm *having* a hectic day, it's not over yet.' He peered over her shoulder at what she was typing. 'What make of typewriter is it?'

She squinted down at the machine, seeking a nameplate. 'I'm not sure — oh yes, it's an Adler, you can just about make out the name —'

'An Adler?' He couldn't keep the sharpness out of his voice.

'What's the matter? What's so extraordinary about this typewriter being an Adler? It's a well-known name.'

'Here, let me see what you've typed.' He bent over the sheet

201

of paper in the carriage. Jean was no professional typist and the spacing and lay-out left much to be desired, but it was the actual letters that leapt to his attention. The centre of the 'a' was blurred and surely 'W' was out of alignment?

'Quick, take that out! He reached for the platten knob and unrolled the sheet.

'Patrick, I haven't finished! What are you doing?'

'Sorry, love, but this is important. Put another sheet in and type what I tell you − please!'

Jean looked at her husband in bewilderment but did as he bid.

'What have I to type?'

'Now how did it go? "There is nothing to look forward to except a lonely old age"', he recited slowly, and after a strange look at him she tapped it out, "and increasing dependence on the bottle. What is the point. I choose to go whilst I still have some self-respect and a few friends." That's all, give it to me.'

He held up the sheet of paper and scrutinised it carefully. 'I just don't believe this! Where did that typewriter come from?'

'Patrick, what is this all about? What on earth's the matter?'

'The typewriter?'

'I told you, it belongs to the Nature Conservation Trust. I borrowed it.'

'Where is it usually kept?'

'In the office at Sheldon House.'

'And who has access to it?'

'Well, theoretically just members of the committee who have a key, but the room's not always kept locked and I think other organisations there use it from time to time and discreetly borrow it − you know what that place is like.'

'Don't I just!' groaned Mansfield.

Sheldon House had originally been built by a Colonel Sheldon who had made his fortune bringing the railway to Felstone. It was a massive Victorian mansion and had been appropriated during the war by an army unit who had inflicted considerable damage on its interior. After the war it had been taken over by the local council, and being in a strategic position near the

202

centre of the town, it had been earmarked for demolition to make way for a modern council office block. After an uproar by conservationists a preservation order had been slapped on to it, and the rambling old building now housed a variety of tenants.

The council used part of it and leased out the rest to various charities and local organisations. The library was housed in the front part of the building, and it was also home to the local Tourist Bureau, the Citizen's Advice Bureau, the Nature Conservation Trust, the Felstone Mission to the Deaf, as well as providing the headquarters for the Scouts and Guides.

'I'm sorry, love, but I'm going to have to take this with me.'

'But I haven't finished using it! Aren't you going to tell me what's wrong?'

'No time now. Open the door, please.'

'But, Pat, you haven't had you tea! You're not going already?'

'Sorry, but this is important. Don't wait dinner for me.'

Jean Mansfield stood aside in resignation as he humped the typewriter out to his car.

Roland had just come through a gruelling session with Superintendent Lacey. The Super hadn't liked the way things were going and had been at great pains to stress this.

'How many more are going to be knocked off before you nail the culprit, that's what I ask myself? It's over two months since that damn skeleton was discovered and where have we got? Two more killings and no nearer the truth!'

'We are getting there, sir. We know the identity of the skeleton, and we're uncovering the background and piecing the story together.'

'Piecing the story together!' Lacey was disgusted. 'You sound like someone on "Watch with Mother". We want a conviction not a lot of theories! How is Evans?'

'He's being discharged tomorrow morning.'

'It's bad enough when the hoi-polloi get scrubbed out, but when one of my own men is attacked and left for dead, I take umbrage! Do you understand that, Inspector? I take umbrage. I want this case cleared up!'

'Don't we all, sir. But we're getting there. I'm following up several promising leads.'

'Which you're going to tell me about?'

'Of course, sir.'

'It's gone on too long,' grumbled Lacey a little while later, having been put in the picture as regards the latest developments, 'I think we ought to call in the Yard. The CC is not going to like this one little bit.'

'And have them take all the glory? Just give me a little more time.'

'All right, but I want results, James, and no more nasty happenings!'

'Thank you, sir.'

Back in his office Roland flipped desultorily through his case-notes and doodled in the margins. Mansfield found him a short while later.

'You look like the cat that got the cream. What's up?'

'I've got something for you.'

'It had better be good. The Super's screaming for results. Our days on this case are numbered unless we come up with the goods PDQ.'

Mansfield handed him the typewritten sheet and he glanced over it.

'What's this? Mucking about with our evidence? You're not supposed to remove . . .'

'Have another look,' cut in Mansfield.

Roland perused it again and looked up in astonishment.

'This is not the original note − give!'

'I think we've found the typewriter.'

'Where was it?'

'You're never going to believe this − in my house!'

Chapter Eleven

Mark Taplin, Simon Dalton's friend, lived with his family in a quiet close in Wallingford on the Croxton side of the village, not far from Mansfield's own house. Mansfield had decided to tackle young Mark first before approaching Simon and his mother, and set out for the Taplin residence early that evening. He netted the two together; Simon was spending the evening with his friend.

Mrs. Taplin opened the door. She was a rather harassed-looking woman who gave the impression of being in a perpetual hurry. Mansfield introduced himself and calmed her down as she reacted worriedly to his visit.

'Mark has done nothing wrong, Mrs. Taplin, we're just hoping he may be able to help us. We know that he and Simon Dalton were friendly with Alfie Coutts. They probably knew him as well as anyone and may be able to help us with some background information; how he used to spend his time, where he went, his local friends − that sort of thing.'

'I never thought it was good for him, being so friendly with that daft old man,' she said fretfully. 'I know one shouldn't speak ill of the dead, but there's no denying it − he was only 90p in the pound. But there, Ginny Dalton, Simon's mother, thought there was no harm in it and it kept them out of mischief.' Mansfield has his doubts about this. 'If I could just have a word with Mark?'

'Simon's here now. They're up in Mark's bedroom playing computer games. I'll get them down.'

'Don't bother, I'll go up. I don't want to alarm them — just an informal little chat. You, of course, must be present.'

Mrs. Taplin led the way upstairs and opened the first door on the left of the landing.

'There's someone to see you.'

The two boys were bending over the unit housing the computer. They turned at the interruption and Mansfield saw recognition spark in Simon's eyes before a pose of studied indifference replaced it.

'You know who I am, don't you? Detective Sergeant Mansfield of the local CID. I've come to enlist your help.'

This caught their interest and he pressed on quickly. 'A poor old man who never did anyone any harm has been killed. Oh, we know he helped himself to the odd rabbit and pheasant, but he never hurt anyone. And yet someone hurt him, fatally. You were friends of Alfie Coutts and I know you will want this wicked person to be caught and punished.' He let this sink in. 'Was anything worrying him? Did he tell you anything that might help us to find out who killed him?'

'We haven't seen him for ages.' This was Mark.

'When did you see him last?'

'I dunno.' He looked at his friend and Simon said hurriedly: 'Not since the hurricane, I think.'

'You're sensible lads. I'm sure that I can confide in you.' Mansfield adopted a conspiratorial tone. 'We think Alfie Coutts saw or heard the person who murdered Mr. Lester in Croxton Woods on the evening before the hurricane. He spoke about this rather rashly, and he may have been killed to stop him telling us about it. So it's very important if he said anything — anything at all — about this, that you tell me. We want to avenge him, don't we?'

'We haven't seen him, he didn't tell us anything.'

'Are you quite sure?'

'He didn't tell us anything.'

They sounded as if they were telling the truth, thought Mansfield. He assumed they were two boys who normally didn't lie and yet he was convinced they knew something. Had young Dalton emphasised the word "tell"? He tried a shot in the dark.

206

'What were you doing on the evening of the hurricane?'
Alarm and fear flashed over their countenances before they
composed their features.
'I don't remember,' said Mark.
'You went to that scout meeting where they showed the
slides of the summer camp, surely you haven't forgotten?'
said his mother sharply. She turned to the sergeant. 'Simon
and Mark went together, and Simon stayed the night here
afterwards. He often does, and it was a good thing on that
occasion. He could have been badly hurt ...'
'Quite,' said Mansfield hurriedly. 'Do you remember
now?' The two boys nodded.
'Well, I'm disappointed. I was counting on your being able
to help us. Never mind, I'll let you get on with your game.
Finished your homework?'
'We don't get any on Wednesday evenings.'
'Lucky you.'
Downstairs again he led Mrs. Taplin on to the subject of
scout meetings.
'I take it that Mark and Simon are both members of the
local scout troop?'
'Yes, they're both very keen, and they both went to the
camp in Norfolk in the summer holidays.'
'Where are their meetings held?' He knew perfectly well but
was edging the conversation round to the topic in which he
was interested.
'There's a hut behind the church hall, they hold the
meetings there.'
'I expect you or your husband pick them up after the
meetings?'
'Well, no,' she looked puzzled, 'it's only a short distance
from here and they have their bikes.'
'Ah, yes, these youngsters like to be independent but I'm
sure you must have picked them up after that meeting on the
evening of the hurricane, it was such a wild night.'
'No, actually we didn't, Sergeant. My husband and I
attended a business "do" that evening, and Simon stayed
here to keep Mark company. We knew we were going to be
late home but one daren't mention babysitters when they are
this age! The wind didn't really get up until the small hours

207

and by that time they had been safely tucked up in bed for hours.'

'Yes, of course. Well, thank you, Mrs. Taplin.'

'I hope you catch the person who killed that poor old man. It's terrible, all the violence about nowadays, no-one's safe. It wasn't like this when I was a child, and that's not all that long ago. I blame the television. It's all you see, even on the News, crime and violence . . .'

Mansfield cut her short and made his escape. As he drove out of the village the spark of an idea was germinating in his mind.

Tony Garfield sat at his desk, scowling at the sheaf of papers on his desk, and re-lived the scene which had taken place that breakfast time. He still couldn't take it in, what Lee had said. She was leaving him! Just like that she'd come out with it, between the bacon and toast, so to speak. He had tried to treat it as a joke but she had been serious, had talked at length about all the excitement and romance being gone from their marriage and how his latest venture − his brainchild, the culmination of hours of planning and wheeling and dealing − was the last straw.

Until this morning he hadn't realised how utterly opposed to his scheme she was. He had thought he could talk her round; after all, once the place was built and in use they would reap handsome financial benefits. It would be a struggle initially but once it got off the ground it would be a little goldmine. He had even tried to appease her by hinting that in a few years time they could move, leave the district and build a dream house in a place of her choice, but she had been adamant. She wanted nothing to do with his − what had she called it? − financial chicanery! That had hurt. He had always taken care to keep within the letter of the law and she had never been averse to spending the money he earned. He had tried to plead and cajole, but when she had insisted that her mind was made up he had lost his temper and demanded where did she think she would go? What would she do if she walked out of his life? And she had told him!

He groaned and rested his head on his hands. She was going

away with Bradley Scott! He couldn't believe it, and yet he had suspected for some time that she was seeing someone else. No, he must face facts. He *knew* there was someone; ever since that night he had returned home unexpectedly and had found her missing. He had never let on, had preferred to hide his head in the sand and deny what was only too obvious. He should have faced her with it then, but he had said nothing, hoping there was an innocent explanation and not daring to put to it to the test. Small joy she would get, throwing in her lot with Bradley Scott, he thought savagely. He knew Scott's type, a typical bachelor, footloose and fancy-free. Scott would never marry her − not that he himself had any intention of giving her a divorce.

How had things come to this pass? He knew he was not the world's most passionate or exciting man but things had been different in the beginning. He let his mind stray back to their courtship and marriage; a dispiriting exercise. He had been on a business trip to the States and they had met in Los Angeles. There had been an immediate rapport between them and after a short courtship they had married in Las Vegas, the town where marriages were easily made and unmade and not too many questions asked.

How ironical! They had come back to England where his business had prospered to the extent of allowing him to live the life of a country gentleman in his spare time. He had thought that Lee had embraced this existence, too, but it appeared that she still craved the excitement and uncertainty of her earlier life. Perhaps it would have been different if they had had children. She had cheated on him there, too, but he had never held it against her.

He had thought they were happy, but in the last couple of months their relationship had deteriorated; thinking back, the present downturn in their affairs seemed to stem from the discovery of Tim's body on the marshes. Tim, whom everyone had thought was alive and well in Australia. The uncovering of this crime had cast a long shadow over everything but it was not going to destroy his marriage. She was not going to run out on him. He wouldn't let her!

He sat back and closed his eyes and tried to blot out the pictures that chased each other across his mind's eye: Lee and Bradley Scott together, lying, laughing, loving . . .

'I have a theory.' Mansfield leaned forward and tapped out the dottle from his pipe into an ashtray on Roland's desk. His superior eased his chair sideways and tried not to get upwind of it.

'Let's have it then. I feel I'm groping about in the dark at the moment.'

'Both those boys insisted that Alfie never let drop a word to them about the events of that night. They were so emphatic about it that I began to get suspicious. They were trying to tell the truth and they seized on the one thing that they could deny in all honesty. So I began thinking around the situation and a startling theory came to mind.'

'Go on, the suspense is killing me!'

'They weren't told anything by Alfie because they'd *seen* it for themselves.'

'What are you getting at?'

'Suppose they were with Alfie that night? Perhaps he was initiating them into the delights of poaching.'

'Is it possible?'

'They were thrown when I asked them what they were doing on that evening. Apparently they should have been at a scout meeting, that's where the parents thought they were, but the Taplins themselves were out that evening and only know that the boys were in bed when they returned late.'

'Well, it should be easy enough to check whether they were at the scout meeting or not. They're not going to admit in front of their respective parents that they were playing hookey but if we can get confirmation from the scout master that they were absent, we can face them with it and see what happens.'

'I don't think, if they were with Coutts, that anything they saw or heard raised any question in their minds of a connection with Lester's murder,' said Mansfield slowly, thinking back. 'They were more concerned with the possibility of being found out.'

'But now you've put the idea in their heads, they may come up with something. We must get onto that scoutmaster. We may be chasing after rainbows but if your theory is right and they did see or hear something, it puts them in a very vulnerable position. They could be in grave danger.'

'Unless . . . Suppose Simon saw his mother that evening? He would probably have assumed that she had a perfectly good reason for being there and would only have been concerned with keeping out of her way, but now . . . he's not going to point the finger at his own mother, is he, even if he's convinced she had nothing to do with the murder?'

'It's a thought. Hell, this case is leaving a nasty taste in my mouth!'

'Any luck with the typewriter?'

'Forensics have confirmed that it was definitely the one on which the suicide note was typed, but it doesn't get us much further forward. There are a mass of blurred fingerprints super-imposed on one another but nothing that can be singled out or matched. And as to who had access to it . . .' Roland flung down his pen in disgust '. . . the whole world and his wife would be as good an answer as any. It was a real freebie as far as I can make out. Committee members of the Trust have keys to the room in which it was kept, but the door was left unlocked for much of the time and people working in other parts of the building wandered in and out and made free with it. It was borrowed overnight or for longer periods of time − a much travelled machine, all in all.'

'So any of our suspects could have used it to type the note?'

'Lee Garfield and Ginny Dalton are committee members − as is your Jean. Presumably Stephen Bates could have got at it if he had had a mind to, and believe it or not, Bradley Scott is known to have borrowed it a few weeks ago when his own typewriter went on the blink! All we can say is that our typist must have been someone living in the Felstone area who knew the whereabouts of the typewriter and how easy it would be to get access to it.'

Roland thrust his hands in his pockets and mooched around the room. 'We're having no more luck with our enquiries into Alfie Coutts' death. Pomroy has finished the house-to-house and nobody saw or heard anything untoward that evening. Our murderer is either so familiar that his presence in the

211

vicinity was taken for granted, or else he took great care not to be seen.'

'What about the American couple?'

'They've been traced. A couple of harmless tourists "doing" East Anglia, but just listen to this.' Roland read from the typescript in front of him: 'I guess I noticed the old fellow because he was holding forth in front of his pals, but there was a young guy sitting in the corner who was acting very suspiciously. He was trying to keep out of the public eye but at the same time doing his damnedest to hear what was going on. He had a very evil-looking face and I said to Mother afterwards that he was up to no good." Quote, unquote. Those were the words of Hiram. J. Cornfellow, the said American tourist.'

Mansfield chuckled. 'Have you told Evans yet?'

'I thought I'd wait until he's fully recovered; that episode certainly knocked the stuffing out of him, and he's not just physically below par. His ego took a bashing too.'

'He's convinced it would never have happened to him in an urban locale; it was all those weird country noises tricking and bewildering him.'

'He's not the only one who's bewildered.' Roland flung himself into his chair. 'I must admit, Patrick, this case has got me beat so far. Here we are with a shortlist of suspects who could have carried out all three murders, but how to find out which one is the guilty person and prove it? I still think the mysterious Leslie Drew is as good a candidate as any but I'm no nearer to discovering who he could be. Bradley Scott appears to be bona fide. He was employed by Shell before he became a freelance traveller and writer, and I can't trace any link between him and old Mrs. Fellingham. It can't be Stephen Bates because he is too old and has been living in the area too long. Unless . . . are we missing something? Is there someone we've overlooked, someone we've had no reason to suspect of being connected with the case but who could be the third cousin?'

'Any other business?' The Chairman, Colonel Pendleton, looked over the top of his glasses at the other members of the Nature Conservation Trust who were seated round the table in

212

the library of The Hermitage. The office in Felstone had been put out of bounds temporarily by the police, pending enquiries; a fact that had given rise to a great deal of speculation and caused Jean Mansfield, the secretary and sometime confidante of her husband, some very awkward moments. So far she had managed to field all the questions and maintain her professed innocence of all matters pertaining to the Constabulary.

As nobody had anything further to say, the Colonel cleared his throat and steepled his fingers.

'I thought somebody else would have raised the matter I am now going to mention. I have heard one or two disturbing rumours about a possible development at Croxton Creek.'

Ginny Dalton turned a startled face to her hostess but Lee Garfield flashed her a warning look and lowered her eyes.

'This is such an environmentally sensitive area,' continued the Colonel, 'that I find it difficult to give credence to such gossip, but I wondered if anyone else has heard anything?'

'Where did you hear this?' asked Ginny Dalton.

'I really can't reveal my sources, it was more in the nature of a nod and a wink, but I thought if anyone would know if there is any truth in the matter it would be you, Mrs. Garfield. You would be the most affected. Your land runs down to the creek, doesn't it?'

'Yes. I've heard nothing, and surely we'd be the first to know if any such thing had been mooted? I wonder how these rumours started?'

'I believe surveyors were seen down on the marshes and somebody must have put two and two together and made five. I'm glad to know there is nothing in it. Development of the creek would be an utter disaster.'

'I couldn't agree more,' murmured Lee Garfield, still not looking her friend in the eye. The Colonel gathered his papers together and looked relieved. 'Well, that seems to be that. Thank you all for coming, and especial thanks to you, Mrs. Garfield, for your hospitality.'

'You're very welcome. I'll get some coffee. Is that all right for everyone, or would anyone like tea?'

She refused offers of help, saying that her housekeeper

would make it, and after she had left the room Miss Thomas, one of the two elderly spinsters who were committee members, looked around appreciatively and twittered: 'What a lovely place this is. Mrs. Garfield is so lucky to live in such a lovely place, don't you agree, Colonel?'

The Colonel, who was impervious to his surroundings, looked startled but hastened to agree.

'Fine place, yes. By the way, have we agreed on who is to go and see the Wallingford vicar?'

'I think I drew the short straw,' said Jean Mansfield wryly.

A large part of the meeting had been taken up by a heated discussion of the pros and cons of either letting country churchyards run wild, thereby establishing useful habitats for struggling flora and fauna, or keeping them clipped and mown, which looked neater but effectively destroyed a good deal of wild life. It had been agreed that the vicar of Wallingford, whose churchyard was inordinately large for a small parish, and hidden for the most part behind a high brick wall, should be approached about allowing at least part of it to be used as a wildlife sanctuary.

'It is very difficult,' said Miss Thomas, looking distressed. 'I agree with our decision in principle, but my poor, dear mother is buried in Wallingford churchyard and I don't like to think of her grave being overrun and lost. When I'm gone there will be no-one to remember where she is buried.'

'Is that such a bad thing?' demanded Lionel Coleman, a local government official who was a keen member of the Trust but who had no time for what he called the "old biddies" on the committee who, in his opinion, rambled and digressed and wasted a lot of time.

'I quite agree with, Mildred.' Her friend Miss Tatum hastened to her defence. 'You'll die one day, and you wouldn't like to think you were forgotten, with not even a headstone to mark your last resting place.'

'When I'm gone, I'm gone. I don't need a memorial. If I've done nothing to make my mark on the world and be remembered by, I deserve to be forgotten. Dust to dust and ashes to ashes, and all that.'

Tony Gorham, the young biology teacher from Ginny Dalton's school, who was another committee member,

214

started to hum "On Ilkley Moor Baht 'At" under his breath. Fortunately, only his colleague beside him realised the significance of the tune.

'Cut it out, Tony,' hissed Ginny, trying not to smile, 'or you'll have everyone at each others' throats.'

'Please, we've already spent far too much time discussing this,' said the Colonel. 'I thought we had come to a decision.'

'That is true,' agreed Miss Thomas, 'I must bow to the majority opinion, but what would your father have thought?' she shot at Ginny.

'Oh, I think he would have been all in favour of nature conservation as long as it didn't interfere with his precious garden.'

'A remarkable man, your father,' said the Colonel, eagerly seizing on another topic, 'but very eccentric, if you don't mind my saying so.'

'I couldn't agree more, and I should know!'

The coffee arrived, arranged on a large tray by Mrs. Collins who was followed by their hostess, carrying a plate of biscuits. The housekeeper deposited the tray on a table and withdrew. After the coffee was handed round the Colonel returned to the subject of the late Reverend Merrivale.

'Mind you, I think he abused his position. I remember him getting up in the pulpit one morning and actually telling people to vote Labour.'

'It didn't have much effect from what I remember,' said Ginny, grinning.

'Who are you discussing?' Lee Garfield had missed the earlier part of the conversation.

'My father. You remember him, don't you?'

'Oh yes, a great character.'

'Quite famous in his day,' said the Colonel, 'but he upset a lot of people. Used to get bees in his bonnet, eh?'

Ginny agreed that this was the truth, and helped to hand round the biscuits.

'I remember how he upset my great nephew,' said Miss Tatum, 'by refusing to christen their baby because he said they weren't giving him a proper name. Gary, they wanted to call him — what was wrong with that?'

'I'm afraid that was one of the subjects on which he held

215

very strong views,' said his daughter. 'If it wasn't in the Oxford Dictionary of English Christian Names, you hadn't got a hope. He hated Americanisms and what he called sloppy derivatives. You'd have been out in the cold ' – she turned to Lee Garfield – 'he would never have accepted Lee as a baptismal name.'

'Ah, but my real name is Leslie, spelt the masculine way. My father wanted a son, and when I came along he was so disappointed that he gave me a boy's name. When I started to talk I couldn't get my tongue round Leslie very easily so I called myself Lee, and it stuck.'

There was a knock on the door and Mrs. Collins popped her head inside the room, a worried look on her face.

'Mr. Garfield is on the phone, madam. There has been an accident.'

'An accident?' Lee jumped to her feet and hurried out of the room. The other committee members looked at each other anxiously.

'Oh dear, I do hope it's not serious,' said Miss Thomas. 'Poor Mrs. Garfield.'

'If her husband is on the phone, he must be all right' pointed out Lionel Coleman. 'I wonder what sort of accident?'

Ginny wondered whether she should follow their hostess, and whilst the others speculated amongst themselves, torn between curiosity and dismay, she got up, intending to go to her friend's side. Before she reached the door, Lee came back into the room.

'What's happened?'

'Tony has had an accident. The car overturned on Bidwell Hill.'

'A notorious blackspot,' said the Colonel. 'Is he badly hurt?'

'No, he had a lucky escape, but the car is damaged. I have to go to the hospital.'

After offering sympathy and help, which was refused, the committee members dispersed to their various homes, leaving only Ginny behind.

'Do you want me to come with you?'

'No, I shall be all right. You go back home to Simon.'

'What actually happened? Was any other vehicle involved?'

'No. Apparently the car went out of control whilst he was negotiating the bend at the top. It left the road and crashed down the hill. He was flung out, fortunately; he says he's just cut and bruised and shocked.'

'Was he ringing from the hospital?'

'No. Another car came along shortly after it happened and the driver took him to the nearest house and rang for the police and an ambulance. He says there is nothing seriously wrong but they are insisting on him being checked out at the Cottage Hospital. The ambulance is taking him there now.'

'Poor Tony, I suppose he must have skidded. I noticed a lot of mud on the road when I went through there last week; a tractor had been along a little while before me. They are supposed to put up warning notices if they drop a lot of mud around but they very rarely do. Are you sure you wouldn't like me to drive you over?'

'No, thanks for the offer. Hopefully they won't keep him in and I'll be able to bring him home once they've checked him out.'

'Have a brandy or something before you go - you look very shaky.'

'And be had up for drinking and driving? I'm okay, it was just a shock. Supposing he had been badly hurt, Ginny?'

'He'd pull through, the medical profession can work miracles these days, and he'd have you to nurse him.'

'That's what I mean - how could I walk out and leave him if he were seriously injured?'

Tony Garfield was treated for shock and minor abrasions at the Cottage Hospital and allowed home. His car fared less well. The 827 Vitesse Rover had somersaulted down the bank and ended up with the front near-side wing embedded in a fallen tree trunk.

The car was towed away for repairs by a breakdown truck from a Woodford garage who reported after an initial examination that the main brake pipe had been tampered with.

Roland, who had been alerted to the fact that Garfield had had an accident via Jean Mansfield and his sergeant, lost no time in following up the incident. The car was examined by police experts who reported that the brake system had been deliberately sabotaged. The brake pipe had been filed through in such a way as almost, but not quite, to sever it. The only fingerprints found were those of Garfield and his wife in the interior of the car, and the garage mechanic's under the bonnet. Roland dropped in on Mansfield early in the evening to bring him up-to-date with the findings and to see if Jean Mansfield could add anything to the report of the accident.

'Stay and share our meal,' she urged. 'It will easily stretch, the children are out. Or are you rushing off somewhere else and taking Pat with you?'

'There's nothing more we can do this evening. Thanks, Jean, I'd love to share your meal if you're sure it won't put you out?'

As they ate, Roland and Mansfield mulled over events.

'First thing in the morning we'll go and see Garfield and ask if he can throw any light on it,' said Roland. 'It was very carefully staged. Whoever did the deed worked it out so that he could apply the brakes about three times and then after that − kaput! Which, when you work it out, means that driving from his home to Woodford they were likely to go as he tried to negotiate Bidwell Hill. Who knew where he was going, and when?'

'According to Lee Garfield, he attended a meeting in Woodford on the same evening each week,' said Jean Mansfield.

'So presumably anyone local who was monitoring his movements would have known this. How did Mrs. Garfield react when she heard?'

'Well, she was very shaken naturally, but the fact that he was ringing her himself must have reassured her that he was not badly hurt.'

'He had a very lucky escape. He could easily have been killed or seriously hurt, which I suppose was the intention of the saboteur.'

'Some more coffee?'

218

'Thanks, Jean, that was a lovely meal. Now I can see why Pat is in such rude health. If he eats like this every day, he'll have to watch the old middle-aged spread.'

'There's not a spare ounce on me,' protested Mansfield, 'I'm just heavily built. What you want is a good woman behind you, and then you too could eat well.'

'Yes, well, we're not all so lucky, are we? To get back to Garfield – who wants him out of the way? And why? And how does it fit in with our case?'

'You think there is a connection?'

'There must be, Pat, or are you saying that one of his business rivals has attempted to bump him off?'

'He can't have got where he has without being pretty ruthless; he must have made enemies on the way up.'

'No, I don't buy it. It's too much of a coincidence – everything points to a local link.'

'Well, it lets him off the hook as a suspect, doesn't it, if he himself is now the subject of an attack?'

'Yes, it does. I wonder . . .' Roland put down his coffee cup and rested his chin on his hand. 'We've got to trace cousin Leslie.'

'Look, if you two want to talk shop, I'll just clear the dishes away and leave you to it,' said Jean Mansfield, gathering the crockery together.

'No, don't go, Jean. Give us the benefit of your wisdom. We're looking for someone in his mid-thirties to mid-forties who has moved into the Croxton district sometime in the last ten years, and has been living here ever since.'

'What did you say his name was?'

'Leslie Drew, but he'll be using an alias. You get around a lot, I know you belong to many local organisations – can you think of anyone you may have met who could fit the bill?'

'That's a tall order,' said her husband, 'there must be hundreds of men in that age range who have moved into the area in the last ten years – it's like looking for a needle in a haystack.'

Jean looked at her husband and his superior thoughtfully, and after some consideration smiled.

'How about "*Cherchez la femme*"?'

219

'What do you mean?'

'I mean, why are you so sure that it's a man? Leslie is a woman's name too.'

'Not spelt this way. The woman's name is spelt Lesley.'

'Not always,' she said triumphantly, 'Lee Garfield's real name is Leslie — spelt the masculine way.'

Chapter Twelve

'What did you say?'

'Say that again!'

The two men pounced on her words and Jean Mansfield gaped at them, taken aback by the speed of their reaction.

'I said, Lee Garfield's real name is Leslie.'

'How do you know?' rapped Roland.

'She happened to mention it, only yesterday evening as a matter of fact. What is this? What have I said?'

'How did it come up?'

'We were talking about old Reverend Merrivale, Ginny Dalton's father; about how he had this thing about only baptising children who had what he called proper Christian names, and she mentioned casually that her real name was Leslie and that Lee was just a nickname that had stuck from childhood.'

The two men looked at each other. 'Is it possible? It could turn the whole thing on its head.'

'You've always thought that maybe a woman was the culprit — perhaps it was the wrong woman.'

'There's one way of finding out if we've gone completely off our rockers. May I use your phone?'

'Help yourself,' said Mansfield. 'Who are you going to ring?'

'Larkin. His firm dealt with the original legacy; surely he'll know whether it was paid out to a man or a woman — or has he been deliberately misleading us?'

Roland went into the hall to use the phone and Jean Mansfield turned to her husband.

'I suppose it's too much to ask that you tell me what's going on?'

'I'll tell you one thing — you may have given us the break we needed. What do you know of Lee Garfield's background?'

'I don't know that I know anything much, only that she and her husband were married in the States and settled here afterwards. I remember her saying once that she had had a very nomadic childhood. Her mother died when she was a baby and her father was a geologist whose work took him all over the place.'

'But she is English?'

'Her parents were but I think she was born overseas, whatever that makes her.'

'And this rumour about her carrying on with someone else — we've heard gossip that she is having an affair with Bradley Scott, the travel writer. Have any more titbits along those lines come to your notice?'

'No, I can't say that they have. As I said, she was very shaken when she heard of her husband's accident so they can't be completely estranged.'

Roland came back into the room at that moment.

'Larkin is meeting us in his office in half an hour. He's not very happy about it, in fact, he did his damnedest to refuse, but I managed to persuade him after dropping little hints about legal malpractice. I'm sorry, Jean, we'll have to leave you.'

'Not even one evening off to relax and forget your work?'

'Come on, you know the score by now — or you should do, you two've been married long enough. I'll help with the washing up next time.'

'You have a winning way with you, Inspector Roland. Is it going to be a late session? Can I fix you a thermos of coffee?'

'No, it shouldn't take too long. I promise I'll send him home before midnight.' Roland grinned at his hostess. 'And thanks again for the meal — you're a fabulous cook.'

'Perhaps you're the one on whom I should try out my experiments in Nouvelle Cuisine.'

'We're working men,' growled her husband, 'we need plates of food, not pretty patterns.'

222

'You see — he's not as ignorant of haute cuisine as he likes to make out!'

Cyril Larkin was waiting for them in his car when they drew up outside the offices of Larkin & Webb. He stepped out on to the pavement, annoyance written all over his face.

'Inspector, this had better be important. You've interrupted my bridge evening.'

'It is important, please open up.'

Larkin unlocked the door and led the way into the reception office, back rigid with displeasure as he switched on lights and pulled down blinds.

'What exactly is it you want?'

'I want to see the will of the late Mrs. Fellingham of Croxton Hall.'

'I told you the terms of that will when you came here before.' "Came here pestering me" was implicit in his peevish tones.

'You told me what you thought were the terms of that will. You insisted that it was drawn up by your late father and implemented by him and that you had nothing to do with it. Am I correct?'

'Well, yes.'

'So what you told me about the contents was only hearsay?'

'Certainly not, Inspector. I know for a fact that the two legatees were Mrs. Fellingham's great-nephews. I resent your implications.'

'You don't know what they are yet,' said Roland wearily. 'Will you please show us the will.'

'This is most unorthodox.'

'Mr. Larkin, Mrs. Fellingham has been a long time dead and I am investigating a murder. Your objections have been noted, now will you please do as I ask? You have still got the will or a copy, I presume?'

'Certainly, it will be with my father's papers. If you had come at a more civilised hour my secretary would have looked it out for you.'

'Are you trying to tell me that you can't lay your hands on it?'

'You surely don't think that the partners in this firm do

223

their own filing? Certainly I can produce it but it may take a little time.'

'Then I suggest you start looking, Mr. Larkin. I am a busy man and unfortunately *I* don't work office hours.'

'Not the most obliging of gents, is he?' Mansfield said as the lawyer disappeared into the inner sanctum.

'I'm afraid he works strictly by the book. Anything like this completely throws him.'

'Are we really on to something, do you think, or is it just a wild goose chase?'

'I refuse to conjecture until we see that will. What do you think of the decor?'

'Old-fashioned, but it spells out wealth and respectability. And how impressive to see current magazines.' Mansfield picked up the copy of *Homes and Gardens*. 'My dentist's waiting room runs to nothing more recent than two-year-old copies of *Punch*.'

After what seemed an age, Larkin returned carrying a box file.

'You haven't joined the computer age and got everything on disc yet?'

'My son assures me that will happen eventually,' said Cyril Larkin, smiling thinly and opening the box. 'I think this is what you want, Inspector. The last will and testament of Gertrude Fellingham.'

'Perhaps you could read out to me the relevant bit — the part dealing with the two main beneficiaries.'

Cyril Larkin adjusted his glasses, cleared his throat, rustled through the papers and started to read.

'. . . after bequests, the residue of my estate to be divided between Anthony Garfield, only child of my nephew Ronald Garfield and his wife Kathleen Fairfield, and Leslie Drew, only child of my niece Mary Burton and her husband Gerald Drew. . .' A slight frown flickered across his face.

'Is anything wrong, Mr. Larkin?'

'Wrong? Oh, no, but this will has been rather carelessly drawn up. I'm afraid my father was getting on in years but he refused to retire and insisted on dealing with all his old clients, right up to the time of his death.'

224

'What are you trying to say?'

'Only that there is a certain slackness in the nomenclature. If I had drawn up this will I would have identified the relationships of the beneficiaries by stating: "Tony Garfield, *son* of my nephew Ronald Garfield", and so forth; but in this case the intentions of the testator were perfectly clear so it was not important.'

'I'm afraid I disagree, it was of the utmost importance. I put it to you, Mr. Larkin, that Leslie Drew was – is – a woman, not a man.'

Cyril Larkin was thunderstuck. To the two police officers watching him closely it was evident that such an idea came as a complete surprise.

'Are you serious, Inspector?'

'Very much so. We have reason to believe that Leslie Drew could indeed be a woman. Perhaps you can correct me by proving that the legacy was paid out to a man?'

'Are you suggesting that the legacy was paid to the wrong person?'

'Oh no, I'm sure it was received by Leslie Drew, but I think you may be under a misapprehension about the sex of this person. How was the transaction implemented?'

'Through the attorney representing Leslie Drew. I have it here . . .' He leafed through the papers in front of him '. . . a Mr. Conrad Dwinger, a partner in an old established firm over there. The transfer of monies was carried out through him. This is quite common practice, Inspector, under the circumstances.' He looked over the top of his glasses at the two men.

'So presumably he would know whether his client was a man or a woman?'

'Well, of course. This is most extraordinary . . . I take it this ties in somehow with your enquiries into the murder of Timothy Spencer?'

Roland ignored the question.

'Will you please put through a call to this Mr. Dwinger and clear up the situation.'

'What, *now*?'

'Yes, Mr. Larkin. Let me see, they are about eight hours behind us in Los Angeles which would make it early afternoon over there — a very respectable time to call.'

'What exactly do you want to know?'

'Leslie Drew's sex. If it is a woman, try and get a description — it's over eight years since the legacy was paid out but your Mr. Dwinger may have a good memory, especially if he carried out other legal business for her. Also check if he knows her present whereabouts or if he has any knowledge of her marital status.'

'I shall make the call in my office. Please wait here.'

When he rejoined Roland and Mansfield a little later, Larkin looked somewhat chastened.

'You were right, Inspector, Leslie Drew *is* a woman. I don't know how you knew, or why my father didn't mention the fact. He must surely have known.'

'Perhaps he took it for granted that because he knew, everyone else did. I presume Mrs. Fellingham must have discussed her family with him when he was drawing up the will so he probably did know, but to you Leslie Drew was just a name on a piece of paper. An understandable mistake.'

'But what significance has this knowledge? I don't understand.'

'It means we are a little closer to discovering who was responsible for killing Timothy Spencer, and for the other deaths that have followed on from that. What else did you learn from Mr. Dwinger?'

'Very little, I'm afraid. He acted as her legal adviser in several small transactions prior to this one, but after the legacy had been paid out he didn't see her again. She refused his offer of advice about investments etc. and he got the impression that she was leaving the district, possibly to get married. He does not know where she is now but presumes her to be living in another part of the States.'

'Could he give you a description?'

'He remembers her as a tall, dark woman in her twenties.'

Roland and Mansfield exchanged looks.

'Well, thank you, Mr. Larkin. You have confirmed what we suspected. I won't trouble you further, but before we leave may I have the address and phone number of Mr. Dwinger?'

A short while later, armed with this information, Roland and Mansfield parted from Cyril Larkin on the steps of his office; he to resume his interrupted bridge party, they to set in motion further investigations.

'We must get a photograph of Lee Garfield,' said Roland, snapping on his seat belt. 'If we can match up Leslie Drew with our Mrs. Garfield, we're really on to something.'

'Jean has some photos that were taken in the summer at a garden party that was held to boost NCT funds. Lee Garfield performed the opening ceremony and I'm pretty certain that she figured clearly in several of them.'

'Good man, let's go and get them.'

Jean Mansfield was curled up in an armchair watching a film on television when they returned to Wallingford. She was surprised to see them.

'That was quick.'

'I'm afraid this is just a flying visit,' said Roland. 'I'm going to borrow him again.'

'Where are those photos of that garden party at Woodford?' asked her husband. 'Can you lay your hands on them?'

'You mean the NCT ones? I think they're in the top drawer of the bureau in the spare room, what do you want them for?'

'Means of identification.'

'Do you want me to look?'

'No, I'll find them.'

'I'll have that other cup of coffee now, Jean, if it's still on offer,' said Roland. 'Criminal investigation is a thirsty business.'

'Come into the kitchen and I'll brew some up, but I expect I'll have to go and help him look. He can never find anything, even if it's staring him in the face, which is odd when you consider that he's a detective. I think it's some sort of defence mechanism; he just cuts out when he crosses this threshold.'

Roland sat down and watched as she spooned coffee into the pot and set out beakers. There was a troubled expression on her face as she joined him at the table.

'James, this case you're on. . . it involves my friends, people I know, doesn't it? What have. . . ?'

'Don't ask questions please, Jean, just carry on as normal.'

227

She banged the sugar bowl down in front of him. 'It's hell being a policeman's wife!'

'So I have been told,' he said dryly.

There was a bellow from upstairs. 'Jean — I can't find them!'

'What did I tell you?' She raised her shoulders in a comic shrug. 'I'm coming dear.'

Patrick didn't know how lucky he was, thought Roland as she joined her husband upstairs. Why hadn't *he* married someone like Jean Mansfield? She was so independent, and yet at the same time very supportive — the complete antithesis of Karen. He caught himself wondering what sort of policeman's wife Ginny Dalton would make, and pulled himself up sharply. Such thoughts were madness. He was working too hard, his brain was addled — and, anyway, she hated his guts. Mansfield interrupted his musings.

'Here we are. As I thought, she's in the foreground in three of them. It's a good likeness, she stands out.'

'Good, these should blow up nicely.'

The two men hastily swallowed their coffee and drove back to Felstone. There had been break-ins in a couple of the high street stores that evening, and a bad accident on the dock road, and the police station was humming with activity.

'Here, take these photos to the lab before anything else crops up and see what they can do for us. I'm calling up Lieutenant Kauffman in Los Angeles to confirm that it was a woman and not a man he checked out for us. I'll fax the photos to him as soon as we get them, and he can try for a positive identification from the lawyer and her ex-colleagues.'

'How come we slipped up on the sex of Leslie Drew when the original information came through from the States?'

'It was a telex and just stated his findings re Leslie Drew. We have always taken it for granted that it was a man; the lieutenant wouldn't have realised this if he had found a woman answering to that name. I really think we are beginning to see the light at the end of the tunnel at last.'

'The one person we never considered in our calculations.'

'Why should we? We were justifiably convinced that Leslie Drew was a man, but she could have done it, Pat. Just think: she comes over to England after receiving Great-aunt's

228

invitation, but secretly. She has already sussed out the situation and knows about the probability of the estate being divided between the only three surviving relatives of the old girl. She wants a bigger bite of the cherry so she somehow manages to shoot Cousin Tim and makes an attempt on the life of Cousin Tony. It must have been a blow to her plans to discover he had survived her hit and run accident. She goes back to the States and then Tony Garfield unknowingly plays into her hands by going there on business. She somehow contrives to meet up with him and decides to recoup that part of the legacy she had lost by marrying him.'

'Are you saying that he is ignorant of the fact that his own wife is the third cousin?'

'Yes. Why should he connect a lively young woman called Lee with a distant relative he has never seen?'

'But surely he must have known through his great-aunt that Leslie was a woman? He must be *au fait* with the family pedigree.'

'Not necessarily. In fact, I'm quite sure that the first time we interviewed him he referred to Leslie as "he". But even if he did know, why should he connect Lee with Cousin Leslie? She is a very attractive woman and if she made a dead set at him he was probably way out of his depth. Tony Garfield strikes me as a man who has had little to do with women; as a younger man he was probably shy and retiring and open to manipulation by any scheming female.'

'So she married him ... could she do this in the States under an assumed name? Wouldn't some sort of ID be required?'

'I think it depends exactly where they married. The rules vary from state to state and some are more lax than others. Of course, her real name should be on her passport. I wonder if she holds dual nationality? Anyway, he brings her back to England and they settle in the ancestral acres; everything seems fine and then, by a stroke of bad luck, Tim Spencer's skeleton is found and identified.'

'How does Julian Lester come into the picture?'

'I think we can make the same suppositions as we did when we suspected Ginny Dalton. Lester must have seen her with Tim Spencer and she probably spun him a yarn on the lines I

229

suggested before, but once Tim's body had turned up she knew he would put two and two together and so he had to be eliminated. She could have visited him that evening, fed him the fatal dose and been home by the time Garfield phoned her at nine o'clock. He was in London that night so she could easily have sneaked back undetected in the morning and removed the suicide note, etc. In fact, I wouldn't put it past her to have had a wild night of passion in between with Bradley Scott.'

'And what about Alfie Coutts?'

'She may have heard rumours about his ramblings, she was certainly in the pub that evening and could have heard him and realised that he could incriminate her; she probably recognised Evans in there too and knew she had to act fast. She tucks hubby up in bed with a nightcap, then doubles back and follows the old boy, avoiding Evans and helping herself to a convenient weapon on the way. Then she attacks Alfie in a dark spot. Evans interrupts her and she knocks him unconscious and then finishes off what she has started.'

'What about the sabotaging of Garfield's car? Do you think she is trying to get rid of him now?'

'We know she's having an affair with Bradley Scott; perhaps Garfield has refused to divorce her and she has decided to try and kill him, hoping it will appear an accident. After three murders, why should she stick at a fourth? If we're right in our supposition she never was in love with him and only married him for money and position; now she's found someone else he has become an encumbrance to her so why should she scruple at removing him from her life permanently? Jean said she was very shaken when his call came through about his mishap; it would have been a very great shock to her to learn that he had walked relatively unscathed from what was supposed to have been a fatal accident.'

'You've made out a good case against her.'

'But I haven't an atom of proof; a good defence would make mincemeat of it. We must get some concrete evidence.'

'The boy?'

'Yes, we must bring pressure to bear on young Simon Dalton. I don't want to frighten him, but if he was in the woods that evening and saw something or someone, then we have got to find out what and who. But first we must interview Tony Garfield again, try and dig out some more facts about his courtship and marriage and see if he has any ideas about who would want him out of the way. It may be a totally unrelated incident.'

'What about Lee Garfield — are you going to face her with our knowledge of her real identity?'

'No way. Firstly we must get proof from the States that Leslie Drew and Lee Garfield are one and the same person, and then . . . then I think we must give her some rope and see what happens. I don't want to alert her until we get some proof. If we can prove that she was in the vicinity of Smoky Cottage at the appropriate time, then we are nearly home and dry.'

'But surely if she was seen in the woods that evening, there could be the simple explanation that she was meeting Bradley Scott?'

'Scott was seen after nine o'clock. He has more or less admitted that he was there about that time and I'm pretty certain that Stephen Bates saw him there when presumably Scott was taking a short cut to The Hermitage. That's not the relevant time. It is earlier in the evening when Lester was entertaining his murderer that we're interested in, and I think that is when Alfie Coutts saw or heard something that made him a witness to the identity of the murderer. Send Evans and Pomroy round to see Bates first thing in the morning and get a sworn statement about when and where he actually saw Scott that evening.'

'Suppose in the meantime she makes another attempt on her husband?'

'I don't think she'd be so foolhardy as to try anything so soon after the other "accident". She's capable, as we know, of grabbing at a chance when it offers, to the point of recklessness. She's an opportunist but also cool and calculating. She thinks she's got away with three murders; she won't jeopardise it all by a second ill-advised attack on her husband quite yet. She must realise by now that we know that the car was tampered with, and that we'll be investigating the incident.'

Roland walked over to the window and stared out at the rooftops of Felstone silhouetted against the luminous white sky that pinpointed the dock basin to the east of the town. This complex was floodlit at night and the harsh unnatural glow revealed the giant skeletal cranes fingering the sky, as busy at night as in the day. Ships plied their trade according to tide tables, there was a continuous coming and going, docking and embarkation; like the police station, the docks never slept. He swung round to face his colleague.

'Are we fantasising, Pat? Is this all a load of old rubbish or could we be getting somewhere at last?'

'Bob Lacey wouldn't be very happy with it.'

'God, no! We'll have to come up with something other than mere supposition to gain his support.'

'The thing that niggles me is why, if she is guilty, did she let drop about her name really being Leslie and not Lee?'

'You have a point. Of course, she doesn't know we've been checking out Leslie Drew and what she said was spoken in confidence to a small group of acquaintances; she wouldn't know it was going to get straight back to us. Besides, by then she was expecting her husband to have had his fatal accident so she probably thought it didn't matter, there would be no way to check with him. Still, there is something we can check: the date of the Garfields' marriage. If it happened before Mrs Fellingham died and the will was implemented then we'll know we're barking up the wrong tree. First thing in the morning we'll pay a call on Mr. Tony Garfield, and if Missus is there we'll have to try and separate them.'

It was the early hours before Roland got to bed, and then he couldn't switch off. The more he tried to relax and snatch a few badly-needed hours of sleep, the more active his brain became. He threshed around in that suspended state between sleeping and waking when he wasn't sure whether the crazy images chasing each other round his brain were dreams or rational ideas.

In his mind's eye he saw Lee Garfield taking her newly-found cousin Tim out for a walk on the marshes. She was dressed in the cords and Barbour jacket in which he had first seen her, and she laughed and pointed towards the river, urging Tim to go on ahead of her. When he did so she swung up the rifle that had been slung over one shoulder, took aim and fired.

The shot reverberated round Roland's head and he jolted back to reality, his heart thumping and sweat breaking out on his forehead. He groaned and punched his pillow and tried to settle back to sleep again, but was sucked back into the living nightmare.

This time he saw her dragging the body through the undergrowth. He was following and saw in front of him the herringbone pattern of the flattened marram grass springing back to cover her tracks; then she was digging, tearing away at the river bank in a fenzied burst of energy, her back to him. He called out to her to stop and she swung round and it was Ginny Dalton's face staring at him, distorted with hate, her belly grotesquely swollen with the child she had borne three years earlier. Then he was in Croxton Woods, somehow suspended above the trees, and below him, through the threshing branches, he saw Ginny Dalton and Bradley Scott emerge from Smoky Cottage, their arms full of manuscript paper which they threw up into the air. The wind snatched at the sheets and carried them upwards so that he was surrounded by a whirling mass like giant snowflakes. Down below Ginny and Scott hugged and congratulated each other and ran off hand-in-hand.

Roland dragged himself back to reality. The suicide note — was there something about the suicide note that he had missed? He yanked the duvet back into position and tried to marshall his thoughts into logical sequence, but his brain refused to function and he was catapaulted back into the world of fantasy and distortion. Lee Garfield was coming towards him, a long-handled shovel held menacingly in front of her. He put up his hands to ward off the blow then, shockingly, she hurled herself into his arms and pressed her lips hard against his. Desire exploded through him and he shot up in bed, gasping and trembling. He snapped on the light and looked at his watch. It was ten to four. He went to the toilet and relieved himself, had a drink of water and climbed back into bed again.

A new theory was clamouring for release at the back of his

233

mind. It was something he and Mansfield had overlooked when they were threshing out ideas the evening before. Suppose the Garfields were both involved, united in conspiracy?

Tony Garfield could have carried out the original killing and Lee the murder of Julian Lester, having established a nice little alibi between them for the night in question. As for Alfie Coutts, either or both of them could have disposed of him, and the sabotage of Garfield's car could have been an attempt to throw the police off the scent. Excitement stirred and then he remembered that Lee Garfield had a lover; the Garfields' marriage was on the rocks, it was public knowledge. If they were guilty they would cleave together, bound by complicity; no way would they reveal a split in their relationship. He sighed and threw himself on to his back.

It was five o'clock before he finally drifted off into a natural sleep. The alarm clock's shrilling at seven o'clock dragged him reluctantly back to the grey, early morning world.

The two policemen set off for The Hermitage armed with the knowledge that confirmation had come through from Lieutenant Kauffman that Leslie Drew was a woman, and he would try for a positive identification from the photo. It was a cold, clear day and as they got out of the car a flock of geese winged overhead towards the river, the thrumming beat of wings sounding unnaturally loud in the still atmosphere.

Mrs. Collins opened the door to them and showed them into the sitting room.

'Is Mrs. Garfield at home?'

'No, sir, she's out shopping. I thought it was Mr. Garfield you wanted to see?'

'It is, please tell him I am here.'

Tony Garfield walked awkwardly into the room a short while later. He was not exactly limping but moving warily. A graze and some scratch marks adorned one side of his face, and his left hand sported a large amount of sticking plaster.

'Mr. Garfield, I hope you have recovered from your mishap?'

234

'I was very lucky, Inspector, came out of it with barely a mark to show, but I must admit every part of my body aches today. I've been told it is reaction to shock.'

'A nasty business. Can you tell us exactly what happened?'

'I was driving over to Woodford. I was late for a meeting, and I must admit I was going faster than perhaps was wise, considering the wet road conditions. However, the car handled well, no problem with the brakes until I got to Bidwell Hill. You know the sharp bend at the top before the road drops to the bridge across the stream? I put my foot on the brake and nothing happened. I was going too fast to turn the corner, the car shot out of control, hit the bank, went over the top and plunged down the embankment. I was thrown clear, fortunately.'

'Were you wearing your seat belt, sir?'

'Yes, but I think I automatically released it as the car started to fall. I have always had a horror of being trapped in a vehicle after an accident.'

'Lucky for you you did, sir. Now, can you think of anyone who wishes you ill?'

'I can't believe it was caused deliberately. The brake pipe must have worn badly, or else some freak friction . . .'

'Mr. Garfield, that brake pipe had been filed through. It was done deliberately. Brake pipes don't wear through on a nearly new Rover. And remember, this is the second attempt on your life.'

'But that was ten years ago.'

'So was the murder I'm investigating.'

'You think there is a connection?'

'I don't know. On the face of it, it is absurd. But in view of the events of the last couple of months . . .'

'You mean the other deaths?'

'Yes, Mr. Garfield, I do.'

'You gave me to understand that they are all connected though I fail to see how.'

'Oh, they are connected, sir, believe me.'

'How is your investigation coming along? I mean, are you any nearer to finding the murderer?'

'I think I can say confidently that we are close to solving the case.'

'Really? Well, this is excellent news, Inspector. If there is any more help I can give you?'

'Tell me, Mr. Garfield, what is your wife's real name?'

'Real name?' The man looked startled. 'What do you mean?'

'I presumed that Lee was a nickname.'

'She's always been called Lee as long as I've known her.'

'But you must have known if that was her given name when you married her?'

'Actually, I believe she was baptised Leslie. But what has this ...?'

'As a matter of interest, when were you married, sir, and where?'

Garfield looked puzzled and worried. 'We married in April 1980 in the States − Las Vegas,' he said slowly.

'Las Vegas? Somehow that is a place I have always associated with quickie divorces rather than marriage.' Roland gave a little deprecating laugh and behind him Mansfield scribbled in his notebook.

'Yes, well ...' Before their astonished eyes the man seemed to fall apart. The confident, portly businessman meta-morphosed into a bewildered, hurt man who seemed to shrink in stature. Roland could have sworn that tears lurked in his brown, spaniel eyes. 'You may as well know, Inspector − she does want a divorce. She says our marriage is over.'

'This is very sorry news, sir. Is it − er − another man?'

'Yes,' Garfield's face worked, 'there is another man. I don't know why I'm telling you this but it's that writer − Bradley Scott. He lives in the village.'

'And has it been going on for long?'

'Long enough. It's my own fault. I know I've been so involved with my work that I've neglected her. I am away a good deal, she gets lonely ... perhaps if we had had children ... This is not the first time, you know. She's had her flings before and I turned a blind eye, hoping they would blow over, and they did, but this time she insists it's serious, wants a divorce.'

'Are you willing to give her one?'

'No, never!' He turned an anguished face to Roland. 'I still love her, you see. She doesn't really mean it − it's just an infatuation. He'll never marry her. She'll come to her senses when she realises that.'

He walked over to the fireplace and leant his head on the high mantelpiece. After a few seconds he raised it and made a visible effort to pull himself together.

'Sorry, Inspector, a shocking display of emotion, please forgive me – I don't normally behave like this. I suppose I'm not fully recovered from the accident.'

'It's understandable, sir. Where is Mrs. Garfield today?'

'She hasn't left me yet,' he gave a wan little smile, 'in fact I've managed to persuade her to carry on as normal for the time being – she's agreed to do nothing rash in the immediate future. I'm hoping a little breathing space . . .' He shrugged.

'So where is she?'

'Shopping in Woodford. We have a shoot tomorrow.'

'Here on your land?'

'Carstairs is the host, the guns will be out on his land and mine. This is the first formal shoot of the season, the hurricane played havoc with much of the terrain. Mrs. Carstairs is putting on the lunch for the guns but she is in poor health and Lee is helping her by organising the refreshment for the beaters.'

'Your wife doesn't shoot herself?'

'It's strange you should ask that. My wife is a crack shot but she doesn't usually turn out with us. She's an official of this Nature Conservation Trust and although she knows that organised shoots don't go against the aims of conservation, rather the opposite in fact, it doesn't go down well with many of the members. However, she insists that tomorrow she will join us. She will lay on the lunch for the beaters herself and take part in the shoot in the afternoon.'

'Mrs. Garfield does all the preparations for the lunch?' asked Roland delicately.

'Good Lord, no. Mrs. Collins will prepare the food, my wife will just transport it over there and set it out. They use the old cart lodge on occasions like this. The guns will be entertained in the house but the beaters prefer something more simple outside.'

"The rich man in his castle, the poor man at his gate." The lines from an old childhood hymn ran through Mansfield's head as he listened and took notes. Each man to his station ... and where did this leave Lee Garfield on the morrow?

'How many guns will be out tomorrow?' asked Roland.

'About fifteen. As I said, the birds were very disturbed by the hurricane, much of their natural cover was destroyed, but Bates has promised us some good sport.'

'And you feel well enough to participate?'

'Yes, I think the exercise will do me good, stop me from stiffening up completely.'

'That is probably wise, sir,' said Mansfield, 'when we get to our age we mustn't let up or it's the beginning of the end, isn't it?'

'Er − quite.' Garfield looked both startled and affronted, and a spurt of anger coiled through the burly sergeant. In Garfield's scheme of things there was obviously a strict line of demarcation between "them" and "us" and it didn't take a genius to guess where he came. No wonder his wife had decided to leave him; for all her faults, snobbishness was not among them. She might have married him to further her ambitions, he thought, but had probably long since regretted it.

'Well, thank you, sir,' said Roland, drawing on his gloves. 'If you have any further ideas on who might have perpetrated the accident, please contact us. The garage assures me that your car should be back on the road by the middle of next week. I hope you'll not be too inconvenienced in the meantime.'

'Thank you for your concern. I have the Range Rover and my wife has her own car.'

He saw them to the door and hesitated as they took their leave.

'Inspector ... what I have told you about my wife and myself ... it was in confidence. I trust it will go no further?'

'We don't indulge in idle gossip just for the sake of it, sir. All information is grist to the mill in our enquiries but we jettison that which is not relevant.'

Tony Garfield hovered in the courtyard looking wretched as they drove off.

'You can't help feeling sorry for him, can you?' said

238

Mansfield. 'All his material possessions haven't brought him much happiness. Which car are you using today — the Panda or the Black Maria?'

'I thought I detected a touch of the envies back there. Be glad you've got Jean and not Lee Garfield to wife. She's a proper bitch, led him a hell of a life quite apart from her homicidal tendencies; and now he's served his purpose, she's set to help him on his way.'

'You think she'll make another attempt?'

'I do, and I tell you what I don't like, Pat — this shoot tomorrow. What an opportunity! *And* she's insisted on taking part.'

'If it were a rough shoot, I'd agree with you. Accidents can and have happened in rough shooting — somebody moves from their given position or accidentally gets ahead of the guns. But I don't see how she could arrange an accidental shooting on a formal shoot, it's too organised and safety conscious.'

'Let's hope you're right. Let's hope we can come up with some evidence to pull her in. I'm pinning my hopes on young Dalton. He'll be at school now and so will his mother. I don't want to draw attention to him by whipping him out of class; we'll catch them at home after school. Wait a minute — he does a paper round, doesn't he? But he should be home by six o'clock. In the meantime we'll try and get details of the Garfields' marriage from the good Lieutenant; they must keep records over there. What worries me is this business of him not knowing who she really was — how did she get away with it? Even if she married under a false name, her passport would have the correct details. You have to produce a birth certificate when applying for a passport.'

'He's admitted that her real name is Leslie,' pointed out Mansfield, 'it's a common enough name in that age group, why should he connect her with the third cousin?'

'You're probably right. Come on, let's go back to the Station. We're going to go over every scrap of evidence again and see if there is anything we've missed that could tie in with Lee Garfield. I can't believe she's covered her tracks so professionally.'

*   *   *

239

Six o'clock found them outside Ginny Dalton's cottage in Duck Lane. In was in darkness, shrouded by massed overgrown shrubs, the windows blank eyes, the undamaged chimney bereft of smoke.

'Damn, it looks as if they're out.' Roland rang the bell without much hope. The silver-grey cat joined them on the doorstep, looking hopeful.

'Here, Tiddles, where is your mistress?' cooed Mansfield bending down to stroke it.

'Her name is Faience, and she's a very superior creature.'

'Well, they're not here. Perhaps there is something on at school.'

'Let us repair to the Duck and Spoon and do some constructive thinking while we wait. We'll try again later.'

'You did say constructive drinking, didn't you?' said Mansfield, following him back to the car.

An hour later they were back again but the cottage was still in darkness.

'Where the devil are they?' grumbled Roland, pressing the bell although he knew it was a waste of time.

'You don't think they might have gone away for the weekend?' suggested Mansfield. 'After all, it is Friday evening.'

'Hell, I hope not! We'd better try the neighbours and see if they know where they are. You stay in the car, I don't want them to recognise us as police officers.'

Roland walked back down the path and turned in at the next gate. He could hear the television booming away as he approached the front door. His ring was answered by an elderly man in slippers and a droopy cardigan. Roland introduced himself as a long lost friend of the Dalton family who had found himself in the area and was looking up his old friends.

'I don't know where they are.' He peered up at the policeman suspiciously. 'But Mother might know. I'll get her, she's a little deaf.'

Roland could well believe this. The television was thundering away in the front room, he could hear the signature tune of a well-known games show and the canned laughter.

'MO-THER!' shouted the old man in a surprisingly loud voice. 'There's someone wants to know where the Daltons are.'

His wife ventured down the hall, trailing her knitting.

'What did you say, Bert?'

'This gentleman here wants to know where Mrs. Dalton is.'

'Well, I really don't know — they could be at school though. What's today? Friday, isn't it? I believe there's a school concert on this evening — I saw a sticker about it in the back of her car.'

'Thank you, I'll come round again when it's more convenient.'

'Do you want me to tell her you've called? What did you say your name is?'

'No, don't bother. I'll give her a ring beforehand next time. Good evening.'

'We're wasting our time,' grumbled Roland as he joined Mansfield in the car. 'They're out at a school concert. There's not much point in our hanging around here any longer; we'll leave it till first thing in the morning. I'll give her a call early to make sure they're in.'

But it was Ginny Dalton who called the police. Roland and Mansfield were in the former's office early the next morning, checking through urgent memoranda, when DC Evans put his head round the door.

'Mrs. Dalton has called. She's asking for you, sir, and she sounds rather distressed.'

'Well, bring her up.'

'No — I mean she's on the phone.'

'Okay, Evans, put her through.' The two men exchanged wary looks and Roland picked up his receiver.

'Detective Inspector Roland here, what can I do for you, Mrs. Dalton?'

Her voice, trembling on the verge of hysteria, cut across his preamble.

'It's Simon — he hasn't come home!'

Chapter Thirteen

Roland felt everything inside him lurch.

'He's missing? When did you last see him?'

'He went out early to do his paper-round and he hasn't come back. He should have been back an hour ago!'

'Have you checked with anyone?'

'The newsagent says he went out with his normal load of papers and they haven't seen him since.' Her voice wobbled. 'I've rung up some of the people I know he delivers to, and they've all received their papers.'

'Who is the last person on his round?'

'Mr. Bradley Scott, I've been trying to get him but there's no reply. What can . . .?'

'Don't worry, Mrs. Dalton, we'll be right over. There's probably a simple explanation, I expect he will be back by the time we get to you. Just stay where you are, and don't panic.'

Panic! He knew in those few seconds what people meant when they said they felt their blood run cold. He was as near to going to pieces as he had ever been in his entire career. He slammed down the receiver.

'Did you get that? Come on, let's go!'

'Do you want me to come as well?' asked Evans, picking up the urgency in his chief's voice.

'No — stay here and get on to The Hermitage. Find out where Mrs. Garfield is, and what she's been doing since yesterday evening. I don't care how you go about it but don't alarm her. I don't want her stampeded into some desperate action. Then stand by. This may mean a full-scale search by the entire workforce.'

'If anything has happened to that boy, I'm resigning forthwith,' Roland rasped as he swung the car out of the Station car park and accelerated towards Croxton. Beside him Mansfield stared grimly through the windscreen and in his imagination went through all the things that could have befallen Simon. None of them were pleasant and he tried not to imagine his daughter in the boy's place. How much more vulnerable you were with kids of your own.

Ginny Dalton was waiting on her doorstep when they arrived in Duck Lane. She was so pale that she looked bleached; even her hair seemed drained of colour and the emerald green tracksuit she was wearing was, by contrast, shockingly garish. The two men jumped out of the car and strode up the path.

'He hasn't returned?'

'No.' She rammed her fists against her mouth as if to stem the flood of hysteria threatening to overwhelm her. Her wrists were fragile, as slender as bird bones, and the veins stood out like livid skeins.

'Come and sit down, Mrs. Dalton, and tell me all you know.' Roland led her indoors. 'Sergeant Mansfield will make us a nice cup of tea.'

'Is everything in the kitchen, ma'am?' asked Mansfield, and she looked at him uncomprehendingly as if he were speaking an unknown language. Roland took her into the sitting room and pushed her gently into a chair and Mansfield busied himself in the kitchen. He could hear their voices as he filled the kettle and found mugs and teapot; hers rising in agitation above Roland's deeper, measured tones.

The breakfast things were still on the table: packets of cereal, a loaf of bread, jam and marmalade. The boy probably had a snack before starting out in the morning and a second breakfast after he returned. There was a photograph of him on the dresser. It had been taken recently by the school's photographer and was the standard product, with an unnatural sky-blue background and the whole enclosed in an oval dark brown mount. Mansfield studied it. Oddly, the boy

243

had a look of the chief about him; when he grew up he would bear a strong resemblance to James Roland. *If* he lived to grow up ... He poured boiling water into the teapot and swore as the gush of steam scolded his hand. Where the hell was the boy? Surely he hadn't been scrubbed out to stop his tongue? Please God, no!

The sound of a car drawing up outside the gate distracted him from his thoughts. He hurried to the window. A Ford Transit van had drawn up behind Roland's car and as he watched the doors opened and Simon Dalton jumped out, followed by Bradley Scott. Relief swamped him. The boy was alive and well and looking remarkably pleased with himself. In the other room Ginny Dalton had also heard the noise. She rushed out of the front door and swooped on her son like an avenging angel.

'Simon − where *have* you been?'

The boy looked startled. 'I had a puncture and Mr. Scott mended it for me, and then we had some breakfast.'

'Do you realise you're over an hour and a half late home? I've been worried stiff!'

'I'm sorry, Mum ... I didn't think.'

'Don't blame the boy, Ginny. It's my fault − I didn't realise you'd be worried,' said Bradley Scott, looking embarassed. 'We mended the puncture and then, as I hadn't had my breakfast, I cooked enough for both of us to share. His bike's in the back of the van, it should be all right now.'

'You could have phoned!' accused Ginny Dalton, trembling now with relief and reaction.

'Well, yes, I suppose I could, but I never dreamt you'd get so uptight you'd call in the police.' He looked curiously at Roland and Mansfield standing by the door.

'Mum, we had wild mushrooms for breakfast. Do you know there are over sixty sorts of fungi in this country that you can eat?'

'Yes, I did, and at this moment I couldn't care less. I've been nearly out of my mind with worry. Don't you ever do that again!'

'I'll get your bike out and leave you to make your peace with your mother,' said Scott, opening the back door of the van and handing out the machine. 'See you around, young

Simon.' He slammed the doors, got into the van, reversed away from the other car and drove off, leaving Ginny standing uncertainly at the gate.

'Why are they here?' Simon indicated the two policemen.

'Don't you understand – I thought something had happened to you!' She frog-marched him up the path.

'I'm sorry, Inspector, for wasting your time.'

'That's all right, Mrs. Dalton. Anyway, you haven't wasted our time; we were coming over this morning to have a word with Simon.' The boy looked startled and threw a questioning glance at Roland.

'What about? What has he done?'

'Suppose we go in and have that cup of tea.'

'Now, young man,' said Roland, putting aside his mug and studying the boy who sat uneasily beside his mother in the living room. 'We asked you before if Alfie Coutts had said anything to you about what he had seen on the evening of the hurricane, and you told me no. Do you still stick to that?'

'Yes.' The boy licked his lips nervously.

'Simon always tells the truth,' said his mother defensively.

'Oh, I think you are telling the truth. Alfie didn't *tell* you anything because he didn't need to. You were with him that evening – you saw for yourself, didn't you?'

Colour flooded into the boy's face and he looked the picture of guilt.

'Simon!' expostulated his mother. 'What is this?'

'Please, Mrs. Dalton, let me handle this.' Roland turned back to the boy. 'I think you and your friend Mark were in Croxton Woods with Alfie Coutts that night while he initiated you into the delights of poaching. Am I right?'

The boy eventually nodded, avoiding his mother's eye.

'But you were at a scout meeting!' said Ginny Dalton. 'I took you over to Wallingford myself.'

'I think you were meant to think that, but they played truant. That right, Simon?'

'We didn't steal anything. Alfie just took us through the woods and showed us things.'

Roland spoke kindly. 'Look, I'm not worried about what you did. Alfie Coutts is dead and will never poach again, and

245

I think you learned your lesson. All I'm interested in is who and what you saw that evening. I'm sure your mother will forgive you and forget about it − ' he threw her a speaking look − 'but it is very important for us to know what happened.'

The boy tossed back the hair which was tumbling over his forehead and glanced nervously at his mother.

'Tell the Inspector what he wants to know,' she said.

He looked down at the floor and scuffled his feet on the carpet, mumbling something under his breath. The only word Roland caught was "Garfield".

'You saw Mrs. Garfield, didn't you, leaving Smoky Cottage?'

The boy looked up in surprise. 'No, it was *Mr.* Garfield.'

'Mr. Garfield − are you sure?' Roland tried to keep the astonishment out of his voice. Beside him, Mansfield stiffened with shock.

'Yes, it was definitely Mr. Garfield we saw. He came out of the door as we were hiding in the bushes outside.'

'Do you know what time it was?'

'I'm not sure . . . about nine o'clock, I think.'

'And what did he do? What happened next?'

'He went into the woods. He looked sort of as if he didn't want anyone to know he was there.'

'He didn't have his car?'

'No, that was in the old hut over the other side of the woods. Alfie said it was still there the next morning after the hurricane. He told us afterwards he had seen it there and Mr. Garfield in it, and he said . . . '

'Yes?'

'That Mr. Garfield must have had a nasty shock.' The boy took on the Suffolk accent and tone of Alfie Coutts' voice in an unnerving way. 'Mrs. Garfield has a − a man friend who visits her when Mr. Garfield is away, and Alfie saw him going there that night and he said − he said that Mr. Garfield must have found out about it and hung around that night to catch them.'

The boy looked very unhappy, obviously upset at betraying Lee Garfield but not realising the significance of what he had said.

246

'Do you know where this hut is where the car was hidden?'

'It's all in ruins now, it's where that man used to keep the chickens,' he appealed to his mother.

'I think I know where he means,' she said. 'There's an old nissen hut, left over from the war. Some years ago someone took it over and started up a smallholding, built several more huts and tried keeping chickens and growing vegetables. He wasn't successful and gave up the project. The buildings are now derelict. That's what you mean, isn't it, Simon? They are off the beaten track, hidden by trees, down a rough track between the back of Croxton Woods and The Hermitage.'

'What did you do after you saw Mr. Garfield leaving Smoky Cottage?'

'It was getting very windy and Alfie said we must go home, he'd take us out another night.'

'So you went back to Wallingford. Are you sure you didn't see anyone else around?'

'As we left the woods we saw Mr. Bates the gamekeeper, and Alfie got frightened and made us hide until he had gone past.'

'How soon after you saw Mr. Garfield was this?'

'I dunno, not very long.'

'Your friend Mark Taplin can confirm all this?'

'Y-e-s, but I don't want to get him into trouble.'

'You should have thought of that before you started all this deception,' retorted his mother.

'Don't be too hard on him, Mrs. Dalton, this information is invaluable.' Roland turned back to the boy. 'Can you show us where this hut is where Mr. Garfield's car was parked?'

'Yes, I suppose so. Do you mean right now?'

'Do as the Inspector asks.'

'But, Mum, I'm supposed to be going out!'

'Out? Where are you thinking of taking yourself off to now?'

'I'm supposed to be going swimming with Mark at Felstone — I did tell you. His dad is taking us.'

'Oh, yes, I'd forgotten. Well ...'

'Suppose you come with us in my car and show us this place,' suggested Roland smoothly, 'and then we'll drop you

247

off at Mark's place on the way back to the Station. Is that all right with you, Mrs. Dalton?'

'Yes, I suppose so. He can't come to much harm with the Taplins in Felstone. Go and get changed and ready,' she told her son, and he shot out of the room and up the stairs.

When she was quite sure he was out of earshot, Ginny Dalton tackled Roland.

'What is this about Tony Garfield?'

'Mrs. Dalton, I can't discuss my case with you.'

'You don't have to, I'm not stupid,' she retorted. 'You think he killed Julian Lester, don't you? That's what you're getting at.'

Roland was silent as she grappled with the idea, a look of horror on her face. 'That means you think he killed Tim too — and Alfie Coutts? But that's preposterous! Tony?'

'Does the idea that he may have killed his own cousin strike you as completely untenable? How did they get on?'

She stared at him and hesitated. 'I . . . they weren't on very good terms, I suppose. Tim always said he had never forgiven him for what he termed wheedling himself into his, Tony's parents, affections. I think he resented Tim and was jealous of him. But even so . . . '

'I understand that his marriage has broken up and that his wife is having an affair with Mr. Scott and urging him to divorce her.'

'Yes — I mean, no. She *is* having an affair with Bradley Scott, but she's not bothered about a divorce. That's not why she is threatening to leave Tony.'

'Then why, Mrs. Dalton?'

'I suppose I can tell you, it will soon be common knowledge. Tony has dreamt up this ghastly scheme for developing the creek. He needs to put up her money — she has private means — as well as his own to get it off the ground. She feels that the only way she can stop him is by walking out.'

'Are you sure of this? I got the idea that she was begging for a divorce?'

'Good heavens, no. Lee is very unconventional in that respect. If she decided to go with someone else, she wouldn't be bothered about remarriage or whether she was still legally

248

married to Tony. Whoever told you that?' She looked worried. 'Was it Tony? I wonder why . . .'

'So do I, Mrs. Dalton. Tell me, do you know anything about this shoot up at the Carstairs place today?'

'Lee is laying on the lunch for the beaters. She asked me to go along and help.'

'And have you agreed?'

'No, Inspector, I'm afraid I don't see eye to eye with her on the subject. She insists that it is an essential part of the country cycle and provides a natural cull, but that is ridiculous. Thoses birds are bred specifically to provide sport for the guns — how can that be a natural cull? And what about the ones that get pricked?'

'Yes, well . . .' Roland had no wish to start a discussion on the ethics or otherwise of shoots, too much else was clamouring for attention. 'I understand that Mrs. Garfield is eager to take part herself and will join the field after lunch.'

'Wrong again, Inspector. She is not at all eager but Tony insisted that she joins them this afternoon — to keep up appearances, I suppose — and she agreed just this last time.'

Roland and Mansfield exchanged glances, both having come to the same alarming conclusion. Mansfield spoke up.

'Has Mrs. Garfield got her own gun, or does she use one of her husbands'?'

'I really don't know.'

At the moment Simon clattered into the room, swinging the duffel bag containing his swimming gear in one hand.

'I'm ready.'

'Right, young man, let's get on our way.' Roland turned to Ginny Dalton. 'I'll make sure he gets to the Taplins' safely. Stay here and don't worry.'

'But . . .'

There was a worried frown on her face as she saw them off, and she stayed by the gate staring after the car long after it was out of sight.

Simon was adept at giving directions. He had seized on the fact that there were going to be no repercussions from his escapade and now settled back to enjoy the excitement. He

249

was disappointed that they were not in an official police car with flashing lights and siren, but somewhat mollified when Roland showed him his personal UHF radio.

Simon directed them down the narrow lane that led behind Croxton Woods and joined the Wallingford road further along. The turn-off was little more than a rough stone track leading through a gap in the hedgerow. This track wound in and out between stubble fields and rough pasture and dipped sharply behind the hill that led up to The Hermitage. At the bottom was a sagging, broken-down, propped-open gate that seemed to lead to nowhere.

'Is this the place?'

'Yes, the buildings are hidden behind those bushes.'

Roland edged the car cautiously forward through the gateway, bumping over the uneven ground, and rounded the thicket. There were a collection of huts and chicken houses in various stages of decay. Amongst them was an old shepherd's hut which looked as if it had been used as living quarters by the ex-crofter. The front end of the nissen hut was missing and a piece of sacking hung over the opening, providing a makeshift door.

'Stay here,' Roland admonished the boy, 'and I mean that!'

He and Mansfield left the car and walked over to the nissen hut. They pushed aside the sacking and went inside. Roland was immediately aware of the smell: an elusive mixture of oil and petrol and exhaust. A car had been kept here not so long ago. Mansfield pulled a torch from his pocket and they crouched on the beaten earth floor, looking for tyremarks.

'Here we are,' grunted Roland. Rain had driven in through the opening at some time and that area of ground had been reduced to mud. This had now dried out, but preserved in the crumbling ruts was a distinctive tyremark. 'This should clinch it.'

'Garfield's car is still at the garage in Wallingford; Forensics can compare his tyres with this. I think we'll get a perfect match. Let's just see if we can find anything else.'

'How did Alfie Coutts come to find the car hidden away in here?' said Mansfield as they searched, with no further success, round the hut.

250

'He probably used this place as a shelter from the weather – just think, it's only a short distance from both Garfield's house and Smoky Cottage, though so out of the way that most people probably don't know of its existence. Pat, it's all falling into place. The only reason we crossed Garfield off our list of suspects was because we couldn't see how he could have driven back from London during the hurricane; but he could have returned immediately after he set up his alibi with the false bomb alert. He could have left the car here and sneaked home before the brunt of the storm struck us.'

'But surely his wife would have known?'

'No, he needn't have gone into the house, there is a flat over the stables – the stable boy used to live there but it's empty now. He could have spent the rest of the night there – and remember, Mrs. Garfield was otherwise occupied!'

'We've got him!'

'Yes, I think we have. We'll get the team out here immediately to deal with this, and with any luck they may find a fingerprint. Our smooth Mr. Garfield is going to find it difficult to talk himself out of this one.'

'You're going to pull him in?'

'Yes, I think we've got enough evidence and time is of the essence – I think Mrs. Garfield is in grave danger.'

'You really believe he is going to make an attempt on her life?'

'Yes. We know that money is his god. If she is holding out on him and preventing his going ahead with this development scheme at the creek, I don't think he'll hesitate to get rid of her. He'll inherit her money if she dies, and there will be no-one to stop him. I think he's already set things up – that car accident was faked to pull the wool over our eyes and make us think that someone has got it in for *him*. And his insistence that *she* wants a divorce – he's planning to kill her in some way so that it will look as if he were the intended victim, not her.'

'The shoot?'

'Yes, but how? You said yourself an accidental shooting couldn't be staged during a formal shoot. He's hardly going to blast off at her in front of a dozen or so witnesses, is he?'

'No.' Mansfield looked crestfallen, then a gleam of

251

excitement came into his face. 'The gun — he could sabotage the gun she is going to use.'

'How? How could he do that and make it appear an accident?'

'It is possible — don't you remember that case up in Norfolk last year? Some chap was out shooting under snowy conditions. He used his shotgun as a prop when climbing over a fence and some ice and snow got rammed up the barrels. The whole thing exploded in his face when he pulled the trigger, and blew his head off!'

'By God, yes! It could be done. He wouldn't have to use anything incriminating — a clod of mud would do the trick. How long have we got? She's not joining the shoot till after lunch.' He glanced at his watch. 'It's just after ten-thirty now — we've got a couple of hours. Firstly, we must get proof that this tyremark matches up with his car; once we've got that, we're home and dry. I'm calling up reinforcements. We'll get that boy to Wallingford and then double back to Croxton.' Roland pulled out his radio. 'Go and see if he's all right, I don't want him to hear my call.'

He was lucky enough to catch DC Evans when he got through to headquarters. He described the location and gave instructions for the scene of crime team to come out immediately. He arranged for reinforcements to rendezvous with them at the boundary gate of Carstairs' estate, and asked for Tom Drake to accompany them as he was familiar with the terrain. He signed off and went back to the car. As they bumped back up the track he informed Mansfield briefly of the measures he had initiated.

Simon, supremely unaware of the train of events his information had set in motion, sat in the back of the car and enjoyed the ride. As they accelerated through the village towards Wallingford, he was convinced the Inspector was speeding.

Ginny Dalton walked slowly back into the cottage, trying to marshall her whirling thoughts. Tony Garfield, who had always behaved towards her in a friendly, avuncular manner, a murderer! She couldn't believe it — and yet . . . Shockingly,

252

she realised that she could indeed swallow the assumption. There had always been something just too plausible, too good to be true, about him. On the surface he appeared considerate and tolerant but he always got his own way. That amiability masked a ruthless will. When you dug deeper you found a disturbing coldness and lack of empathy.

Poor Lee, what would this mean to her? At least she wasn't still in love with him, thought Ginny, thank God for Bradley Scott. But even if you had stopped loving your husband years ago, it would still come as a terrible shock if he were arrested for murder. And that surely was precisely what James Roland was about to do. Lee must be warned, prepared for the event. Ginny grabbed her coat from the peg and hurried out to the garage. With any luck she would catch Lee at the Carstairs' place, preparing the food for the beaters' lunch.

Flinging herself into the driving seat, she fumbled with the ignition. Pray God the Mini wouldn't choose this morning to be temperamental! Thankfully, the engine fired. She backed out of the garage and reversed into the lane. She would tell Lee the dreadful facts and bring her back here, leaving the field free for the Inspector and his posse.

Lee Garfield was unpacking sandwiches and piling them onto the trays set out on makeshift tables when she heard the Mini approaching. She looked out and smiled when she recognised the car and driver.

'You've changed your mind?'

Ginny Dalton stared at her friend and found she couldn't speak. Lee looked so carefree, dressed in lovat green jacket and breeches with matching trilby pulled down over her black hair. How could Ginny shatter her complacency? How did one break the news to a friend that her husband was a triple murderer?

'What's the matter, Ginny, is anything wrong?'

'They're going to arrest Tony!' she blurted out 'Inspector Roland has just left me — the police are sure he committed the murders!'

'Oh, God!' Lee clutched at the wooden partition for support and sank down on a bale of hay. She shook her head

253

slowly from side to side. 'Why? What have they got against him — have they any proof?'

'I think they must have, Simon has just produced some incriminating evidence.' She briefly brought the other woman up-to-date with the events of the morning.

'Oh, my God — it's worse than I thought! How did they find out?'

'You mean you *knew*?' Ginny was aghast.

'No, not really. I sometimes suspected that he had had something to do with Cousin Tim's death, but I couldn't believe he was involved in the other murders. I've been trying to tell myself there is no way he could be connected with their deaths, and yet . . . he's been behaving very strangely just lately. I thought it was because he'd found out about me and Brad, but now . . . what you've told me is beginning to make horrible sense!'

'Lee, this is terrible — are you sure?'

'That night of the hurricane, I thought he was in London. He rang me from there, or so I thought — he must have been *here* all the time. Someone had been in the stable flat that night. I told Tony later and he said it was probably a tramp, but it must have been him all the while. He must have been there while I was having it off with Brad only a few yards away in the house!' She laughed hysterically. 'My dear husband, a murderer! He killed my cousin all those years ago, and now he's killed Julian Lester and that poor old fool to cover his tracks!'

'*Your* cousin? What do you mean?' Ginny pounced on the unknown fact.

'Tim Spencer was my cousin as much as he was Tony's. I am the third descendant of Great-aunt Gertrude.' She saw the look on her friend's face and paused. 'Yes, it's true. I was in the States when she died and I inherited part of her estate. Tony came over to the States and we met up — accidentally, I thought at the time, but now I'm not so sure. After we married and came here he said it would be wiser if we kept my real identity a secret, and I was quite happy to go along with that. It didn't bother me, though I couldn't see the point. All sorts of things are becoming clear now — he married me for my money, Ginny. That's not a very comforting thought.'

254

And he killed the father of my child, thought Ginny, staring mesmerised at her friend who was working herself into a fine rage.

'What are you going to do?'

'I'll tell you what I'm going to do — I'm going after him. He'll regret the day he tricked me!'

The Range Rover was parked to one side of the cart lodge, and Lee ran towards it.

'You're going to warn him?'

'Warn him? I'm going to stop him once and for all!' She yanked open the door of the vehicle and reached inside.

'Lee, that's a gun!'

'Too true. Darling Tony left it for my use. I'm going to make good use of it, but not in the way he expected!'

'Lee — you're not going to shoot him? Is it loaded?'

'It soon will be.' She fumbled in her jacket pocket and produced two cartridges. She broke open the shotgun and slipped them into the breech.

'He's your husband, — you can't shoot him' Ginny was horrified. 'That makes you a murderer too!'

'I'm not a murderer, I'm ridding the world of a menace. You shoot vermin, don't you? He's killed three innocent people, but he's not going to get away with it!'

'He won't — the police are on to him.'

'You don't understand, Ginny, they'll never make any charges stick. He'll get a good lawyer and talk himself out of it; I've seen him do it before with dubious business deals. He thinks he's above the law, probably thinks he's justified in what he did. People like that can't be allowed to walk around — they're too dangerous. I can't let him get away with it!'

She threw the shotgun on to the front seat and swung herself up behind the wheel.

'Lee, you can't drive with a loaded shotgun beside you — it might go off and kill you!' Ginny was clutching at straws.

'I'm breaking all the rules for once, and it's not me who is going to get hurt!'

The engine roared into life and she tugged at the wheel, swung the vehicle round and scorched off down the track, scattering pebbles and mud in her wake.

255

'Let the police deal with it!' bawled Ginny after her but she was shouting to empty air.

Roland toiled up the slope that demarcated the eastern side of the Carstairs' estate. He hauled himself up on to the wall that followed the contour of the slope uphill, away from the massive wrought iron gates. He swung up his binoculars and focussed on the scene below him. To the left, in the near distance, a stand of young sycamore trees, still miraculously upright, curved round the boundary of a field that fell into a shallow bowl between them and the distant line of scrubby trees and bushes that marked the perimeter of the valley. Stretched across this little valley was the line of guns, carefully spaced, remote figures from this distance.

It was a bright, frosty morning and a pale sun illuminated the autumn colours. Sound carried clearly through the still air. Roland could hear as well as see the beaters tapping through the far thicket. Even as he watched, the first birds erupted from cover and arched upwards, silhouetted against the cerulean sky. The guns barked and the birds fell from the sky and toy puffs of smoke clouded the scene and the movement of the dogs. It was, he thought, like watching a macabre firework display taking place in daylight. Wave after wave of birds arched and looped and fell back to earth, accompanied by the thunder of gunpowder.

Christ! All those lethal firearms around — should he have got authorisation for a police marksman? He heard the cars in the distance and jumped down and rejoined Mansfield at the gate as two police cars drew up and disgorged their passengers.

'I want those cars off the road,' said Roland sharply. 'We don't want to advertise our presence yet. Draw in behind that hedge — where is PC Drake?'

'Sir, he's taking part in the shoot, he's one of the beaters.' Evans stepped forward, looking worried.

'Oh, well, that could work to our advantage, especially if we can set up a line of communication. Anything else I should know?'

'The CC is one of the guns.'

Roland swore softly. 'You're having me on?'

'No, sir, it's true.' Evans looked even more unhappy.

The Chief Constable, thought Roland, of all the bad luck. Well, this would either make or break his career; to arrest a friend of the Chief Constable's in front of him was not a situation in which an ambitious inspector cared to find himself. Pray God he had enough evidence to make the charges stick.

He explained the situation to the men, and gave instructions.

'The guns will be moving on to the next position now. I want you to make your way parallel to them, keeping under cover. No-one is to get up in front of them, I don't want any accidents. I don't know whereabouts in the next line-up Garfield will be; if he is near either end it will be easier to take him out, but I don't want any heroics – remember, he is armed and liable to react dangerously if he thinks we have rumbled him. I am going to try and get hold of the game-keeper, he controls the shoot. Now, any questions?'

'What about Mrs. Garfield?' asked Mansfield, shielding his eyes from the sun and squinting up at the distant farm buildings.

'Yes, I was coming to that. You go round the back of the house to the outbuildings and check that she is there busy with the lunch preparations. Don't alert her, and join me when you've done that.'

Patrick Mansfield was annoyed. He wasn't a bloody minder sent to look after the women; he wanted to be in on the action. As the men moved off he grunted and took to the driveway leading up to the house. He skirted that building and made for the complex of farm buildings which lay a little distance beyond this. As he neared the barn he thought he heard the sound of a vehicle being driven speedily away in the other direction.

She had to be stopped! Ginny looked after the disappearing vehicle. Would it be quicker to take the Mini and follow her, or could she take a short cut across the meadows and catch up with Lee before she reached the shooting party? Even as Ginny hesitated she heard the sound of approaching footsteps scrunching on the gravel of the track that led up the hill to the cart lodge. She ran out and recognised the sergeant, Roland's side-kick, toiling in her direction. Never had she thought to be pleased to see him or his chief again. She ran to meet him.

Mansfield saw the woman rushing down the hill towards him and stopped in surprise. What the hell was Ginny Dalton doing here? She looked as if the devil were snapping at her heels, and where was Lee Garfield?

'She's going to shoot him!' Ginny tripped as she reached him. She stumbled and he put out a hand to help her. 'You've got to stop her!'

'Who? What are you talking about?' But he knew who she meant and his heart sank. Surely they hadn't made a mistake, surely it wasn't Lee Garfield after all?

'Lee — she knows about Tony — she's gone after him!'

'What did you tell her, Mrs. Dalton?'

'That the police are going to arrest Tony — I had to warn her, prepare her — I didn't expect her to react like this. She's gone berserk!'

'Has she got a gun?'

'Yes, a shotgun.'

'Where did she get it from?'

'Tony left it out for her — she's supposed to join the shoot after lunch.'

This was worse than he had thought. If the gun had been fixed, and it was beginning to look increasingly likely, then she was in dreadful danger. A pot-shot at her husband — and in the state she was in, she was unlikely to check the gun first — and it was curtains for her. Or at the very least, a nasty, maiming accident.

'Where has she gone?'

'To catch up with Tony. The shoot is making its way through Longbottom meadows towards Hermitage land. She took the Range Rover — the track goes behind the woods and comes out further down.'

'Is there a shortcut on foot?'

'Ye-es. It's rough going but you can cut down the back of the hill and get to the meadows that way.'

'Show me.'

She was already running round the side of the cart lodge and he quickly followed her.

'It's down here, through these hawthorn bushes. We'll have to squeeze through the barbed wire fence and then it's downhill till we reach the stream.'

'Not we, Mrs. Dalton. You wait here and I'll go on my own.'

'I'm coming with you.'

'Please, Mrs. Dalton, do as I ask. Stay here and leave this to me.'

'You don't know the way. You've got to get across the stream — I know where there's a crossing.'

She was plunging through the hedgerow and he followed helplessly, ducking to avoid the branches that sprang back in her wake. The going was rough. They pulled the strands of wire apart for each other to climb through the fence and Mansfield, being bulkier, got hooked up and ripped his anorak as he pulled free. They waded through a sea of bracken and brambles and then dodged down the hillside, avoiding the mole-hills that littered the cobweb-spun grass, turning it into an obstacle course. As they neared the stream, the going got wetter. They squelched across the marshy ground and Mansfield stopped as they reached the bank.

'Where exactly are we in relation to the shoot?'

'The stream leads through to the bottom of the meadows. They can't be all that far ahead.'

'And what point is Mrs. Garfield likely to have reached?'

'The track ends, just over there behind those trees.' She pointed to the thicket beyond the far bank of the stream.

'So how do we get across?' With distaste he eyed the grey, chilly water slipping past the etiolated reeds and the black, mud-pocked margins.

'We follow it down to that clump of alders. Years ago, in another gale one blew down across the stream and formed a natural bridge. We used to play here as kids.'

It was as she said. The alder had crashed down, embedding itself in the opposite bank, and the forked, moss-covered bole looked rocksteady, slippery and highly dangerous. Ginny Dalton negotiated it nimbly and Mansfield took a deep breath

259

and launched himself after her. He teetered unsteadily on the slender trunk that suddenly seemed far to fragile to bear his weight, and forced himself to scramble across to the other side. From there he could see a glint of metal through the trees, and beyond, in the distance, he could hear voices and the excited bark of a dog, abruptly silenced.

'The Range Rover is over there. Is it any use asking you to wait there and not come any further?'

She shook her head and leant back against a tree stump, fighting to get her breath. 'Are you going after Tony?'

'Forget Mr. Garfield. It's his wife we've got to stop.'

'You're not going to arrest her?'

'I'm not arresting anybody. I just want to avoid a nasty accident. She mustn't use that gun.'

'No ... What do you mean?'

'I think,' said Mansfield heavily, deciding he might as well take her into his confidence, 'that gun may have been deliberately sabotaged. It's likely to explode in her face.'

She cottoned on remarkably quickly. 'You mean ... Tony? Oh, my God!'

'Isn't that her ahead of us now?' Mansfield could hear rather than see the progress of somebody moving away from them through the undergrowth. If it were Lee Garfield she was making no attempt to silence her movements, but at least she was keeping under cover, behaving circumspectly; not charging forward like the avenging virago Ginny Dalton had led him to expect.

'Yes, I think so.'

'Keep behind me and don't startle her. When we get close, I'll try and get her attention. I may need you to back me up.'

Ginny Dalton's presence might be vindicated after all, he thought as they hurried after the retreating figure. She might be able to persuade her friend better than him. The only trouble was, there was no way they were going to be able to keep their identity secret from the shooting party. Ginny Dalton looked like an exotic parakeet with her red-gold hair tumbling over her scarlet jacket and her bright green-clad legs working like pistons. If Garfield saw her he would be immediately alerted. Still, that couldn't be helped. Lee

Garfield's safety was of paramount importance. The rest of the police presence could deal with her husband. Where the hell was Roland?

'He's the third one from the left in the line-up,' Roland spoke softly into his radio, 'the one with the liver and white spaniel. They are in position now for the next drive. Let the birds go up and afterwards we'll move in. Have you got Bates the gamekeeper with you?'

'No, sir, he's in the middle of the line, ready to give the go-ahead to the beaters when the guns are ready. There's no way we can get hold of him without disrupting everything.'

'What about Tom Drake?'

'Sorry, sir, he's up ahead with the other beaters. There's no way we could get hold of him either.'

'Never mind. Can you see me from where you are?'

An affirmative came over the air.

'If I raise my arm suddenly, close in. Is that understood? Over and out.'

Roland pocketed his radio and looked around him with satisfaction. Everything was working to plan. It was fortunate that Garfield was positioned near the end of the line, it made it so much easier to get close to him without being seen. The concentration of the guns on their feathered quarry was such that the police officers had managed to get into position, using what cover there was, undetected. The dogs were remarkably well trained too. He had been afraid that one of them might give the police away and a burst of barking a few minutes ago had almost confirmed this fear, but it had turned out to be a young dog belonging to one of the "pickers-up" who had disgraced himself, and his owner, by anticipating the fall of game and forgetting his training in the excitement of the chase.

Roland edged forward, keeping the low lying blackthorn hedge between him and the guns, and behind him two more police officers moved into place. Over on the far side of the field the Chief Constable, resplendent in shaggy tweed, waited at the ready. Thank God he was not near Garfield, thought Roland. Let the next flush of game go up, and let Garfield discharge his barrels, and then he'd get him.

A flash of colour back amongst the trees behind the meadow caught his attention. He thought he saw a glimpse of red hair bobbing amongst the foliage. What the hell was William Evans doing back there? Evans should be over on the far side, parallel to himself. He swung up his glasses and froze with shock.

It couldn't be Ginny Dalton! He was obsessed by her, hallucinating at a time when he needed all his wits about him. He studied the figure darting through the trees; unless Evans was in drag and sporting flowing lovelocks it was indeed Ginny Dalton, and just ahead of her, surely, was Patrick Mansfield. Sweet Jesus, what was his sergeant playing at? He'd spoil everything. They looked as if they were chasing someone. Roland lost them momentarily behind a thicket of bush and focussed on the terrain in front of them.

He saw then what he had missed a few seconds earlier; another figure plunging through the undergrowth, only a few yards away from the edge of the meadow. It was Lee Garfield. She was carrying a gun and there was an air of frightening determination about her steady progress towards the field of sportsmen.

Everything seemed to happen at once then. Afterwards he wasn't sure whether he had actually heard the click as she slipped off the safety catch or whether he had imagined it. He saw her swing up the gun and draw a bead on Garfield. He started to run forward and at the same time Mansfield's voice rang out: 'Don't fire that gun, Mrs. Garfield – it's been fixed!'

Tony Garfield swung round and simultaneously a fusillade of shots rang out as the beaters put up the first wave of birds. Someone screamed and Lee Garfield checked, her concentration broken.

For a few seconds husband and wife faced each other across lowered guns, and the scene froze into a tableau. Then Mansfield reached the woman and removed the shotgun from her unresisting grip, and Roland and his officers surrounded Garfield.

'Your gun, please.'

Roland put out his hands and the man gave a shrug.

Unbelievably, the trace of a wry smile flickered across his face as he complied.

'You win, Inspector.'

'Anthony Garfield, I arrest you on suspicion of the murders of Timothy Spencer, Julian Lester and Alfred Coutts. You are not obliged to say anything unless you wish to do so, but anything you do say may be given in evidence.'

Chapter Fourteen

'Collapsed like a pricked balloon. Talk about sing — he couldn't warble quickly enough once we'd pulled him in.'

It was a week later. Tony Garfield had been remanded in custody pending trial, and Superintendent Bob Lacey, expressing himself in clichés as was his wont, was talking over the case with his colleagues. He eased his bulk on his office chair and beamed round at the assembled company.

'By the way, James, the CC thinks you made a reasonable job of nabbing him in the circumstances, although it ruined his day's sport.'

'That's comforting to know. I don't think I have ever before made such a public arrest.'

'Was his wife really going to shoot him?'

'She wasn't aiming at head or heart. I think she'd had a chance to cool down and come to her senses on the dash to get to him; she just wanted to hurt him.'

'Well, it's a good job she didn't pull that trigger. The gun had certainly been sabotaged — a wad of clay and pebbles rammed up each barrel. It would have made a nasty mess of her.'

'Is he going to be charged with her attempted murder as well?'

'That's up to the powers-that-be. He's confessed to the three other murders and the attempted murder of his great-aunt, Mrs. Fellingham.'

'I thought the insurance investigators had ruled out arson,' said Mansfield, fiddling with his pipe and tobacco tin. 'How did they manage to slip up?'

'It was caused by a dropped cigarette smouldering in the bedclothes, only he was the one to drop it, creeping back into her room after she was asleep. It didn't quite work out as he had planned; he didn't intend the Hall to burn down and she didn't kick the bucket straight away.'

'But he inherited from her, didn't he?' asked Evans. 'Why did he decide to kill Tim Spencer?'

'Go on, Inspector, you tell the tale,' said Bob Lacey, leaning back and scratching his head. 'It's your baby.'

'It all started back in early 1978.' Roland tipped his chair back and prepared to reveal all to those amongst his colleagues who weren't yet in full possession of the facts.'

'He was just a small businessman waiting for the chance to break into the big-time. Then the opportunity arose for him to become a partner in the business consortium with which he is now associated, but he had to buy himself in. Suddenly he found himself in the position of having to find a considerable sum of money within the next couple of years.'

'He confidently expected to inherit the entire estate from his great-aunt. Timothy Spencer had disgraced himself and been banished to Australia, and the other cousin in America hadn't been heard of for years. Then, to his horror, he learnt that Tim had been summoned home to attend the old lady's eightieth birthday party. He had always been pathologically jealous of the younger man, whom he thought had transplanted him in his parents' affections, and he feared Tim might wheedle his way back into favour and scoop the lot. That was when he started on the road to murder. He met Tim off the train and somehow persuaded him to walk down to the creek on the pretence of having something important to tell him before he went up to the Hall.'

'He shot Spencer and buried the body in the river bank. He must have had a horrible shock when Julian Lester later mentioned that he had seen Tim on the train and wondered what had happened to him. Garfield told him that Tim had discovered that Ginny Dalton was about to marry someone else, and was so upset that he had decided to go back to Australia and give the party a miss. He persuaded Lester that it would be wiser not to mention to Ginny Dalton that he had turned up – something along the lines of letting sleeping dogs lie — and of course Lester was not on social terms with the old lady so there was no chance of her getting to hear of it.'

'Having removed Tim he now set about plotting his great-aunt's demise. As we've seen, things didn't go quite according to plan but she died as a direct result of the "accident". Then he discovered that Leslie Drew, the third cousin, was sharing the legacy with him. He went over to the States and deliberately sought her out. I don't know whether he planned to kill her, too, but when he met her I think he genuinely fell for her. He made himself known to her, wooed and won her and brought her back here, somehow managing to persuade her not to reveal to the locals her relationship to the old lady.'

'He now considered he had virtual control over all the money he had originally thought was due solely to him. I think the marriage was reasonably happy in the first year or two, but he discovered that his wife was unable to have children and thought she had cheated him. She for her part soon became disillusioned with her sober, staid husband whose business interests seemed all-consuming. She is an attractive, highly-sexed woman and she started to look elsewhere. However, they were still content to jog along together and that was the state of affairs until we come to the end of this summer.'

'Then Tim Spencer's skeleton was discovered, and not only discovered but identified, a chance in a thousand. Garfield thought he was safe and prepared to ride out the enquiry, and then Julian Lester, who had been away on holiday at the time of the skeleton's identification came home and started to wonder. I think Lester must have suspected Garfield of being involved in Tim's death, and got in touch with the idea of putting on the screws. Garfield know then that he would never be safe whilst Lester was alive, so he plotted his death.'

'He set up an alibi for himself at his London flat, making sure he was seen there in the early evening and just before midnight, and ringing his wife halfway through the evening, making her think he was calling from London when actually he was using the phone in Smoky Cottage. He drove up from the City and visited Lester between eight and nine o'clock, taking a bottle of Oude Jenever as a gift. He got Lester tipsy, slipped the barbiturates into his drink, and when he passed

266

out, removed his own glass, wiped his fingerprints off everything, left the pill bottle behind and put the suicide note, which he had typed out beforehand, in Lester's typewriter.'

'How did he get hold of the typewriter?' asked Pomroy.

'Borrowed his wife's keys to the NCT office and went there on the pretext of picking up some pamphlets for her. He made sure there was no-one within earshot and typed it out on the old Adler; it would only have taken him a few minutes.'

'He then drove back to London, set up the false bomb alarm, but afterwards got cold feet. He wasn't sure if he had given Lester a lethal dose and he was afraid he might have left something incriminating behind, so he decided to drive back to Croxton. By this time the wind was strengthening and he found himself coping with a force 10 gale. He decided to leave the car at the abandoned smallholding, sneak up to his house and spend the rest of the night in the stable flat which was unoccupied. At first light he would go back to check Smoky Cottage.

'This he did — it must have taken some courage to battle his way through the woods under those horrific conditions — and found to his astonishment that Lester had somehow roused himself in the night, gone outside and got himself killed by a falling tree — or so Garfield thought. After the initial shock he realised that this was going to work in his favour. He removed the pill bottle, took the suicide note out of the typewriter and shoved it in the boiler, which he proceeded to top up from the hod — a bad mistake. He went back to his car, in which he spent the next few hours, and eventually turned up late that morning, having obstensibly just driven up from London.

'He now expected Lester's death to be accepted as accidental and must have been a very worried man when he realised that we were treating it as suspicious. However, he had set up his alibi on the chance that something might go wrong and was convinced we couldn't break it. And he was right. We worked out that he could have committed the murder, but as far as we could see there was no way he could have driven up from London in the hurricane and destroyed the suicide evidence, so he was in the clear.

'But the police were interviewing everyone locally and

267

asking awkward questions. There were rumours flying about that Alfie Coutts, the local simpleton, knew something about the death. Garfield realised that he must have been seen by Alfie in the woods or Smoky Cottage that night. He persuaded his wife to drive with him to the Duck and Spoon, which he knew Alfie frequented, on the pretext of buying a bottle of whisky. Whilst she was doing this he hung around and overheard enough to know that Alfie could finger him if he was so minded. He also recognised Evans and knew that he had to get to Alfie before him.

'His wife tucked him up in bed with a nightcap to ease his make-believe cold, and as soon as she had left, Garfield upped and crept out of the house on Alfie's trail. He waited until Alfie had parted from his companions, and realising that he was going to take the short cut home, doubled round ahead and got there first, having grabbed a suitable weapon on the way. He laid in wait for the old man, and when Alfie appeared, befuddled with drink, he was an easy victim. However, he hadn't counted on you, Evans, being so on the ball. He was interrupted in his task, darted into hiding, and then when you bent over the body he laid you out and finished off the job he'd started. I reckon you were lucky, William — he was getting in the habit of murder — you could have ended up as dead as his other victims.'

'He wiped the evidence off the shovel, returned it to the place from whence it came, and sneaked back home, taking care that nobody saw him. By now he was beginning to think that he was omnimpotent. The police were as unsuccessful in solving Alfie's death as they had been over the other two murders. He thought he was safe — and then his wife dealt him a nasty blow. He knew that she had been carrying on with Bradley Scott but he had turned a blind eye because she still had control of her part of the legacy. Garfield had come up with this ambitious scheme to develop the creek. It would turn him into a millionaire but he had first to invest money in it, more money than he could put his hand to. He needed her money as well, and was convinced she'd back him. But this is where he came unstuck.'

'She flatly refused even to contemplate the idea. He had forgotten how involved she was with nature conservation and how strongly she felt about the despoiling of the countryside. She wouldn't allow her money to be used to further his plans, and in fact was determined to stop him by leaving him and going off with Bradley Scott. He had to have her money; if she wouldn't play ball, the only other way was to dispose of her so that he inherited her wealth. I think from the time she told him she was walking out on him, she was in deadly danger. He began to plot ways in which he could get rid of her and make it appear an accident.'

'He was so confident and cunning that he sabotaged his own car and faked an accident, so that if his wife died and he came under suspicion later it would appear that *he* was the intended victim, not her. Incidentally, he also faked the hit-and-run accident around the time of Tim's murder as an insurance policy in the same way.

'He never knew that we were on the trail of the third cousin, that we had discovered that Leslie Drew was not the man Garfield had led us to believe, but a woman and his wife to boot. But when we questioned him about his wife's real name, he began to get suspicious and fed us this sob-story about the break-up of his marriage. He did his damnedest to persuade us that he was heart-broken about it and was refusing her the divorce she wanted because he hoped to win her back. In fact, he was laying the seeds of another plot − to make us think that *she* was trying to kill him. He hoped we might think that it was she who had tampered with his brakes, and I'm sure he had it all worked out that when she was killed by the gun he would be able to prove that it was his gun that she had got hold of by mistake after disabling it herself.'

'Yes, he's a cunning bastard but he over-reached himself. He forgot that not everyone is as cold and calulating as himself; he didn't allow for human error in other people, or for his wife to react with such passion and not keep to the script he had written for her. Apart from that, and the fact that he was seen by two other witnesses on the night of Lester's murder, he would probably have got away with it. After all, we were playing into his hands by thinking that Lee Garfield was responsible for the whole thing, that he was just the poor, ignorant husband.'

Roland was still having nightmares about what could have

happened to Simon and Mark if Garfield had realised that they also had witnessed his movements on the night of Julian Lester's murder and knew that he had been seen the following morning in the vicinity. There had been so many "ifs" and "buts" in this case that he hadn't seen the wood for the trees, but he wasn't going to admit to Lacey that it had really been luck that had enabled him to clinch the case before anyone else had met with an untimely end.

'I still don't quite see how he faked those two accidents. He was injured, wasn't he?' Mansfield was trying to remember what had gone into the record book about the first accident ten years ago.

'Easy enough,' said Roland, 'there were no witnesses to the said hit-and-run accident. He mentioned that he still had scars on his legs from it — self-inflicted, I imagine, and who could prove otherwise if he had said at the time that he was knocked unconscious? As for the recent one: he drove to Bidwell Hill, parked somewhere off the road where no-one could see him, filed almost through the brake pipe, then applied the brakes violently a few times so that it was completely ruptured. And then, choosing his moment carefully when no other vehicle was in sight, he sent the car over the edge, jumping out of the way himself. When it had come to grief he pushed through the hedge and rolled down the bank, collecting some very telling scratches and bruises on the way. He then pretended to be suffering from shock when a witness came along. He had it all worked out: he's the possessor of a very devious, cunning mind and yet as we've seen was also capable of grabbing chances when they offered — a diabolical combination.'

'The sooner he's permanently behind bars, the better.' Bob Lacey gathered up his papers. 'Those two boys are key witnesses and they don't want something like this hanging over them for long. His pleading guilty will help to speed things up a little, but still, knowing boys of that age, they're probably having the time of their lives. They mustn't blab to their schoolfellows though, or discuss the case before it comes to court — I leave you, Inspector, to impress that on their parents.'

Roland assured him he would do just this.

*   *   *

He had deliberated at length on the choice of a gift. Flowers? And if so what sort of flowers – a bouquet or a pot plant? Chocolates? Wine? In the end he had reluctantly decided that it would be strictly unethical with the case still pending. And, anyway, she would probably throw his offering back in his face.

So he stood on her doorstep one Thursday evening, empty-handed, and rang the bell. She was such a long while answering that he was afraid she was out, but eventually she opened the door. Her eyes widened in surprise when she saw him.

'Oh, it's you.' She seemed at a loss and he stepped forward, afraid that she was going to close the door on him.

'May I come in please?'

She shrugged and stood aside and he preceded her into the living room. It was in chaos. Bags full of brightly coloured materials and wools had spilled their contents across the floor and colonised every surface.

'I was just sorting out some stuff for a craft session whilst Simon is out. I wasn't expecting any callers.' She swept two chairs clear of the jumbled textiles and he sat down.

'Where is Simon?'

'At a scout meeting. And he really is,' a smile flickered briefly across her face, 'I made sure of it.'

So had Roland.

'Good, I wanted to talk to you about him. The case comes up in six months. Simon and Mark will be called to give evidence but there is no need for them to worry about it; under the circumstances, they will be dealt with gently.'

'If he has confessed, I don't understand why they need to be bothered,' she said fretfully.

'I understand he is pleading guilty to the charges but you know how British justice works; every man is innocent until he is proved guilty, so he will have a fair trial. In the meantime the two boys mustn't talk about the case, tempting though it may be to boast to their schoolfriends or fellow scouts. Can you make sure he understands this?'

'Yes.' She got up from her chair and wandered round the room, picking up and discarding bunches of gaudy taffetas and silks. She looked troubled and he waited silently for her to bring up the topic that was worrying her. 'Inspector ...' she hesitated '... does everything have to come out?'

'You mean about Simon's birth and adoption?' he asked crisply, and she nodded.

'As it has no bearing on the case, I can see no reason why it should. The defence and prosecution councils will only be interested in what he saw on the evening of the 15th October.'

She let out her breath in a long-drawn out sigh and sat down on the sofa, stroking the cat, Faience, whom Roland had not noticed before. She was curled up, almost hidden, in a multi-coloured bed of remnants.

'But you should tell him, you know. A child should always be aware of the fact of his or her adoption. It can save a lot of heartbreak later on.'

'I will ... in time, when all this is over. Surely you can see that it would be most traumatic at the moment for him to learn that he is really Tim's son?'

'Yes, I understand.'

'I've told Lee, though. I felt she should know.' Ginny spoke a little defiantly and he raised his eyebrows.

'How did she take the news?'

'She wants to settle some money on Simon. She thinks he should have the share of her great-aunt's legacy that should have gone to Tim.'

'And are you agreeable?'

'No,' she said sharply, 'that inheritance has caused enough trouble already. It's tainted money and I want none of it for Simon. Besides, how could it be explained away?'

'Perhaps you are right.'

'I'm sure I am. I just want to forget the whole horrible business. I'm thinking of leaving the district, starting somewhere new.'

Shock curled through him.

'Are you sure that is wise? Surely Simon has had enough upheaval in the last couple of years. Is it fair to uproot him from all his friends and the setting in which he has grown up?'

'He would adjust, and what is there left here for me? Only bad memories and reminders of the past.'

'That's not true.' It came out with more force than he had intended and she looked at him in surprise.

272

It was his turn now to get up and wander round the room. Eventually he swung round to face her and said abruptly: 'There are things I want to say to you, to discuss – things about you and me. At the moment my hands are tied. I am involved in the case in which Simon is a key witness, and it would be strictly out of order for me to ... to embark on any sort of personal relationship. Do you understand what I'm saying?'

'I'm ... I'm not sure.' She looked dazed.

'When this case is over, I want to see you again.'

'What do you mean?'

'Look!' He threw himself down in the chair opposite her and spoke urgently. 'I am not a clone of Tim Spencer. I am a hardworking policeman whose wife left him because she couldn't stand his commitment to his work. You've seen it from the other side, you've been at the receiving end of a criminal investigation and I can't blame you if you want to have no more truck with me, but I feel differently. God knows, we got off to a disastrous start at that Rotary Ball but you must take some share of the blame for that.' He leaned forward and spread out his hands.

'Do you think, Ginny Dalton, that some time in the latter half of next year we could start over again?'

She sat very still and stared at him, and he wondered what was going on behind those odd-coloured eyes. Suddenly she seemed to come to a decision.

'Would you like a drink, James Roland, or are you still on duty?'

'On duty? I finished my official visit when we stopped discussing your son. You surely don't think I go around dropping proposals in the lap of every woman I interview in the course of duty?'

'Don't you? I've heard you have a bad reputation as far as women are concerned. You haven't answered my question.'

'I should like a drink.'

'I'm afraid there's little choice.' She got up and went over to the sideboard. 'I have sherry, there's some whisky or a bottle of redcurrant wine?'

'I'll sample the wine. Did you make it?'

'No. Mathew Betts, who lives up the lane, goes in for

273

winemaking in a big way and he often gives me a bottle to try.'

He uncorked the bottle whilst she fetched glasses then filled them with the ruby liquid.

'To what do we drink?'

'The future? You realise that I'd lose my scalp if the Powers-that-be could see us now?'

'Then we must make sure that they don't get to know.'

A little while later he put aside his empty glass and stood up. 'I am going out of that door and you won't see me, except officially, for six months. Will you have left the district by then?'

She got to her feet and ushered him through the door to the front doorstep. He thought she was not going to give him an answer, there was something so final, so irrevocable in her action. In another few seconds he was going to be outside on the path, banished forever, helpless to prevent his exile. As her hand curled round the doorknob, she looked up and caught his eye. A slight smile flickered across her face, and she gave a little shrug.

'I reckon I may stick around a little longer,' she said in an offhand voice.